Merciless Encounter

"Stay," he shouted. "It's the axeman. He's trying to divide us."

"And let them burn?" one man yelled. He turned and plunged into the darkness in the direction of the screams from the second pyre. Another man followed him.

"Stay!" the leader repeated. A yell sounded from somewhere near the first fire. "See? He's out there. He's waiting. Call in the other sentries. He's out—"

But suddenly, in a blur, Tor was in the firelight swinging his axe, downing four men in aroing swings too fast to mark. The leader jumped back, holding the dully glowing short-sword in one hand, the captive's throat in the other.

"Come closer and I'll ..."

THE PELBAR CYCLE
by Paul O. Williams
Published by Ballantine Books:

The Song of the Axe:

Book Six of the Pelbar Cycle

Paul O. Williams

A Del Rey Book

BALLANTINE BOOKS • NEW YORK

For Ted, Colin, Carl, and Bill, esteemed colleagues

A Del Rey Book
Published by Ballantine Books

Library of Congress Catalog Card Number: 84-90856

ISBN 0-345-31658-4

Manufactured in the United States of America

First Edition: July 1984

Cover art by Darrell K. Sweet

Maps by Shelly Shapiro

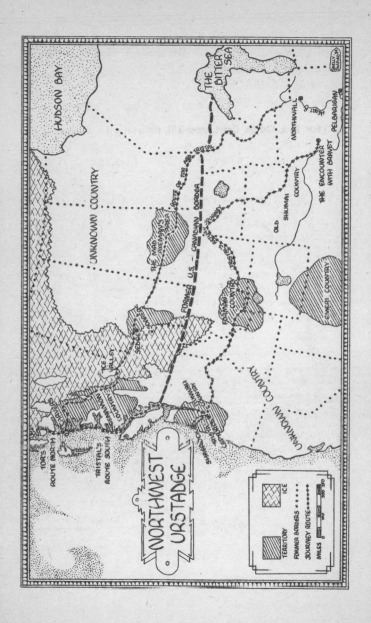

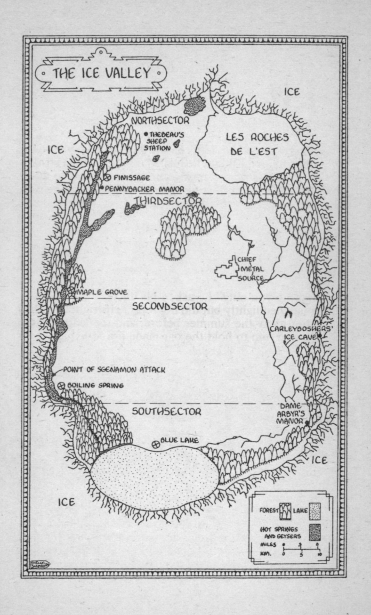

THE ICE VALLEY

ICE

NORTHSECTOR

ICE

LES ROCHES
DE L'EST

• THEBEAU'S
   SHEEP
   STATION

⊗ FINISSAGE
• PENNYBACKER MANOR

THIRDSECTOR

CHIEF
METAL
SOURCE

• MAPLE GROVE

SECONDSECTOR

CARLEYBOSHERS'
ICE CAVE

POINT OF SGENAMON ATTACK
⊗ BOILING SPRING

SOUTHSECTOR

DAME
ARBYR'S
MANOR

⊗ BLUE LAKE

ICE

ICE

FOREST   LAKE

HOT SPRINGS
AND GEYSERS

MILES 0   5   10
KM.   0   5   10

1

TRISTAL seethed with chaotic feeling. Every time the idea roiled up in his mind, he leaned into his paddle strokes harder, mindless of the spring current, reluctant to shear away from the wood floating downriver on the spring rise, surging, holding himself at the high edge of his breathing.

"Easy, Tris," his uncle said from the stern of the arrowboat. It was well past high sun on the third day after they had left Northwall on the long journey to the ice country. Raran, Tristal's dog, sat at ease in the center of the long arrowboat, lifting her ears as Tristal shot a glance behind her.

"Wearing you out?" he asked his uncle.

Tor laughed lightly but did not reply. His right hand had been shot away the summer before, and the leather strap that allowed him to hold the oar made it a little harder for him to match Tristal stroke for stroke. His long axe lay between his feet, in its sheath, blade up.

They stroked on again for some time without speaking. Finally Tor said, "You don't have to come, Tris. You can go back. I'll give you the boat. It's better for me running anyhow. At least I have two feet. But—"

"I'll come. But what?"

"But . . . if you drink honey at the beginning of the race, what reward is there if you win it?"

"Honey? Aven knows I've drunk little enough honey, Uncle."

"And once you climb to a lovely plateaued land and live there, it's difficult to think about climbing higher up."

Tristal felt anger boil up and paddled on in silence. Who had told his uncle? Had he guessed, divined, surmised as usual? The young man had said nothing about his startling encounter with Fahna the evening before he left Northwall.

He was afraid of her, an abrupt and beautiful teenager

1

who made even grown men draw in their breath when she passed. Once, when he had ventured to call her Thistle, as her family did, she had given him a shriveling look and turned her back on him. He avoided her.

But as he had stood on the edge of the hill near Jestak's house, before descending the path to the river, he had heard a slight scuff behind him and had whirled almost into Fahna, whose quick breath he felt on his cheek as she reached to kiss him. "You don't have to go," she had hissed at him. "You can stay. Let him go. I—I can't have you go off and never return."

"But I do have to," he had said. "And what are you..."

"Shut up, you ninny. What's wrong with you? Kiss me," she whispered. He paused. She looked up in dim ferocity in the dark. "Not tomorrow!"

Bewildered, he had put his arms around her, felt her soft lips reach up to his and the bands of her arms clasp him, and the bloom of strange light start from the sough of her young breath against his, as she murmured through the kiss, the bloom spreading through him, lifting him, then setting him down gently, as she slowly unclasped herself from him and stood back slightly, shivering a little, gasping once.

"Damn you," she whispered. "Go on, then. I will wait for you. Even up to seven years. Not a sunwidth longer. Then if you don't come, I'll never look at you again. You're not like the others. Either they are blind or you are. Which is it?"

She reached up and kissed him again, lightly, on the cheek, then said, "Well..."

"I'll come," he said, bewildered.

Then she ran off, leaving him standing like a post, only then really feeling, in remembrance, the hard, yet soft, fact of her body against his, so strange, so perfect, so impossible for him. He had heard Raran barking down by the river then, and turned to join Tor there, stumbling in the dark, so distracted that he caught Tor watching him as they cinched up the last of their supplies for the journey.

He realized then that he had made the simple Shumai promise that precedes marriage, and had done it with scarcely a thought, and it had been *demanded* of him by the prickly but lovely Fahna, the light of all eyes. It all seemed impossible.

Now, as they paddled, he went over his encounter again and again. Fahna, the beautiful, the inaccessible. He was too young to settle down. He had few real skills but Shumai ones. She was desired by every other young man around. Was she toying with him? He didn't know. But it could not be. He started through the whole memory again, timing his reminiscence to the strokes of the paddles, reaching and thrusting, as though in anxiety to escape the whole thing through physical exhaustion.

He glanced again at Tor, but his uncle simply paddled with him, stroke for stroke, twisting his long body to make up for his shorter right arm. Tor's mouth was set with his effort, but his expression was a mild joy. Raran flapped her tail lightly as she looked up at Tristal, ears cocked.

TRISTAL lay under a screen of brush on a river island. His face ran with sweat in his fever, and he barely had the strength to wave away flies and mosquitoes. He turned his head, looking for Tor. The afternoon sun sifted through the heavy leaves of the cottonwoods and silver maples, and its shafts of light rayed down clearly in the smoke of the damp leaf fire Tor had built to keep off the insects.

"Tor," he murmured. No answer came. "Tor," he croaked more loudly. He felt vague, and in his present weakness being alone was terrifying. Even Raran was gone. He reached for his short-sword and felt its smooth wooden handle, then relaxed and let his hand lie across it. "Tor," he called, but little sound came out. Again Tor did not appear. Tristal pulled his light blanket up to his chin and then again touched the handle of the short-sword.

In his distress and drowsiness, the leaves over his head seemed to be swimming, churning. He felt a hot breath, and opening his eyes, expecting Raran, he found a giant brown muzzle close to his face, like a bull's muzzle, but sharper, with canine teeth under it. It moved nearly against him snuffling, then opened its jaws, showing its teeth burning with white fire. Tristal rolled over and ran.

The river was gone and he was out in the long grass in snow, running toward a looming rock. Turning, he saw the giant mouth pursuing, nearly on him. Its tongue writhed and slathered. It snapped its teeth with sharp sounds. The rush of its breath was like a campfire. He ran on.

He hoped to find some crevice in the rocks ahead, but as he drew closer to them, they rose, transformed into a standing creature, hair covered, slope shouldered, gray and menacing. Arms tore out of the mass and reached up and out. Tristal fell flat, and the pursuing mouth yawned then drove its long teeth into the chest of the looming *thing*. It roared in response, grappling with the head and falling to the ground, thrashing, nearly crushing Tristal, who rolled again, desperately, over and over, rising and running again, tripping over a strange log, which turned into a snake, which curled and snapped up at the ends, enveloping him. He pushed and fought against it, losing his breath in its crushing spiral, refusing to give in and relax, refusing, refusing, and rolling backward, downward, as blackness came on him and he fell into its vortex, spinning, rolling, through nothing, down toward stars, in blackness, blackness, an endless fall.

As he fell, slowly turning, he saw something tiny, but bright, rising toward him or falling in the opposite direction. It grew larger, rushing, and he saw it was Fahna. He cried out, but no sound came, and he could see her open mouth as she too cried soundlessly, reaching out for him as her body turned helplessly, rolling her arm away from his, rushing by, diminishing in the other direction as he shot away. Blackness intensified, became total, but then within it Tristal seemed to feel a hand grasping him, holding him. Reaching for it, he could not touch it, yet it held him.

In the distance a light grew, dull and red. He squeezed his eyelids against it. Then he opened them and felt a stab of light and briefly saw trees, leaves, before he shut his eyes again. He opened his eyes once more, cautiously, and found their camp on the river island with the morning sun lancing through the leaves to his eyes. Tor knelt by him.

"Tor."

"You're better now. Cooler. Good. Can you eat?"

"No."

"Drink? Try." Tor held out a cup of warm broth.

Tristal sipped at it and felt it suffuse him with flavor. His lips were cracked. He drank again, slowly taking the whole noggin, then leaned back, feeling weak but clearheaded. He tried to remember what they were doing. Yes. Going north to the ice country. Why didn't he want to go? He couldn't remember. It was . . . it was . . . It didn't matter. He closed his eyes and fell back to sleep, but this time it was a sweet sleep. Tor felt his forehead, then took a cloth and wiped it again. He leaned down and put his cheek against Tristal's cheek, then sat up again and closed his eyes, a slight smile on his face.

Raran, nestled on the other side of Tristal, sighed and turned, settling back again. Tristal never moved, his chest rising and falling slowly with his breathing.

Finally Tor rose and said to Raran, "Stay now. Watch him. Be still." He turned and trotted to the riverbank to check the fish traps.

TRISTAL grew well rapidly after the night of the crisis in his fever, and in two days he and Tor set out again upriver, Tristal paddling for a while, then resting in the bow of the arrowboat. They had been traveling for nearly three weeks, and with the delay caused by Tristal's illness, spring was advancing northward more rapidly than they.

Tor had been unusually silent, paddling steadily near the east bank, but finally he said, in an abstracted tone, "Tris, has it ever seemed to you that everything is singing? I don't mean in actual song, of course, but as a radiance of what it is? Have you heard it? Can you? This may sound strange, but it's important."

"Singing?"

"Yes. Stating itself. Singing."

Tristal pondered. "I've heard the old people say something like that maybe, when I was a child."

"You. Do *you* sense anything?"

Again Tristal pondered. "No," he said.

"Start with an easy thing. What is our furred companion telling you?"

Tristal looked at Raran, lying at ease between them, panting lightly, at first unaware that she was being talked about, then more alert, looking from one to the other.

"You see, Tris, she feels your thinking of her. That is not precisely what I mean, but a simpler aspect of it. You know that because every hunter knows it. And Raran is a hunter. We may have shifted our posture very slightly when we began thinking about her. So slightly we didn't know it. But Raran sensed it. Husbands and wives can be the same after a while. They know when the other one holds her head just so that she is tired, or the lift of her shoulders shows that she is just slightly peeved.

"But I don't mean that. Start with the river. What is the river singing?"

Tristal was slightly startled. He listened a long time. He could feel the river as a presence, even though it was much smaller where they were than down at the Pelbar cities. He still had not given himself to the idea, though. Finally he said, "Tor, you have never married. How can you tell?..."

"About husbands and wives? There is a little of the Shumai axeman in the best of them. They sense things. You can watch it happen. Now listen to the river."

Tristal tried again. The idea made him uneasy. Finally he said, "Tor, why have you never married?"

"I am married to all this." He waved his left hand. "It is wholly satisfying to me. And my best contribution has always been to be that way. I'll always be a Shumai axeman, even though there are no more running bands. We axeman bound all Shumai country together, even though there were so few of us. We practiced this way of knowing. I see now how it accords with Pelbar prayer. It is different, of course."

"You mean everything has a spirit—"

"No, no. The Peshtak think that, so I hear—spirits of love and of hate and all that. No. Sertine, the Shumai sense of God, was the binder of all things, and if there was any spirit, it was Sertine's. When you sense the singing of things, you aren't thinking of the things themselves. You'd have to do that if you were thinking of spirits. You are thinking behind the things to what lies behind them—their reason. Their nature.

"This is hard for me to explain because it is not something I have thought about the way the Pelbar ministers do. I haven't stood away back from it and said, This is the way it is. Our theology, which is what the Pelbar would call it, is simple and unspoken."

"It makes me uneasy, Tor, the idea that things *sing*. It sounds weird, magical. It sounds like what we are warned against by everyone. Trying to explain things by ways that make no sense."

"You've drunk in a great gulp of Pelbar rationalism, and it's sitting in your stomach like a rock. But so often this rationalism isn't the origin of knowledge, but only a means of explaining what has already been decided, way down in the guts somewhere, by some wholly nonrational sense."

"I don't understand."

"Think of it like the old Pelbar minister, Omed. You know her—in her mountains of robes? I've watched her at her business. People see the robes moving. They hear the practiced voice coming out of the robes. She isn't the best of the Pelbar ministers. She has mistaken the appearance of what she does for the whole thing. I used to amuse myself by thinking of her body beneath the coverings—wrinkled, stooped, potbellied, wholly undisciplined. That is where the singing really came from—from her, not the coverings."

"You mean that ugly bodies—"

"No, no. People can't help what bodies they have been given. Only what they do with them. More than that, what the bodies say about what they are. What they are uses the body because that's all it has to use. The slow piling up of the results of that makes a statement."

Tristal pondered that, running his hands through Raran's fur and releasing the shedding clouds of it to the light breeze. He looked at his uncle's ruined right arm thinking of this. "Why are you telling me this?" he finally asked.

"It is the way of things. But also important is this—if you hear the song of everything, you hear danger before it arrives. You know it is coming. You have heard it singing itself. That is what Stel calls my intuition. It isn't as simple as that, of course. But what I can teach of it most easily includes this listening."

"Danger?"

"Of course. If everything is declaring itself, can we not be aware of the unspoken thought?"

"But what of a rock hanging, loosened by frost, ready to fall? That has no thought."

"Yes. That is different. That's another problem. But even there there is some awareness. I don't understand it. I am myself too rational about it, I suppose."

"Even there?...I don't understand."

"Neither do I. But it is so. Rocks declare themselves, too, you know. When you throw one and it bounces, it has, so the Pelbar thinkers have said, acknowledged the presence of the thing it bounced off. That is like thinking. It also asserts its own solidity. It tells its history and origin. The shells in the rock of the river bluffs tell us the rock was once something else. That is a declaration."

"But all that is simple observation. You are making it something else."

"I wondered that for a long time. I no longer think so. You have heard bird song, of course."

"Yes."

"Birds sing—that is, they declare themselves—even when they are silent." Tor pointed up at a vulture lazily circling. "Him. Do you feel something coming from him—as to what he is?"

Tristal squinted upward, then shaded his eyes. He looked and thought hard. "No. I don't think so."

"Even a dead bird is declaring itself. It is sharp, active, delicate, transforming itself with all due speed."

"It gives a sharp impression, Tor. *We* feel pity. It is *us. We* are thinking those things."

"Perhaps, Tris—but the bird is active. It is changing. It has been invaded by other things. It has the complete repose of relinquishment, but the giving up involves enormous activity. It is not a matter of its own will, and yet it is."

"Well, this all seems very strange."

"Maybe. But I am trying to determine how I know things. There must be a reason, a set of reasons."

"The Pelbar would say that Aven tells you when you need to know."

"But why me? More than others?"

"Stel said once that all are told but you are listening."

"I know I am listening. That's what I mean to say. The question is to what—and how to develop and sharpen the listening."

"Stel says he thinks it is partly a matter of courage and resolve."

"Maybe. I think it is a matter of stillness."

"Stillness?"

"I have no interests. I'm not so distracted by other noises. Stel thinks of Ahroe, of his position at Pelbarigan, of his child and this one to come. He thinks of them in an interruptive way. He doesn't include them in the overall singing of things."

Tristal pondered this. He felt vaguely uneasy about what Tor had said. "What of me? Do you hear a singing from me?"

"A very clear singing now, different from before the fever. A sturdiness and directness. An honesty and yearning. A hickory toughness."

"Toughness?"

"Yes."

Tristal squinted back at his uncle who was paddling steadily in the still strong spring current. Tor's strokes were even and wiry. Yet there was still that extra twist of the back with each stroke because of his right arm. Tristal felt it as pain, though it was clear there was no pain. It was a wrenching. There was a bearing up. Was that a part of Tor's song? Tristal wondered. Then, almost without thinking, he turned, sat up, and took his paddle, stroking with Tor, who watched his back. A quiet smile of pride budded on Tor's face.

"In another week we'll be leaving the boat and running," he said.

Raran thumped her tail once, then unbalanced the boat as she moved, stood, and leaned over the side for a few laps of water.

IV

FINALLY they reached the limits of the river, portaged through several lakes, and decided to abandon the arrow-boat. As they tied it upside down in a low tree, Tor remarked, "If nothing else, it may shelter some bird."

"Maybe the starband will come up here again for a winter hunt."

"Maybe. What do you see?"

Tristal had stooped and picked up a curious stone. He was scuffing the dirt off against his thumb. "An arrow point. But made of stone."

Tor took it from him and looked at it, turning it over. He handed it back. Tristal held it in his open palm. Slightly pink, chipped chert, it lay perfect and symmetrical.

"I've seen two or three of them," Tor said. "It was probably a spear point."

"But . . . the ancients didn't need anything like—"

"No. I think it came from before the ancients. The hunters they replaced. When the running bands find one, they always bury it again. They are very rare. But they have several at Pelbarigan. The Protector showed me."

"Should I bury it, then?" Tristal was disappointed.

"Not for me. We aren't a running band. It was for luck or respect. Maybe it'll be useful. Doesn't weigh much."

Tristal tucked it in his leather pouch then slung it over his back. "Let's start walking," said Tor. "I'm still cramped from the boat."

They walked all that first day. The next day they began a slow running pace northwestward, taking their time, stopping occasionally to rest, fish, cook, or chat. Tristal kept them supplied with small game with his shortbow.

As usual, Tor insisted on playing catch with his axe, tossing it at first easily to Tristal, then with increasing force.

Tristal noticed something grim in Tor's face when the axe came fast. Its edge was knife-sharp, and it was unsheathed. Tristal was uneasy, but the handle always came first, and he always tossed it back with the same force with which Tor threw it. Tris's handling wasn't always true, either, and Tor had to dodge aside at times and reach for it. But he never missed, nor did he say anything.

They continued to travel northwestward for some time, the landscape changing, with more pine forest. Finally they came to the shore of a very extensive lake and spent three days trotting around it to the west. Increasingly the country-side looked like the familiar Shumai grasslands, though colder and a little drier for so far east. They had seen flat-horned deer in the forests and swamps farther south, but they began to encounter small herds of deer with sweeping, spreading antlers.

At first Tristal found the going tedious; the landscape seemed so endless and slow to change. But Tor exulted in it, and his delight was contagious. He clearly was in no hurry to return. Tristal also no longer felt any anxiety about getting back to Northwall. Somehow that had all vanished with his fever. He knew he would return some day, but there seemed a vast stretch of time available. After all, he had a full seven years before the traditional Shumai promise he had made to Fahna would lapse.

Days of slow running unraveled into weeks as they progressed through a seemingly infinite, rolling prairie country, making their way farther north and west, into drier land, all empty, with shorter grass and much gullying, and into a steadily cooler climate. These changes unfolded so gradually that only someone as sensitive to slight differences in surroundings as a Shumai could watch it happening.

Shortly before noon one day, as they trotted slowly down an incline toward a stream, Tor slowed and turned aside. By the time Tristal was even with him, he was already kneeling.

"What do you see?" he asked, panting lightly.

"Bones. Large animal. One of those giant deer."

"Yes. What else?"

"It had antlers. They are gone. Cut off. Someone cut them off. There are people. Then the country isn't all empty. We may meet someone."

"Yes. What else?"

"They cut the hide off at the ankle, here. Scratches here. No side split, though. They took the hooves. For glue, probably. They took the lower jaw."

"Good. What else?"

"Else?" Tristal pondered. "I . . ." He fell silent.

"What did they use to butcher with?"

"A knife. Good sharp one. What else?"

"What kind?"

Tristal pondered. "Steel. Straight edged."

"Yes. Probably from the south. See what you said about the leg bone? The northern Shumai sometimes didn't use that side slit. They turned the leg hide inside out for stockings, against the cold."

"Shumai then?"

"Could be."

"It must be incredibly cold up here in the winter."

"Maybe. But with all this game, they could get along all right. But this has an odd feeling."

"You mean, like Disdan? Another wild group?"

"I've heard of Shumai avoiding justice by going north. For many years. Disdan did. Not common. I've heard of it."

"Could we run with them? Would they mind us?"

"Who knows? I'd as soon not. We wouldn't know why they were up here. They could be anything. This must be at least a couple of months old—a spring kill. Now, where would they be going? I don't know this northern game. There seems plenty of it everywhere."

Tristal did not reply. He would enjoy some human company—and to hear of Shumai life in the north. But Tor seemed uneasy. There was something he was not saying.

"Let's just run west for a few days," Tor said. "I'd as soon not meet them."

Tristal was disappointed, but he said nothing.

Two days later they found another kill site, more recent. Tor again studied it carefully. "No women," he said.

"And no children," said Tristal. "None of the marrow has been taken. No blood broth cooked. Or the tripod marks are gone. It's old."

"No small children anyhow. Maybe none at all. A lot of carelessness. Look how that hide was staked. Any old way."

"And they camped right among their butchering."

"Probably not long, though." Tor stood and looked around, sighing. "Let's run west again. Keep your nose awake for smoke. They have some reason to live away from the rest of us. It may be preference. But it may be . . ."

"What?"

"Some crime."

Tristal was unsure. Tor seemed too cautious. "Does your listening hear any danger?" Tristal asked. Tor looked at him. "No, Uncle, I don't mean any disrespect."

"No. I don't hear any danger—except what these signs tell me about the people. That is just good sense. There are only two of us. Now, we need to provide for every eventuality." Tor squatted down to explain what seemed to Tristal an overly elaborate set of procedures for dealing with anyone they might meet. But the younger man could see that Tor was in earnest, and when quizzed, he could repeat precisely what he had been told.

The next day they came upon some tracks. Tor stooped along the sand of a small prairie stream to read them. "At least four men," said Tristal. "How do you read it?"

"The same. About three days old. They aren't young either. And? . . ."

"They seem heavy."

"Good. That would be good for us, too. Heavy. But I'm not young either. Now. Let's take a run dead north awhile. Keep Raran close."

Two days later, Tor crested a rise and instantly gave Tristal a hand signal to fade off. Tristal saw him continue over, disappearing. He hissed Raran to his side and drifted off to the north into the grass, careful to leave little sign. He heard Tor's greeting call float back over the hill. Slowly he worked his way up to the ridge about fifty arms north of their path, holding Raran by the collar. He saw Tor advancing at an easy walking pace toward a group of men seated and standing down in an open place near a stream. They had no fire yet, though one man had kindling in his hands. They all looked at Tor. Tristal saw only spears and throwers—weapons of the sort the Shumai had used before the fight at Northwall, more than fifteen years before. Tristal settled down on his stomach to watch.

Tor approached the group, holding up his hand. Their axeman walked slightly forward. He was as tall as Tor and heavier, bare chested, his Shumai leggings worn and slick with grease. The two men approached each other. Several others crowded behind the axeman.

"Tor, here," said Tor. "From the bowbend far to the south."

"Everything is far to the south from here," said the axeman. His dialect was northern. "You wear an axe. Where is your band?"

"No band. In the south there are no running bands anymore. Since the fight at Northwall, they are settling down on the Heart and the Isso and farming or raising cattle and horses."

For a moment the man looked startled. "Fight at Northwall? Did we kill off the Pelbar, then?"

"No. We are allied to them. And the Sentani. It was against the Tantal, who had invaded. You haven't heard? That is almost twenty years ago now."

"I had heard of the fight," said a tall, sandy-haired man from behind the axeman. "I didn't believe it. Vale knows, too. We never thought it worth mentioning."

The axeman turned slowly. "It isn't. Nothing like that concerns us. But this man does. What're you doing here? And with your axe. We don't need an axeman."

Tor held out his arms. "I'm used to it. It seems a part of me." He smiled slightly. "You never told me your name."

"No. I didn't. What happened to your arm?"

"I lost it when we opened the dome. A long story. Where the rod rises in the spring. Have any of you heard of that?"

"Of course."

"There was a building under it. Some people had lived in it since the Time of Fire. Had all their supplies inside. It eroded out. We tried to get them out. They thought we were attacking and shot me."

The axeman laughed a low, ugly chuckle in his throat. "I think that may not be all you lost," he remarked. The men behind him laughed.

Tor cocked his hip. "Maybe not. It was enough. Too much," he said slowly.

"That's a long-handled axe. Let me see it."

"Guess not. You have one."

"There's room enough around here for only one, I think."

"There's plenty of room. I'll go back and around you. Never come back."

"I'd like to see the axe."

"Is yours old, then?" A couple of the men laughed, but stopped when the axeman turned and swept his eyes across them.

"Not old," he said quietly, turning back. "Very sharp. I think it could take a man's head off in one stroke."

Tor smiled. "Well, let's not try on me."

"There might be no need to. But I'm the axeman here. And I'd like to see yours. I am asking politely."

Tor shifted his position and behind his back gave the finger flick that told Tristal to turn and start to run. Tristal hesitated, but then backed slowly down from the hilltop and started to run north. Raran whined, but Tristal cuffed her hard and she dropped her ears and ran.

"He signaled," the axeman called. "Take him. Watch the hill for a running band. Now, take him." The men rushed forward, as Tor had backed, whirled, and started to run southeast, turning in time to dodge three spears, wrenching one free from the ground as he ran. With high, wailing yells the whole band followed him.

As Tor came back over the ridge, a wave of relief passed over him. Tristal was out of sight. He pounded down the slope, counting his steps, and when they measured thirty, he turned and threw the spear back over his path. The axeman came up over and met the spear, but dodged. It caught a runner behind him through the leg. The man cried out and went down. The axeman turned a moment and then came on, followed by the rest. Tor ran, dodging, trying to watch for more spears. He saw he was gaining as he passed through a small woods near a stream and looked back again. As he had noted, they were mostly older men and not truly running hardened. Tor settled down for a long run, arcing very slowly northward. He wondered how far away Tristal was.

He wasn't shaking off the runners as he thought he would, though he gained ground. He could see they had paced themselves for a long chase. Well, he could match them in that, and after sunset, their greater number would make less difference.

They had fanned out slightly behind him, well back, but driving him forward. He didn't like that. It was too much like an animal drive. Perhaps he could turn to the flank and confront the end man—no. They had thought of that. On both ends two men ran together.

After about seventy sunwidths of running, they had covered more than ten ayas. The country was still open. Tor had lengthened his lead, but not by a great deal. The men were tougher than he had thought. He came down off a ridge and decided to spurt north, trying to outdistance all but the end men. Tristal was out there somewhere. Tor wondered where, and how much he saw.

As Tor hit the valley floor and ran along the bottom, he suddenly saw a flat trap for large animals ahead of him. It was too late to dodge around it. He leaped but didn't quite make the far edge, falling through with only his arm over the edge. He saw the two end men speeding up, racing down the hill. One sent back a long ululating call. Tor struggled to throw himself up out of the pit, but with one arm he could not. The flankers ran nearer. Tor could feel the pounding of their feet through the dirt. One raised his spear, yelling, as two others appeared at the ridge-top behind. Tor desperately threw his leg up on the lip of the pit, glancing at the spearman, saw a flash and a short arrow in his chest to the fletching. Tor rolled up out of the hole as another arrow took the second man in the side.

Tor scooped up the near man's spear and ran north, Tristal ahead of him. Behind them they heard yells from the running band and turned to see the first of them sweep by the downed men and follow up the hill. Tristal ran slowly to wait for Tor, but Tor waved him on. Raran ran by his side.

They continued running, well ahead now, but their pursuers showed no signs of quitting. Finally Tor caught up with Tristal. Both were tired and lagging, but Tor motioned to run on. "We have to make it . . . at least to twilight," he panted out, "then run tonight."

"Why . . . did they try to . . . kill you?"

"Something to hide."

"What?"

"Don't know. Think they are . . . man-lovers."

"Oh. But . . ."

"Don't know any more. Don't want to."

"How many? I counted nineteen."

"Sixteen now . . . minus any who are taking care of that first man."

"The others?"

"They won't... need care."

"Oh. I... there seemed no... other way."

"There wasn't."

The pair ran on, slowly now, doggedly, as the sun faded. Occasionally they caught sight of a pursuer behind them, but the running band was clearly tired, too.

"We'd better settle in for a long night's run," Tor said.

"How late?"

"Most of the night?"

"Will they really follow?"

"Don't know. It's the axeman. He's determined... I think he will. We better keep going."

"Can we fight them? When they have separated, strung out?"

"No." Tor said nothing more for a time, then continued, "We would have to kill them. Rather run than kill. Besides..."

"What?"

"People who kill tend to die doing it. This... is safer."

Tristal mused on that as they ran into the dark, slowly, steadily, an easy, ground-eating trot. Gradually they swung westward until, by high night, they were heading nearly dead west. After another half quarter past high night, Tor slowed to a walk as they ran up a grade and at the top called a halt.

"I'll watch first," he said. "You sleep."

Tristal didn't argue, but lay down and unrolled his thin blanket. Their backpacks were the usual Shumai kind, running packs that hadn't hindered their progress much. Raran curled up by him and she soon sank into an exhausted slumber, twitching slightly as her muscles relived the run.

Tristal took his watch before morning. Somehow, as the sun rose, the country seemed more empty than ever, especially since they knew now that it wasn't, that out there somewhere people were looking for them.

Soon after, Tor jerked awake and sat up. "We'd better go," he said. They trotted down the hill, chewing a small strip of dried meat each, then headed northwest toward a narrow stream, where they quickly washed—except for their feet—and set out again.

With slight breaks, they trotted all day, stopping to cook and eat near sundown. Then they walked well into the night. Tristal began to think that Tor was taking their escape too seriously. After all, they were many ayas away now, and they had hid their tracks carefully.

That night they both slept with stomachs full of prairie dog. Raran, too, had eaten well. But Tor shook Tristal awake again before light, and they set out.

"This is not a pleasure, I know," he said. "But we're going this way anyhow. I sense..."

"Danger?"

"Determination. That axeman's determination. The men weren't hostile when I came down the hill. They were glad for a fresh face. I felt fear from them. But that man radiated hostility. He is holding them here, and they aren't strong enough to break free. He may have chased some of them down just the way he has chased us."

"Why did you go over the hill at all?"

"They'd seen me. I was sure of it. I wanted to give you some time."

"I didn't need it. We could have run together."

"It saved me, Tristal. They'd have had me except for your arrows."

Late that afternoon they stopped for a rest and a full meal. Tor felt easier, but was watchful. They walked on into the evening again, not hurriedly, but steadily.

The next afternoon they came upon a wooded slope, and Tor rested while Tristal took his shortbow for a hunt. Raran followed along, staying close. Tristal moved silently, his shortbow strung, and arrow already nocked.

As he eased around a large rock, suddenly a rope snaked over his neck and jerked him to the ground, choking. He was dragged a little way while trying to grasp the rope then the world began to go vague. Then he saw the form of the unnamed axeman loom up over him.

"Loosen it. Don't want to kill him yet," he said, grinning. He deliberately stepped on Tristal's ankle. Tristal whirled his other foot out at him, but the axeman jumped back and the man with the rope yanked it tight again. The axeman laughed. "Keep a watch for old one arm," he called.

Tristal was flipped over and tied, then carried, slung from a pole. "The dog. Did you get the dog?" the axeman asked.

"No. He run off."

The axeman frowned. "Fine. What kind of belly-picking

grovelers are you? 'He run off.'" He pondered. "We'll move out into the open. Maybe he'll attract the one arm. That is, unless he's deserted his young suckling here." He laughed.

They found an open area and built a camp. The axeman squatted by Tristal, questioning him about his origins and the purpose of his trip. Tristal refused to answer, and the axeman slapped his face repeatedly, then took a knife and dug its point into Tristal's belly, almost breaking the skin.

"You'd best explain yourself," he said.

Tristal did not reply. The knife dug in farther, and a trickle of blood came out around it.

"There is nothing to say. We came to see the country."

"Nobody just comes to see this frostbitten country. Just comes. Now. The truth." He moved the knife. Tristal winced.

"That is the truth. A running band came down the Heart last winter. A man named Disdan. They had been up here since before the fight at Northwall. They didn't even wear cloth—"

"You won't be either in a little while." Two men nearby laughed.

"They hadn't heard of the peace with the Pelbar. We were cutting wood for the Pelbar. They talked to us a long while. We thought we would come see the country."

"What did you do? One of us?"

Tristal writhed. "We did nothing. My uncle didn't want to be a farmer. He couldn't see himself there. I have no family. I came with him. That's all."

The axeman twisted the knife. Tristal squeezed his eyes shut. Then he sighed and said, "There's no use talking to you. You don't believe anything anyhow."

"Where's this uncle?"

"Who knows? He's a coward. He has probably run off and left me."

"A coward?" the axeman laughed. "Now I suppose you'll call that the truth. He may run, but I've seen enough to know he's no coward. Too bad he won't be able to help you. But you'll make a good enough bait to draw him in."

The axeman stood. "It's nearly sundown now. Get a good long pole we can tie this suckling to. And some firewood. Keep a watch out. His uncle can look on, but he won't be able to do anything. He'll try, though. He'll try."

The axeman's men were weary and silent, but they rolled to their feet and did what he said. Tristal wondered where Tor was. There had been no sign of him. Surely he would do something. But what could he do against sixteen alert men? As it grew dark, Tristal felt some sense of relief. That would change the odds. But he was less sure as time passed. The axeman set up his camp and its defenses. The men ate, paying Tristal little attention except to look and chuckle occasionally from a distance as they talked in low tones. He was now tied to the thick pole that had been brought for him. His short-sword lay with its point reddening in the fire, dandelion yellow around the edges.

Tristal worked on his bonds. They were so tight his hands were swollen and hard to move. He felt desperate. If Tor were so prescient, why hadn't he seen this? He had really led them right to this vicious running band and then abandoned Tristal. All that talk about hearing the singing of things—what good had it done? In the whole empty country, they had to blunder into the one gang of madmen. Tristal felt a helpless fury. He wondered what his uncle would have felt. Tor probably would be trying to pray, especially since he'd been with the Pelbar. But how could anybody pray at such a time?

He could almost hear Tor saying, "When would be a better time?" He was too desperate and angry to pray. But he could hear Tor's voice: "Then it's time to stop being desperate and angry. You at least have control over that— if not over much else." And what about Raran? She hadn't stood with Tristal either. She must have gone to get Tor. A lot of good that had done. Tristal took a deep breath and sighed to himself. He knew he ought to try to pray. He hadn't thought about that as much as Tor had. He'd resisted most of Tor's efforts to practice any sort of discipline like that. He would try.

He was interrupted by the axeman's calling to his four sentries, set well out from camp in a square. All were in the open. They all called back. The axeman then walked up and stood facing Tristal. He smiled. "This will be a pleasure. After pain. After the pain you've caused us. And the three men."

"I'm sorry about them," said Tristal. "We meant no harm. We only wished to save ourselves."

"We meant no harm. We only wished to save ourselves,"

shrilled the axeman, mimicking him in a woman's voice. Several men laughed.

The axeman stooped, took the handle of the short-sword, dropped it, then got a rag of animal skin and picked it up. He advanced on Tristal and waved it in front of his face. "Now, do you want to tell us more about what you're doing here?" he asked in a mild voice.

"You don't want to know anything about that," said Tristal. "You just want to hurt people."

"You think so?" The axeman waved the sword in front of Tristal's eyes, then touched it to his shoulder. Tristal yelled out as pain stabbed through him.

"Now, can't we be more pleasant?" he asked.

"You certainly could."

Again the axeman dipped the tip of the sword and Tristal felt another heavy splash of pain. He gritted his teeth, his head trembling, but said nothing. His breath hissed out.

"Very brave," said the axeman.

"Tor!" Tristal yelled. "Tor, Tor, Tor!" He hadn't known himself so capable of abject agony.

"Observe. There is no answer," said the axeman. "It is time to get serious." He lowered the tip of the sword again and drew a line from high on Tristal's left shoulder, down across his chest. Tristal shrieked out in the rush of pain, and as his cry died out, it seemed to echo from the distance. The men watching turned. In the distance they could see that a sentry had been tied to a bush. It was on fire, and he was yelling and shrieking.

"It's Doomy," one man shouted. Three men rushed out, spears in their hands, and as they did another fire bloomed from another sentry quadrant. Again a man shrieked from the middle of it.

"Stay," the axeman shouted. "It's the axeman. He's dividing us."

"And let them burn?" one man yelled. He turned and plunged into the darkness in the direction of the second pyre. Another man followed him.

"Stay," the axeman repeated. A yell came from the darkness toward the first fire. "See?" the axeman yelled. "He's there. He's waiting. Call in the other sentries. He's out—"

In a blur, Tor was in the firelight swinging his axe, downing four men in arcing swings too fast to mark. The axeman jumped back, holding the dully glowing short-sword in one hand, Tristal's throat in the other.

"Come closer and I'll—" A rush behind him struck him, knocking him forward as Raran hit him from behind, and before he could recover himself, Tor had leaped forward and sliced his shoulder with a quick downward stroke. The man screamed, as Tor raced behind Tristal and cut his bonds in a series of quick strokes. Tristal slumped to the ground.

"Up," said Tor. "Two other sentries and at least two men are out there." As he said this he swept Raran aside and finished the axeman. "Up." He lifted Tristal in the crook of his ruined right arm and shoved him toward the darkness, sheathing his axe, stooping and grabbing the short-sword.

Footsteps came from the darkness. He threw the short-sword. It flipped weirdly through the air. A cry sounded. Tristal stumbled into the dark. Raran snarled and leaped out. Tor followed. Tristal slumped down again, then forced himself upright. He turned and ran blindly toward the action, finding his short-sword lying in a small oval of burning grass. A body lay nearby. He took the sword, its handle still hot, and, turning, saw two of the running band returning to the firelight. One had a spear. Without a cry, Tristal ran toward him, bursting into the light, sweeping aside the spear and plunging the hissing sword into the one man. The other raised his hands and cried out. His legs were red and blistered. Tristal shoved him down and ran back the way he came.

Far ahead he heard Raran barking. He followed the sound, his chest throbbing with pain, running out into the darkness, steadily now, his arms fluttering with nervous agony, gripping the short-sword.

"Raran," he yelled. He heard a rush, and the dog was with him, wagging and prancing, but also whining in her anxiety. The dog turned and rushed off, and Tristal followed.

Ahead he saw a shape. "Tris. How bad is it? Can you run? I don't think they will give us any more trouble. But we don't know."

"I can run," said Tristal, grimly.

"Good. I think I saw a place in the woods that'll be safe. Even with a fire."

V

Once well away from the hostile Shumai, Tor and Tristal slowed to a walk. Only now was Tristal aware that Tor had a deep gash in his side. He walked along uncomplaining, blunting Tristal's bewildered resentment that he had not been rescued earlier.

Out in the open, short grass area, Tor stopped and listened. "Nothing yet," he murmured. No moon showed, but the starshine lit the scene with a ghostly brightness. "I'm sorry I couldn't get to you sooner. How is your chest?"

"Like fire."

"I heard you scream out as I was coming to the second sentry. Good thing, too. It distracted him. He got out a short yell, but you masked it with yours. It was a tight thing."

"You burned them?"

"I set the fires around them, with grass tied to them and fuel under them. I knew they'd yell. Maybe they did burn some. So did you."

"Yes, I did. I don't want to go through that again."

"Let's move on, then."

They continued toward and into the woods, over several ridges, and finally rested on the shoulder of a ridge with a good view below them. Once they were settled, Tristal fell into a fitful sleep. He awakened near sunrise to find Tor sewing his wound shut while biting on a shaved stick. Raran sat nearby, ears down.

Tor glanced over at Tristal, his eyes swimming. "Goodbye, darkness," he said. "Can you watch awhile?"

"Yes."

Tor held out a noggin of water, and Tristal took it and drank deeply. Tor finished his work, wiped his hands in pine straw, and curled up to sleep.

Tristal lay back at ease, thinking of the strangeness of

it all, of most of his life of wandering, of Tor's near total footlooseness. Again he felt a yearning to be back with Fahna and a strange, contrary realization that he really scarcely knew her. His chest felt tight and fragile as the skin attempted to heal over the burn. The sun flared the hurt, but he could not stand to wear anything on the wound, so he held up his hands to shade it.

Toward high sun, Raran, who had been off on a hunt, loped back, turned, and growled. Tor sat up. Approaching slowly over the eastern hill were three of the Shumai. One limped. They carried spears.

"Sharpen that shaft, Tris," said Tor.

"I have no speartip."

"Anything will help. Any shaft you can hold. I don't think they want a fight."

The two groups looked at each other across the narrow, wooded valley. The three Shumai conferred. Then one of them stuck his spear in the ground and came on alone. As he approached, slowly, walking up the hill, Tor called, "That's far enough. We can hear you." It was the sandy haired man who had spoken when Tor first met the band.

"Will you help us?" the man said. "We have three men badly hurt."

"You help yourselves."

"None of us has ever led."

Tor unsheathed his axe. "Come up here."

The man advanced up the hill, slowly, then squatted down as he came up to them.

"You do it," Tor said. "You take the axe."

"They wouldn't accept me."

"It doesn't matter. Just take it and leave. If any of them follow you, well and good. If not, you go alone. They will probably follow."

"I can't do it. I have no skills."

"They are there. You have let them sleep. Your axeman isn't the kind that would want them awake. I'm surprised at the hold he had over you."

"Well, you know—"

"There are some things you can't permit, even though you may want them more than life."

The man sighed. "You're like all the others. You—"

"Don't understand."

The man started. "Yes. You don't understand."

"I understand that some things are like stepping off a ledge and finding there is nothing below at all to break your fall. Ever. Nothing. Once you take your step, you are on your way. There is a good way and a bad way to be whatever way you happen to be. If the way you are leads to such submission, then you cannot permit it."

"It doesn't have to be that way."

"The potential is there. It happens with an axeman like yours. He knows there'll be no resistance. Why don't you go south? To the Pelbar."

"We can't. You know that. Not with their views."

"The question comes to whether the few of you would like to live up here with each other, and loneliness, or go south and endure frustration. Or contemptuous rejection. I didn't say it was just. But it will happen."

The man picked up a stick and snapped it. "No choice."

"When you have no choices, you've overlooked some. Go south to the Sentani winter country. It's easier than this one. Live there. If you want, find something you can trade south. Visit once a year. Contain yourselves. You will never make a running band. A real one."

The man bridled, then looked chagrined. Tor continued, "Because there are qualities an axeman must have that are closed to you. You don't see that, do you. An axeman has to deny what you exaggerate. I am not condemning you. But you have to be realistic."

"Exaggerate."

"Anything that so focuses the urges exaggerates them. You have to concentrate your thinking on things which do not involve any urges, normal or abnormal."

"Abnormal." The man snorted. "You are a person of no understanding. The way *you* are has to be the only way a person can be. Unimaginative. It is because of people like you that we've been driven off like cattle to a frozen waste like this. Just because your kind is in the majority. We're normal enough."

"Is it normal to be so dominated by a ferocious axeman like that one?"

"That was a mistake."

"But one not possible for me. Is it normal for me to have one hand?" Tor asked mildly. "I can't accept myself as any less a man, any less worthy, but it is not normal. It is a variance from the norm. It is a disability. You have to compensate. You have to struggle. You will never have anything but a struggle until you drop the whole question and look somewhere else."

"Where?"

Tor gave him a crooked smile. "A hard question. Service. Exploration. Curiosity. Complete freedom. A probing of the meaning of things. I'm still looking."

The man's return smile was just as crooked. "We thought you might help us."

"You hoped I might go along with you."

The man looked back at his companions across the valley. They stood still, leaning on their spears. "We thought at first we might follow you and try to kill you."

"That might work. What would it get you?"

"Revenge. Something to do."

"It's strange being what I am. As we came, we saw your signs. Everything I did to try to avoid you seemed to lead me to you."

"Sertine. It was Sertine who decreed you had to come. Because of the axeman."

"Or whatever. But that's why you won't trail us. You know that you had to be freed from the axeman. Aven knows we tried hard enough to avoid it. It wasn't permitted."

"What does that mean?"

"I don't know. But you are free. You are being allowed to change—to grow—to step back from the edge. Don't go over it again. It's a long fall."

"That's old meat and bitter water, axeman."

"I said I was not normal," Tor replied. "For awhile I was so stunned by the loss of my arm, I thought I would die. Who ever heard of an axeman with a ruined right arm? I was lifted out of it by truth spoken with love—by the Pelbar couple, Stel and Ahroe. And I found a purpose temporarily. I don't claim what I am doing now is 'normal.' My nephew, here, worries about that enough for both of us. But it falls within the broad boundaries of the normal. It isn't vicious. There are good ways to be abnormal. Judging by the hold your axeman had over you, that wasn't one."

"Help us find one."

"That has to come from you."

The man stood. "You are afraid you can't do it."

"I know I couldn't do it. Every building stands on its foundation. Everyone knows that."

"That's a riddle."

"No. Anything I would build on your foundation would depend on that foundation. You like the foundation. You build on it. Good-bye. You take the axe yourself. Never really trust yourself. You can't mistrust yourself enough. But you can keep that to yourself. In fact you'll have to. If the axe rusts, let it be with water, not blood. When you find other people willing to do what you ask, you have to withhold asking. The last axeman didn't. He carried domination to the point of entire perversion. Look at the result. Misery. As I said, there is a good way to be, however a man is. And a bad one. It's a real skill not to confuse them."

The man stood silently. "Doomy says to thank you for setting the fire away from him. He's not bad off. Neither is Gome. You are Tor?"

"Yes. This is my nephew, Tristal."

"I am Agon. Good-bye."

They palmed a Shumai parting, and the man went down the hill alone. Tristal released Raran's collar.

"When they go over the hill, we will have to move," said Tor.

"Will they follow?"

"Don't know. I don't think so. But we have to assume it. They are uncanny trackers. We'll have to be better than ever. We'll have to find someplace we can rest. I'm deadly hungry. I know you are, too. We'd best walk."

 VI

Tor and Tristal walked on for two days, slowly, hunting and watching, before they settled down to rest. They were in short grass prairie again, cold and wind-swept. Tristal had found a winding stream, small and clear until a wild thunderstorm raised it into a foaming, muddy torrent.

They had built a shelter in the bank above it, but it proved no match for the storm, and streams of muddy water soon snaked through the back wall and down across its small floor. Their tiny fire, on a platform in the front of the shelter, smoked with the blown mist and weighed the air down with the stink of the dried dung of grazing animals with which it was largely fueled.

Tor leaned back in a corner on a bed of grass, chewing on a stem, brooding over something. Tristal resented both his own misery, and his uncle's nonchalance. Nervous with the thunder, Raran snuggled against Tristal, who had tired of the conundrums and math games the Shumai used to amuse themselves at such times. Tor had an endless supply of them and never seemed to use the same problems twice. Tristal had asked his uncle to stop posing questions. He reclined in a dark moodiness.

"You sat out enough storms like this one in the old life not to worry about it, Tris. It will end."

Tristal held silent a long time, sewing a patch in his running boots. "But I've sat them out in Pelbarigan, too. It was more comfortable."

Tor threw the straw out into the rain. "The old way was a bad one at times. We know that. We know it from the speed we all dropped it when a new way opened up. But it had its good side, too. I wouldn't have missed this for anything."

"This? You wouldn't have missed this?"

"No."

Tristal looked out at the gray scene, the blowing rain, the seething stream below them. He felt disheartened, almost to despair. Tor had admitted to abnormality in talking to the Shumai survivor. Tristal began to wonder if he'd allowed himself to be guided into a place of entire misery by a truly strange man.

"Before you judge my statement, think about it at least a quarter of the afternoon," Tor said.

Raran growled. Across the stream they could see forms in the driving rain—animals trotting north along the rim of the stream gully. The beasts smelled the fire and turned, slowing to a walk then stopping. They loomed almost as large as wild cattle. Their shaggy hair blew in the gusts. They held their heads low. Horns swept down the sides of their faces and curved outward. One of them snuffled loudly, and they turned and loped heavily away eastward.

For Tristal they seemed a sudden animation of his feeling of the strangeness of the place. He turned to Tor and saw his uncle's eyes were gleaming.

"What were they?"

"I don't know. But they are used to the cold. All that hair. That would make a winter coat! I know what I hope it means."

"What?"

"That we are coming to some new place. Maybe Disdan's ice country."

Tristal stared at the rain, his threaded needle and soft boot held idly in his hands. Raran rooted her nose in under Tristal's arm. Tor shifted, and Tristal saw his eyes were closed, a rapt look on his face.

The next morning dawned clear, the air washed and cool. When Tristal awakened, Tor was already wrapping strips of dried meat carefully in the soft leather of his food pouch.

"Ready to go?"

"No good reason to stay here," Tristal replied.

As it turned out, they found nothing new that day or the next. The third brought rolling country and some rocky outcrops. Far to the north they saw more of the strange beasts, grazing. Pines appeared on higher knobs, and spruce. In the afternoon, Tristal looked ahead and said, "Looks as though we're in for another line of storms."

The horizon gleamed with a dull white, hovering over the landscape. Tor squinted. "Mmm."

Tristal whirled around, looked again. "Ice? Is that the ice? We are going to go over that?" He turned to his uncle and found him laughing.

"Who knows? Let's go and see."

Tor lay on his belly in the rocks looking down at a small group of people that was seated around a campfire. They had traveled for two more days, the ice in the northwest slowly growing before them. The country had grown rougher and higher. Then a whiff of smoke had sent them to cover in the rocks, and Tor had worked his way forward to see.

Below, an old man sat by the fire surrounded by three boys and a young woman. He held a thick skin over his knee, and on it pressed a large flake of stone down onto his thigh as he worked a long bone tool into it, shaping it. Around him a litter of pieces of broken stone told of his long work on such tools.

One of the boys helped the woman to cook. The others played the Shumai game *na*, *na*. Yet they were not like any Shumai Tor knew. They stood shorter and tended to be darker, though the girl's braided hair gleamed yellow in the sun.

The old man held up the piece he worked on, squinting at it. Then he blew at it. He wiped his hands and picked up a knob of bone and rubbed the edge of the piece. Then he returned to picking at the stone's edges, sending out small snapping sounds. Tor was fascinated. Two spears lay nearby—shafts with hollow ends—and a small stack of stone-tipped sticks that obviously fit into the shafts.

Suddenly the man paused as though listening. He began to work again, but again paused. "Abry," he said to the largest boy. "Tell man in rock he can come down here if he want to watch." His voice was crisp, the accent different, but not hard to understand.

Abry cried out and rushed for a spear, but Tor immediately stood up and began picking his way down the rocks. He looked at the old man and laughed.

The old man laughed back. "Abry," he called. "Put that up." The boy looked confused.

"Tristal," Tor yelled over his shoulder. "Bring Raran."

Tristal rose from above Tor and followed him, holding Raran's collar.

Tor held out his hand to Abry, but the lad didn't understand palming. Tor passed the staring boy and approached the old man. "Tor," he said. "My nephew, Tristal. The dog, Raran."

"Alone? No band this time?"

"You've seen Shumai before? Yes. We're alone."

"Only long ago. We traded. Two or three time. And the mad tribe."

"I must be getting careless. Or I must smell. How did you?..."

The old man waved his hand. "I felt your interest. You reached out with your mind."

Tor felt a slight inward chill. "Teach me to make those," he said.

"You can't learn overnight."

"No. I imagine not."

Tristal turned his eyes from the young woman, stooped, and rummaged in his pack. "Here" he said. "I found this one. Way back."

He handed the old man his ancient spear point. The old man took it and turned it over and over, murmuring. He held it out at arm's length.

"Would you like it? Take it," said Tristal.

The old man laughed. "No. Keep it. You'll need later. I can make them. It is very nice. We have some old ones. At Sedge. Our place. Here. I am Tegrit. You've met Abry, my grandson. His brothers, Prent and Doce. My grand-daughter, Orsel. Are you hungry? We will soon eat. You got anything to add?"

Tristal handed Orsel two ptarmigan he carried on his belt. She smiled at him. Tristal found her features slightly blunt, her eyes clear blue and upsettingly direct. He smiled back as he turned again toward Tegrit.

"There is none of right rock at Sedge," Tegrit explained. "It is easier to make tool here than to carry back all rock and make them at home. Of course we will take some back. And we leave most of what we do here rough. Finish it at home. If you come, we can take more."

"Yes. Of course."

"Now, Tristal, you stir while Orsel clean bird. Boy, you get more wood. And straw for bed. You—Tor—you want to watch? I think you can do it with one hand. Not easy, though. You'll want to make hide pad to hold down rock. Or get your nephew to do heavy first cracking."

Tor merely murmured in reply and squatted down to watch the old man work the stone into a long, leaf-shaped point.

"I'll finish this one well so you can see," said Tegrit. Waving his bone tool, he said, "Only older people seem to want to do this. Younger one let older one make all tool." The two men looked at each other grinning in instant rapport. But Tor was worried, too. Tegrit had *felt* his presence. What else could he divine? His ability was too definite to be like Tor's own. He felt no danger, but he would be wary.

They stayed on four days while Tegrit worked on tools, Tor with him all the time, his own attempts laughably clumsy. Tegrit instructed and commented. Tristal spent most of his time hunting with the boys, who had never seen a bow before. At first contemptuous of it, they soon began to marvel at its accuracy and the distance of the flight of its arrows.

Orsel sometimes came along, too. She was largely silent, but Tristal could sense her presence, her looking at him. By the third night she contrived to sleep next to him in their line between the fire and a large rock.

He felt her foot move against his leg, then her arm come over him as they all lay still, the dying fire flickering. As it rested across him, her arm radiated smoke and sweat odor. He lay very still as though asleep. She twisted closer. The weight of her arm pressed Tristal into the rough straw under him. At least three sticks, pointed, jabbed his down side. Her knee came up over his, and her ankle hooked around his shin. Tristal found sticks down there, too. He remained perfectly motionless, breathing with a practiced evenness, his body crying out for relief, for movement. Orsel was warm, her skin smooth and fine as the fur between Raran's ears. Her breath came close to his ear, tickling him. It smelled faintly like apples.

"Stop pretending, Tristal," she whispered.

Tegrit rolled over and stood up, brushing himself. He went to the fire and trimmed it, adding wood, then walked off into the dark. The flare of light lit up the sleepers. Orsel rolled away. Tristal still didn't move, his oppressed arm nagging him for relief. Finally Tegrit returned, looked at the fire again, trimmed it again, dropping a small log. Tristal sat up as though awakened, turned and stretched.

Tegrit looked at him and smiled dimly. Tristal lay back down, turning and settling. He never looked at Orsel, but soon from her breathing he could tell she was genuinely asleep.

In the morning Tegrit roused Tristal at sunup and sent him hunting with the boys. When they returned, in late afternoon, the old man was still chipping stone with Tor, whose hand was cut and bloody. His mouth was set with frustrated determination. Tegrit seemed amused. Orsel was not there. When she returned, she would not look at Tristal. He was relieved but somehow vaguely upset by this. What had he done? He was promised. Did he have to announce that to everybody he met?

That night the boys lay down after sunset, but Tor kept

working at his stone chipping while Tegrit watched and commented by firelight. Tristal watched, stiffly, slowly and elaborately making an arrow. Somehow the air was tense.

Finally Tegrit stood and brushed his hands on his thighs. "You, Tristal. You and Orsel take walk. Not too far in dark." They both looked at him. "Go on," he said. "Take walk. Not too far, I said." He turned to Tor. "One of problem of knowing thinking is noise of it. With these two it is almost deafening. You understand, don't you?"

Tor looked wry. "I don't hear thoughts that clearly. If you think it is all right, though. They probably ought to talk to each other. But Tristal is promised."

"I never told you that," said Tristal.

"You know thing, too!" Tegrit was amused.

"Some things. Some things are obvious."

"What does 'promised' mean?"

"It means that when he returns home, he will marry. They have settled it."

"Is it that settled then?"

"It normally is. Ask him."

Tristal was vaguely irritated. Who was Tor to wedge himself in and settle everything? Of course he was right. It was settled. But it all seemed too brutal, so ridiculous way out here.

"I don't wish to take a walk," Orsel said.

"I'm your grandfather, and I'm telling you to take one. I can't stand your shouting at each other."

"We've said nothing."

"I've heard it all. Now go. Don't say a word to each other if you don't want to. But go. Off far enough to make thing quiet around here."

"Aren't you even afraid for me?" Orsel asked, suddenly weepy. "Don't you think I have shame? Any future?"

"Tristal is good enough boy. Neither of you know what you want anyway. Go. Now, Tor. Edge too messy. Take bone joint and rub it across. You need flatter place to work from."

Neither man would look at Tristal and Orsel any more. They concentrated on the rough stone Tor was attempting to chip. Tor hit the stump of his right wrist again, and waved it, whistling softly. Tegrit chuckled.

Tristal looked at Orsel. She dropped her eyes. They met on the far side of the fire and walked out onto the dark grassland. Tristal took her hand. Eventually they stopped and faced each other, wrapping their arms around each other's waists. Orsel still smelled of sweat and smoke. It occurred to Tristal that he probably did, too. Her breath still smelled like apples, and, when he found her mouth, he found the same apple sweetness.

"How promised are you?" Orsel asked.

"All promised. Enough to be lonely. What do they mean for us?"

"Not that much." Orsel kissed his ear. "You have lovely ear. Not everything. Something in between."

"How will we know?"

"Grandfather say you are good boy." She paused and snickered at that idea. "Good boy," she repeated, drawing it out. "He mean you will know. If you don't, I will. I have my limit. You will not stay. I will probably marry man named Dardan. Much bigger than you. Good catch. Now stop talking." She bumped her forehead against his.

The stars were somewhat different in the north, and, after a time, Tristal told Orsel the Shumai names for many of them. But that was a diversion. The moon on Orsel made her seem smooth and almost light green, unreal, like a Pelbar carving that moved and murmured. At one point she sighed and said, "We've been out here a while. Grandfather work slowly and talk. And my cousin. It's good thing you came. You are so tall. What happened to your chest? No. Don't tell me. Some other time."

☐ VII

AFTER Orsel and Tristal had left the firelight, Tor and Tegrit worked for a time in near silence. Then Tegrit said, "Do you mean to stay with us? Long?"

"I don't know. Not long, I think. I mean to cross the ice."

"No one cross ice. No one knows if it even has far side."

"It must have a far side. Everything does. It has this side."

"Priest only people who go up on ice. They do not permit other to go. They say it has no far side. It is braced against beginning of thing, pushing. Only their power hold it back."

"They hold it back? You ... accept that, then? I mean no disrespect. If we're to meet them, though, maybe you could tell me something about them."

"Priest? They have been here long time, but not as long as hunter, I think. Story say they came many year ago, far beyond memory of any living person, or of any oldest has talked to. But not so long ago as hunter."

"Came?"

"Yes. They said they had mission to us. But they didn't come from southeast, way rest of us think we did. They came around ice from west. They are generally darker than us, as you will see, though they intermarry some. I mean they take some women, good and pretty one."

"You don't like that."

"They use people. Use them up. They keep their secret of mind influence. I see you are skeptical about their mission, their holding back of ice. Any person would be. Until they knot thinking up. They train each other. Eat some special thing from far to south. Send messenger for it every year again. But are very careful. I know that from reading thought. They are on guard against some people living far to south."

"How far?"

"Some week running, I think. Don't know. They are very secretive. Teach their secret only to each other and guard them. No one tell them on fear of death. No one dare ask either. They say it is all necessary to power of holding back ice. You will see. They do have power. Some knowledge, some mystery, some manipulation of thought, something they eat. When I touch thought of older priest, I find it mad and spinning. I know when they will die. Always madness first, then quick death. I think other one quietly kill them, then mourn them."

Tor shuddered. "Is it worth all that, then, to control other people?"

"They say it is all sacrifice needed to hold back ice so it will not fill up all space."

"I take it you don't believe them."

"No. You know I have ability to read thought. I never asked for it. It was always there. I know what they think. I know they say one thing, think another. They now have come to know they can't control me. That is one reason I am out here. It is safer to be away. Hunter feel that, too, and are out from Sedge as much as they can be. You must know what I mean. You read thought as well."

"No. I've been watching you. You simply know what people think as though they said it. I *feel* the way things are. It is wholly different. I've been wondering."

"I know you believe that. Maybe it is so. But I fear for you and your boy. The priest will not like you. They will try to control you. I sense you don't control easily. They will try to destroy you with thought. They can do it. I have seen it. I had hoped that you could resist. Now you say you can't."

"In your way, you mean? I see what you mean. How have you stopped them? They don't like you."

"You have to feel thought is *your* thought first. If you know *they* are thinking it, then its edge is dull. They are very devious. You think, 'I hate that man. I am going to kill him.' And you do. Then they call you murderer and do away with you. But all time it was their idea you thought your idea. They put thought in your mind. When you know it is their thought, you laugh to yourself and nothing happen. You see?"

"Why? Why do they do this?"

"For control. You know some people like to control. Soarer set up that way. We are Soarer. Named that way because we fly from ice with wing every year four time. It is ceremony. Only certain one do it. They are held up in air by strength of priest of ice. So priest say. It is really wing themself—something from ancient time. They know that so I know it. If anyone else want to try it, they let them. But they change wing so they fold and person fall down and die. They also throw thought that wing is good, so people believe it."

"How have you managed to survive? This is a harsh climate. Such a burden on your society should destroy it. How many are you?"

"We are about five hundred. Priest have not helped. But much of time you don't notice. Only when you are really *aware* can you tell. Priest of ice and Soarer not all that many. But they control everything. They are satisfied to control. It is easier than working. Rest of us feed them, build their shelter, weave their clothing, tan their skin, go to their ceremony. Give them best women. To marry sometime. To have other.

"They are careful. They don't go too far. We are people of honor in part. It is hunter. You know hunter. They are independent people. Have to be. Have to be good comrade, too.

"Now one hunter, young man named Dardan—him they call ox arm—is on verge. He is very powerful. Obvious leader. He is away much of time. Priest of ice fear him. They know he cannot continue as he is. They want him to join. He has some contempt for them. Know something is wrong. If he doesn't join, I fear they will kill him. If he escape them, then maybe something will change. I have tried to talk to him. He won't listen, but I know that that is because they have made me kind of outcast out of fear. My family have suffered for it. They are afraid that other will believe me. None do."

"But they haven't harmed your family?"

"Not yet. There are only five hundred of us. And half now are far south with potato crop. They can't kill too many. We need each other to survive. But they do kill. Now and again. It keep us afraid."

Tor pondered this. The old man seemed to be telling the truth. He was aware of attempts to influence thought from his early time with the Alats. They didn't do it by thought projection but by endless haranguing and attempts to instill their ideas to the exclusion of all others. The Soarers' way was far more insidious. Tor felt he could resist it all right; he thought of Tristal with some fear.

"Tegrit, what if we made it seem that Tristal were a little simpleminded? Would they accept that?"

"You are more worried about your nephew? I wouldn't try it. Simpleminded people are easy to influence. If he didn't follow their lead, they would know. Then they would know you were danger. They would think I have influenced you. They are not fond of me. You must realize that. I am valuable, though. I am best of toolmaker. We have little metal—all of it from ancient ruin. So I make many tool. So do other, but mostly old people, and we don't have many old people."

"The life is too hard, then?"

"No. When you know how to manage it, it is not bad to live here. Up near ice, where we live, many animal migrate from north in autumn. We store much meat for winter. We grow potato root near steam hole to south. That carry us through. We bring wood on snow. We are comfortable enough—except for priest of ice."

"Do you have no God, then? I know some Shumai, some of my people, must be in your makeup. Way back, maybe. I see the blood and some of the habits. But some other group as well. Is there no mention of Sertine, the Shumai God?"

"There is mention. But he is forbidden. Some of hunter talk of Sertine, but only out on hunt." The old man smiled. "I think integrity of that has helped to carry us along. Sertine is idea of integrity. My father was hunter. I was named for integrity. My father named me. But he hid name since it was not traditional one. You are like them, hunter. I sense it from you, but much more. You could change us. You could make all difference. I sense it. But it would be dangerous."

"Danger is nothing, but . . ."

"But your nephew. He is not as aware."

"No. He is not responding as I had hoped. But that may be the right thing. I am not bound to people as he is. If he has that and also what I can teach him, he'll be a true leader."

"Think about these thing. You may not be strong enough. They are very clever. I do not think you can cross ice. I can't read why you want to. I sense your deep desire to. I have not long to live. No. Do not protest. Priest of ice do not like old people. They tend to go mad as they grow old."

"It is what they do with their minds that makes that happen."

"Yes. I think so. They feel old people are burden when they can no longer work. So they get them out of the way. Sometimes it is direct. Sometimes it is through someone else. With me, I fear it may be Dardan."

"The hunter. I see. That would be very efficient. Two threats removed with one incident."

Tegrit looked at Tor, surprised. "You do read thought."

"No. I have seen tyranny before."

"Tyranny?"

"The rule of some by others through force and deceit. It is common enough in human societies. Do you pray?"

"Pray? Say prayer to ice or to Sertine? No."

"But you know some prayers to Sertine?"

"Yes. I have heard hunter say them. I have said them too when hunting. But they are nothing. You think they are something. I can see that. Well, it is too late for me."

"Never. But let that go. We will get along. But I am going to cross that ice, Tegrit. If it is so bad a thing to think in your society—the Soarers?—then you should not tell."

"No. Tristal. He must not tell either."

"I will try to see to it."

"You must do more than try." Tegrit fell into silence, staring at the fire. Finally he said, "Well, I'm going to lie down. These old bone are getting stiff. I think young people back soon."

Tor looked at him quizzically.

Tegrit laughed. "Some thing I don't say," he said, getting up, looking at his hands. "You've kept me at tool making. But we've got good lot this time. Time to go to summer soaring. I will tell you about that tomorrow."

"I'd like to ask you one more thing. It will sound strange. Do you hear a singing from things?"

"Singing?"

"Then you don't. All right. Tristal doesn't either. For me everything has its own voice. Not sound. Its part in a great song all sung together."

Tegrit looked at him silently, then murmured, "No. I don't hear that. Only thought of other people." He turned and walked toward where the three boys were sleeping. Then he paused and turned. "What kind of song does ice sing?"

"I haven't been close to it. So far it is a song of grandeur, threat, command, danger, fear. Not a good song, except for the grandeur. And a kind of purity. But a purity in which there is no life."

"No life, then. That is song of priest of ice." The old man sighed and prepared to lie down.

Tor remained by the fire a long time, looking at it and thinking. Perhaps they shouldn't join the Soarers, as he gathered they called themselves. He didn't mind for himself though it might be dangerous. But for Tristal . . . Tor placed his palm against his eyes as the Pelbar did while praying and remained that way a long time thinking.

Finally he heard Tristal and Orsel coming. They moved to him and sat by him, one on either side.

Orsel took Tor's hand in hers and looked at it. "You better stop working stone. Your hand is cut bad."

"Not so bad."

"There will be time. Let it heal."

"What's the matter, Uncle?" Tristal asked.

"The matter?"

"We did nothing," said Orsel. She laughed lightly and leaned over, kissing Tor's cheek. Tristal shot a glance at her. She grinned at him. Tor put his arm around her and squeezed her lightly against his side. She laughed quietly.

"You both go to sleep," said Tor. "I have some thinking to do."

"You do, Orsel. I'll sit with my uncle a little."

Orsel stood and thrust out her lower lip playfully. "I'll save a place for you," she said. "Don't be long."

"I won't." He glanced at Tor. "Not too long," he added. "Don't go away."

She laughed quietly and found her sleeping robe. The two Shumai watched her, smiling. When she settled down, Tristal turned to Tor and whispered, "Now. What is it?"

 VIII

SEDGE was a low village of half-buried log huts heaped over with dirt. From the outside each looked like a mound with smoke rising from its center. They were circular, and inside each contained one very large room for an extended family. Booths around the sides of the room, neat and cozy, could be partitioned off by hanging heavy skins across the entrance area, but during the day, except when someone wanted privacy, they were left open.

Tegrit's family was not a large one for Sedge. Two of

Tegrit's sons had died, one in hunting, the other in response to the collective will of the priests.

It was impossible for Tor and Tristal to melt into the crowd unnoticed. The arrival of strangers was so rare among the Soarers that the two moved at the center of a group of children continually. They also stood taller than almost all the Soarers, and while there was a fair sprinkling of light-haired Shumai types, they were interspersed with a shorter and darker strain of people. Others seemed a mixture. Most of the priests of the ice were from the darker group.

Many of the Soarers regarded the two with suspicion. It had helped that they arrived with heavy loads of Tegrit's worked stone, the boys carrying their light packs.

The day following their arrival, a dark young man in a long decorated robe stopped at Tegrit's house to ask that Tor and Tristal come for an interview with the priests' council. Tegrit didn't look up from his work, but Tor felt his warning.

They were ushered into a structure with walls of stone instead of logs. It was also somewhat larger than the family homes but otherwise not much different. The support posts inside were carved and polished, and around the ceiling hung the wings used in the ceremony of soaring. The two Shumai were asked to sit on the floor in front of a semicircle of four men and a woman, all elaborately dressed in dyed skin robes and tall boots. The man in the center wore a tall hat trimmed with goose feathers.

He raised his hand. "We understand that you have come from far off."

"Yes," said Tor. "Very far. From the country of the Pelbar, far down the Heart River."

"Why have you come here?"

"A hunting band described the ice country to me last year. Since my own running band had broken up, I wanted to come and see it. This is my nephew. He came with me also for the sake of exploration." Tor felt strangely uneasy. He had expected that, though, and forced it out of himself. He had asked Tristal to try to remain silent and concentrate on things he had memorized or to work mathematical problems if he thought he felt any attack on his peace of mind.

"If we are a trouble to your people, we will gladly move on. It is a large country. I see it is almost all empty. I am sure there need be no further encounters."

The central priest waved his hand. "You have come in time for midsummer ceremony of soaring. You must stay. You will see force with which priest hold back ice. You may stay on longer if you wish and if you obey law. We need hunter. Always can use hunter. Now, you must tell us of encounter with mad band. We have heard you met them."

Tor recounted their meeting, flight, and briefly, without detail, the defeat of the axeman. He ended saying, "My nephew bears a bad scar from them and I was cut myself. We were fortunate to escape alive."

"It was ability, young man," said the priest. "Obviously it was ability." Tor thought he saw a frown or two shade across the impassive countenances of the priests. Then he wasn't sure.

The priest turned to Tristal, smiled slightly, and asked, "Young man, have you very much education?"

"Education? No. Only in the Shumai way. I know the stars some, and some things about hunting."

"I know Shumai love mathematic. Have you any knowledge of that?" He smiled strangely.

"I . . . only a little."

"Can you tell me square root of one hundred ninety-six?"

"Of course, it is . . ." Tristal felt something hit his mind and seem to scoop everything out of it. He tried to speak but could not seem to make his mouth work. He tried again. He looked at Tor for help, but his uncle seemed to be picking at a hangnail abstractedly. "It is . . . nine," he stammered.

"Are you sure of that?"

Tristal seemed to see the answer gleam out in perfect light. "Yes, it is nine," he said, smiling.

"Very well," said the priest. "Now, have you any other reason for being here? I mean, of course, reason of your own other than your uncle."

"We mean to . . ." Tristal felt a slow clarifying of his thought and a bewilderment about his previous answer.

"Yes?" Darkness seemed once more to fight for his mind. Tor continued to pick at his hangnail.

"We mean to see the new country. It was hard to believe what Disdan said about the ice."

"And what do you think now?"

"It is beyond what he said of it. If we went home now and told what we had seen, I think few people would really believe us. And no one would understand about it who had not seen it. An endless mountain of ice. It must be strange to live near it all the time and never have it out of your sight."

"It is our duty. We keep it at bay through strength of our mind, just as hunter keep great brown bear at bay."

"Keep . . . what? I don't understand. What are they?"

The priest laughed and pointed at a giant brown pelt hanging on the wall. "Those," he said. "More powerful than ox or flat-horned deer. Much faster than man. Roar like falling of face of ice. Eat man if it can. Come mostly in early winter, near ice or from north. If you stay, you will see."

"You don't object to our staying, then?"

"No. We see no danger in you. You may stay. You have come, as I said, in time for ceremony of soaring. Good. You will see wonder such as you have never imagined."

Tor glanced up at the wing structure spread out against the ceiling. "With those?" he asked.

"With those and our strength of thought. Our duty," said the priest.

Tor stared at the wings with a strange fixity. "Remarkable," he said.

"We thank you for coming. You may go." The two Shumai rose. As they walked toward the entrance, both were hit with a strange weakness and their knees wobbled. Then it passed and they left.

After they had gone, the woman turned to the central priest and said, "What do you think?"

"Young one is child. Older one is not. He is dangerous man. He forced our thought out of younger one. He knew. Tegrit has told him thing."

"How did he do it, then? Is he adept?"

"I don't know. But he is hunter. It give him courage. He is man who know no fear. No fear at all. You felt his courage? Young one full of courage, too, but lack experience. We can get to young one. Did you mark how older one let us take young one thought in question of mathematic but not of why they are here? There is more to it."

"But you saw how we took strength from their leg."

"I saw them let us."

"Should we eliminate them or send them off?"

"Not us. We get argument to eliminate them. And we do same with Tegrit."

"What of his tool making? He is best."

"Other will have to learn. It is necessary. We must have order. We cannot let disorder enter Sedge. It is too important. Better that he die than whole society thrown into disorder and danger."

"We have waited far too long already," said a small man on the end of the arc of priests. "He know our thought; we cannot have him warning other. He has done much damage."

"What will his grandnephew think? One will soar tomorrow."

"He is trained enough. He will know we are right."

"Mage, you will see to that."

"He is trained. I will need help."

"We will all contribute. Let us give it some thought now."

Outside, Tor asked Tristal, "Tris, what is the square root of one hundred ninety-six?"

"Fourteen, of course," he replied, looking puzzled.

"You don't recall the priest asking you at all, then?"

"Asking me that? No."

"You told him it was nine."

"Nine! I . . ."

"His thought told you to. You let it take you. We will have to be more wary than any hunt ever made us. Believe nothing that makes you angry. Believe nothing that makes you doubt me or Tegrit. Test every thought. Do not be tempted to any violence."

"Are you sure it's all that bad? They aren't monsters."

Tor shot him a look. "What did I just tell you?"

"But I need to be allowed my own independence of judgment."

"Yes. Exactly. Your own. Not mine. Not theirs. You will find it in concentrating on the values you have always known. Test everything continually. Test it. Take no action at all until you have."

"What about you? I saw your knees wobble as we left. They were laughing at us. They were telling us they could do anything they wanted to, but that they chose not to."

"Yes. I won't say I let them wobble. But when I saw they were, I knew the source."

"What good is that?"

Tor laughed. "It let me know I wasn't just getting old." He put his arm around Tristal, but his nephew shrugged it off. "They have you already, then?" Tor asked mildly. Tristal looked at him, astonished.

The entire population of Sedge went to the ice face early in the morning, a walk of about three ayas. Near the face, the ground lay soggy and running with melt water. The side of the ice sheet was not smooth, as Tor had expected, but a series of complex and crumbling ridges, gullied like eroded dry country, occasionally falling off in gigantic chunks that rumbled and crashed as they fell. The ice itself seemed to gleam with blue-green light.

The priests had selected for the ceremony a comparatively stable ice mass. For some time they and their apprentices had been chiseling a series of steps into the ice, reaching far up the steep shoulder of the great mass so that figures on top looked like fine dark seeds. Two sets of wings were already at the top when the crowd arrived and arranged themselves on a slight rise opposite the ice.

A group of twelve priests seated in a row were already chanting in a slow monotone, using words that made no sense to Tor. Above this strange collective voice a high wandering woman's voice ran, but Tor could not hear at all what she was saying.

Suddenly, at a gesture from the central priest, the chanting stopped. He raised his hands and called out, "My children. We are gathered here once again to show our mastery of ice and sky. It is our duty to remain here to hold back ice from rest of land. Only we can do this, through our training and ability and fact that ice fear us, so shrink back. We have special opportunity today to show our visitor how great our mastery is. It is fact that Soarer, through dedication of priest of ice, control air and sky. There is much danger in this. You shall see. Let singing begin again. Be silent all other." As the chant resumed, louder than before, the central priest could barely be heard shouting, "Let soaring begin."

High on the ice face a figure was being strapped under broad V-shape wings of thin, scraped hide painted yellow and red. Again the priest raised his hands, and the figure dropped out and away from the ice, falling swiftly, then suddenly swooping upward, turning toward the ice again, rising, gliding along near its vertical surface, turning again, rising, swinging in lazy arcs like a vulture, gaining altitude, soaring away from the ice toward Sedge, gliding back again, performing the same lazy circles, mounting higher, then spiraling down in broad circles to land lightly near the priests. All the while Tor studied the techniques and pattern of the flight.

The crowd yelled and danced, forming a ring around the flier and the priests, chanting the priests' chant, marching and waving their arms. The celebration continued for some time. Then the soaring was repeated by the second man.

Tor tried to get close to the wing devices, but tradition held that the crowd had to keep back.

Tristal saw him staring at the wings fixedly. "What? What is it?" he asked.

"What? Oh. Just seeing how they are made. Judging the measurements."

"It's amazing, Tor. It's as they say. They really flew."

"Yes. I've always wanted to do that, watching hawks."

"I'd like to be a priest of ice and do it, too. It'd be worth staying for, Tor, to fly like that."

Tor looked at him hard, then shut his eyes. "Think, Tris. Think hard. Do the birds need priests?"

"But they aren't birds. They are men."

"With *made* wings. Now. I want you to study the wings as carefully as you can, so you can draw them out if you need to. Every detail. Even the dimensions as you estimate them."

Tristal looked disgusted. Tor gripped his arm and shook him hard. "I didn't know you'd be so easily put to sleep," he said.

"You just don't believe what's in front of you."

"I am the one who does. What is in front of you? Just facts. No interpretation. Two men, using wing structures, have glided down from the face of the ice. I would think it was the priests—maybe—if they did it without wings. Now. Study the wings. Remember every detail."

Tristal fell silent. He stared at the wings, but they seemed unremarkable to him. Tor was being more stubborn than usual. Still, he was Tor and had to be regarded.

After the soaring, the people returned to Sedge, still chanting, ready for celebration and gift giving. As was their custom, they gave away even precious possessions, and if anyone asked for something, it was turned over without question. The two Shumai watched Tegrit give away a large portion of the flaked tools he had worked on.

"You will have nothing to show for your work," Tor said.

Tegrit looked surprised. "Maybe not. But they will remember when they use tool. They will bring meat and other thing. And if I ask, they will give me thing, too. It is good custom."

"I don't see you asking."

"I need nothing. Not now, anyhow."

A shout came from the north end of the settlement. A group of five hunters had just arrived, dragging sledges of meat and skins. They had missed the soaring and looked worn and tired. One was taller than the Shumai, a dark man hugely framed.

"That is Dardan," Tegrit remarked, following Tristal's glance. "He has been gone long time. He and Orsel are friend."

Dardan looked slightly sour as much of the meat and most of the skins were given over to people who asked for them. It was only after some time that he noticed the two Shumai with Tegrit. The old man motioned him over and introduced them. Dardan eyed them warily.

"Don't worry, Dardan." Tegrit laughed. "They are not like last Shumai."

"I see your axe, Shumai," Dardan remarked, gesturing. "Metal. Very nice. May I handle it?"

Tor lifted it from its sheath and tossed it across to him, smiling.

Dardan looked at it for a time, murmuring, "Nice work. Haven't seen much metal. Never seen one like this. I'd like to have it."

"Sorry, Dardan," Tor said very quietly. "That is the one thing I keep."

A hush fell over the crowd. Dardan looked at him narrowly. "It is ceremony of soaring. I have given away most of my meat and skin. It is our custom. You must not understand. It is mine now."

"Dardan, they are not Soarer," Tegrit said.

"No matter. They eat meat, use skin."

"Dardan, you would not ask the priests for their wings, the head priest for his feathered hat," Tor said. "I'm sorry. It is the same. It is my office. I will give you anything else you ask."

Dardan's anger deepened. Suddenly he said, "Take it back, then," and threw the axe at Tor with furious strength.

Tor caught it, dodging aside, tossed it in the air, caught it again, and sheathed it. "Now," he said, in the same very quiet voice, "what may I give you instead?"

"Your clothing. Give me your clothing."

Tor laughed. "All of it? It's poor enough."

"All of it." The crowd murmured. Nakedness was a source of shame among the Soarers, and as they watched Tor take off his clothes, smiling wryly, tossing them over to Dardan, they closed around him with fur robes and covered him. A tense hush fell over them.

"I have something you might like, Dardan," Tristal said, rummaging in his pocket. He held out the stone projectile point. "It is from before the ancients. I found it far back on the upper Heart River, a thousand ayas from here."

Dardan took the point and looked at it. Such things were prized rarities among the Soarers.

"Don't be angry with us. There is no need," said Tristal.

Dardan laughed. "All right. This I'll keep. Clothing are too worn and dirty. You may have them back. Nice cloth, though. Where did you get cloth?"

"From the Pelbar, far down the Heart River."

"Pelbar? I know nothing of them."

"They are very far away. Much farther than you have ever been, in a country much warmer than this."

"Much warmer? Easier to live, then. This is hard country."

"But we are needed here so priest can keep back ice from rest of land," said a girl nearby.

Dardan gave her a glance, then smiled slightly at Tegrit and Tor. "Of course," he said. "And they do it well. Now. I am tired and dirty. Must go." He held up his hands and palmed Tor and Tristal. "Sorry I got angry. It—"

"It is nothing at all," said Tor.

Two days after the ceremony of soaring, Tor and Tristal set out northward with a small band of hunters. They were gone a full fifteen days. On their return, the priests called one of them, Fatch, to their quarters. He sat before the priests' council as Tor and Tristal had.

The central priest said, "Well, Fatch, what did you learn of them?"

"Very little, my father. They are good hunter. Excellent. Better runner than any of us. Tristal bow is so good we all ought to have them. He is making some—also making long-bow."

"Longbow?"

"Much larger. Can kill big droop-horned ox, he say. One shot. Saw him shoot goose out of sky, though quite high up. We have feather for you from it. And . . . Tor. He is odd man."

"Odd?"

"Yes. He has way of knowing."

"Knowing? Knowing what?"

"He know when game is around. He say he can't tell how. He know. They are good men. Both of them very good hunter. Their dog best ever. Drive animal. Good dog. And . . ."

"Go on."

"They tell us of great extent of land to east and south. Many people. Some hostile, many friendly. Great dwelling of stone. Several. Great lake of bitter water, stretching many kiloms. Many. Big animal people can ride. Other kind of ox that people keep inside fence. Take care of like dog. Eat when they need to. Warmer country. Country covered in big tree. Wide empty place from what they call Time of Fire. Remain of ancient. All this they call Urstadge. They tell us of battle and war, of people called Pelbar, Tantal, Shumai, Sentani, Peshtak—some evil, some good."

"Is all this true?"

"I think so. Too much to make up. All consistent."

"Ah. We must not be too sure."

"Yes, my father."

"Thank you, Fatch. You may go now."

Outside, Fatch met Dardan and remarked to him, "I don't understand. Two Shumai good hunter, good men. They tell us much. Priest not want me to believe them."

"Hummm," Dardan muttered. "Well, no chance to ask now. They've already gone hunting again."

"Alone?"

"Just two. Yes. And dog, Raran."

"Where?"

"North again. Around priest-forbidden area then close to ice. Tor want to see more of ice." Dardan frowned.

Three days later, Tor and Tristal lay in the grass deep in the forbidden area watching apprentice priests practice gliding with the wings from a low rise. Generally, as at the ceremony, a line of priests chanted. But several flights were made without chanting. From the one low, large, dirt-covered hut smoke curled up. They saw one of the apprentices return from hunting with a drag containing meat.

"Now we know how they fly, Tris."

"What are you going to do?"

"Nothing. It isn't our affair. I may tell Tegrit. Now we'd better learn what we can of how the wings are made. Question each other about every detail. Maybe even make a small model. Then swing east and north. Get some meat and dry it."

"How did you know?"

"The fliers had real skill. It meant practice. It's a transparent story that they need this place for chanting and privacy to force back the ice. The people are afraid not to believe it."

They arrived in Sedge over a week later each dragging a load of dried meat, hides piled on top. Tor immediately sensed tension. As they let down the drags in the open ground in the middle of the circle of mounded huts, only older women came to pick from the bounty. Several hunters waved but none came forward to greet them.

Then Tegrit appeared at Tor's elbow and said, "Be careful. Priest have given out that you told many lie about other place. People upset. Watch Dardan. I sense them trying to use him. He is coming. He is not himself."

Dardan had ducked out of his family hut and was striding across the open ground, his spear strapped on his back.

"Ho, Dardan," Tor called, grinning. "Want some meat?"

"I can get all meat I want, Shumai."

"True. Are you well?"

"Well enough. Want some answer. All hunter full of lie you tell about other place. Why did you do that? I want you to admit it. This is hard place. We cannot have disruption with lie. Can't have people going off to see. Now. I have decided. I will call hunter and you admit lie. Tell all. You will do it. Then maybe I take some meat."

"Dardan, no!" Tegrit said.

Dardan glared at him. Hostility seemed to grow like a dust cloud in a freshening breeze. "Did the priests ask you to say this?" Tor asked mildly.

"Ox turd! No. It is too obvious. Tale of wonder. Winter story. You, Tor, shameless liar. Cloud of bug. Log rot. House of excrement. Fatherless lout. Mess of maggot. Rotten meat. Thieving wolf." Dardan leaned over Tor, shouting his insults.

"Calm down, Dardan, please," said Tegrit. "Be—"

"Quiet, you old bird dung!" Dardan shouted.

"All right," said Tor, again quietly. "I admit it. It was all lies. All. Every word a lie. Now, are you happy?"

"Not enough!" Dardan shouted. "You tell all. Then you crawl. Crawl across this place asking our pardon."

Tor took two steps back as Tegrit forced his way between, saying, "Dardan. Dardan. He admitted it. Don't ask too . . ." Dardan swept him aside, the old man thudding hard against his woodpile and sprawling forward.

"Ah," Tegrit murmured. Tristal stooped down to him. Blood flowed from Tegrit's nose. The old man struggled to his feet and stepped forward again, saying, "Dardan, you must not . . . it is the priest wanting you . . ."

Tor moved forward, Tegrit waved him aside, and Dardan, bellowing, reached for Tor with his stone belt knife all in one blur of motion. Somehow Tegrit had forced himself between and took the raking thrust into his chest. Tor took Dardan's wrist, yanked him forward, twisting it behind him and throwing him. Others began running toward them. Dardan flailed under Tor, but soon others held him.

Tristal cradled the old man. Bubbles of blood came from his mouth. He waved his arm weakly. "Let me down, Tristal," he murmured weakly. "Don't blame Dardan. You, Ardit, Roten, Juni, look. Don't blame Dardan. You know . . . what Tor has said is true. So does . . . Now, see what good knife . . . I make?" He chuckled slightly and then his eyes misted over.

Orsel shrieked, clutching him. Dardan was dragged to his feet, held by four men. He stared blankly. "You," Orsel shrilled, "you've killed him!" She gave herself up to weeping.

Dardan suddenly became passive and limp. He glared at Tor. "We will still settle this," he rumbled.

"Easy, Dard," said Ardit. "You done enough already. Easy."

"Stop!" a priest called. "I saw it. Is he dead, then?"

"Aaaahhhhh!" Orsel yelled.

"Then, Dardan, you have murdered. Take him to dark house. The council will decide about him. This terrible day for Soarer. To kill their own. I saw it all. Tegrit tried to make peace. Died for it. We will have to judge. Not easy. There is matter of story of Tor. Provocation. Very bad. Bad."

Tor caught Tristal's eye, then dropped his own. The young man stood nonplussed, anguished, helpless.

Dardan roared and twisted in his captors' arms. "Tor, you liar. You will account for this."

"Don't blame yourself, Dardan. Everyone knows you meant the knife for me. It was an accident. The priests will see that."

Dardan roared again incoherently.

"You, Tor. Priest will decide what priest will decide. Not for you to say."

"No. Of course not. You will decide." Under his breath he said. "What you have already decided."

IX

NEAR the face of the ice mountain five men dug feverishly, trying to finish Tegrit's grave, scrabbling in the crushed rock and thin soil that ran with mud. Back a little, on a slight rise, Tor and Tristal and four others stood waiting with Tegrit's body, which was wrapped in strips of old hides. Two priests of the ice stood, nearby, silent, impassive, waiting. The grave was still shallow when the hunters digging it signaled that it was ready, waving their hands. Nearby, from high on the face of the ice, a large chunk calved off and rumbled down the face of the glacier then struck the ground, spewing ice in the air. The diggers started to run, but then returned to stand by the grave.

"Take body," one of the priests commanded. They lifted the old man on their shoulders and walked forward to the narrow and shallow hole.

The other men lowered the body into the hole, and Tor and Tristal stood back as the diggers scraped dirt and rock over him with their wooden spades. Tegrit's family stood off a little way, tonelessly chanting a death cry. Like the priests' chant at the soaring, it seemed to have no meaning. Tristal thought he could pick Orsel's voice out of the crowd, but he wasn't sure.

They had been somewhat isolated after the killing of Tegrit. The family had asked that he and Tor be included among the carriers of Tegrit, but few other Soarers spoke to them. Dardan lay in the dark house awaiting the priests' decision on him. Tristal sensed a deep resentment about that among the hunters, but Tor wouldn't talk about it.

After the shallow grave had been mounded over, one priest raised his hands and said, "Now, ice, you have won this man from us, but we still fight on. Priest of ice will hold you back with their mind. You will not win. We will hold you by our chanting and our power and our soaring. That is all. Come. Draw back from face of ice now."

"Priest, we wish to say a prayer for our friend Tegrit," said Tor.

The priest stared at him. "Say what?"

"A prayer. A statement of our wishes to Sertine."

"What is that? We must go before ice fall on us all."

"You go, then, and we will follow."

The priests retreated rapidly, and the diggers followed, but the four hunters who had borne Tegrit stayed with glances at each other. Tor stooped down on one knee. Tristal wondered, having never seen him do that before, but he followed suit. So did the hunters.

Tor closed his eyes and said, "Sertine, whom the Pelbar call Aven, watch over this man, Tegrit, and guide him if there is indeed a journey after death. May your justice resolve the issue with Dardan, and preserve him, whose blow in anger was not his own and who, as Tegrit himself said, is not to blame, is no more to blame than the inert knife he held, himself being a knife held by other minds. Let no blame fall on the innocent. Keep us all from evil, as the scroll of Pell says. Guide us all in our sometimes frightening walk through the unknown."

Tor stood and brushed off his hand. The others, watching him, also stood and walked back to the group on the rise. As they neared, the priest said, "This delay not good. We cannot hold back each part of face of ice forever, though we hold back all."

"Thank you for doing it, though," said Tor, smiling slightly. As if in response, a gigantic mass of ice cracked and slipped, grinding and bouncing, splitting up and falling, finally hitting with a ground-jarring thud, spraying Tegrit's grave with large chunks. "Thank you, indeed," said Tor.

As they walked back to Sedge, one of the hunters came beside Tor and asked him, "What was that thing you said back there? I don't understand."

"It is a custom among many peoples. It is talking to the maker of all and telling him—her if you are Pelbar—of your wishes.

"Talking to what?"

"Sertine, or Aven, or whatever he is called. Sometimes he is called God. The maker."

"I have heard hunter speak of Sertine. But they do not talk to Sertine that way. They recite thing—careful thing, all prepared so as not to offend. Now. I do not understand what you said. Thing are not made. They are alway there. Ice sent out to crush everything, and we hold it back for all other." The man growled this out, adding, "You come with strange idea. Not good. Confusing. Every time Shumai come, trouble come."

"We must leave, then. But you seem to have trouble enough without considering us."

The hunter made no response. Tor could see him pondering, mouth turned down. Then Tor added, "This matter of Dardan is very troubling, though. I would like to stay that out."

The man looked startled. "What is there to see out? Priest take care of it. Not your affair."

"No. But . . . there is a people far to the southeast. The Peshtak. I've met them—fought them. They are very deceiving. I haven't seen it, but I've heard they have shamans who kill people with the power of their hatred. I don't like it. Dardan was upset. But I felt his mind in the grip of others. Tegrit himself said as much."

"Priest can make us die. They say that keep order. Bad must go. 'Keep order alway to hold back ice,' they say."

"That's a nice thing to say if you want to kill somebody."

The man frowned as he thought that over. "I don't know," he finally said. "Dardan our leader, alway my friend. But you must go or they will kill you. All this too much. I like this talking to . . . the nature of thing, the maker, though, even if it is not real. It give some comfort. I feel it. I would like to hear more about it. Even illusion helpful sometime. But not so priest could know it. Many time in winter, cold, alone, waiting on hunting station, feeling ice only, I would like to talk to something like that."

Tor was uneasy. He was cutting at the foundation of the whole society, mad as it was. That was never good or safe. But maybe this time it had to be done.

The man then said, under his breath, "When you took all that back for Dardan, that was not true, was it?"

"No. It was to appease him. I knew he was wild with anger."

"Hunter will ask you that. They are waiting."

"What should I say? Will they? . . ."

"No. You tell them. They liked Tegrit. Dardan was not right to kill him. Look. They are waiting. Be careful, though. Some of them priest men."

Ahead a small knot of hunters stood waiting a short way out from Sedge. One, a large man named Stawn, asked, "Well, what does he say now?"

"That it was true, what he said. That there are these place."

A man stepped forward and said, "He lie again. Priest say we die if we leave. They have proven that. Men have died. We've seen it. He lie."

A strange feeling came over Tor. "You won't surely die," he said. "The priests know that if you get far enough away from here your eyes will be opened to the way of things. You will see some good as well as all this cold and evil you are used to. You've had enough cold, enough hardness, enough death, for a lifetime. You'll know there is warmth as well. You can't imagine how vast Urstadge is. The land we've come through is so huge, so various in range and season, so rich, so filled with game, ducks, herons, places of easy living, almost endless forests, and far to the east and south the Pelbar cities, and now the Shumai farms around them—it's a wonder to think of it. There is ice in winter, but winter is short, and farther south there is no winter at all, or hardly so."

Stawn snorted. "If all this is so, then why did you come here?"

"To see. To see the limits of things."

"This is the limit of things?"

"Yes. Unless you could cross that ice."

"No one can cross ice."

"No. I see it is immense. And winter is soon to come."

"If we leave, and not support priest, ice will soon follow and fill all land you speak of, even if what you say is true." The speaker was an older man, short and gray.

Tor looked at him. "If you think this is paradise, a garden of ease, then you have no reason to leave. But there is good land east of here, and south, where you can run naked if you want, and be warm."

"We do not do that."

"No. But you could. I am wondering. You are men of courage. Has no one ever raised these issues before?"

"We do not do that," said one man. All of them looked uneasy. "Even if you right, men still die when they make trouble. I say we let this alone. You need to leave soon."

"Yes. I would leave now but want to help Dardan."

"Dardan is best of hunter. He killed Tegrit. That was not right. But we cannot want to lose him. Not bad man. He was not himself then. Must make some exception. None of this bring back Tegrit. Now Splay will have to make our tool. No one did it like Tegrit."

"That for priest to decide," the short gray man said.

"Yes. But Orsel, too. She probably was to marry him."

"Hmmm," one thin man snorted. "I know one priest who will like this change."

A general murmur followed that. Tristal looked around. Orsel was not in sight. Now he was confused. She had seemed to love him. He knew now that it was a common custom for the young Soarers to test each other's limits on dark walks though fidelity in marriage seemed the norm. Still, he experienced a regret for the impossibility of what he didn't really want anyway. He was committed. But all that seemed long ago and very distant. Perhaps they could go back soon, as soon as the issue of the Soarers was settled—if they could escape it. Tristal could see that it was very serious, and that Tor seemed to be embroiling them even further. For such an individualist, Tor surely had a way of getting into social difficulties.

A priest was coming, and the hunters broke up their group with practiced nonchalance. Tristal decided to look for Orsel, finding her inside her family's earth house, grimly working at weaving with her grandmother and aunt. All three had been crying. Both older women were widows now, women with faces drained of life. None of the women looked up when Tristal came in and sat on his heels near Orsel. He felt a brittle tension in the air.

Finally Orsel said, "Don't say anything. You have your Tor. Now I have lost grandfather and future husband at once." Orsel deftly twirled a yarn of the hair of the droop-horned ox that her aunt fed her from the mass her grandmother was smoothing together. She used a distaff made from some large animal bone.

"Dardan will be condemned then? How do you know?"

"Once in the dark house, they generally are," said Orsel's grandmother, sighing. "I can remember when old hunter named Lacon was told he was evil and would be condemned to ice—before they alway put people in dark house for time, then judged them. He said that since he was condemned, he would have his revenge ahead of time. He killed five priest before hunter stopped him. Ever since, it has been three day in dark house, and they come out meek as moss."

Tristal felt as though something crawled up his spine. As Tor suggested, the priests must work on the minds of prisoners to avoid any trouble from them.

"Now Ojam will want me to serve him," Orsel spat.

"Ojam? The scrawny priest?"

"That one."

"Can you not refuse?"

"No. There is no way. It is service to those who hold us all in life, whose work is necessary to whole land. It is small thing, they say, and little to ask for their comfort." Orsel spoke sarcastically.

"You will accept this then?"

"No. I will not. I care nothing for what they will do.

Even if it is death. It does not matter. Life is cold and ugly thing at best. Look at what has happened."

Tristal stood. "No. It isn't. Only here. It has its bad side but is not cold and ugly. I should know. I've had enough bad."

Orsel's grandmother snorted. Her aunt shook her head sadly. "You see?" said Orsel. "They are older, know more than you. There is only one way out I see."

"What? I will help."

"For you and Tor to help. Would you do that?"

"Yes. You know we would."

"Then this is way. You must take me and flee. You will have to outsmart hunter. Can you do that?"

"I know some you can outsmart," said Orsel's grandmother. "They will want to be outsmarted—as it is now. They will come along. I want to come myself. What about you, Ulpan?"

"I will come," said Orsel's aunt, "even if it means dying."

"Then it is decided," said Orsel. She stopped twirling the yarn and snipped it off. Tristal felt uneasy but committed. He turned to get Tor. Things were getting out of hand. As he stooped out of the hut, though, he nearly bumped into one of the young priests, who leaned in and said, "Orsel, it is time for you to come and say poem of commitment to Ojam. He has waited long enough. You need relief from sorrow. He need some help and service. I would suggest you say traditional poem like 'Bridal Flower.' I'm sure you know it. We have arranged it and will attend you in two turn of sand clock. You must dress."

"Now? In this hurry? Cannot you see I am still mourning for my grandfather?"

"That is just what Ojam thought best. Would take your mind off your sorrow. He would bring you much joy and enlightenment. Service easy."

"Enough. I will come. You may depend on it." Orsel's voice was grim.

The priest smiled. "Remember. Ojam would like 'Bridal Flower.' You know it, of course."

"Yes. Of course. But I have one of my own I have been saving."

"Uh. If you wish. If it is a good one."

"Ah, yes. Very appropriate."

The priest bowed and left. The women stared at one

another. Ulpan began to sob, and her mother put her arms around her, keening.

"If you despise these people so, why do you keep doing what they say?"

"No help for it," said Orsel. "Save one. I will take it now. There is no time to run with you now, Tristal. Too bad. You are not Dardan, but better than Ojam by far."

Tristal didn't know how to react. He simply said, "I'll go get Tor," and left.

Tor received the news silently. He pondered and finally said, "It would do no good for you to run with her. The hunters would catch you. Besides, what would you do with her? You are promised. There must be a better way. It has to involve Dardan. As I see it now, the hunters are divided. Dardan was a natural leader. Some are deeply disaffected by his condemnation. Others follow the priests wholly. We have to get Dardan out, somehow."

"Would he come?"

"I don't know. He is steeped in these ideas. And they've been grinding him down in here." He gestured toward the old storage building used as the dark house. "Him and the potatoes."

As the two talked, they heard music, drumming on stretched animal skins, fluting, beating of ox bones. A procession was approaching Tegrit's house to accompany Orsel to her service. They were chanting another of the Soarers' monotones. As Tristal watched, Tor slipped away.

As they neared, she emerged from the house, freshly dressed in a bleached skin robe, her hair bobbed up, her feet in high white boots with wood-splint weaving. She was staring down, either modestly or grimly. The procession gathered her into their midst and led her to the open ground in front of the priests' house. Several other chants were taken up, the Soarers march-dancing slowly in a circle, in the center of which Ojam sat in a chair, with Orsel kneeling on the ground in front of him. The central priest gave a short speech about dedication to the great task before them of holding back the ice for all mankind, and then invited Orsel to say her poem of commitment to Ojam, who smiled stupidly and benignly down at her.

As the ceremony wound on, Tristal watched in growing despair until Tor suddenly reappeared and drew Tristal aside.

"I've talked to Dardan," he murmured.

"How? He is guarded."

"This is a distraction. I came up the back and ducked down the smokehole."

"How is he?"

"Profoundly depressed. But the priests have made less progress with him than they suppose."

"I don't understand."

"No time to explain. But he is a man of courage and determination. And now I have given him a few instructions in defending his moods."

"How?"

"I have told you everything; most of it you didn't hear. But forget that. Listen. I don't know what's going to happen, but he is willing enough to try anything to save Orsel."

"It's too late for that. It'll be dark soon, and—"

"Exactly. Dark. That may be our chance. I've already sent Ulpan and her daughter south toward the first rest shelter on the way to the potato growing. And seven others went along—all old. No fighters. Burdens, really. It will be up to you to get Orsel out. I have other jobs—freeing Dardan the main one."

"Well, Orsel is beginning her poem."

The Soarer girl continued kneeling, but lifted her arms and said in a clear chanting voice, "Hear now my song of commitment, drawn from me like the heart's blood."

"That's some beginning," Tor whispered.

Tristal gave an impatient hunter's silence sign. Orsel began in a singing monotone:

"It is always said, 'walk soft
on tiny tundra flowers—
who can walk soft enough for them,
barefoot, in cold wind?'
But you, oh Ojam, slender shod
with chipped stone knives, edge down,
years after you pass rise or vale,
your trail of wind-blown desolation there
gathers its ice and frigid wind,
prepares its way for greatest ice,
mountain of ice, moving to crush,
forever, all land, all flowers, all earth,
reaching for sun, for sky, to snuff out all,

  out air, out light, out freedom, joy,
  out pleasure, warmth, out children, food,
  and here you start by wringing out,
  with iron-cold hands, my hot heart's blood."

Having sung this, clearly and quietly, Orsel folded her hands in her lap and looked down. A general murmur drifted through the crowd, most of it angry. Ojam's look had turned from stupid pleasure to slow apprehension of his rejection, to shame, to rage. He and the other priests silently glared at her. Suddenly she rose, with wild hands, looking ahead of her in total terror, and shrieked, then fell in a heap and lay still. Tristal glanced at his uncle but found him standing silently, palm against his eyes. Then Tor looked up, smiled, and strode to the circle around the girl, parted them, and picked her up.

The central priest suddenly stood at his elbow. "You've interfered enough," he hissed. "Put her down."

"I will. In her own house," said Tor, and strode off with the limp girl. No one tried to stop him.

"You have seen her ingratitude toward her protector and guide," the priest shouted. "You need do no more. She will see no more than two weeks sunrise before she follow her grandfather. She is friend of ice who will not help priest in need. Evil. Foul. Shameful to dedicated worker for people. Infected by Shumai visitor. Hunter, await our counsel in front of our house."

He strode off toward the priests' house, the other priests following. Tristal heard some laughter as they vanished and saw others glare at those who laughed. He hurried to Tegrit's house and found Tor kneeling beside Orsel, who said in a near whisper, "I saw it. I saw ice rise up with face of bear and come at me."

"No. You saw an image in their minds. Ah, Tristal. How light is it?"

"Getting dark."

"Good. Dig through the back wall, then, up toward the roof. Work fast. No. No protests. Orsel, you have to pull yourself together. You are leaving. Don't worry. They won't be able to reach you. Their power gives out when they are far off. I will keep the others off guard until you are gone. Then I'll see about getting Dardan out."

As he spoke, he built up the fire in the center of the

room, throwing on a dampened rag for smudge. Then he stooped out the front door and sat by it, taking up Tegrit's stone-working tools and practicing on some of the unfinished tool blanks the old man had left behind. A circle of hunters approached and stood around him silently.

One said, "Who you think you are coming here and interfering?"

"I didn't mean to interfere. How did I?"

"Telling the girl to sing that, then picking her up? You need her for your nephew? Know you wouldn't want her, sterile old man."

"Only reason we don't kill you is we are waiting what priest say," said another.

"You aren't saving Orsel. You know that," said a third. "She finished. Done. Nobody treat priest that bad."

"Yes. That was too bad," said Tor. "Never should have done it. She should have accepted him, slept with him, helped him pick his pimples, washed his feet. You'd have liked that. You can see your women do those things."

A murmur of anger went through the group and they began to close in on Tor, who simply sat looking up at them. From behind they could hear a crowd coming and turned to wait for them, then parted as the central priest came through and stood in front of Tor.

"We have decided," he said abruptly. "Evil Orsel will never rise again from her bed. Not see late-summer soaring tomorrow. Take this one to dark house. Bring Dardan to watch Orsel die. Then he will serve Angler for two year and then be free. All disruption stem from arrival of these Shumai. Bring young one, too. They will fly at soaring. We will see their great prowess."

"He's inside," said one hunter, moving toward the door. Tor stood across it. "One side, trash," the man said, shoving at Tor. Three others grabbed him and bundled him aside. The first hunter stooped in and found the house full of thick smoke. Coughing, he reemerged. "Can't see," he said. "Fire."

Another man ducked inside and crawled around feeling, three others following. Soon they came back out. "Nobody's in there," one said, the others running around the house and finding the hole in the back.

Amid shouts, a party prepared to track the fugitives. The priests rang a bell, and the central priest called for

Dardan to be brought. When he came, still logy and cramped, the priest addressed him. "Orsel and young Shumai have escaped us. Both guilty. You find them and bring them back. You then freed after serving two year to prove worthiness. You lead other. Now, take this one to dark house until tomorrow soaring. He will show us his great strength in air. Here, give me his axe."

Dardan gathered a band of ten hunters and set out with torches, tracking Tristal and Orsel in the dark. Tor found himself bound to one of the posts of the dark house. Ojam was among those who bound him, and as a last gesture, he leaned down and pinched Tor between his thumb and forefinger until the axeman twisted and threw him aside. Two of the hunters then knelt by Tor and pummeled him in the face and body as he writhed helplessly away from their blows.

"Enough," said an older priest. "We want him to fly like goose tomorrow."

The hunters laughed. "Speared goose," one of them said. They laughed again. Tor didn't reply. He ran his tongue up against his split lip, sucking the blood.

They checked the bindings again and left him there. Tor sat up and drew in his breath fully, then let it out in a long sigh. He wanted to try to relax, as much as his ropes would permit, but he had thinking to do. That would take much of the night.

 X

As the night progressed, Tor sat straight in the pitch dark thinking through his situation. He knew he would be the next victim in the soaring game. From what he gathered, the combination of his lack of skill and some fault in the wings were expected to result in his fall from the ice.

Painstakingly he went over every detail in the wing structure as he had committed it to memory. He tried to recall how the apprentice priests had managed the wings under the eyes of their instructors.

Now and then he felt waves of fear tapping at the doors of his mind, but he held them shut and would not let any terror in. He knew that this was suggestion from the priests, probably sitting in conclave.

Eventually the door skins were pushed aside and torch-light flared in the dark house. Tor found himself sitting among bags of partly rotten old potatoes and racks of dried meat. Two priests entered and stood over him. Tor smiled up at them, then looked above them. An old, rusted piece of sheet metal gathered from some structure of the ancients had been stretched across the roof braces under the grass and dirt covering.

Looking carefully, Tor saw it had some discernable writing on it—printing that had rusted differently under what had been different colors of paint.

"Interesting," he said. "Hold the torch up a little, please. Your roof has writing on it."

The priests had not expected this reaction. The younger one looked up. "Writing? What is that?"

"Silence," said the older man. "Writing is way ancient had of placing speech on object so other could tell what it was even without speech."

"'Think it over: to live and die in your sins is to spend eternity in the flames,'" Tor read aloud. He laughed.

"What? What do you mean?"

"I? I'm just reading what it says on your roof. A fit sentiment for a place like this."

"I don't understand," the younger priest said. "Is he fooling with us?"

The older priest tried to look up with dignity, moving aside the torch that the younger man held. It was clear to Tor the old priest couldn't read either.

"That's above the line," said Tor. "There is more below, but it is obscured by the beams—and rust. Let's see. I don't understand that part." He frowned, pausing. "Ah," he continued. *"Réfléchez vous...mourir...dans le pêche ...éternité...l'enfer...*I can't make it out. I think it is in the language of the Rits and probably says the same thing. A cheerful notion. Eternity in the flames. If they are right, you two will spend a long time burning for all your lies and murders."

The older priest slapped Tor hard across the face. "You made that up. Those are chance mark. It make no sense anyhow. Sin. We keep order when order is necessary to survival. You are disorder. But tomorrow we will give you chance to prove yourself in soaring. If you can fly without our help, then you can show your worth and will go free. If not, well . . . then you will have fallen from weight of your own evil."

"You agree then that evil things fall from the weight of their evil? I'm glad you perceive that. You're talking about yourself there. Remember that as you weigh yourself down. You are making yourself inflammable for eternity."

"Nonsense. There is no eternity. There is only this short and desperate life by side of ice. This is to be lived well, because that is all there is. But we have come to offer you bargain. If you tell us where your nephew went, we will chant for you when you fly. It may help, though force of ice must hate you for your rebelliousness."

"My nephew? Tristal? Where he went? I hope far away. From all this evil for which you will burn in eternity. Because you are living and dying in your sins."

"I see you are intractable. Very well. Maybe later in night when you have thought over your fate—terrible fall from ice, left locked in fold of ice forever, maybe to thaw out sometime, black and putrid mass of rot—or fall into crevasse, breaking leg, where we will leave you to slowly freeze, begging for help—maybe then you will be more agreeable." He whirled and struck Tor across the face with a sharp smack.

Tor laughed again. "Remember that sin, too, as you burn in the flames for eternity. It says so right in your own building. I didn't make it up. Look. There it is. The wisdom of the ancients. *Regardez ça, mes amis.* We all know how wise the ancients were. As you return to bed, wholly steeped in your evil, think it over. Remember . . . the pain will be forever. You will deserve it. You are losing your only chance to—"

Tor stopped talking because the two had left the dark house and no longer listened. He could hear the younger man saying, "Did he really read that? Is it true? It can't be . . ." The older priest spit an angry rejoinder. Tor chuckled to himself and set about remaining calm. The priest's blows had set his lip bleeding again, and he ran his tongue across it.

Meanwhile, Tristal and Orsel had gone east, then turned south, then east again, before turning south and catching up with the older people. Then, leaving all pretense of confusing trackers behind, they walked steadily south through the night. At one point, they could see the torches of the trackers far behind, but they seemed at a fault.

"I will reason with them," said Orsel. "I think priest made mistake. If hunter catch us, I don't think they will kill us—unless priest along with them. That is unlikely. They like their sleep enough."

Later in the night the two priests again came into the dark house. Tor remained silent, his head down. "We withdraw our proposal," the older priest said. "We will not chant for you. You are too evil. You will have to fend for yourself."

"Perhaps you are right," Tor said, slurring his words. "Perhaps the ice is all. I will be in the flames of eternity, just as any sinful person would be—anyone who dominates the lives of others. It is too late for me now, too late."

The older priest glared at him, unsure.

"Now I am very sleepy. You must let me sleep," Tor murmured.

The older priest smiled. "Yes. Sleep. Sleep well. Sleep deep. Sleep without dreams to trouble you. Rest in your sleep, preparing for your last sleep. No one will trouble your sleep. It will be good sleep. Perfect sleep. Deep sleep. Rest. Relax. Sleep. You are safe here. No one will hurt you. Sleep well."

Tor looked up slowly. "You will not disturb me, then? Let me sleep?"

"Yes. Sleep now. We are going."

Tor's head slowly sank toward his chest. The old priest looked, watchful. He motioned to the younger man, and they quietly left. Quietness settled in the dark house like unseen dust. Tor sat up again, straight as a spear shaft. He flexed his arms against the ropes.

Early in the morning dark, the older priest came alone, a tiny oil lamp in hand, and slipped into the dark house. Tor sat slumped in his ropes, breathing deeply and evenly. The priest looked down at him a long time, frowning slightly. Then he lifted the lamp and studied the ancient sheet of metal on the ceiling. In nearly perfect silence, he stole out of the hut, easing the skin flaps back. Tor sat up again, shaking his head.

Sometime after sunrise, one of the hunters with Dardan found the trail leading south and called the others. They came and stared at it. "I don't understand," one said. "Look. No attempt to hide trail at all. Look. That's my great aunt. She with them. Carrying something, too."

"You sure?"

"Look how she turn her left foot in. Yes."

Dardan frowned. His mind was a whirl of contradictory notions. "We won't catch them standing here," he said. The hunters took up the track, trotting behind him.

It was midmorning before Tor was roused and unfastened from the post in the dark house. Most of the people of Sedge watched him brought out, looking on silently as he shuffled along, head down, on the path toward the ice. At the edge of the town he was given the half-folded set of wings he was to wear and made to carry them. Some of the people jeered at him, but others watched without a word. The wings were surprisingly heavy to Tor, though not in relation to their expanse.

One child threw a mudball at him. Glancing over, Tor saw the child's mother shaking him by the arm. At last he reached the steps the priests had cut into the ice and began walking upward, struggling to keep from falling with the awkward shape of the folded wings on his back. He concentrated on keeping his footing, and eventually, breathing hard and cramped in his shoulders, he reached the soaring platform the priests' men had chiseled onto the face of the ice. Far below he could see the priests' pavilion and the crowd of Soarers, their faces like tiny flecks of batter flicked on a dark griddle.

Below a priest was giving a speech, which Tor could not hear, as the priests on the ice assembled the wings, deftly fastening everything together and testing it. A young man with dark curly hair was cinched into the harness.

"I don't like it," he said. "This wind is picking up. It almost too strong."

"Let us hope it pick you up," another said. "Too late to cancel now."

"Don't worry," said Tor. "The priests will hold you up.

With their chanting." He tried to look sincere.

The flier cast a look at another man. "I am not worried," he said sardonically. "It is you will worry, Shumai. No one will be chanting for you."

Tor hung his head. He heard the chant taken up from below, like the murmuring of a far wind. The flier advanced to the platform, assisted by three men. "It's slightly from the north," one of them said. "You'd better get out from the ice fast."

"I know what I'm doing. You want to try it?"

"Not today. Not good day."

The flier breathed in deeply, sighed, and ran to the edge of the platform, launching out swiftly, dropping away from them, easing back, lifting over the crowd, swinging around, coming back at them. Tor saw that he caught an updraft where the wind hit the line of ice and rose to pass over it. It was like hawks and gulls riding the river bluffs far back in Pelbar country. They would soar for miles without moving a wing.

The flier banked in front of them, teetered in a gust, then mounted higher, swooped back over the crowd and returned again, banking again as he neared the ice wall. At that point a swelling gust took him up and back behind them to the west, well up onto the ice field. Tor could see that he had lost the advantage of the updraft and turned back into the wind as soon as he could, gliding down, flaring up, faltering a moment, gliding down again, nearing the edge of the ice, flashing out beyond it, as the distant crowd let out an audible murmur, and banking out well east of the ice, wheeling, circling, and settling toward the crowd and the landing place.

As he landed, one of the other priests said, "Showman. He almost ruined that one." Then he glanced at the hunters guarding Tor and said, "He tested limit of chanting." Tor laughed. The man glared at him.

One of the priests brought Tor's axe forward and hung it around his neck on a cord, looping another around his waist. Tor could see that the priests below were addressing the crowd again. The ones on the ice began moving Tor into his harness.

"Wait," he said. "Ardit. Juni. I don't know you well, but we have hunted together. I know you for honest men . . ."

"You. Don't listen. You. Do your part."

"Ardit," Tor continued. "If I die, you can have my axe if you help here. Look. They removed a brace. Take the axe and tie it in there. On the right. To match the bracing on the left. See?"

"Don't touch it," a priest hissed.

"It is the chanting that holds up the wings," Tor said. "Isn't that right? What will it matter? I haven't practiced either, as you all do in the forbidden area. Let me fasten it in."

"Hold him!" the priest yelled.

"Then this is an execution, not a test or a ritual," Tor said mildly. "What are you going to do—tamper with their minds so they believe it? It is all so transparent—like air itself. A foolish deception. Must keep you endlessly busy reinforcing it?"

"You," said Juni. "Let him fix brace. Soarer can be fair. Priest will not chant. He will fall. You said it yourself."

"Get away!" the man screeched. "Who are you to?..."

Juni had lowered his spearpoint at the man's chest. "First you want to kill Dardan, now want to rig this man death. I have no objection to you killing him. But admit it. This is vile. Like child game."

Without another word, Tor wriggled free of the harness, untied his axe, and tied it in, using the thongs from his neck and waist, biting them as he tied with his one hand. Then he went over all the bindings of the wings, finding one weak and refastening it with the cord from his shirt front. One of the priests moved toward the rig as though to help. Tor pointed a finger at him and said, "You. Keep back. If I'm going to die here, I'd as soon do it by myself."

"Fool," the man said.

Tor felt a wave of giddiness sweep across him. He shook his head and refocused on facts. He got Juni to strap him in. The hunter looked dead serious. He whispered to Tor, "Get far away if you can." Tor looked at him and didn't reply.

Finally he stepped to the back of the platform. Again two of the priests of the ice moved forward. Without hesitation, Tor ran forward and dove off the platform, rushing downward, going through all the procedures he had memorized, seeing the crowd growing, trying to lean back, finding everything going fuzzy, shaking his head to clear it, somehow shifting weight, suddenly feeling himself rising, gliding with unbelievable speed over the shouting crowd, gaining altitude, crying out with the pleasure of it.

Tor managed to bank around and race toward the ice, hearing angry yelling from below. He seemed to be settling, but finally caught the updraft and turned away from the face of the ice, wobbling, catching a sudden gust, and rising above the level of the ice wall. He managed to turn south, feeling exultant, shaking that off as more priestly deceit, and riding the updraft away from Sedge. One glance back showed the small group on the ice as tiny dark dots.

Tor let out a long Shumai yell and glided away, heading toward where he felt Tristal might be. He found he could ride the updraft, gliding rapidly, moving his body little. Once he nearly lost the pattern crossing a wide gap in the ice, but he managed to pick it up again by wheeling slowly east into the wind, as he had watched vultures do, and then circling around again.

As Tor made his shaky flight, Tristal, turning, saw the hunters running steadily toward them with Dardan in the lead. Raran growled deep in her throat and turned to trot back with Tristal as he hastily nocked an arrow and stood between the fugitives and their pursuers. Orsel and the others stopped, and two old men put their spears at ready. The hunters fanned out and moved toward them.

"That's far enough," Tristal yelled. The hunters paid him no heed. He drew an arrow and aimed it at Dardan. The hunters slowed to a walk and came on. "Five more steps and you'll be looking at my fletching in your belly," Tristal shouted. They stopped. The man on the east end continued forward.

"Stop," Dardan yelled. "It is my belly. Shumai muck rot mean it. You, Tristal, put up your bow. We will talk first—then maybe fight."

"Stay there, then. What do you want?"

"Orsel to come back. Priest say so. Other—you have no right here either."

Orsel had come up beside Tristal. Now she shrieked at Dardan, breaking into furious tears. "Dardan—murderer. Stupid ox head. So they let you go—to catch me. Fool. Hollow noggin. Mass of meat. Brain of rat. Is that all you are worth? To help them who condemn you? Where is your brain at all?" She fell weeping in a heap by Tristal. He reached out a hand to her, but she slapped it away.

The man on the east took several steps forward. Tristal drew on him and shouted, "Back up." The man didn't move. "Ten steps back or you die."

"You will die too at that," said Dardan.

"No matter," said Tristal. "I'll take you, too. Now. I'll give this turd pile five. One. Two. Three. Four..." At that the man moved. "Now stay there," Tristal said.

Orsel got to her knees, then stood up. "Dardan, you fat head," she shrieked. "Can't you see anything? They'll only kill you when you get back—whenever they want to. You come with us. Leave there."

"You got your lover," Dardan replied.

"Him? Tristal? You crazy? He friend. More friend than you, priest slave. Now, give your word. Come."

"Easy, Dard," said another hunter. "She deceiving you. We can take them."

Orsel let out another bellow and ran at Dardan. As she came up to him, he put his spear aside and caught her as she struck at him, flailing her arms and crying. Then she went limp as he grabbed at her arms, dropping his spear. Another hunter came toward them. "Keep away," Dardan said. The man stopped. He held Orsel to him and she gave herself up to weeping, her head against his chest.

"Come with us," she whispered.

Dardan sighed. "How can I do that?" he asked. He looked up and saw a strange look on Tristal's face, as the young Shumai looked out beyond the hunters. Tristal's expression then went from face to face among the fugitives. Orsel's aunt gave a frightened cry and began running away. Dardan stole a look over his shoulder and saw a set of Soarer wings gliding toward them, turning east, rising, wheeling, and coming on again. Soon both sides watched, the hunters turning, fearful that one of the priests had come to observe. Tristal drew his bow, then realized it was Tor.

"Come down," he shouted up. "Over here."

"Can't," Tor shouted back. "Don't know how." He wobbled in his flight, caught on another gust, wheeling again, losing altitude, heading into the wind and toward a scrubby cluster of pine trees on a rocky rise. Both groups watched him try to turn, falter, and plunge into the trees with a sound of splintering.

Tristal was running toward him before he crashed, and soon came up to the place, panting out, "Tor! Tor!"

"Up here."

Tristal looked up and saw his uncle hanging upside down in the twisted harness. Glancing behind him, Tristal saw no one had followed. He scrambled up and began cutting Tor loose with his short-sword.

"Cut the axe loose, too," said Tor.

"What's it doing there?"

"Those foul-swill priests tried to fly me off with a brace missing. I got the hunters to let me tie the axe in."

Tristal laughed. Looking back, he could see the cluster of Soarers conferring. Tor came loose, hung swinging by one arm, and dropped. He was scraped in a number of places and ran blood. Tristal retrieved the axe and tossed it down to him.

"I don't like it. Looks like they're getting together," said Tristal.

"We'll wait here then," said Tor.

After a time, Dardan and Orsel came toward them. Tristal put his arrow back in its quiver. Orsel was laughing through her tears. "Dardan is coming with us," she said. "And six of hunter. Other won't come." The others had, in fact, already begun running back toward Sedge for help.

"You'd better get moving, then," Tor said. "If you head south and east, a long way, longer than you can imagine, you'll eventually come to water flowing south and east. Then you'll know you're in Shumai country. Follow the water and you'll come to the Heart. Then eventually you'll be in Pelbar country. But not this season. You'll probably winter on the plains. It's easier than this, but hard enough. There's plenty of game, though. You'll find wild cattle, larger than the droop-horned ox if you go far enough south. And tougher to kill. But you'll have no trouble. Only with shelter. Go south quickly, but bear east."

"You have uprooted our life."

"Better than dying."

"Yes. But not easy."

"Here," said Tristal, unstrapping his short-sword. "Take this. It lasts better than stone tools. If you get to the Pelbar, they'll ask you where you got it. Tell them I gave it to you. It's been mistreated by heating, but it ought to serve."

Dardan took the short-sword without a word. He glanced at Tor, who was looking northwest. "That must be the third flier," he said.

It was. The young priest circled overhead, screaming curses down at them, but well up in the air. Then he planed off northward, looking for a thermal.

"A good flier," said Tor. "But he's still going to have a long walk home." He laughed. They could see the man losing altitude without the air current across the ice face to work with.

"What will you do?" Dardan asked.

"Leave," said Tor. "We can't stay around here."

"Come with us, then."

"No. Too soon."

Dardan looked at the two Shumai, then held up his hands and palmed them, as he knew was their custom. "Good-bye, then."

"Good-bye. May Aven be with you and guard you on your journey. May you sleep warm and you two have many babies. May you find peace and a kinder country."

Dardan and Orsel looked at each other. Orsel smiled, her face still wet and dirty with her tears. They turned and walked away toward the others, who waited for them, mostly squatting on the ground, all in one group.

 XI

AFTER the fugitive Soarers left, Tor and Tristal moved six ayas east. They took practiced care to leave little trace of their passage, finally finding a small tangle of rocks and spruce trees to bed down in. Tristal had a large twist of dried meat they divided into thirds, chewing slowly. Raran gnawed her share with great relish, but looked up afterward, still hungry.

"We'd as soon have more, too, girl," Tor murmured, adding, "Tris, you sleep first. I'll take a turn in a while."

"Then what?"

"Then we'll have to put distance between us and the Soarers. They won't take this easy."

"I'd think they'd leave us alone."

"Hsst. Look there." High overhead, to the west, they could see two Soarers circling, well up above ice-wall height, scanning the area.

"Have they seen us?"

"I don't think so. Hold Raran. Stay still and down. I'll watch."

Tristal didn't think he could sleep with the fliers nearby, but he soon sunk into a troubled slumber, dreaming of ice, crumbling and roaring. Tor watched the Soarers slowly working their way southward. He felt waves of fatigue rush over him, unsure if it was genuine or the influence of the Soarer priests. Finally he aroused Tristal in late afternoon and lay down between the rocks himself. Near dusk, Tor sat up suddenly out of his deep drowsing.

"What? Hear something?"

"No. I feel it. Presence. String your bow. We need to move out—north."

"Right toward them?"

"It's the only way open."

"How do you know? I can't—"

"Don't know how. They send out their anxiety ahead of them. Their troubled song. You sense nothing at all?"

Tristal paused. "Nothing."

Suddenly Raran pricked her ears and growled low. Tristal put his hand on her back. Then he strung the bow. Still tired, they began trotting north. After a time, they heard a shout to their west and then a long sustained reply from the south. The two Shumai speeded up further, but ran steadily. Tristal began to feel waves of terror and hopelessness lap at the shores of his mind.

"They have priests along," Tor panted. "Or they are working from Sedge. Feel it?"

"What?"

"The artificial fear."

"It's real enough."

"It isn't real. Try to trisect an angle."

"It can't be done."

"Not yet. Think about it. Hard."

"Will you?"

"Won't have to. I'm mentally rereading one of the rolls of Aven—one I read with Celeste when she was sick."

Tristal thought back but could remember nothing significant about the Pelbar scripture. "I'll work on the trisection," he said.

"We'll have to run into the night," Tor said. "Well into it."

"Where to?"

"The priests' forbidden area."

"There! Why? That isn't safe."

"Nowhere is safe now. But there are supplies. And more stable ice. And if the priests want us . . . they'll have to explain some things to the hunters."

"It's a long way. You mean, then, we are . . . going on the ice?"

"They won't follow us there."

"I hope you're right."

The two ran on in silence, with Raran ahead, for some time. At first they heard distant shouts from their pursuers, but then it seemed as though they waded completely alone through a world of scrub bushes, grass, and islands of evergreens. It was unnerving. Tristal felt a series of fears trying to seize him. He fought them away by working through a succession of mathematical conundrums and trying to make up new ones. He could hear Tor humming under his breath, calmly, but clearly enough so he knew it was a discipline and defense.

As darkness neared, they saw a flier circling high overhead. The man clearly had seen them and wheeled slowly high up like a signal flare. The effect on Tristal was unnerving, and when the man eventually lost his altitude and drifted toward them in the dusk, Tristal stopped and nocked an arrow.

"No, Tris," Tor gasped out. "You don't have to kill him."

Tristal felt a surge of resentment rise, but he fought that off, too. That was one of Tor's long-held principles. They ran on into the late light. The flier drifted away, slowly sinking. The same strange stillness of the previous time settled back over them.

Tristal looked far out over the grass and tree clumps. No pursuers showed. "Can't we stop now?" he said.

"They are right close."

"Where?"

"I feel it."

"They're confusing you."

"Maybe. But I doubt it."

"I can't run forever."

"Nor I. But..."

Ahead, as though out of nowhere, a huge, brown-haired creature rose out of the scrubby grass, its long-clawed front paws hanging, slightly raised. Tor, in the lead, raced toward it. Tris cried out, reached for an arrow, and fumbled it onto the bowstring as they ran. "Tor," he shouted, as his uncle ran on as though oblivious. "Stop!"

The beast let out a roar and dropped on all fours as Tristal drew, but Tor ran right through him. Shivering, Tristal followed, as the cry of the Soarer hunters behind them, ragged with distance, pursued.

"We must be passing beyond Sedge," Tor called, over his shoulder.

"How did you know? The beast?"

"Raran didn't sense him. The priests. Still fooling with our minds."

They ran on into the dusk, passing two main trails to Sedge. Tristal found himself eager, anxious, to get to the forbidden territory. Tor suddenly slowed, turning with a frown. "I don't understand."

"What?"

"They want us in the forbidden zone. Can you feel it? Them saying it?"

"I...don't know."

"Let's turn west."

"That's Sedge."

"Maybe they won't expect us. We have options. We could even hide in the dark house. Eat old potatoes."

Tristal hesitated. It seemed like a good idea, somehow. They turned and ran a short way, but Tor suddenly stopped so abruptly Tristal almost ran into him. "What?" he gasped.

Tor squatted down, panting, Raran nuzzling his arm. "I can't...I'm sorting it out. Fooled."

"What?"

"Quiet a moment." Tor pressed the palm of his hand against his eyes, his breath slowing. It was full dark now. Tristal squatted down, nervous.

"Turn north."

"You said they were telling..."

"They were. Loud. They still are—so loud we can feel

their saying it—know it's them. They're also enticing us to Sedge. So softly I was fooled. Now. We'd better move."

"Are you sure?"

"Yes. Common sense is always better than clever madness. I should have seen it."

"I'm afraid."

"No. You aren't. Let's run. As we go, say over and over to yourself, 'We are coming to Sedge. We are coming to Sedge.' Let's see if we can fool them."

That seemed ridiculous, but Tristal tried it. As they ran, his mind began to whirl. He felt nauseous. Tor cried out and held his head, falling. Tristal stopped and took his shaking shoulders. He could hear his uncle murmuring, finally panting out, "A mistake. A mistake."

Tristal felt wrung out by fear. "What?" he panted out.

"I was wrong. Don't fool them by their own methods. They are better at it. The method is wrong. I can see it. We have a better."

"What?"

"Truth. Honesty. Fact. Even in defense never adopt theirs."

"Tor. We'd better go."

"I can't." Tor was trembling violently.

"We'll walk." Tristal hauled him upright, Tor swaying.

"Did you find out how to trisect that angle?" his uncle asked irrelevantly.

"Almost. Almost."

Tor began to laugh, softly, and Tristal joined him.

At Sedge, the central priest sighed. "We've lost them. We've lost them."

"Perhaps not."

"Yes. I'm afraid so. I don't understand how. Now we have to send hunter into forbidden area."

"What will we say?"

"I don't know. Yet. We will work on having them believe it, whatever."

"Of course."

"I mean very hard."

"Why not just let them go? Somehow shift their image in mind of people?"

"Yes. We'll do that. But having their body laid out is very convincing."

"We need to be quiet and work on what we're doing," said the woman priest.

"In other word, shut your mouth?" said the central priest pleasantly.

"I thought to have Dardan serve me out of this."

"Perhaps you still will."

"Perhaps. But there are more pressing matter. Flier have not reported seeing them. They are far off."

"Hunter will find them. They have old with them."

"When Shumai come, trouble come."

"So it has been."

Tor and Tristal finally rested, hungry, nibbling grass seeds under a pine. Shortly before dawn they started out again, straight north, and with the light came the familiar cry of their pursuers, now spread along the west. Tristal was ahead at the time, bow strung and nocked, hoping for a quick shot at small game. The Soarers seemed to be gaining on them.

"It must mean we're near the forbidden area," Tor panted out. "They aren't pacing themselves. Look. Ahead. Is that a marker?" On the rise ahead, south of the top, stood a tall pole topped with red streamers.

"They'll cut us off," Tristal called.

"Slant east," Tor replied.

Suddenly, ahead, another brown-furred beast rose up and looked at them. Tristal ran on toward it. The Soarers behind them shouted. "Tris!" Tor yelled, spurting up as Tristal neared it. Raran shot by him, hitting the animal in a flurry of barking. Tor shouldered Tristal aside, swinging his axe down across the beasts' muzzle as it charged, dodging as it whirled, enraged, and with two quick strokes blinding it. It flailed in pain and anger, roaring, raking Tristal once across the chest, although lightly, leaving four parallel groves, as Tor yanked him back. The Soarers shrilled in triumph, but the blinded bear turned at the sound and charged, scattering them. The Shumai ran on, up, over the rim of the hill, and down, Tristal's chest streaming blood now, his nocked arrow snapped but still clutched in his hand, with the bow.

In half an ayas, Tor slowed to a walk and turned. No Soarers came over the hill after them.

"How did you know?" Tristal said.

"Saw flies. Flies around it. And Raran knew. Here. Let me look at you." He parted Tristal's torn shirt. "Uhh. Not good. But not bad. Two more ridges and we'll be at their shelter."

"What if there are priests?"

"There better not be. For them. I'm sick of them. But we can't stay there long."

"Will they come, then? You think? What good are they?"

"Little. But they'll find some contorted reason to send the hunters. You know they will. They don't give up. We've slit the belly of their bag of illusions, and it's draining."

"Where will we be safe then?"

"Nowhere. But safest up on the ice."

"The ice? You mean cross it? After what we've seen? We've heard?"

"Yes."

Tristal looked at the distant ice wall rising, looming, shimmering in the sun of the short northern summer. He bit his lip and looked down at his bloody, throbbing chest.

☐ XII

TOR and Tristal stood at the head of the priests' steps, high on the ice face, looking down, resting. Behind them was a sledge loaded with fur robes, hide rope, potatoes, dried meat, grease. Far below, a line of twelve hunters watched them from in front of the priests' house. Two priests stood with them, and as the Shumai watched, two others stooped out of the shelter. One of the priests pointed. Tor waved back with both arms.

"Come, Tris. We'd better get moving," he said. Tristal sat still, his chest aching, leaning against Raran, who panted quietly, watching. Tor looked down at him. "We can stay if you want. I don't think they'll come up here. Of course they may."

Tristal rose and took his place on the sledge rope. Slowly

they worked their way up, on, higher and higher on the ice face, walking the crest of a hogback ridge, only to find it end about two ayas up, with precipitous ice gullies all around them. Tor seemed unperturbed. He loosened a coil of hide rope from the sled, fastened it, and lowered the burden down the break. But it didn't quite reach the bottom.

"Let it go," said Tristal.

"No. It may go anywhere. We'll have to bring it up."

They did, with much labor. Their only course was to retrace their steps almost halfway back, finding a branch. Here Tristal sat with the sledge while Tor scouted on ahead. Raran lay with him. Tristal's chest throbbed with angry pain. He thought back to Pelbarigan, to Fahna, to the danger and arduousness of their trek north. Squinting out on the blue-white world of the ice, he wondered what he was doing there. Tor's distant figure appeared, trotting on the ice toward them.

"Found a way," he said, coming up, taking the sledge rope. "Rested?"

Tristal picked up the rope without a word and they started forward.

Far below, at the priests' house, a priest was saying, "You saw. They vanished up on ice. I see it now. They ice men. Not Shumai. Ice in form of man come to defeat us. Almost did. Now we know. We know how to test. Will not succeed again." He looked out at the circle of hunters regarding him silently. He tried to force the thought on them. He saw it would take some time.

A long way south, Dardan's party watched the approach of a dozen hunters from Sedge. Dardan strode out from the others, his hands raised, spear on his back. The hunters stopped and sent a man to meet him.

"You have to come back, Dardan. Priest say you die otherwise."

"We'll die then. You come with us. Alway use a good hunter. All of you come."

"What are you saying? Can you really say that?"

"No choice. You know they made tool of me. I didn't want to kill Tegrit. See that now. Tegrit right. Tor also right. Never go back to priest again. We've been fool. You see that."

"Come, Dard. Otherwise we have to kill you. Priest say so. If we don't have priest, then what do we have? Nothing."

"Everything. Ourself. Come. Join us."

"No. I will draw back now. When we reach our group, truce ended."

"Come with us," Dardan repeated.

"No," the hunter called back over his shoulder. Dardan retreated slowly, watching the man join his party. He saw them discussing, looking at the others. Dardan looked over at Orsel. She was impassive. She held Tristal's short-sword.

"I think they won't come," she said. "But if they do, I am willing to die here. As good as any place."

"Why should we wait?" her mother asked. The older woman picked up her burden and started south. Several other older people followed.

"Look at them," Dardan said. "Leaving us."

"It as well," said Fyl, one of the hunters. "If they fight us, what good old one? Might as well go. We ought to follow. Look. They're still arguing."

After a time, Dardan and Orsel stood alone, watching the hunters argue. "Dard, let's go," Orsel said. "If they want us, they can catch us." She looked at him and laughed.

He regarded her in return. It seemed unwise to go. But on impulse he took her arm, and they followed the others. That evening they picked up five more hunters. They never saw the other seven again.

Far southeast, the goldenrod bloomed on the bluffs and hills near the Heart. Fahna stood on the riverbank watching an arrowboat with a single man in it come downriver. Eventually she realized it was not Tristal, but another young Shumai near his age and size. Disheartened, she sat on a timber pile smoothing her hair.

The young man drew close, grinning and sweating. He looked up at her, let out a whoop, and called, "Waiting for me? The word goes on ahead. Bravet is coming." He laughed as she turned and walked away, then stopped suddenly as he saw the lithe grace of her body. He stared after her, shaking his head. Then he laughed again and released another whoop, long and loud, cupping his hands. On the bank, two guardsmen looked out at him. He shook his head at them, grinning, then stopped at their look.

"Some woman," he ventured.

"What's your business?" one of the guardsmen replied in a flat voice.

                              *   *   *

By their tenth day on the ice, Tor and Tristal had grown
used to the toil, the backtracking, the frustration. Tristal
had also begun to be frightened as he watched their pro-
visions, which still were ample, disappear daily. When they
reached a rise, all they could see ahead was more ice,
gullied and tangled, stretching west and still upward. Tor
seemed content enough, and curiously silent.

On the nineteenth day, Tristal found a rock pinnacle
thrusting up through the ice. "I don't understand," he said.

"A mountaintop, I think," Tor said. "The mountains
have generated the ice—with help. From the climate. And
some change. Some change since the Time of Fire."

"How you know?"

"The ruins. Back in Soarer country. Don't think the
ancients would have built all that near this much ice."

"The ancients. They might have done almost anything."

"Perhaps. But look. This means we've gone somewhere.
Maybe there are more mountains. West of here. Maybe we
are going to start down soon."

"We'd better. If we turned around now, we'd be out of
food before we got back."

"It'd be faster. But then there's Raran. I think she's
going to have puppies."

"Juni's dog? She has no taste." Tristal said this with a
laugh, but he looked at his dog with real concern. This was
not time for a litter of pups.

By the thirtieth day, they seemed no further out of the
ice, though they had found no more peaks. Tristal had
grown more gloomy. There was no going back now. The
frustrations of the ice, which seemed so routine to Tor,
grew more and more maddening to him. His uncle still
treated the whole trek like an amusement, an afternoon
stroll somehow extended. Yet even he had become more
gaunt, seemed to eat less, to ponder more. Finally he had
begun cutting Tristal's ration, too.

Three light snows had fallen, making the ice more slip-
pery, the crevasses more hidden.

On the thirty-fourth day Tristal suddenly slipped, sliding
down a slope, breaking through snow, and finding himself
hanging suspended by his rope over a narrow crevasse so
deep he could not see the bottom for the ice protrusions
on the way down. Looking up, he could see nothing but

the jut of ice at the lip of the ice chasm. He was secure enough, but trapped. He could feel light tugging at the rope. Whatever Tor was doing, it didn't help. He could envision his uncle somehow holding the sledge, and himself, on the steep slope above the drop. He seemed to hang for a quarter of the morning, shouting occasionally but receiving no reply. Faintly he thought he heard Raran barking at one point, but then it stopped.

More time passed. Tristal looked around in growing resignation. His stillness had made the sweat of his walking cool and he began to shiver. He thought he heard dull chopping above, methodical, continuous, but then he thought it was his own blood. No. It was chopping.

Eventually it stopped, and Tristal's isolation seemed to return with greater force. He shouted repeatedly but heard nothing. He was in a world of curving ice, except for one small patch of sky he could see above between the incurving rims of the crevasse. He found himself giving in to a terror greater than he had felt ever, even though he had resigned himself to death.

The chopping resumed, louder now. Scattered ice chunks began to sift by him; then, looking up, he could see larger pieces rolling by the suspended rope where it disappeared. Suddenly the rope shifted, dropping him several spans as he cried out in fear, ice falling around him. The pinch of the rope around his shoulders tended to cut off the circulation to his arms. His hands were numb even in their furred mittens.

He heard Tor calling. What was he saying? "Swing?" How could he do that? He was too terrified to move. "Swing, Tris," the voice said again. He tried, gritting his teeth, and found he could, gaining momentum. Then, on the upstroke, he felt the rope lift. He swung again, lifted once more, gaining now, swinging with more force, slipping slightly, gaining again, finally nearing the groove in the rim of the crevasse above, losing swinging distance, hanging again, hearing the axe again, now loud, still methodical, holding his face away from the flying chunks, then, in a pause opening his eyes and seeing Tor's face, grim and determined, above him.

"Don't hit the rope," he called.

"Try not to," Tor panted. "How are you?"

"Cold."

A large ice chunk came away, tearing at Tristal, leaving a gap through which he could see Tor above, another rope, around him and disappearing up over the rim of the slope. At the top, Raran peered down at him. Tristal was too cold to help, so Tor had to haul him up the slope, bracing against steps he had cut into the ice. Finally Tristal got a foot against the lowest step and began crawling upward, his hands useless, using his elbows instead. He reached the top and lay there, panting.

Tor routinely began winding up the rope and preparing to continue, staggering a little from the recent strain. Tristal looked at him in growing resentment.

"How can you do this? Doesn't all that mean anything to you?"

"If you don't walk, you may freeze."

"Why did I come here? What am I ever doing here? You. You're a false leader if ever there was one."

Tor looked at him, startled, but said nothing.

"Of all the fool things—to voluntarily come somewhere no one could ever live. Only to die. We're going to die. You know that? And Raran with us. Look. You don't know how far west all this goes. We could fall in another of these in two sunwidths. That would be the end. What would it be for? I could be home."

"Home?"

"With the Pelbar. With Fahna."

Tor turned to him, somewhat fiercely. "True. But you're here. And you have to walk or you'll freeze. Now. Walk. That way. I'll bring the sledge."

Tristal felt a whirl of despair. He looked west, squinting against the glare, even though the sky was overcast. Then he took one step, another, another. They were moving again.

Thirteen days later they ran out of food, even though they had been on short rations for over two weeks. Ahead, the ice continued in its peaks and gullies. Raran had lost all the spring from her gait. It had snowed several more times, and finally, the next day, they were stopped completely by the first mountain storm of the winter.

The three lay under fur together by the sledge. Tristal had not yet recovered from his resentment. Finally he said, "Tor, I think we're going to die. I'd just like to know why we're doing this? Why? What am I doing here?"

"I went. You came with me. No more than that. We aren't going to die. Forget that."

"Look out. You can't even tell which way is up. What if the ice continues even half as far as we've come?"

"We've been trending downhill for almost two weeks. It ends. I know it ends."

"How do you know? You've said yourself that one thing about truth is that it is understandable. If one man knows a thing, and it is true, then it should be clear to all others."

Tor was silent a long time. "Answer," said Tristal. "I deserve an answer."

"Is a man who conducts you down a wide path a leader?"

"If you don't know it. If he is showing you."

"If there is a path, there is no need."

"But to come here! This is false leading. Did you have to come just to prove you could lead? And one man and a dog? What can you be thinking?"

"My coming is nothing—though I enjoy it. It is you. You are the whole thing, the whole reason. But it hasn't been working. You have the social sense I do not. I am fine with Shumai hunters. But that way is gone. Even those who persist in it are mere anachronisms. Nothings. They have no real function. You do—or you will if you learn. But you haven't. You won't listen. You have to hear both the people and the pulse of things."

"This pulse of things. It's too mysterious. It's a personal gift. You have it. I never will."

"I don't believe in personal gifts. Well, Tegrit had one—you've seen people before who could hear and influence the thoughts of others. That's mysterious. But ultimately unhelpful. You saw he thought of it as a burden. The only real gifts are ones anybody can develop. The pulse of things. It is a matter of listening. Ideal listening. I've found I can't teach it. I wonder if anyone can teach anything. But it can be learned. You can't keep wilting, you know. Giving up. You think everything is too much—well, not everything. But if you want to win, to persist, really want to, then you'll look for a way. You can't do anything—unless some foolish thing—without an idea of what to do. If you don't know, you keep very still and ask. There is always an answer, you know. Nothing is without its answer."

"None of this makes any sense."

Tor would say no more. Tristal thought he would try it

then, this listening. He heard the hiss of snow and the wild wind. He felt Raran snuggle closer against him, hungry and frightened. He put his arm around her. Her nose came against his ear, nudged, and went away.

Two days later dawned clear. Tor put Tristal and Raran on the sledge and began towing them, slowly, placing a rope anchor ahead, then bringing up the sledge. By afternoon Tristal insisted on helping. He could see it. They were trending downhill.

The following day, at high sun, Tor, ahead, stood still a long time, shading his eyes. Tristal brought the sledge up, plodding, dizzy. "What?" he said.

"Trees. Thick trees," Tor said. "A long way yet. But we should be in them tomorrow."

Tristal looked. In a gap in the ice he could see trees. Not so far. Then he looked at the grooved and gullied ice between.

 XIII

AMI was late for supper, but she commanded Unsit to bring another bowl of barley stew. The long table was set on its trestles in the main room of the small manor house. All ate together, even the nine farm workers and the cheese maids. They regarded Ami with mock severity since she was a universal favorite, at five, with dimples and frank, wide brown eyes. No one in the room had failed at one time or another to reach down and kiss her soft, bulging cheek. Ami paid little attention, taking it as her due.

"Not only are you late, young one. You don't seem hungry. Been up with the shepherds?"

"No, Mother. With the hair-clothed men. I ate some of their sheep."

"Hair-clothed men? What do you mean?"

"They are up in the woods. With their animal. They say

its a dog, but it's much too large. It is this high. But it's lying down now."

"That high? It must be bigger than a sheep then."

"Oh, yes, James. Much bigger. With long teeth. This long. I felt them."

"Ah. You felt them. And what did this giant dog do then?"

"He cried. Just a little. And he licked me. On the hand."

"And how big are these hair-clothed men, little one? Like the barn, perhaps?"

"No. But very tall. Taller than anyone. With light hair— lighter than Uncle Bartram's—and strange eyes."

"Strange? You mean like a cat's—yellow and slitty?"

"No, Francis. No. Blue. Almost like the sky."

"Do you know your colors, then, eh?"

"Yes, Em. Some of them. I'm learning. Ernest has taught me."

"And where is Ernest? With the shepherds, I imagine. I've told him to tell me when he's going to sleep with the shepherds."

"No. He's with the men. He says he's going to sleep up there with them. They aren't feeling well. Especially the young one. He has four scratches across his front. Like this. Like a big hand came down and scratched him, but much deeper. They are both very thin. And the dog. His name is Raran and he's going to have puppies soon."

The whole table erupted in a long laugh. "I see. You may be learning your colors, but there are some other things..."

"Enough," said Ami's mother, Dame Arbyr. "There will be time. Too much time. Raran, you say. His name sounds like a dog barking, then. Did he growl at you?"

"A little. When we came. They had a fire. They were cooking a sheep. Ernest told them they were in bad trouble for that. Bad trouble."

"What did they say?"

"They said they were hungry. They said they would pay it back. They seemed not to understand. They said they ran out of food while crossing the ice. They..."

"Crossing the ice?" Immediately the whole table was silent and alert, the men rising.

"Yes. What's the matter? They are very nice. They said it took them more than a whole month to cross the ice.

They are very hard to understand. They talk like this." Ami screwed up her face and squeaked out some high nasal sounds. Everyone laughed.

James frowned. "Did they have anything with them— swords?"

"Oh, no. The older one had an axe—very strange, with a thin handle. I told him it would break when he chopped wood with it."

"What did he say?"

"He laughed at me." She put out her bottom lip. "Then he kissed me like you all do. On the cheek." She indicated with a tiny finger.

"Show me the mark."

"Oh, it doesn't make a mark. I'm glad. It would be all worn out if it did." They all laughed again, rising from the table to go about evening chores.

Randall, a large, redhaired man, the manor reeve, came up beside Dame Arbyr, frowning. "You think there's anything to that? Want me to check?"

"No. Someone has been telling her stories. They have never come on this side. Never. They don't send little girls home to tell stories."

"Even so..."

"Ah, Randy. I'm sure it's all right. Ernest has gone up with the shepherds before. We've all been alarmed. This is the safe side of the valley. We all know—that ice goes forever. This season you can't even get up on it, running as it is on this face with melt. And in winter... winter's almost on us, too. How is the haying?"

"All finished in three days if the snow holds off. I've seen some way off over the ice already. But we've done all right."

"Good. Now. I'm troubled about the way the new loggers have been looking at Elayna. I don't like it. They're from the fourth sector, aren't they? Do you understand what they're saying?"

"More than I'd like. I'll see to it, ma'am. Don't worry."

But Dame Frith Arbyr did worry about it, as well as about the strange detail in Ami's imagined account. As Unsit was putting the child to bed, she came into the loft room and sat on a stool by her. Unsit sang her prayer with her, curtsied, and left.

"Where did you hear about such men as these, little one?"

"Didn't hear, ma'am. I talked to them. They are very nice. The older one sang me some songs."

"What of the younger one?"

"He was too sick. The older one fed him. He held his head, like this."

"Did the younger one say anything?"

"Only a few things. I told him my poem about the man with the huge nose."

"Yes. I hope he liked it."

"Yes. He made up some more for it."

"More?"

"Yes. He sang it, too. Then we all sang it. So many times I remember it. I think." She pondered, then smiled. "Yes.

'Oh, the man's great huge nose grew so fat,
It toppled him down when he sat.
Each leg was so narrow,
As thin as an arrow,
They looked like two spoons in a vat.'"

"That's very nice. Thick as . . . what?"

"It's called an arrow—like a long crossbow bolt. They had some. With feathers on one end and a sharp point on the . . . what's the matter? Ma'am?"

Dame Arbyr had rushed from the loft room and down the ladder, then out into the farmyard. It was full dark. She looked out at the woods toward the distant ice front. The wind was chill. She hugged her arms against her sides and ran across to the barn. The stretch of spruce forest lay dark and silent except for the cold breeze. She whirled around, scanning the buildings for Randall.

Hearing a slight sound, she turned again. A tall figure, swallowed in the dark, loomed up in front of her. She caught her breath.

"Don't worry," said a strange voice. "I've brought the boy. Ernest? He's asleep. He grew frightened when it got full dark. We let the fire go out."

"Who? Ernest? Where?"

"Here. He said he could stay. But I thought it unlikely. He said he did it often. My name is Tor. We came over the ice. My nephew, Tristal, and I. And his bitch, Raran. Here. He's small enough. Can you carry him?"

She ran forward with a cry. Ernest stirred. The two came together. She smelled smoke and sweat as he gently put the boy on her shoulder. The two looked dimly at each other in the dark.

"Ernest said we were in bad trouble. For the beast we killed. I'm sorry about him. We will make it good to you. We had to. It's been days up on the ice without food. My name is Tor, as I said. I am a Shumai from far to the south and east. And you—you must be Dame Arbyr. Isn't that what Ernest said?"

"How did you—"

"You're the mother. Servants don't come out in the night and take children from strangers. Mothers do that."

Dame Arbyr felt somehow safe. "Come to the house," she said.

"No. I can't. Thank you, though. Tristal needs watching. He was hurt before we got up on the ice. It weakened him. And we've been on it for fifty-two days. He's near frayed out. And Raran. I think she's about to have pups. Not a good thing to be making pups when you're starving. Do you understand?"

"Most of it."

Ernest stirred on Dame Arbyr's shoulder. "Tor, let me watch the puppies," he murmured, drifting off again.

"My men will come up in the morning," she said.

"Are you angry?"

"Angry? No. I am so frightened I—I—You're not a Raider, then? No. Raiders take the children."

"Raider? No. I don't think so. We saw no one on the ice. If I were a Raider, I wouldn't go there. They must come from elsewhere. Who lives to the west?"

"We . . . don't know."

"I don't understand. Don't you go . . ." He paused. "Ice?"

"Yes. This is a large country—surrounded with ice. The Raiders come over the ice. In the west. They've never come from the east before."

"Before? They never will. Can't you follow them over the ice and put a stop to it? Are there too many?"

"No one can get up on the ice."

"And yet they get down."

"With long ropes. We think. They seldom come. But

they come. We cannot get over the ice. No one has ever done it. You will see."

Tor sat down abruptly. "I will get out," he said. After a pause, he added, "And yet, if it is like this last trip, I dread it. And if it is much farther, it . . . would be too far. Who is that?"

"What?"

"That shadow."

Dame Arbyr called, "Randall. Randall, come here." The shadow turned, paused, strolled up the hill. "Randall, this is . . ."

"Tor." Randall started, stiffened. Tor stood.

"He has brought Ernest back. Here, take him. He's getting heavy. Ernest grew frightened in the dark." Her voice seemed high, seemed to tremble. "He won't come to the house. Another man and a dog are up in the forest and he is going back to them. Perhaps in the morning—"

"We'll go get them any time you want, ma'am. Now if you want."

"Randall, it's not like that. Now don't start trouble. He's . . . all right. I think."

"I think so, too, Randall. But Ernest says I'm in trouble for the beast we have been eating."

"What, a sheep-stealer? We're standing here talkin' to a sheep-stealer?"

"Randall, use your head."

"We were hungry, Randall. I have told the . . . owner we would pay it back."

"Come, Randall. Bring Ernest to the house. Good evening, then   "

"Tor."

"Yes. Good evening, Tor. Come."

Randall hesitated a moment. Tor chuckled. "Don't worry. You could push me over with a twig right now. I am that worn out. But there's no need." He turned abruptly and silently vanished into the dark.

"Did I see?" said Randall. "He seemed to have only one hand."

"He lost the other in a war," Ernest murmured.

"Likely. More likely he's a thief. A sheep thief."

"I don't think so, Randall. He doesn't act like one. Randall . . ."

"Yes."

"Hold me a moment. I'm so frightened, I think..."

"It doesn't have to be a moment only," Randall muttered.

"No, not that again. All I'm asking is for steadiness. You know my mourning period has years yet to run. Besides..." Dame Arbyr sighed, then added, "All right, take me back to the house."

The southsector sheriff was there by morning with thirty men, standing in the farmyard with mugs of hot barley drink in their hands, their breath steaming in the cold air. He looked grim. All the men carried long-swords, most of them old and worn. Several also hefted dark-stocked crossbows with well-packed quivers.

"Now then, Randy, which way?" he asked.

"Up there, I think. The children were with them. Ernest and Ami. They would know."

"The children? They're that dangerous, eh?"

"The one I saw had one hand. He admitted sheep-stealing."

"But he was hungry? Come over the ice? The other sick?"

"Well, sheriff, it seemed only reasonable to call you. What do we know of them? Of what they're doing here? And there's the sheep."

"Alf," the sheriff called. "Get someone to get the children, eh? For directions."

In a few moments, Ami was brought by Unsit. The child rubbed her eyes and squinted against the light. Unsit was obviously frightened. "The boy? He's with you?"

"No. You think he's..." Sheriff Janus squinted eastward, against the new light. "Look. That smoke?"

"Looks like it, sir."

"Well, then. Come. We've drunk enough. We won't need you then, little one." He leaned over and kissed Ami on her cheek.

"Take me, though. I want to see the puppies."

"Puppies?"

"The dog," said Randall. "Their dog is soon to drop a litter."

"That puts them at some disadvantage, then, doesn't it." The sheriff's eyes gleamed.

The men entered the spruce woods in a column, but after they neared the camp of Tor and Tristal, they fanned out, swords drawn, crossbows nocked. Sheriff Janus took the lead in the center, advancing toward the column of light smoke. Ahead he could see a tall man standing. Ernest was squatted down near him, his back to the advancing men.

"You know him, Ernest?" Tor asked.

The boy stood and yelled down through the trees. "Sheriff. Come here. You should see these puppies. Four of them." His voice was shrill and ringing.

The sheriff motioned to his men to stop and walked up through the trees. Tor was standing at ease holding a wooden noggin of sheep broth.

"Your name, Sheriff?" Tor asked. "I'm Tor. My nephew, Tristal. This one's the mother, Raran. Ernest has been naming the puppies, but he can't tell them apart yet. You understand me?"

"Some," said the sheriff. He held out his right hand. Tor looked, frowned, then set down his noggin and held out his left.

"Only got one," he said. The sheriff grasped his hand and shook it briefly, then dropped it. "Your men don't do much walking up on people, do they? In the woods."

"What?"

"They sound like a herd of something. Why have them stand out there? Bring them up. Is all this about the beast? I told the woman—Dame Arbyr?—we'd make it up. Must be some work we can do."

Raran whined, looking at the advancing men. Sheriff Janus looked at her and whistled. "That's a dog, eh? Can't be. Too big."

"Always been one," said Tor. "I've seen bigger. All yours little? The woman said last night you're surrounded by ice. That was hard to take for me. I've had enough ice for a lifetime."

"What? What do you mean?"

"Uh? To climb over. Go west. Surely don't want to go back."

The other men had come up and stood in a ring around the camp.

"I'd offer you some of my ill-got beast," said Tor. "But I suppose you've eaten."

"Eh? Yeah. Look, you—Tor? You can't stay up here. We have orders. You'll have to come down. All of you. This business of the sheep has to be adjudicated. You may be all right, but we have Raiders. We can't have strangers like this. I'll take that axe now. And those."

"I'll come. I'd as soon wait a day more for Tris to rest. And the pups. I'll keep the axe, too."

At that most of the men drew swords again. Tor laughed. "Ernest," he said. "What's this all about? Am I the enemy?"

"What?" the boy said. Three men moved in around the boy and drew him away.

"Don't step on the pups," Tor said. "Well, it's like that? You—Sheriff? Here. Take the axe. Remember. If it's your sheep, that's my axe. Now. Tris will need some help walking, I think."

"No," said Tristal, standing, swaying. "I'm all right. You. Ernest. Help me carry the pups. Here, Raran. It's all right. Stop that. It's all right." He stumbled, then stood again. Tor came to him, but he shrugged his uncle away. Then he sat down. "Tor, you carry the pups. You. Maybe your men can help with the gear." One of the men moved up on each side of him, taking his arms. "I need a good washing," Tristal said, abashed.

"Plenty of time for that," the sheriff said. "You, Ben, Jeff, Pierre. Bring the stuff. What?"

Ben had turned over the bearskin and stared at its inside, whistling.

"What?" Tor asked.

"That's one animal? No seams? Where did you get?..."

"Never mind that," said Sheriff Janus. "Come. Let's get down to the manor."

"I can carry a pup. I can," said Ernest. Tor and the sheriff looked at each other. Tor gave one to the boy, lifting it carefully into his arms, as Raran looked on anxiously.

As they came down from the woods, they were met by a large crowd from the manor and nearby farms, all standing silently.

"You don't get many strangers, I guess," Tor said.

"None. None but the Raiders," the sheriff replied. Then, when they were well out into the farmyard, he faced Tor and said, "I hereby charge you with the willful theft of one sheep belonging to Dame Arbyr. I hereby take you into custody before your trial. Now, both of you, come with me."

"It's all right about the sheep," said Dame Arbyr from the crowd. "I can let them work it off."

"Not this time," the sheriff said.

"This custody," said Tor. "What is that? Prison?"

"Prison? Not until the trial."

"Is there food and a place to rest? What about Raran? How long do you mean?"

"No questions. Come. Men, bring the other one."

"Dame Arbyr," said Tor. "What is this?"

She looked disgusted. "The law," she said.

"The pups. Will you take care of Raran and the pups?"

"Of course."

"And my axe. Will you keep my axe for me?"

"No. That belongs to the state," said the sheriff.

"It belongs to me," said Tor. "You just took it."

"What do you know of our law? It belongs to the state."

Someone in the crowd blubbered his lips, and the rest laughed. The sheriff glared around at them, then urged the weary Shumai forward. They were tied in a cart with a long shaft, pulled by four men.

As they left, down a rocky road, followed by most of the crowd, Elayna said, "Mother, the young one. Is he all right?"

"I don't know," said Dame Arbyr. "I am angry. I will see my brother about this. This is not right. Not right at all."

"Who are they?"

"Men from far away. From over the ice."

"The young one. He's so tall."

"They're both tall. The tallest men in Ice Valley now. But you saw just the young one, eh? Now. There's wool to card. Let's get to it."

XIV

Tor and Tristal were finally released from the jolting cart in the small stone city of Blue Lake, governmental seat of the southsector, and led into a large building and up a set of stairs, leaving behind the usual crowd of the curious.

Entering a dim room, they saw in front of them a dais, hung on three sides with wool cloth, surrounding an ornate chair, in which sat a smallish, middle-aged man.

The charges against them—sheep-stealing, trespassing, unauthorized presence—were read. Judge Caspar Morton regarded them silently down his upturned face. He drummed his hands on the arms of his chair. Finally he lifted his right hand and said one word, "Prison."

"The sheriff said we would be tried before prison," said Tor.

Morton raised his eyebrows. "You have been."

"Where?"

"Take him away, jailer."

"How long? How long will we be there?"

"Your sentence is indeterminate, but you certainly are not helping it by your impertinence."

"What impertinence? Trying to find out what is going on? Is this another society without justice?"

Morton rose, sniffed, and left the room.

"Come on, boys," said the jailer. The two Shumai looked at each other. Tor dropped his eyes.

Two months later, in deep winter, Judge Morton again sat on his dais. Before him stood a smallish man dressed like the farmers on Dame Arbyr's manor, in a blouse, over-shirt without sleeves, and belling pants.

"Well, what have you learned?"

"They won't talk to me, sir."

"Ah. Then they are angry."

"No sir. They are very popular with the men. They saw immediately that I . . . was a spy. The older one did."

"What have they done? What trouble?"

"Trouble? None. Well, they've stopped Durke's bullying. And they got the jailer to do something about the rats."

"The rats?" Morton drew back.

"Yes. They trapped them. All kinds of ways. Put them in his desk. In his cabinets. In—"

"Yes?"

"His lunch."

Morton stood. "You saw them do this?"

"No. No one saw. It . . . just never happened before."

"But you didn't see them."

"No. And they read to the men."

"Read? They can read? What do they read?"

"Things from the library. They asked and the jailer brought some things. They laughed so much the others had them read. Good stories. Old ones. From their cells. At night."

"I thought you worked."

"We work enough. From the stew they saved grease skim for oil and made lamps. Now we all have lamps. From hollowed stone waste."

"Well. We can put a stop to that."

"Why?"

"Irregular. Not punishment if there is that. What else?"

"Not much. They fit in. They tell stories. They run up the wall."

"They what?"

"Run up the wall and then flip over. Landing on their feet. Astor tried it. But he fell on his bloomin' back. Laid up a couple of days. It's not that hard, though. I did it. Fell a few times."

"Did they teach you, then?"

"No. They don't talk to me. Sir, I think I ought to be let go. It's uncomfortable. They all know. Reese would have coshed me if he could. No fun being a slimer."

"Well. You seem to have botched it. Perhaps so. You'll have to stay off the swigging. No more barley mash."

"Yes. Oh, yes. And, sir, if you want to put them out on a farm next summer . . ."

"Yes?"

"I'd be glad to have 'em."

"Even on the west side? Where their friends would come?"

"Friends? They're not Raiders. I've seen the Raiders. Nothing like them. I'd feel safe. The older one...He'd know they were coming. I'm sure of it."

"Know? How would he know?"

"He'd just know."

Morton raised his eyebrows again. "Yes. Of course. He would just know. Well, Blake, I suppose you may go home. Don't want to see you here again. No fights. No barley mash."

"No, sir. Thank you, sir. Glad to go. Those stones are a wirsle-warsle."

Winter seemed to deepen even further, the snow driving down from the western ice face, blowing across the open lands, burying farmsteads and sheepshelters. In the middle of this, three weeks after Morton's interview with Garey Blake, he had another visitor, who was admitted by the sector judge's servant, stamping and shaking off the cold, driven snow, cuffing it out of his beard. It was Second-sector-judge Fenbaker, one of the four chief men of the valley.

With some surprise, Morton admitted him to his inner room, with its troughfire, handing him steaming barley drink as he entered.

"I must say, this must be a matter of enormous importance. Had you no one you could send?" Morton began.

"It is. Indeed. Very troubling. I need your help. My daughter—"

"Blanche?"

"Emily. The younger one. She's been spirited off. Carleyboshed. A forced marriage in the offing—unless we can stop pregnancy."

"Stolen! Emily? No complicity?"

"No! Not this one. Some northsector loggers who saw her this summer. Or one of them. I'm sure of it. I'm certain it's not her will. We've done a rapid search. Dupin and his men have been cooperative. In fact, they are somewhat shamed. But they've come up blank."

"Surely you don't suppose they came south. We'd know."

"Ah, I well know that. I've come to ask the loan of your prisoners. The two . . . strangers. I've heard of them—how they hunted giant animals before they came here. Like ones from the old time, the storied time. How the older one has his instincts."

"A problem, I'm afraid. The older one. Almost two weeks ago he refused to work."

"Refused . . . I don't understand."

"Said they'd worked enough for any small beast. Said he was being exploited. I said then if he wouldn't work, he wouldn't eat. He's stuck to it. He's weak now, but not working. So he's not being fed."

"You would starve him? That's against the regulations."

"What would you do?"

"Why, perhaps reduce his ration—or confine him alone. But to starve him . . ."

"I won't have him running my prison, Jeffrey. I thought he'd give in."

"From what I've heard, he isn't the kind to give in. Then he's too weak. What of the other one? Might he be convinced?"

"He's angry about his uncle. I'll have him brought. But you better prepare yourself for some insults."

Fenbaker sat down, staring at his drink. "I don't like it, this interfering. But I'm desperate. I can't see Emily jabbering like that for the rest of her life."

"No. I'll have him brought."

When Tristal was led in, Fenbaker marveled at his height, then quailed slightly at the grim anger in his expression.

"Judge Fenbaker wishes to speak with you," said Morton.

"About feeding my uncle? Some society you have here. Even the Peshtak feed prisoners sometimes. The Tantal. The most degraded societies—except for this one."

"Yes, yes. We'll see about that. Perhaps an arrangement can be made if you help me."

"If I help you? What if I don't? Going to starve me?"

"No, no. Try to be courteous. It'll be easier."

"We were courteous enough when we came. We've been thrown in prison and worked. Courtesy got us no place."

"For the Lord's sake, man. Sit down. Jailer, let go of

him. You won't flee, will you? Please? Perhaps I can help. You can help me, I think."

"That's the real point, isn't it. You're another of these so-called judges, I've been told. Helping you is what this whole setup is all about."

"It's no use," said Morton. "See? He's a savage."

"I? I a savage? What savagery have I done? Starving a man is savagery."

"I'll hear no more of it. Jailer, take him back."

"No! No! No!" Fenbaker shrilled, rising, clinging to Tristal. "Morton, please. Go out. Please? Take the jailer. Let me talk to him. Please? It's my daughter."

The room fell silent. Morton left with the jailer. Tristal could feel Fenbaker's arms trembling. "Sit down, please. Just listen, please. It's my daughter. She's been taken. Carleyboshed. She's out there somewhere with a man and his friends. If she becomes pregnant, she will have to marry him. It's the law. Not often used. Most marriages come from previous pregnancy. That's normal."

"Normal? Never heard of that. That brings only trouble."

Fenbaker looked at him, his eyes swimming. "Yes. Well, among us, it works well enough. No one wants to make anyone pregnant unless they mean to take care of them. I mean pregnant, you see."

"And you want me to find him first. Because we are hunters and you people can't hunt your way out of dark room."

"Must you be so insulting?"

"Why not? Unless ... you can get my uncle fed. Put him back on food and I will go and hunt your daughter. But ... what happens if I don't find her?"

"I'm afraid I can promise nothing."

"What happens if I do?"

"I ... will ask to have you transferred to secondsector, and I promise you I will consider setting you free. And your uncle."

"So our freedom depends on our success."

Fenbaker pondered. "Perhaps so. Otherwise I wouldn't have come. It's not easy out there. We've looked everywhere. Everywhere."

"But the right place. All right. I will go. But I see it

now. I have to take my uncle. On a sledge if necessary.
With men if I need them. Otherwise I'll go back to prison."

"All right. All right. I'll see if I can arrange all that. With
the judge."

"He'll go free, too, then."

"I . . . I don't know."

"You'd better know. Or I won't go."

"Young man, you are in a poor position to be so difficult."

"It's plain you're not in much of a position yourself.
One other thing . . ."

"Yes?"

"What if we kill somebody?"

"They are outlaws. Carleyboshers. They can be killed.
We don't approve of it if there is another way."

"Like starving them. I'll need my bow, too. And Tor
his axe."

"Bow? I don't understand. Crossbow?"

"No. Different. Be sure I have it. And all the arrows.
Seven."

"Different?"

"Big. Morton will know it. Just get the gear."

Two days later, out in a flat area of blown snow, Tristal
stood gazing blankly at the empty whiteness. Behind him
lay two sledges. Tor, wrapped in piled blankets, was on
one, supplies on the other. The secondsector sheriff and
six men stood with him.

"You've checked all the farms."

"Yes."

"And the hay."

"No chance."

"And the forests."

"Nothing to support them there. But we sent men
through. The third- and northsector men have, too. No
trace. But they must have gone to ground before traveling
that far. Too cold."

"He worked in the forest."

"Yes. To the east."

"What of the west?"

"He couldn't have made it."

"But he has friends."

"All northsector people. We think we know them. Their

families are silent. Ashamed. But they wouldn't dare harbor them."

Tor threw off the robes and stood up, leaning on the sledge back. "What of the ice?" he asked.

"The last place. Impossible."

"Why?"

"Cold. Nothing to eat. Danger from its shifting."

"In winter, too? Have you been up there to check?"

"No need. Only a madman would do that."

"The whole plan sounds mad enough. It'd be just the place for a madman."

"Not as mad as you might think. It's done often enough. Every child must have its father if that father be known. He'll have to pay. But his blood may some time rule the secondsector—if he can carry it off."

"What of the girl—Emily? Will she agree to it?"

"It works out surprisingly well. But you didn't come here to talk. We'd better get back to those farmsteads again."

"No. To the ice face," said Tor.

The sheriff looked at him scornfully. Tor smiled wanly and put a hand on the man's shoulder. "Look," he said. "I was there. Not all that long ago. It has caverns in it. Hidden places. Surely they would freeze up. Where better to store food? They could have been killing those yellow-fronted woodchucks and storing the meat up there all fall. Wood, too. The smoke might well vent back from the ice face, up some fissure. And they could insulate themselves with some kind of shelter. All this rock you use. Not necessary. It really drains the heat away. Grass or hay would be better."

"We'll go to the ice face," said Tristal.

"Not me. Not my men."

"Give me two. You take the rest."

The sheriff considered. "All right. Johnny, Bob. Go with these men. Watch out, you understand."

Tristal smiled, seeing he picked the two biggest, men nearly as tall as the Shumai. "Here. We'll take turns pulling Tor."

"Madness," said the sheriff. "Madness."

Tor eased himself down on the sledge. "Sheriff, I've had much more experience at these things than you. You know your territory. But you have to think of habits of mind. This whole plan may seem mad. It's surely flamboyant. But how did it come into being? From what I've been thinking, and know of young men, it may well have pecked open its shell as they climbed up to the ice face after work. Don't treat them like plodding farmers. They have a certain . . . sense of play. You have to be dull to hide a girl in a haypile, even in the best of barns."

"Maybe. But we can't chase dreams. This is the sectorjudge's daughter."

But as he watched them fading into the whiteness eastward, he began to wonder. "Pierre. What do you think, eh?" he said in a low voice.

Tristal lay on his belly near the fissure. Only the faintest of tracks led in, but he could smell the slight acridness of woodsmoke. He turned and motioned to Bob, pointing to the other side of the opening. The Ice Valley man slid his skis over that way, sword drawn. Tristal nocked an arrow and silently kicked off his skis, motioning Johnny Dowder to his position. Below he saw Tor trying to stand up off the sledge, then sitting down again.

Tristal started to move inside, but saw Tor beckoning him. He was disgusted. What this time? He slid back and knelt, putting his skis on again and gliding down to his uncle.

"What?"

"I can't refrain. They can hardly miss you in there. They have these stocked bows—crossbows."

"So?"

"Here. Put this in your coat." He held out a frame of boards he had been whittling silently, with his axe, as they traveled. It was roughly curved to fit Tristal's trunk.

"How can I bend with this?"

"If it comes to that, discard it." Tor smiled slightly, putting a hand on Tristal's shoulder. "Go now. Do it well. Aven keep you."

Tristal returned to the entrance of the ice fissure, again shook off his skis. Then he slipped inside. Instantly the wind ceased, though cold seemed to reach at him from the walls of ice. Yes, here were more tracks. Tristal stooped— as well as he could with the boards across his chest. In the dimness he could read six sets of tracks. One was a woman's. Irritated, he started to remove the wooden framework, but then thought a moment and left it.

Ahead the fissure forked. Both passages had tracks.

Again he pondered, then took the north fork. In twenty more steps he heard voices. The passage narrowed. The floor was disturbed. He stared at it. A trap. So that was it. That bad. They meant to be tough. Tristal backed up slowly, then took the other path. In the dimness he barely saw the gut string across that one. He stepped over it, tracing the path of what must have been an alarm.

Ahead was a flickering orange light. Tristal moved forward. The voices were plainer. He nocked an arrow and checked his belt knife. It seemed mad to confront them. But he had the authority behind him—and it was a way out of prison.

He breathed deeply and stepped around the corner, bow ready, saying, "All right. Sheriff's authority. Nobody move at all. Now. You, over to the right. There. You, Emily . . ."

As the one man moved, a man behind him sent a short bolt at Tristal from a crossbow. It flashed across at him and whacked into his stomach. Three of the five cried out and rushed at him, but he drew the bow and stood still, yelling, "Back now."

"*Je ne comprends*" . . . one began.

Another cried out, "*Taisez vous. A l'instant. Quand je commencerai a courir, battez le retraite! Détournez-vous. Maintenant. Allez vite.*"

The five moved fast, vanishing around a curve in the tunnel as Tristal advanced toward the bound girl. He turned as a man with a loaded and drawn crossbow slipped around the bend behind him. The man loosed the bolt low and it pierced Tristal's leg near the outside of the hip. Tristal's anger surged as the man dodged back out of sight and he hobbled after the fellow, rounding the bend as the man was reaching for another bolt. Tristal drew an arrow and put it through the man's thighs, then turned in time to dodge a sword thrust from someone behind him.

He whipped his bow across the man's face, driving him back, then tripped him, disarmed him, and turned again, as another man raced at him, yelling, "*Pour l' amour!*" Tristal parried his blow, and on a return stroke hacked the man's sword arm down. Turning as the man he had felled reached for him, he thrust through his leg, then raced back toward the opening, meeting a fourth man, who shrieked, turned, and fled for the entrance.

Tristal turned, scooped up the crossbow from the ice as

he stepped again over the man lying in the path with the arrow in his legs. The man was moaning, *"Ahh. Les jambes. Quelle douleur. Je voudrais que . . . que . . . ah, je meurs."*

Tristal limped over to Emily and tore aside her gag. She cried out. He turned to see a grim young man with a sword out, advancing on him. *"Vous êtes un homme sauvage, mais maintenant vous allez mourir."* Behind him, Bob, the sheriff's man, appeared and felled him with a single blow from the flat of his sword. The young man dropped with a slight grunt and lay still.

"You, Tristal. You all right?"

"My leg. This short arrow is all. This one's sticking in some wood. We have them all?"

"I think so. Here, Emily, how are you? All right?"

Emily wilted with anguish and crying.

"How could she be all right?" Tristal muttered.. "Here, Emily. Come. We have a sledge. You can ride home. We'll have to make another. For these wounded."

"And you," said Bob. "What of you?"

"Ahh," said Tristal, at last feeling the pain in his leg. "What a mess. Look at all of us."

Emily, freed, stood up, still crying. She hid her face in her hands. "I . . . I can ski," she said.

"Brave girl," said Bob. "You don't have to."

"I will. I will." She fled from the ice fissure, slipping and crying out as she stepped over the wounded men in the passage.

By the time Tristal had reached the entrance, Emily was at the sledge. Tor's arm was around her, and she was weeping into his shoulder. Tristal sniffed at that, then laughed to himself. He looked over at the man who had tied him. The sheriff's men had bound his arms behind him. He spat at Tristal.

"You're a brave one,". Tristal said. "You're probably the lover, the would-be father. A fine lot. To steal a girl. You'd better steal another. None would pick you."

"Savage," the man said. "Savage." He spat again.

Nightfall found them at a scanty sheepshelter down from the spruce forest. One of the sheriff's men, Bob Landy, had gone ahead for help. Tristal lay in the straw, his leg throbbing, watching Tor work on the carleyboshers, as the locals called men who stole women for wives. The man who had been shot through the thighs was gravely hurt.

Tor had cut the arrow and worked it out carefully as the man lay in the ice fissure, stanching the blood as well as he could, binding the wound with pressure compresses.

Now he took them off and looked at the wounds once more. In the dim light of their fire he looked up at the others. The four bound carleyboshers muttered among themselves. Tor dressed the wounds once again and tried to put the man at his ease. Then he took the man with the head wound onto his lap, took out his Pelbar folding knife, and began to shave the hair back from the wound. The man cursed him. *"Vous êtes un esclave,"* he murmured. *"Un chameau. Un porceau. Jean, est-ce que c'est un porceau? Ah, oui. Alors, mes amis, j'ai pieds et poings liés, mais les cordes sont mal tendues. Après que ce chameau-ci se sera endormi, je serai libre."*

"Hold still," said Tor, frowning. "I'm going to sew it. It will hurt some."

"Ce n'est rien."

"That 'tchamow' part sounded bad. What is a 'tchamow'?"

"Vous êtes un chameau. Un gros chameau—ahhhhh."

"Clumsy, too. Hold still. I'm worried about your friend. Very worried. He's in bad shape."

Before he moved to the next man, Tor checked his patient's bonds, found them loose, and tightened them. The man continued to curse him.

The arm cut was also quite deep. Tor washed it, getting Emily to hold a bowl of hot water. She turned her head away, her mouth down. Tor gave the man a leather strap to bite down on and sewed his wound. Then he wiped the sweat away from the man's forehead.

The man Tristal had immobilized with a thrust to the leg had also lost much blood. He also cursed Tor as the Shumai worked on him, mildly, smiling up at the man benignly. Then he returned to the first and cradled his head against his leg, wrapping him carefully in blankets brought from the ice fissure. When Emily brought stew Bob had fixed, Tor fed the man, spoon by spoon, wiping his mouth occasionally. The others glared at him.

"Emily," he said. "Which one wanted . . . is the one?"

She pointed at the unwounded man, then shrank back, crying.

"I'm sorry. I thought that was the one. The coward. Depending on his friends. Must have some position."

"Don't talk about it," said Tristal.

"He does. His uncle is northsectorjudge."

"Great uncle," the gravely wounded man murmured. "*Son oncle est èleveur de moutons. Et ce n'est pas un poltron.*"

"Easy now. Don't concern yourself," said Tor. He had the crossbow in his hand, studying it. "Tris, I think I could use this," he said. "Especially tonight. I'll watch. Bob, you trade-off maybe. The rest of you sleep. You, what is your name?"

"*Ça ne vous regarde pas.*"

"It's Roland. Roland Thebeau. Ah, Roland, I'm so sorry you're this way. But it was bound to happen," said Emily.

"Not bound. Hadn't thought of *les hommes sauvages*," Roland murmured.

Tristal looked over at Tor in disgust. Tor lifted his shoulders slightly. "You see how it is," Tristal said. "I wonder . . ."

"I don't think so," Tor said. "There's the people."

"They're hard to tell from the sheep."

"What are you two talking about?" Bob said in a severe tone.

"The future. Just the future," said Tor.

"You make no sense, but just don't try anything. There is authority, you know."

"Ah. So we've been hearing. And hearing. And hearing," said Tor.

Emily looked at him. "I don't understand. I don't understand at all," she said, whimpering.

"You never will if you don't now," said Tor. "I hope you've just been through the most severe experience you'll ever have. But everything's freezing over again, just the way it was."

"It'll never be the same. Never."

"Perhaps. Not for Roland here, surely."

"I don't see why you're being so careful with him," said Tristal. "He tried hard enough to kill me."

Tor shuddered slightly. "But you are Shumai," he said. "You know how to conduct yourself. He . . . he's only a badly hurt young one. He tried to be gallant for his friend." Tor rested the stump of his right arm across Roland Thebeau's side.

"Don't concern yourself for me," said the wounded man.

"What you have to learn is that you have to concern yourself for everybody," said Tor. "Everybody. Even Emily. See what that would have saved you."

"Tais-toi, chameau," Roland muttered.

"'Tchamow' again. Always 'tchamow.' Ah. It's the sheriff's men. Already."

"Where?"

"Listen. Well, Tris, are we the hunter or the game?"

 XV

EMILY stared at the high window in her room, a massive room with cut stone walls hung with thick woolen tapestries. She toyed with the barley bread on her plate, sighed, drank a sip of spruce tea, gagged, sat back in her tall-backed chair.

Her father entered the room. "Emily," he said softly, sitting opposite. She glanced up, then down at her lap. "Your mother says you've spoken harshly again. It's been long enough. You need to straighten up. It's no shame. Everyone knows."

"You put them in prison."

"Who? The carleyboshers? Northsector will come for them when the weather breaks. They have to be punished. If you say that in public, everybody'll think you enticed them."

"Enticed them! Who'd dare? I don't mean them. I mean the savages."

"Ah. Them. What else was I to do? What shall we do with them? They don't fit. Embarrassing enough it was to the sheriff to have them go right to you. As though led."

"That's what you got them for. You promised them."

"Only to consider their release. Only to consider it."

"Have you been out in the town lately?"

"No. Busy. Why?"

"Mother has. She defends you. But she's seen the backs turn to her."

"Backs turn! I'll have none a' that. Just let her give me some names."

"Names? Going to imprison all of Boiling Springs? I'd swither at that, I would."

Sectorjudge Fenbaker pondered, shaking his head. "After all I've done for you. Goin' ta get them and all, in the severest weather."

"The young one would've been killed but for his uncle's shield under his coat, and you'd have swallowed that quick enough. Too bad. But only a savage. No matter. Truth is, you don't know what to do with 'em."

"No. I don't. It's partly Morton. Partly Dupin. He's coming, you know. Angry about Roland Thebeau. How is he? You've heard?"

"Better. Won't walk right, they say. He took his chance, he did. No question. Claude would be nothing without him. Never would've happened. You let me talk to Dupin. I'll burn his ear. To think of Tristal grinding rock again..."

Fenbaker paused, looked at his daughter, and said softly, "And the older one?"

"Tor? Him, too. Of course." She looked at her father. "Nothing like that. Don't try me so, Father. But he is so...self-contained. He's...remote. In another world."

"What world?"

"He...seems to want nothing. But to see. To know. He wants to know everything. He it was led them to me."

"The sheriff told me about that. Nothing mysterious. He even explained it. Put his mind in the mind of the north-sectorers."

"And why didn't the sheriff do that?"

Fenbaker considered. "Couldn't. Just couldn't. All so plain later. He thought about it as they left. Eventually he turned back, you know. He was on his way."

Emily stamped her foot. "Father, you know if it was up to him, I'd still be up there in the ice, with that cheese face on me every two—"

"Emily!"

"Face it. You got two men to save me. They did. One was hurt. Now you're through with them, you're just crushing them up and throwing them out. Like broken dishes."

"What would you have me do?"

"Free them. Free them, of course."

"To do what? They belong to no guild. They have no family here. Their skills are savage ones. They don't belong to the Brotherhood, perhaps know nothing of the Sacred Way. They simply have no place."

Emily stared out the window a long time. "I can hardly believe it."

"What?"

"Tor told me it would be like this. He almost used your words."

"I'm growing a little tired of that man's divinings. There's something strange about him."

"No. Nothing. Here's something, though. When I ran from the ice, he smiled at me and put his arm around me. I don't remember what he said, but it . . . made life . . . possible. You—you didn't do that. You just sat down when I came in."

"The Lord! How can you say that? I was weak with relief. Maybe you'd prefer the savage as a father. No. No, don't say that."

They sat in silence a long time. At last Emily said, "Father."

"Yes?"

"Have them to dinner."

"Dinner! Them? They live in the forest. How can you . . ." He looked at her a long time. "All right. Next week."

"Tonight."

"But—"

"If you send now, they'll have time to clean up. I'll meet them. I'll tell them . . . not to insult you. No doubt they are angry. I would be. I am. But they're very gentle."

"Gentle!"

"Tor held Roland on his lap and fed him with a spoon— all the while he spat insults."

"No doubt in jibber-jabber which Tor didn't understand."

"He understood the purport of it. Made nothing of it."

Fenbaker threw up his hands. "All right. Tonight. I'll send for—" Emily had thrown herself on his lap and squeezed him. "The Lord, Emily."

It was a small dinner, prepared in protest by Dame Fenbaker. Present were Tor and Tristal, the sectorjudge and his wife, Blanche, Emily, and Colin, the Fenbaker's nine-year-old son, whose eyes beamed at the Shumai with fear and excitement. Also present were five men standing at ease near the wall looking on. Tor smiled at them. Only Bob smiled back.

"Is it enough, then?" said Mistress Fenbaker.

"Yes. Very nice. Much better than over at the prison."

"Tristal, you promised," said Emily.

"What? Did I say something wrong? I thought I said..."

"You all eat much the same things, ma'am," said Tor, musing. "I think I could go a lifetime without the turnips. Given the choice. We've been turniped daily for quite a while. But I can see you've few vegetables. Beyond the ice there's a great variety. I wish it weren't so far. The Soarers grow potatoes. They'd go well here. Good food with little work. Never had barley before. And your only meat's the sheep. The ill-fated sheep. There must be water-fowl here in summer. Do you take them?"

"Ducks? Geese? Eat them? Feather meat?"

Tor laughed. "Is that bad, then? Whole societies eat them—some as developed as you are. Some like us—savages, dripping with gore, you know. Slathering for the kill."

"Tor!"

"Ah, Emily. I'm sorry. I did promise. I'm impressed with your flax. Never seen it before. I could get used to wearing that."

"It's endless work, and hard on the ground. It and the sheep. We have to be very careful."

"We've been learning about your country. You have hot springs here."

"You've seen them before?"

"Far to the south there are some. I've never been there. It's in the edge of Forman country. Some of the Shumai used to trade with them. They've seen them. Water and steam gushing up from the ground. In high country. I always thought someday to go there. Maybe yet...though everywhere I go here, people say nobody can cross the ice."

"No. It is impossible. Many have tried."

"I will. Tris will, too—right, Tris?"

Tris finished his mouthful. "I suppose," he murmured.

"We've heard of the Raiders. They cross it. If they can..."

"They come down with ropes. In places no one has ever

climbed," said Fenbaker. "Many have tried. Some have been killed trying. After all, the Raiders take children. They kill, burn farms, take some clothing, but mostly children. You can imagine how raging angry it makes the parents—and eager to get their bairns back. But no one has managed it. The ice is crumbling and melty from the steam springs. It breaks off."

"How do the Raiders manage it?"

"Few see. They come and go very fast. But from what we can tell, they have a series of long ropes, and they let them down in stages, with men at each stage watching. They take up the ropes, then let them down when their men come back."

"And lift the children up?"

"Reckon so. Mostly at night."

"Children," Tor mused. "They must lack children for some reason. It's a big risk for children. The ice must not be so wide on the west."

"Why do you say?"

"If we carried that much rope as far as we came, we'd never of made it. What defenses do you have? You ought to be able to stop them."

"Little. We've set them up, but then they may not come for seven or eight years. Everything relaxes."

Tor laughed. "It's like down on the Heart. Some places flood in the spring, but not often. After a big flood, people move out. Move back the fishing camps, the butchering camps. Then they think, 'Ah, well. We won't have a big flood like that one in my lifetime,' and they move back. Then the water takes it all away again."

"But not the Pelbar," said Tristal. "They're the ones who live by the river but really take care."

"I don't understand a thing you're saying," said Dame Fenbaker.

"Far to the south and east is the Heart River," said Tor, his eyes seeming to mist over with musing. "It drains an area of Urstadge so large it is hard to conceive of. I have been on over a thousand kilometers of this river—as you measure distance—and Tris at least seven hundred. Where the Pelbar live, the river is over a kilometer wide, though not deep. It has over another thousand kilometers to flow before it reaches the southern salt water. It has several major rivers to empty into it yet. When you watch it flowing on and on, so massive, so quiet, yet rising sometimes in spring and caving off whole sections of islands with all their trees, it's... very moving.

"In the winter the eagles come, then thousands of ducks and geese. They leave for the north in spring, with the seagulls, and the vultures return and circle the river and ride the winds above the bluffs. In it are fish as big as a man. Around it is all thick with trees, of course, close to the water, hanging over it, in it, and all wide-leaved trees, like your aspens, or birches. Almost no evergreens."

"You wouldn't like it, though," said Tristal. "It's hot and very buggy. Mosquitoes all over."

"We have our share of them," said the judge. Then he paused. "Is this all the truth? Why did you come way out here, then?"

Tristal snorted. "Tor has to know what's over the horizon," he said.

"Tris is getting tired of it," said Tor. "Especially after the ice. I seem to find trouble wherever I go. This has been no exception, has it?"

"Perhaps Tristal could stay, then," said Emily. "I'm sure there's swinking enough here for any man."

Tristal frowned, puzzled. "Work, she means," said her father. "There is that. If you are to be out of prison, you have to have work. There isn't any hunting here, as you describe it. But there's plenty of labor, if you don't mind it."

"I intend to leave, when I can," said Tor. "I imagine Tris will come. But the best way I can help you, I think..."

"Yes?"

"Is to tell you about the world outside, and..."

"Never you mind about the world outside," said Dame Fenbaker. "No need to make us dissatisfied over what'll never be ours."

"And?"

"To find a way to defend you against the Raiders. I hesitate about that. I keep trying to get away from such things. But I can do them. It would seem—"

Tor paused as a commotion from outside in the hall interrupted him. *"Pour le dîner!"* they heard. *"Les assassins avec la famille. Cèla passe les bornes."* A thin man burst into the room, pushing aside the attending men who went to meet him. "*Vous!*" he shouted. "*Fenbaker! Où sont les hommes sauvages?*"

"*Qu'appelle?*" said Tor.

"*Vous? Oui. Mais* ..."

"*C'est moi. Et celui-ci est l'autre. Tristal. À votre disposition, monsieur. Nous sommes furieux et sommes assoiffés de sang. Mais pour la défense de nos actions, peut-être vous avez oublie que votre relation a assisté a un elevement. Ce n'est pas très beau.*"

"Another surprise," said Sectorjudge Fenbaker. Dupin, the northsectorjudge, stood openmouthed. He shifted his eyes from Tor to Tristal and back.

"*Alors,*" he said. "*Vous parlez comme un homme honnête. Mais* ..."

"I only know a little," said Tor. "It's the language of the Rits, who live on the north edge of the Bitter Sea. I haven't been there, but when I was a *petit garçon*, a lonely old Rit woman lived in the Shumai winter camp, and she taught us—the children—so she could hear the sound of home."

Dupin sat down abruptly. "*Il y en a d'autres hommes ...aussi...qui parlent comme* ..."

"*Oui,*" said Tor. "Far away. Farther than you can think of distance. But it's true."

"*Et vous?*" said Dupin, looking at Tristal.

"No," he replied. "I've heard Tor a few times, but I've never been to the country of the Rits."

"*Les Rits,*" Dupin mused. "*Sont ils nombreux?*"

"*Mais oui,*" Tor began, but Dame Fenbaker coughed and frowned. "Yes. There are many, I think. No one has counted, but they hold a great deal of land. The Shumai, my people, traded with them sometimes, and on occasion—in former times—fought with them."

"Fought? But no more?"

"Not since the great fight at Northwall. Against the Tantal. I was very young then. The separate surviving peoples are getting together again—as they were before the Time of Fire."

"*Je ne comprends pas. Une époque du feu?*"

"Long ago, we know, all the land was filled with people, all speaking languages understandable to each other, probably governed by one set of laws and one government. Something terrible happened, killing nearly everyone. Here and there a pocket survived and, in the aftermath, lost all knowledge of the former time. Now these survivors have become numerous enough to interact regularly. They are discovering likenesses, identities. Obviously you and the Rits had some common ancestry. Your language proves it. What could be more obvious?

"Now you're cut off by distance and ice. On the other side of the ice I saw an ancient sign in both your languages. It is plain that the society—"

"What did it say?"

"Something nonsensical about sinners burning for eternity."

Dupin and Fenbaker stared at each other. "What is nonsensical about that?" Sectorjudge Fenbaker said sternly.

Tor glanced at Tristal. "You believe it, then. In the Heart River societies, your custom of getting pregnant before marrying would be thought of as extremely sinful. I must admit it seems so to me. That would mean that your whole society is going to burn for eternity. I can't think that Aven, or the Lord, as you call him, would do such a thing."

"And yet. . ." Tristal began.

"Qu'est'ce? . . ." Dupin queried.

"He allowed the Time of Fire."

"Would anyone like some turnips?" Dame Fenbaker asked. "That is, anyone but Tor?"

Everyone laughed. *"Les navets,"* said Dupin. *"Ce sont des modestes légumes mais utiles. Dans le fort de l'hiver on éruct des navets tous les jours."*

"Cést vrai," said Tor. "And now, down on the Heart, the eagles are leaving, the shadbush is white with flowers, and the willow trees near the water are already a haze of green. But it still is, as you say, the depth of winter here."

They fell silent a moment, then continued talking about the travels of Tor and Tristal, the fight at Northwall, the layout of all of Urstadge as the two Shumai knew it. Tor kept turning the conversation to the ice, but everyone was firm in the opinion that it could not be crossed.

Fenbaker summarized what Tor and Tristal had been learning already. Ice Valley was roughly elliptical. Its rocky north end was used largely for sheep pasture. It was rimmed all around by forests, mostly of evergreen. A line of hot springs ran up the west side near the ice face. Rain was scarce on the west side and not very plentiful on the east.

But glacial melt water was channeled and stored for irrigation. Peas, turnips, barley, hay, and oats were grown, as well as flax for linen cloth. Drainage led all the surplus water in the valley down to the lake that gave the south-sector city its name. While the lake was rimmed with ice on the south side, it had some kind of hidden outlet, since it rose in summer with meltwater, but then slowly fell again in the fall until hard freezes seemed to halt the process.

Tor wanted to know whether the ice was gaining on the valley or receding, but no one had thought to look closely. The ice was the ice. It had always been there, they thought, and so they accepted it. Tor and Tristal had much enlarged their hosts' view of the world in the evening's conversation, but most of what they had said had not been absorbed, though Dupin seemed most eager to contemplate the notion that somewhere far off there were speakers like those of the northsector, where all the francophones lived.

It was clear, also, that Tor had completely won Dupin over, and that any resentment he had felt over the wounding of Roland Thebeau had been dissipated. Tor managed to suggest to him that Thebeau ought really to propose marriage to Emily, by rights—and even do so before the usual intimate courtship. Dupin raised his eyebrows but said little. He ended the evening by inviting Tor to the northsector to visit and perfect his speech, assuring him he had a drasty pronunciation, badly in need of improvement. The north-sector was sparsely populated, containing only about eight hundred residents. The other three sectors totaled an additional thirty-five hundred, making the Ice Valley people one of the more populous of the Urstadge groups, especially for residents of so small a region.

The evening ended with Dupin walking Tor and Tristal back across to the prison, where they were still to be housed until a place could be found for them—but not as prisoners. As he left them, he put his hands on Tor's arms and said, *"Mon ami, ta présence est une affaire d'une signification très important, et peut-être cela sera une chose important pour notre futur."*

"Tu es tres bienfaisant," Tor replied, smiling. *"J'espére que c'est vrai."*

At that moment Dame Fenbaker was saying to her husband, as they prepared for bed, "Imagine, he didn't even believe that people will burn forever for being sinful and unrepentant!"

"Ah. I'm sure we can teach him that, my love."

"And all that middle-maddle about giant rivers and endless countryside. I don't want to hear about that. It's hard enough to run a household—especially when savages come to dinner and old jibber-jabber busts in."

"Yes, my love. But I'm very pleased to have it settled. Dupin likes them. They can jibber with him—at least Tor can. He is a rare man, Nannie. No doubt about it. Rare. I'm pleased to have met him. I have hopes, too."

"Hopes? Not Emily! No, not to that giant."

Fenbaker laughed. "No. But that finally we'll get a man who can handle the Raiders."

"If he's not one of them."

"Nannie. You're still not mad about the turnips!"

"No. I...I'm a bit frightened. It dizzies the head, all these new things."

"Indeed it does, Nan. A whirlie business."

Tor was right about the season on the Heart, too. The shadbush was in bloom, and the long log booms from winter cutting had been floated down to Northwall. Again Fahna was momentarily startled when she saw Bravet, once more mistaking him for Tristal. But no. He was nearly as tall, and wide-shouldered. But he lacked the haunted grace of Tristal, and the slightly cocky runner's stance. His hair was blond, but not light-filled gold.

But Bravet caught her look and grinned back, yelling, "Here I am, ready for the lucky." She spun away, walking up the riverbank. Bravet and his two close cronies laughed. An old Shumai on the bank, now a farmer, spat into the grass just slightly ostentatiously.

"You got some trouble?" said Bravet, looking narrowly at him.

"She mistook you," the man said, undaunted. "I was in the narrow valley in the south when the man she mistook you for killed his first Peshtak. You look just a shade like him. But not really. He grew up a running hunter and still is one. Not a farmer. Not a chopper. He lives every day with the old Shumai spirit we've all lost."

"Listen, you one-eyed slime digger..."

"And not a one of those hunters would yell at a woman like a stepped-on duck," said the man mildly, turning, spitting again, and walking away.

 XVI

FINALLY the weather in Ice Valley began to moderate, reaching above freezing during the days. The high snowdrifts glistened with thawing snow that formed crusts at night.

Randall Stonewright, Dame Arbyr's manor reeve, was walking across the farmyard when Raran suddenly ran out of the log barn, followed by four flop-eared, knob-legged dogs, already big. The clot of animals flew by him heading northwest. He shaded his eyes, looking, and saw a single skier far out across the pasture, coming toward the manor.

As the dogs neared the distant man, he squatted down on his skis. Raran bowled him over and leaped around him, the other dogs coming up and standing in a high-tailed wiggling circle around Raran and the man, who wrestled in the snow.

"What's that, sir?" asked one of the manor sawyers, Billy Rantool, coming up to Stonewright.

"I imagine it's one of the savages, come back for his dogs. Good thing, that. They'd of eaten the whole flock by fall. As much as two men and not a bit of work out of them."

"Strange dogs. That Raran, though. She's a lollapalooza. She even brought Justin's gloves and dropped 'em at his feet when he'd forgot 'em. You talk to her and she seems to understand."

"Yeah. I know. I watched her push Ami out of the ram's pen with her head. Butting her just like the ram himself would. But the pups! Useless. They undo four times what good the bitch does."

Finally Tristal came up to the two men in the yard. "Hello," he said. "I'm dog hair all over. Raran has spread hair from one end of Urstadge to the other almost. You remember me, I guess. Tristal."

"I remember," said Randall. "Come for your dogs?"

"Raran anyway. You've raised the others. If you don't want 'em, I'll take 'em along."

"She's the good one of the lot. They're nothin' but trouble."

"Still young. Half Soarer dog. But they have to be trained. They'd be good trained. Might make good herd dogs."

"Let 'em near a flock and they'd as like drive it off a rock ledge."

"Not when they're trained. I'll train one for you if you'd like. All of 'em for that matter."

"Never heard of it. We can make our little ones roll over and the like. But dogs are of very small use."

"Don't know where you got those tiny ones. Must've been in this valley as long as you've been here. Never saw any like 'em anywhere. They don't mind worth fish guts."

Randall frowned at Tristal, not knowing what he meant. "I imagine you'll stay to supper," he said. "Billy's sawing some logs if you want to get on beneath him. Then I can let Coleman move some hay."

"All right. Let me stow this gear."

Dame Arbyr was scandalized that Tristal had been put right to work. She sat at supper with her mouth straight and her head down. Randall knew she was out of sorts, and why, but she continued to eat, blandly, asking questions of the young Shumai, as they all did.

"Where did your uncle get to?" Dame Arbyr finally said.

"He's finally getting his chance to travel the perimeter of the valley. The sheriff's man, Bob, is with him."

"To watch him, no doubt," said Dame Arbyr with some disgust.

"I suppose," said Tristal. "That seems only wise. After all, what do you know of us? Little. He'll learn, as well."

"Learn? What?" said Randall.

"Things he never imagined existed. We're from a different world, you know. We do have some things to teach."

"I imagine you've learned from us as well," said Unsit.

"Yes. About flax and linen. Your judicial system. Sheep.

We'd only seen wild ones. Your songs. The plays at Boiling Springs. Very nice in winter. And Tor has a crossbow now. He can use it with one hand."

"Not his axe?"

"That's a symbol as much as anything. But he's used it well enough." Tristal proceeded to tell them about the fighting with the Peshtak, and of the outlaw Shumai.

A silence fell over the table. "If that is what crossing the ice will bring, I'm glad the ice keeps us in. I don't want any part of it," said Dame Arbyr.

"Yes. I know. But it seems to want a part of you. I mean the Raiders."

"They are a nuisance. Terrible, too. But they won't destroy us. And they come so seldom."

"Tor thinks there's something wrong with them. To come as far under as dangerous conditions as they do—he thinks they are ill or poisoned, or something."

"Ill? I don't understand."

"They mainly seem to take children. Girls preferred. Tor says that's a sign there's something wrong with their reproduction. They want to replace themselves. Something they don't understand. Perhaps an empty place from the Time of Fire."

"We've heard a little of your tales of a Time of Fire. An empty place? What is it?"

Tristal explained at length about such places, glass surfaces poisoned by radiation from ancient times. He explained about the dome from which Celeste had come, and how Stel the Pelbar had opened it, with their final help. He could see incredulity on their faces.

"Ah, you don't believe," he said. "But sure you must have some echoes and reminiscences of the old times. Like your metal. Your steel. It must be from a ruin."

"It is," said Randall. "Expensive enough, too. It comes in rods, which we hack out of rock . . . ."

"Concrete," said Tristal. "Before the dome, we always called it artificial stone."

"Well, whatever. And then long beams of it, and pipes. Almost all in one place in the thirdsector. We have to pay for it, too. Hay enough, and timber. Wool and meat and barley and firewood. Not fair, really."

"The Soarers had almost no metal. They chipped tools out of stone."

"I've heard your uncle does that," said Elayna.

Tristal raised his eyebrows. "Word does get around. He does. Did. In prison. He became fascinated with that kind of work when we were with the Soarers. One man named Tegrit tried to teach him. It isn't easy. Especially for a man with one hand. He's getting it, though."

"And you. Do you do it?"

"I've tried it. It seems futile. But there was little to do in prison, and I learned some."

"Why does your uncle do this?"

"Because he . . . wants to be wholly independent. It lets him think that if he were the last man in Urstadge he could have his necessary tools without help. I think that's it."

"He's never grown up," said Randall.

There was a slight silence. "That may be," said Tristal. "But if you ever saw him in an emergency, you wouldn't say that."

"You did well enough yourself with the carleyboshers," said Elayna.

"I was only the arm. Tor was the guiding mind. I'd have been dead there but for his body shield. He's been trying to teach me how to know things—the way he does—but it hasn't sunk in yet. I . . . lack something. Some mysterious thing all the Shumai axemen used to have."

"Hmm. Well, we have axes, and a need to use 'em if you want to help," said Randall. "To pay for some of what those dogs've eaten."

"Randall, that doesn't matter," said Dame Arbyr.

"But it does," said Tristal. "I know enough to see this is no easy country. I'll work for the dogs. Train 'em, too. Might as well. You'll find 'em useful enough as working dogs. But maybe we can take 'em over on the west side as watchdogs. Need some geese, too."

"Geese?"

"Wild ones. Clip their wings. Feed 'em. I know you won't eat 'em. But they do watch. Way south, the Alats used 'em—white ones—so Tor says."

Randall made a face. "Well," he began. "I'll need help with chores and then I'm ready for the kip. You, Tristal. I'll show you a place . . ."

"Later, Randy, please. Leave him with me this once. I'll talk with him a bit. You can work him as much as he likes later."

Randall paused, swept the room with his eyes, and rose, saying "Yes'm. Any way you'd like it."

"May I stay, Mother?" Elayna asked.

Dame Arbyr raised her eyebrows. "So long as you knit up that kersey."

Elayna dropped her eyes. "Yes'm," she murmured.

"Your uncle—how is he?"

"Fine. Frustrated by the ice. But fine."

"My brother it was that starved him some. I'm guilty about that."

"I heard it was. No matter. Tor bears no grudges."

"A shame, though."

"Nothing to him, ma'am. He's seen much worse times."

"He's welcome here anytime he wants, you know."

"Thank you. I'm sure he'll come. But he'll be in the west most times, I expect."

"The west?"

"Because of the Raiders. It fascinates him. He wants to end the raids. He's trying to get the sectorjudges to set up a defense force."

Dame Arbyr pondered. "Ah," she finally said. "They come so seldom. It's almost a new surprise each time. Like a dry season on the manor. Now, tell me about your uncle. And the Pelbar. Of all the people you've talked about; I wish I could meet them."

It was past midsummer. Tor lay by a fire in the spruce forest, one of Raran's puppies, now big, with him. He heard someone coming. He put his fingers in his mouth and whistled.

Soon Bob came through the trees. "We missed you," he said.

"I saw a place I thought I could climb. Got up quite far. Then I fell."

"You all right?"

"Can't walk. Don't know. I don't think anything's broken."

"Want me to carry you?"

Tor snorted. "No. Give me till tomorrow. Now don't look sklent at me, as you'd say. I'm worried, though."

"Your leg? What?"

"Raiders. With all the questions I've asked, this is the time of year they most come. Stands to reason."

"You sense anything?"

"I . . . don't know. It's not the right kind of year. Not enough rain. I've tried to make a pattern. It's been rainy years as far as I can tell."

"Want me to stay with you?"

"No. Go down the next five farms. Make sure they have their kern alert. Standing their watches. As we set it up. Tell 'em tonight only. I'll be moving soon."

"Will you come down?"

"No. They have to come down the ice. We need to patrol the edge. Trouble is, all I find are tracks of couples, coming up into the woods. Half the young in the valley seem to wander around up here."

"They're looking for something."

"Looking . . . the tracks say . . . looking for what?"

"Babies. Marriage."

"I'm sure the Raiders just don't come sweeping down off the ice. They send advance people. By the time of a raid, they've been watching for some time."

"You're sure?"

"Who can be sure? But we've talked to all the living people in the west who can remember raids. Right? They are too good, too sure. They know. There's only one way that can be done. Scouting."

"You're sure?"

"Ever been on a raid?"

"No."

"I have."

The two agreed to meet at Granite Point the next noon. When Bob climbed to the spot, Tor was there, leaning on a stick, gazing at the ground. "Look," he said. "That's Blake's girl, Martha. She's been up here with Ralph Stewart."

"I can't see anything."

"Here. Look. I'll outline the track for you."

"I can see something. But how can you? . . ."

"It can be only five women in this area. Right? Look. The left foot toes out more than the right."

Bob shook his head. "If you say so. The sleekit lass! She's supposed to be sweet with Arly Robbins. You're sure this is right?"

"Yes. The tracks are clearer down below. The problem

is we can't set traps at all. Can't go catching the young people. Are there ever some who just disappear? Couples?"

Bob pondered. "I recall one set. West side, too. You think . . . we always thought ice fell on 'em."

"Why raid if they come to you? We'll have to make a study. Ask more questions. There must be sheriffs' records. If we can catch 'em prowling before a raid, that'll be a good defense."

"How's your leg?"

"Oh. Some better. Skinned my back some, too."

"How far'd you fall?"

"Most of the way."

Bob looked up and whistled lightly.

"Not straight. Did a lot of skidding and catching."

A light snow was falling by the time Tor came back to Dame Arbyr's manor. It was late afternoon, and the main house lay empty except for Dame Arbyr herself and Unsit. Tristal, she told him, was helping with the logging about four kilometers to the north.

"No raids this year, at least," she said.

"True. Good thing, too. Those farms are so lax, so open. It's hard to believe. Some have lost daughters, sons. Some have been burned out and lost much of their hay crop. It made them poor for several years."

"It happens so seldom. I've been hearing you've learned some things. My brother has been telling me."

"Him. As the southsector judge I've had enough dealings with him to last me. No offense."

"No. I understand. Are you staying with us?"

"Do you realize we've been here now over a year? And I'm no closer to finding a way out than I was when we came."

"Why be so anxious to get out? This is a good place. Good people. A useful life. Much to do. You could marry, settle down."

"I could've done that back at Northwall. I . . . it isn't me, Dame Arbyr. I've always been in the open. I still have a sense of some . . . unfulfilled destiny. I know that sounds odd. But it will happen. I'm sure."

"Call me Frith. And what about Tristal?"

"Tristal?" Tor fell silent a long time. "He has it in him

to be a true leader. More than I'll ever be. Because of his attachment to people—which I don't have."

"Surely you do. Everyone knows your concern. When I met you, you were carrying Ernest home to bed."

"Doing for people isn't needing them. They are often in the way."

"In the way? Of what?"

"Seeing. Knowing. Reaching out to something . . . I don't know what. This doesn't make much sense, does it?"

Dame Arbyr pondered. "No, it doesn't. I don't understand it. But I suppose that's what your special talent comes from. Your way of knowing."

Ami entered the room and walked to her mother's knee, leaning across it, looking over at Tor. Then she went to him, climbing up on his lap and curling up there.

Dame Arbyr looked at the two with something of an ironic smile on her face. "Well, you're welcome with us as long as you want to stay. There's plenty of work. You seem to be able to do most everything."

"Yes. I'd like to stay awhile, if I could. I'd . . . like to build a small boat . . . this winter. If you can spare the wood."

"A boat? To go on the water? Where? Blue Lake?"

"For a start. The water must go somewhere. Maybe an outlet I could navigate."

"And Tristal?"

"Tristal, too, if he wants to come. I sense . . . I hear . . ."

"Elayna?" Dame Arbyr laughed. "A dreamer's tale, that. No offense, but it's a matter of position. You must understand."

"I was puzzled. Yes. But—"

"You mean they're young? Eager? More eager than the older folks."

"I mean I've found strange pairs of tracks in the west woods this summer. Only some I've described. But it's rich with poor, handsome with ugly. Just the way marriages turn out."

"She could do worse than with Tristal. But the manor will be Ernest's. That's the way it works. She has to marry well to live well. I don't want her to be a farm worker's wife. That's what it would be with Tristal."

"Yes. I thought as much. That's the thing of it in the west, too. The manors don't lose children. It's the workers.

The manors aren't so concerned. They determine policy. Some of the workers are quite bitter."

"It's nothing I can change. I just have to live with it. Now. You want to work? Heavy or light? I see you can do most anything, in spite of—"

"Anything that's needed."

"The flax is ready. We need some help with weaving. You should know that, too. If you don't get out of here, every skill is worthwhile. There'll be time for the boat. One thing—"

"Yes?"

"When you tire of the boat, when you find no way out, I want it. There aren't more than two or three in the whole valley. A bargain?"

"Of course."

Soon after, far away at Northwall, the leaves began turning, and with the harvest a fall festival was held, with feasting, dancing, speeches, games. As she watched a line dance, Fahna sensed someone sidle up next to her. She turned and found Bravet looking down at her. "Want some apple crisp?" He held some out.

She looked at him, sensing some indeterminate quality she didn't like. "No. No, thank you."

"Well, you can talk, can't you? You can be a little friendly. After all, I don't bite."

"You're a stranger."

"Everybody starts that way."

"Some ought to continue that way. No offense. I—"

"I what?"

"I'm sorry. I want to be alone."

"Alone? In this crowd? I'll take you someplace to be alone if you want that. Why do you think you're so much better than everybody? It's that whimperer, isn't it? Tagging along with his uncle someplace. The future axeman. He'll never come back. You want an axeman? I handle an axe all winter. Look . . ."

She didn't reply, but stared at him for a few moments, startled, then walked away. Bravet watched her go, angry, then melting with the grace of her walk. He crushed the apple crisp in his hand, feeling it run over the paper cone and between his fingers. Then he looked at the mess and whispered, "Fish guts. You haven't put me off yet, sky nose."

Early the next summer, Tor stopped in to see Fenbaker, the secondsectorjudge, at the judge's request. It was evening, and they sipped spruce tea together.

"What I miss as much as anything is something sweet," Tor mused.

"We tap the few maples near the steam springs, but it's expensive, with everybody wanting it."

"Yes."

"I understand you've been out on Blue Lake with your boat."

"All around it. I need to go back. Later. There is an outlet. It's obvious. As expected. Where the two ice masses flow together, but very deep. I let down a long weighted line. I had sixty meters out, but it didn't touch. It's truly deep there—an old valley, I think, now filled with ice and water."

"You're sure it's that deep?"

"You bounce the line when you find bottom. You can feel the weight come off. I found it easily enough toward the north end."

Emily came in and sat down after pouring tea for the two men and taking some for herself. After they talked a while longer, she said, a little imperiously, "Take me. Next time you go, I want to come."

"Can you swim?"

"Swim? No. Of course not. You do that, too?"

Tor chuckled. "Not that it would do much good, with the water as cold as it is. It's not a big boat, young lady. What would your mother say?"

"You mustn't tell her until afterward."

"A conspiracy? If your father agrees, I'll take you out a ways. Maybe not the whole way."

Emily leaped up, leaned over, and kissed Tor. Then she quickly gathered the tea things and left.

"She's not happy, is she?" Tor said.

"Happy? Happy enough, I think."

Tor looked at him. "I mean I think people regard her as . . . different since her misadventure. And she does."

"She does?"

"Yes. It's a common reaction from a woman so viciously

mistreated. They value themselves less." Tor looked at Fenbaker, who seemed startled. "But that's not what you wanted to see me about, of course."

"Yes. It's the demands you've been making on the west-side manors. The owners are complaining. All this making of bows and requesting that the workers train with them. It cuts into work time. And already one of them has used an arrow on another. Killed him. I've talked to the sheriff. We've decided it has to be diminished. Or discontinued."

Tor looked down at his palm. "I saw that coming. You know, I've checked the sheriff's records. I've found that along the west side, in this and thirdsector, four young couples have vanished in the last twenty-five years. All but one has occurred in years of raids."

"And that means to you . . ."

"They were taken. And the Raiders don't just climb down the ice and attack. They come down and study the whole situation. They've lost only one man in the last twenty-five years."

"We think they've lost more, but they take them with them."

"Even so, not many. You've never captured any."

"No. They come fast and then go. By the time we are organized, they've gone. But you're making too much of this. We haven't had a raid in seven years now. Maybe they'll never come again."

"Maybe. I've found a certain amount of patterning to what they do, but something is missing. I don't know why I can't see it. How about this? Suppose I find work on the west side. I don't want to be in the way. Is that possible? I'd like to continue. Besides . . ."

"Yes?"

"If I find a way out, it'll have to be there."

But that summer, Tor found no way out. Nor were there any Raiders. He did take Emily out in the boat, somewhat scandalizing the town of Blue Lake. She had been largely silent, though eager to see the ice up close. The ice made a wall without a break. Tor was disappointed.

As summer waned, and new snow already was visible high on the ice, Tor left the west and traveled north. Near a small, high, ice-fed lake, Roland Thebeau sat watching a flock of sheep. He strummed idly on an instrument quite like a pellute, leaning against a rock. Suddenly a large dog thrust her muzzle under his arm, jerking it upward. Thebeau jumped up, saying, *"Le Saint-Esprit!"*

Turning, he saw Tor. *"Toi! Va-t'en! Porceau!"*

"Do you know what a 'porceau' is? I haven't seen any here."

"Un animal atroce. Comme toi."

"Not so bad as that. They run wild down along the lower Heart River. Taste good. I think the ancients must have raised them. The Peshtak still do."

"Va-t'en. Je n'ai pas besoin de te parler."

"Sit down, Thebeau. I need to talk to you. You need to listen."

"Non. Je ne veux..."

"Oh, *fermez la bouche* and all that. Sit down. It's *très* important."

Thebeau looked at him, then abruptly sat down. "Look at me," he said. "I can't walk right. Not yet. Not ever."

"You could. You just don't. I could teach you. That's part of what I want to see you about. You're not trying. I saw you last year—"

"When? Where?"

"Oh, visiting the valley edges. Let that go. Winter's coming. Can you get to Boiling Springs for the winter?"

"Are you mad? That's where Fenbaker...what is this?"

"An idea. You haven't seen Emily. She's very troubled. Nobody will take her seriously. Not now. No one says anything about it. But they won't. That carleyboshing was all too public."

"It ruined me. Ruined me. It would have worked."

"No. It's a nasty business. Claude Pennybacker—what kind of a husband would he have made? Poor. He ran. He ran and left you. You know it. You let him use you because of his position. Now. Even after what happened, you saw how distressed Emily Fenbaker was about your wounds. Maybe you owe it to each other to try to put something together from what was smashed. Maybe—"

"Pah. Tu es un homme sauvage. Tu es stupide, sans cervelle. Quelle bêtise. Tu es trop fouinard. Maintenant. Va-t'en." Thebeau turned his back on Tor and would not respond to anything else he said.

Tor stood up and said, "Lady, here." The dog, which

had been nosing the bushes, turned and ran to him. "Well, Thebeau, if you change your mind about walking, I know something about it. You can't sit around here and restore yourself. Sorry to bother you."

"At least something will do your bidding, even if it's only a dog," said Thebeau. "Go back to your dithering about Raiders. Seems to suit you. You give everybody a laugh with that."

Tor left without saying anything further.

That third winter in the valley Tor did not return to Dame Arbyr's. There had been some tension about Tristal and Elayna, but Tristal had surprised enough people with his knowledge of mathematics to earn him a job teaching in Blue Lake for the winter. And Tristal was drawing back from Tor as well—because of his widely known fixation with the Raiders.

Tor got a job with a logging crew on the west slope, staying much to himself, with Lady, living in a crew shack high on the slope. He tried climbing the ice in the winter but had no success at all. Once when Tristal came to see him he was astonished at his uncle's remoteness and gaunt silence. He found sketches of the Soarers' gliding wings, much scratched out and redone. Tor tried to get Tristal to look at them and recall what he had forgotten, but Tristal remembered less than he did.

The third summer Tor remained in the logging shack and patroled the west side by himself, with occasional visits from the sheriff's man, Bob, who had grown to like him and who now worried about him. On one occasion, Bob found him building a set of gliding wings.

Bob nodded at Tor's explanations, then finally asked, "You're not really going to try those out, are you?"

"Why not? I'll start with an easy glide and work up. Good suffering bull's milk, Bob, I have to do something. I've been well up in the ice again, but it's a maze, a honeycomb. I'd never make it. I'm getting out of here. Somehow. Sometime."

"Well, promise me something."

"What?"

"You'll come get me before you do anything like this. Somebody has to be around to scrape you off the ground."

"I will if you promise not to tell. I'm being laughed at enough. I don't care except for the Raiders. I want somebody to be serious about that."

"I'll promise. Oh. I almost forgot. I have a note for you from Emily Fenbaker. She's not pleased about something."

"Along with everyone else," said Tor, taking it and sitting down to read. He held it out quite far. In a fine hand it read,

> I have been told that you asked Roland Thebeau to come and save me from my desolation. You had no right. You are trying to run everything. Foolish old man. Things are not good, but they are much worse now. Thebeau will spread it all over. He is angry and prideful. How could you do such a thing to me? I never want to see or speak to you again, and absolutely forbid you to interfere with me again in any way.

"Not good, huh?" said Bob. Tor held out the letter. "I can't read, you know," he added.

"I'm not going to read it to you."

"That bad. Is there an answer?"

Tor sighed. "I don't know if she will read it. Well, I'll write something."

With a sharpened piece of charcoal, he wrote,

> I am sorry, little one. The scorn wil all come on me. I love you and wil not interfer. Lets hope my mistake is not so bad as you say. Goodby then. Tor.

It was deep in the third summer Tor and Tristal had been in the Ice Valley. The snow had nearly all melted. Bob stood near Tor on a rise in a remote part of the western sheep pasture.

"You're sure you want to do this?" he said.

"No. Have to try. If it doesn't work, I'll try to change it some."

"You're not a bird, you know."

Tor didn't reply but ran to the edge of the small escarpment and launched off, gliding rapidly downward, lifting a little in the north wind, then sinking, running as rapidly as he could, finally falling and dragging downhill, the wings collapsing. Bob ran down the slope toward him as he struggled to get up. Neither saw the two shepherds looking over the rise from the east.

As Bob came up, he saw Tor's right leg running blood from being scraped on gravel. "You all right?"

"Yes."

"You picked up a little. I saw that. But it'll never work."

"I just have to remember·how it's done. I did fly one once."

"That was from high up, you said."

"Bob, how can I try that now? All I'd manage to do is kill myself."

"Well, you're doing a fair job of doing that right now."

"I can't argue that." Tor looked at the ruin of his careful construction, then sat down and laughed. Bob laughed with him.

Not long after, two farmers' sons encountered Tor putting rocks in one of the streams that ran down from the hot springs.

"What is that for?" one asked.

"To swim in. Lake's too cold. Like to wash off the sweat."

"Swim? Some of us take baths."

"Ah, yes, young man. You're all so civilized. No doubt you take baths. But *les hommes sauvages. Nous nous plongons dans le bone.*"

"Done any flying lately?" said one, snickering.

Tor looked at him. "No. Not since the first time. I haven't got it right yet. Not yet." He submerged in the deepening pool and glided off underwater, rising on the far side about twenty meters away.

The boys looked at each other. "No," said Tor. "This is not for you. You stay out of here. I don't want you drowning. I've got enough trouble—not to mention the difficulty it'll be for you, being dead."

"We'll be careful, eh, Denny?"

"You won't tell?"

"No. We won't. Not a word."

"I'm sure."

The next day, eighteen boys were there. A few learned some basic things about swimming. The day following three farmers came and dismantled the pool. Tor helped them.

"You," one said. "You need a job. Your nephew is doing

well enough. Working for Dame Arbyr again. Nothing wrong with him. He's been teaching, too. Knows more mathematics than anybody in the whole valley."

"Except me," said Tor. "Who you think taught him?"

The two men looked at him. "I don't get you at all," the other said.

"You wouldn't. Anybody who won't even teach his son to swim wouldn't. But don't worry. I'll try not to interfere. Really. It's your place. As anybody'll tell you, I'm trying my best to get out of it."

"Well, you're not going to fly out," said one, smiling.

"Looks not. I may give it one more try. I just don't remember enough of the structure. Or the way to control it. The Soarers did it easy enough. I'm scared to launch out from the ice face the way I did. Probably just drop like a shot goose."

Both men laughed. "Look, we like you well enough," the first one said. "It'd be easier if you tried to be more like us, eh?"

"I'd like to try, but it's not in my blood to have Raiders coming and not make it so bitter for them they'd quit."

"Ah. Them. They don't come all that much. It's like accidents. You put a crew on logging. You know sooner or later somebody's going to roll a log off on himself."

"But you work to prevent it."

"Here, Basil, get on the end of this one. How'd you get this rock here?"

"I lifted it." In frustration, Tor moved between the two men and picked up the rock, tossing it aside as the water poured around his legs.

Late in the summer, Emily turned a corner in Boiling Springs and met Roland Thebeau toiling along with two canes. Both stopped and stared. She started to brush by him, then turned. "You must not think that I had anything to do with that fool's coming to see you. I never want to see any of you jibber-jabbers, ever. Ever." She swept by him and walked away.

He turned and called after her, *"Non. Moi non plus. Vous êtes laide a faire peur."*

She turned and said, *"Vous, monsieur, êtes vraiment un monstre. Vous avez ruiné ma dignité personnelle, et maintenant vous êtes arrivé ici, dans Boiling Springs, quand vous*

avez une maison. Si vous venez ici, où est-ce que je vais?"
She burst out crying and hurried away.

Thebeau stared after her astounded. He had no idea she
would understand him.

He felt somebody jostle him. "You have business here?"
It was a heavy man in a sweat-stained shirt. "Haven't done
enough? Want to come back and make more trouble?"

Thebeau swung one of his canes at the man, who blocked
it and yanked it away, throwing him down. He tried to get
up but felt a foot on his neck. "Now, carleybosher. Up.
Go on home. You aren't wanted here."

A crowd was gathering. Thebeau stood up, furious, helpless.

"All right, move it along," somebody said. One of the
sheriff's men stood by him. "You. Come with me," he said
to Thebeau.

Later, in the sheriff's office, the law officer said, "A
letter of apology will get you out of here. Then you can go
home."

"Of apology! I was set upon. A free citizen in a street,
just walking."

"Like Miss Fenbaker some time ago. Set upon. Carried
off. Don't act like injured innocence."

"Have I not paid for that? A year in prison and life as
a cripple?"

A man came in and handed the sheriff a note. He read
it, then said, "All right, Thebeau. You can go. Miss Fenbaker wants you out of here."

"She! She wants me out of here! Who is she, the Lord
Himself?"

"Up."

"No. If she wants me out of here, then she can come
and tell me to get out."

"Look, Thebeau, haven't you given her enough trouble?
Just ruined her chances is all. Now the more scene you
make, the more people know, and the more embarrassing
it is for her. Do that and I tell you now, you'll pay for it."

"All the fault of *l'homme sauvage*. Stupid."

"That, too. But you spread it around. Bigmouth."

"You can give me all the trouble you want. I am not
moving until I'm ready."

The sheriff wrote a note and handed it to one of his men.
Then he jerked his head to another man, and the two of

them picked Thebeau up and dragged him to one of the cells at the back of the office. The sheriff opened the door and threw him in. Then he broke Thebeau's two canes over his knee and threw them after him and slammed the door.

Some time later, Thebeau was sitting by the door, monotonously beating on it with one of the pieces of his cane, when it suddenly opened. He fell into the hallway and found himself looking down at the small shoes of a woman. He looked up. It was Emily. He drew back and struggled to his feet, backing into the cell. "What?" he said. She followed him in.

"Sit down, please," she said. He did. "I implore you not to make more of this than you have. Don't you know how hard it is to live here? I have nowhere else to go. I can't go out somewhere and watch sheep. Please? What have I done to you that you should continue to torment me? I am begging you. The men are angry. I don't want anything to happen to you—because of you but, also, I am selfish. Because of me. If anything does happen, there will be more pointing, more whispering." She sat on the bed in the cell, covering her eyes with her hands and sobbing.

Thebeau looked at the floor. "The stupid savage. All because of him." Emily Fenbaker continued to cry. "I will go," Thebeau said. "Stop that. I heard enough of it in the ice. I still hear it. I hear it in my sleep."

"You! You hear it in your sleep. How do you think it is with me?"

"Why would I not hear it, saying to myself, 'How did I get into this? What have I done? How can I support this?' It was wrong. I knew it as soon as we were well into it. No turning back then." Thebeau sighed. "I might as well admit it. It's been *un cauchemar* enough. But it's done, isn't it? Done. No undoing it. The fool Tor. If he hadn't come, you'd be Madame Claude Pennybacker now."

"No," said Emily. "No. I'd of killed him by now. Some people can take that. Not me. He's the monster. Fat. Leaning on his position for safety. Hardly anything happened to him."

"No. He was in prison. But he didn't have to work. Ah, Miss Fenbaker, I should have found some way to tell you long ago. I am sorry. For me as well as for you. It was not a good thing."

It had all come out suddenly, his pride caught asleep.

The two looked at each other. "Well, you've found a way," Emily said quietly.

"I—I'll go. I have no canes, though. That beast broke them."

"I'll get you some more. If you promise?"

"Very well."

"What do you want here anyhow? You couldn't think . . ."

"That savage. He told me he could help me walk better. Fool that I am, I decided to come ask him how."

"Don't. It means nothing. Look at him, losing his head, trying to fly, wandering around in the forest."

Thebeau started to get up and found Emily's hands on his arm, lifting him. They stared at each other, then both dropped their eyes. "I'll get the canes," Emily said, turning away.

Three west-side farmers were working together forking up the last hay of the summer when one suddenly turned and gasped. The others looked in time to see Tor planing down at them with his second, larger, set of double wings, linen covered, well braced. The farmers ran aside, yelling, as he pulled out of his downward plunge, caught a gust, soared up, teetered, wheeled around, and plunged downward through the roof of a log barn.

By the time they got to him, he had wormed himself free of the harness and dropped into the hay below. His side was skinned and bloody.

"You all right?"

"Mostly."

"Look what you did to my barn."

"I'll work it off. When I get better."

"You're crazy," the second man said, "but I never saw anybody do that before. You really flew. Some."

"Don't encourage him, Ben."

"Don't worry. Won't try again. Now. I seem to have . . . damaged my leg."

"Broke it? The Lord."

"Broke it. Ribs, too, I think. Sorry. Really thought it would work this time."

Tristal heard three days later and ran all the way across the valley, angry and out of condition. He couldn't make the trip in one day. At the farm he found himself among a constant passage of new visitors to view the hole in the barn roof. Laughter was general, but quiet, and everyone looked at the distant launch point with some disbelief. One fistfight started over it.

Tor was not there. He had been taken to Boiling Springs and, for lack of a better place, housed in the jail, his splinted leg stiff and outthrust. When Tristal finally found him there, Tor looked up at him sheepishly and said, "Aven was really with me when I jumped off that ice wall back with the Soarers. Won't try that again."

"You are making fools of us."

"You mean of you, don't you?"

"If we're stuck here, we might as well make the best of it."

"'If' is right. I don't think we are. Just haven't found the way out yet. What about Fahna? Given up on her? Going to let her wait her seven years and then find somebody else?"

"Damn you, what are we doing here anyway? I could have been home now. Now. Last year. Could've been married. Some leader you are. The mighty axeman. Why I let you bring me here, I'll never know. Fool."

"Yeah, well, do me a favor, will you? Help with that farmer's roof. I'll make it up to you. Some way. Are you too busy to do that?"

"Stonewright's got a lot of work this time of year, you know."

"Well, never mind then. I'll get better. Is it Elayna, then?"

"What business is that of yours if it is?"

"None. None at all."

"You going to Dame Arbyr's for the winter? She asked me to ask. Said you could help with the linen. Or she has some woodwork."

"No. I don't think so."

"She said to come. Don't worry. I won't bother you. I won't be there."

"I didn't know you were that bitter."

"You're all right in your own world, but this isn't it."

Tor laughed. "You're right there. I left the Heart because I found no place there any more. Then to be plunged right back into the same thing. It's too ironic. But with a difference. Here I'm too progressive. I'm the one who wants to fly."

Tristal shook his head in disgust.

"I found a good section of stream with trout in it. Really. Want some trout?"

"You know they don't eat fish here."

"They don't. I do. But in secret." Tor laughed again. "I even bagged a goose a while back. And some nameless person tried some with me, even though it's a vile abomination. He found it greasy. But he had seconds."

"Don't you take anything seriously? What's happened to you?"

Tor suddenly sat up, then winced. "Yes. I do. More things than you. The Raiders, for one. The ice for another. Have you looked at it? On the east side it's gained a full four handspans since we came here. Then there's the steam and hot springs. They're fine to pipe around for heating. And without them you know this valley would cool. Did you feel the earth tremble last summer. Know what the means? Instability."

"If the ice gains that slowly, they'll have lifetimes to think about it."

"You're the famous mathematician. Take the four handspans and find the area assuming the valley is seventy ayas long. Think about the effect on climate, not only the land loss. Years ago the Forman iron workers told Ovair's band that their hot springs changed radically after a big earth tremor. What of that? I'm not saying these people should leave. Just that there should be a way out. Only a way."

Tristal sat silently, sobered by Tor's thoughts.

"One thing I'd like you to tell me—at least think it over."

"Don't talk about Elayna. That's my problem."

"I won't. I'd like to know sometime—when I leave, are you going to come?"

"When you leave? When will that be? Not by flying through barn roofs. When you're ready, then ask. I don't think you ever will be. Going east, I don't know if we'd make it. If we did, we'd be in fine shape to handle the Soarers. The west side is too hard to climb. You found that out."

"All right. Unless I go suddenly, I'll ask then."

"Suddenly?" What did Tor mean? Well, it didn't matter. Now he had this new disaster to live down. Tristal turned to go, then noticed some leaf-shaped snippets of linen shoved under Tor's cot.

"What? Not more wings. Will you never..."

"Enough. Close your conservative little mouth, child." Tor's eyes blazed, then when Tristal paused, grew mild again. "No. Not wings. Remember what Cohen-Davies said? About cloth structures that trap hot air and rise? That's what. Just thinking as I watched the sparks rise up the chimney."

"You can't. You can't mean that you..."

"Just a toy now. You must see how boring it is to sit around mending. In a jail, too."

"A toy now. But what later?"

Tor emitted a throaty chuckle. "Who knows what later. I may try a larger model. I may give it up. It's amusing enough."

Tristal threw up his hands and slapped them on his thighs. That evening he left for Dame Arbyr's, sober and dissatisfied.

Tor did spend that winter at Dame Arbyr's. He could see her growing fond of him, counseling him to be more careful, not to be a fool, yet delighting in it, having him waited on as his leg healed fully. This worried him since her period of mourning was nearing its end. Randall Stonewright clearly had his eye on her, too, and saw Tor as an unbelievable choice, a threat, an offense to sense and taste.

Tor was easily well enough to help with the spring plowing, which was done with humans in harness since there were no draft animals. Tor designed a block and tackle affair to ease the strain of such work. Again he was much laughed at, especially because of the amount of rope needed. But he noticed that the idea caught on, especially in the east-side kitchen gardens, where the rows were short.

Though Dame Arbyr objected, he left for the west when the weather moderated and took up his post again in the logging shack. He told no one about the iron spurs he had made to help in ice climbing—nor about the quantity of linen he bought in Boiling Springs with all his pay bills. It was not new cloth, but it was still strong. He felt that he had to get out soon—to give Tristal the option of a long run back to Northwall in time to keep his promise to Fahna. Something would happen. It had to.

XVII

JUST past midsummer, on a surprisingly sultry day, Tor appeared on the Johnston tenancy, near the west edge of the secondsector. Mother Johnston rose from her pea shelling to meet him.

"You, Tor. Everything all right? No boys to teach swimming?"

"Thought I'd come help you with the hay. I think it's going to rain before night."

"Rain, eh? Stan never mentioned it. Can't, though. Can't pay you."

"No matter. I have the time. Plenty of it."

"You're no farmer then. You'll find them in the meadow. Forks in the barn. I'm sure they'd be able to use an extra hand. You're not worried, then? The Raiders, I mean."

"Yes. But not in the daylight. And I've been down the whole secondsector ice face. Nothing but the usual couples' tracks."

Dame Johnston watched him stride off toward the barn, not limping now. She smiled slightly. She liked him. The valley lacked eccentrics. He was a misplaced figure from legend.

As the afternoon wore on, Tor worked with the rest, the fork passing through a leather loop around his right forearm. But he grew more and more restless. Eventually he stopped, looked across the wide strip of woodland rising, dipping, and then rising far up toward the ice face. Something was wrong. The other men, moving down the windrow, looked back at him. He wasn't moving at all. Was he imagining things? He came out of his reverie and worked silently until supper break.

As he had predicted, thunder clouds were piling up, raining on the west face of the ice far off. They were thick enough to begin stretching their high leading clouds out over the forest and west farms.

Tor didn't sit down at the outdoor table, but stood eating a barley cake. "Be glad for your help this evening, long as the light lasts and the rain holds off," Stanley Johnston said.

"Something's wrong."

Johnston looked at Tor. "It's an obsession, Tor. Just an obsession."

"No. Never felt this here before. I'm surprised you don't, having lost a child to them. Even so long ago. I always know. That's my profession. Wish I could help you here. This is more important. Listen. I know you're going to be tired, but set a watch the way I told you—years back now. Probably nothing will happen. Not yet."

Johnston snorted. "We've got to gulp supper and get haying before the rain. Well, thanks for your help anyway."

Tor was already moving away. He waved his hand in reply. By the time he had climbed to the ice face, rain was sheeting down, running from the ice in narrow waterfalls. He found one of his small shelters under a spruce and sat down. As the rain diminished, it began to grow dark. Tor moved in silence along a narrow trace leading toward the logging shack. Something was different. He could taste his fear. The forest floor had lost its brittleness in the rain, which still dripped from the trees and ran audibly in the darkness down the slopes.

The darkness became nearly total before Tor heard the first sound, a slight one, but out of place. He slipped his axe from its sheath. Another sound followed, farther off. Tor moved ahead slowly, crouched, then stopped. He heard nothing but sensed a presence.

He held his position in absolute stillness for at least twenty sunwidths. The presence didn't move. The clouds thinned, and a pearly moonlight began to suffuse them, bathing the forest with ghostly light. Tor still held his relaxed stillness.

Time passed, the night reaching its height and slowly beginning its long fall toward morning. From far below Tor heard a muffled sound again, then another, slight but significant, closer.

Suddenly he heard a slight rustle, then a thrum as an arrow flicked throught the dark, deflected from an unseen twig, and pierced his right arm. In the same instant, he rose, raced toward the sound, dodged, swung his axe, felt it bite into flesh, heard a scream, another rush, turned, arced the axe again, again felt the slice, heard another rush, turned, pointed the axe to blunt the charge and turn it, then raced behind a fir as an arrow thwacked into it. He came back out and caught the dim figure nocking again, swung down hard, feeling the skull catch and give. One of the figures still writhed on the ground.

Tor raced away a full twenty arms and knelt, panting, behind another tree, finally finding time to work on the arrow. The wound was not serious, though it sent out needles of pain. He tried to maintain silence, knowing that whoever was below would have heard the fight. Tor cut the arrow shaft, slipped it out, and bound the wound, his eyes running with the pain. Then he held still once again. From above came slight sounds of thrashing and groaning. One of the attackers was still conscious.

Another slight sound, startlingly close, caused Tor to shift his eyes, though not his body. He strained to see. The trees continued to drip, slowly. He dimly made out a single figure moving very slowly up the slope in front of him. Was it a trick? The figure seemed not to see him, even to sense him. A moment of certain proximity came, and Tor took it, covering the distance between in two bounds and giving the figure one quick rap on the side of the head with the flat of his axe. The sound was startlingly hollow. The figure crumpled with a grunt. Tor knelt on him, found his belt, cut it with the edge of his axe, and bound the man's hands behind him. The man was wholly limp. Tor felt his head, finding it bloody. Then he returned to his tree and listened for another ten sunwidths. The trees continued to drip. His right arm throbbed with a blunt pain like that of lying on a branch. Tor then strode forward, took up the man he had tied, heaved him up on his shoulder, and started down the hill slowly, as quietly as he could. The figure was fairly light, but lithe and well formed.

Stanley Johnston was still stiff with his late evening's work, but he rose with the dawn and stood in his farmyard stretching. What was that coming? Tor again? He was dragging something on two poles? A man! Johnston ran to the bunkhouse and shouted in the door, "All right. All hands now. Quick."

They ran their farmers' run toward Tor in various stages of undress. As they neared, he lowered his travois, standing, eyes vague with fatigue, panting slightly.

The men crowded around, looking down at a young man, dressed in black leather, his face darkened, his hair long enough to be gathered in a greasy queue. His cheeks showed three parallel scars on each side. The left side of his face was swollen where Tor had hit him. He was awake now, blinking in fear.

Tor sat down abruptly. "There are three more up there. At least. All three are at least hurt. Two probably dead."

"You, Tor. You all right? Let's see that arm. You'd think it had its share of trouble already." Stan Johnston looked at the wound, frowned, glanced at the Raider, and said, "You'd better go in and have Mag wash it up again. We'll take care of this one."

Tor whirled up on his feet. "What? What do you mean, take care of him? He goes to the sheriff."

"Listen, now. I lost my boy to 'em years ago. They killed my uncle, burned his farm. There's only one place for men like this. Leave him to me. Now, we humor you, and maybe you help. But move aside." Johnston reached for Tor, found himself lifted, twisted, dumped on the ground.

"All right, you men, back off now," Tor said in a deep, level voice. "What good is he dead? Never learn anything from him. Never make contact, reach agreements with dead men."

"You, Tor," said Jase Smythe. "You go too far. You got no call to hurt Mr. Johnston. Now. Hand him over before somebody gets hurt." He looked, turned, and swept up a post in one motion, and then felt it knocked out of his hand with the next. He looked at Tor's unsheathed axe and backed up a couple of paces.

"If any of you has any rag of decency or respect for the law, you'll run for the sheriff or his men. Now."

"You're a laugh, wild man. All we have to do is go back to the house and get one of them bows you taught us to use. Then what good is that toy in your hand?"

"You, Smythe. Ever kill anybody?"

The big man hesitated. "There's always a first time," he said.

"I just killed three. With this toy. Two had bows. Now go get the sheriff."

The men looked at each other, most of them not feeling Johnston's anger or Smythe's bravado. But nobody moved.

"All right," said Tor. "Have it your way. I'll take him myself. Never call yourselves decent again, though." He picked up the crossbar on the end of his travois and began to walk around them. Two men moved toward him. He dropped the burden abruptly, causing the man on it to cry out, and faced them.

From a distance, he could see Mother Johnston running toward them, wiping her hands on her apron. Her anger and distress were evident. "You, Tor. You got one. Give him to us. Give him." She ran up at him and tried to shove him aside. He stiff-armed her and she sat down with a thump. "You going to take that? From him?" she shrieked. "From a no-good savage?"

They began to move in. "We're talking about a man's life," Tor shouted. "And they'd have all been down here if it'd been up to you." Out of the corner of his eye, Tor could see curious people coming toward them from nearby fields, some of them running. It looked bad. Then he saw Bob striding down the dirt road and felt a wave of relief.

"All right," he said. "No more need to worry about the savage. Here's the sheriff's man." They fell back like a receding wave.

Bob strode up and swept his eyes around the crowd. "Anybody here want to make trouble? What's this, Tor? Finally got your Raider? Here, Johnston, Smythe, get on the ends of this litter and carry him to town. Tor, you all right? You make it all right to the sheriff's?"

"Better send a party up to look at the others," Tor said. "I'll tell 'em how to get there. They'd better go armed."

It was late afternoon before Tor was able to rest. His arm was bound up again, and a narrative of what had happened was taken. News came back that the party that went up to the ice face found the place where the fight had taken place, and plenty of blood, but no bodies. They also found an arrow in a tree. Tracks led into a fissure in the ice face, then vanished.

When Fenbaker stopped in to see the captive, and Tor, early in the evening, he found them both asleep in separate cells. The door to Tor's was open. Fenbaker walked in and sat on the straight wooden chair near the bed. Instantly, Tor's eyes were open. "Well, you got your Raider."

"This is only a start, Judge. We need to talk to him, find out what we can about them, see if we can make an agreement of some kind with them. We need to set up a watch for the rest of the season. You can see—I hope—that they were just scouting. There will be a big band somewhere, waiting. This may scare them off. If they come here to get more people, they don't want to lose the ones they have. Maybe they'll quit for the time now that surprise is gone. But it's hard to tell what'll happen. I'd of loved to follow them."

"Follow them?"

"They got up on the ice." Tor laughed, then sat up.

"Yes, there is that. Have you eaten?"

"Yes. Right now I think I'd like a bottle of barley wine."

"I didn't know you drank."

"Never have here. As Smythe said this morning as he contemplated killing me, 'There's always a first time.'"

"Smythe? A farm worker?"

"Yeah. That wasn't so bad, though. It was Mother Johnston who nearly got blood flowing. I had to set her on her butt. That was a first-time thing, too. She's been smoldering ever since they took her son—Billy, I think he was. It's odd to see such anger flare and burn after all this time."

"No. Not odd. A judge sees it all the time. But not from the best people. It's a form of paralysis, a fixation in time."

Tor regarded him mildly. "The whole valley is fixed in time, Judge."

XVIII

TOR returned to the jail with half his barley wine inside him, his head already whirling. The sheriff's night man held out a glass, which Tor filled. Then he plumped down in a chair, staring at the floor, trying to get it to stop swaying. It didn't. He took another drink.

"Isn't that strong," said the man. "You're not used to it."

"No. When I was a child, living with the Alats, I drank some. Hard alky, cut back with river water. Not since. Here. You take the rest."

"Not here. Can't take much while I'm working. What's the matter?"

"Does no good. I can still remember all the facts."

"But at least they feel different."

"Yeah. Some."

"You'd better rest. It'll all sift out."

Tor rose and looked at him, swaying. "You're right," he said.

Two days later he tried talking to the Raider, but the young man wouldn't even look at him, sullenly turning his head. While he was there, Sectorjudge Fenbaker stopped in and watched Tor's attempts. He shook his head. "I'm having him moved to the sector prison," he said.

"The prison?"

"Yes. He'll be around a long time. And he'll be safer."

"You mean the farmers?"

"I had no idea they'd be so riled up. But he's the first objective enemy they've had at hand. The first chance to get back. It's the tenants, the workers. They've suffered the direct losses."

"As always. About getting back, I wonder how the Raiders feel—about their little defeat. They may want vengeance, too."

"I've put the sheriff's spare men on the situation. One more thing—the farmers don't want you around there. They're angry."

"About my . . . saving the boy from them?"

"Yes. And pushing Mother Johnston . . ."

"She almost had the boy murdered on the spot."

"But she's a woman. You don't push women. She lost a boy, too. I know. It's crazy, eh? But they're my people. It's the way we are. A tendency to glauting and gloom. It's the cold. They're also furious with you for being right. They wanted to think of you as an eccentric, a savage. They sense you had a firmer feel for the law than they. They know the Sacred Way, supposedly, but you showed the mercy. Johnston says if you come back, they'll larrup you good. Together they might, if you let them. You'd better stay away."

"I'm afraid. Not of them. Of the Raiders. There's still something I don't understand—not only why they do these things, but how. How do they get on and off the ice? You don't know how hard I've tried."

"You're not the first. We've all tried. Not collectively. I'm sure it could be done by building giant scaffolds."

"Someday you may need to. If the climate changes. Anyway, the west may be safe if they follow the plan we laid out—though I doubt they will. They've let their bows and crossbows go stringless. Half of them can't find the warning horns. I'm sure most of them have forgotten the defense plans, farm by farm. If the sheriff's men can stir them up, they'll do much better in a raid. It may be that all they have to do is put up one really strong defense—and I mean kill a lot of Raiders—and the raids may cease."

"I hope that's not wishful thinking."

"Maybe. But beyond the ice, where predation is common, you see big animals who will never take on smaller ones that defend themselves. A tanwolf will take a rabbit with ease, because it's running. But it will leave a badger alone, because if the badger got in a good bite, then the wolf would be that much less able to hunt the next day. Predators look for the helpless. Wolves take old cows and calves, not young bulls; they want meals, not wounds and heroism. It's a matter of survival."

"I only half know what you're saying. But these are men, and men do things for irrational reasons. That reminds me, could you stop by the house this evening, please? Emily would like to see you."

"Emily? I thought she was through with me. I nosed in where I shouldn't have."

"Perhaps you did. Just come."

Before Tor left for the Fenbakers' big stone house at the head of the central street of Boiling Springs, Tristal arrived. He had been at Dame Arbyr's when he heard about Tor's encounter. His hair was cropped short in the style of Ice Valley in the summer. He wore a light linen blouse, spruce dyed, with elbow-length sleeves and light knee pants with sandals. His hair had been sun-bleached nearly white.

"Dame Arbyr wanted me to come see how you were," he said. "Hurt again?"

"As usual. Not badly. A little angry now, but healing."

"One of these times you won't get off so easily."

"Maybe not. Listen, Tris, can you go help watch the west? There isn't a hunter in the flock. These Raiders are all hunters. They're as good as the Peshtak. They see at night and move with the quiet of a light breeze. I'm afraid. For the farmers."

"You mean if the Raiders want revenge? You should have thought of that before you attacked them."

"I didn't attack. I was in the woods and got wounded with an arrow. You seem to be thinking like the manor owners—the Raiders are like tax collectors. Let them have what they want and tolerate it. Don't bother."

"A lot think that."

"Listen, Tris. I'm going to get out of here before another year is out. Are you going to come? Or will you stay?"

"You're not getting out. That's just spit upwind. You'll die here of old age. The sooner you admit that, the better you'll get along."

"You wouldn't even go east then—if that were the only way?"

"East? Of course not. If we somehow managed to get across the ice, we'd have to deal with the Soarers."

"That's what you don't understand. You could feel the Soarers manipulating your mind. You could see it and see them doing it. These people do the same thing, but they do it with custom, with law, with refusals to move, to change, to adapt."

"They do all right. What about you? You're the only one I see who's not adapting."

"It's a matter of values, of perceptions. Some things lie beyond convenience. I'm not talking about livelihood—whether to be a farmer or hunter. I'm talking about personal conduct."

"I don't know what you mean."

"You don't?"

"No."

"I've seen your tracks—with Elayna."

"What's wrong with that? Not everybody is old and sterile. Anybody can take a walk."

"I've seen where you sat, where you lay."

Tristal stood up, furious. "I see what the farmers mean. You really do nose in."

"If I had a son, I'd like to raise him myself."

"Meaning what?"

"Suppose you did break your promise? Suppose it was lightly given. Maybe suppose you have adapted and do manage to get Elayna pregnant. What do you think that will get you?"

"It's not so bad to marry that well—and someone . . . you love."

"It wouldn't happen. I've been told as much flat out."

"You think so. What about the baby?"

"There are those from her class who would accept it. The class protects itself. All of them. Even Fenbaker, who is a decent man, is very aware of his class."

"How . . . fish guts to you. You just don't know. And that promise. It was a world away, years ago. Fahna exacted it by chance. It was the first time she ever treated me with anything other than dislike. What does that amount to?"

"A promise? You made it. I promise you here and now, Tris—I'll be out of here within a year. I'd try to go now, but I have another promise—to myself—to stay and see out this season of potential raids. All promises are really made to oneself. Any one who breaks one compromises with himself. You know that—or you ought to. So you won't help watch the west?"

"No. And if you had any sense, neither would you. They

aren't grateful for it. You stopped the Raider scouts and they tried to mob you for it. You're a fool."

Tor was silent awhile. "All right. I see I was. About you, mainly. I had thought . . . you had it in you . . ."

"Had what in me? To be a Shumai axeman? What an archaism. There are no such things anymore."

"No. But they had qualities that should not be lost. And that Urstadge will need. But you seem incapable of them. Never mind."

"You exaggerate. The Sentani could beat them. All they ever did was wander around the prairie taking game."

"It was a hard and good life. But they led—and not for what they could get, the way they do here. They led for what they gave, what they saw. It was a pure thing with the best of them."

"A lot of poetic nonsense."

"I remember . . . you were a poet once."

"I've been branded, run out, manipulated, and kicked. I've burned and frozen. I want to try living moderately warm."

"You picked the wrong place for that."

"You picked it. The great leader. If you only had the sense, you'd see that Dame Arbyr would marry you in an instant, and you'd have the production of twenty-five farms at your disposal. You'd be able to lead something then. Not a raw boy and a dog."

"Dame Arbyr ought by rights to marry Stonewright. He deserves it. He would give himself to it. Not me."

Tris tightened his face in disgust. "Well, then, I'll tell Dame Arbyr you're all right. She wants you to come."

"Please thank her for me. Tell her the boat is hers now. I won't need it anymore."

Tris looked at him, puzzled. Well, the break had been made, as much as was needed. He still felt a deep love for his uncle, and it was hard. But he couldn't be attached to the old fool forever. Even Elayna said as much.

Tor found Emily waiting with her mother in a large front room with soft, linen-covered chairs. They made general conversation for a time, then Emily said, "Mother, would you mind if I talked with Tor alone?"

Dame Fenbaker looked startled. "Tor indeed. Would

you mind if I called you 'Theodore'? It's much more becoming."

"If you prefer. I've heard from the Pelbar that 'being is becoming.' I enjoy being. If being called Theodore would make me more becoming, perhaps it would give me more of being."

Dame Fenbaker frowned, puzzled.

"Mother," Emily murmured.

The older woman rose and left, saying, "I'll be in my room if you need me."

"Now," said Emily. "You told Roland Thebeau that you could make him walk right. I have made it up with him. He's much too embarrassed to ask you how you propose to do this, but you must have had some idea. How—"

"Just a series of exercises. There's nothing really wrong with his legs. Some muscle was cut. He lay still a long time in healing it. He hasn't worked his legs heavily since."

"There's pain."

"Pain. There's always pain. A part of living. I'll draw you out a series of diagrams. There will be pain. You could help him. It'll take time. But he will improve. Now . . . why do you want to do this?" He looked at her. "He is a good man, but he's only a shepherd. Being a friend of Pennybacker wouldn't help him any. Besides, they are trying to put the whole incident back into silence. Are you able to be a shepherd's wife? Ah. It's never been the same, has it? Jason Morton wouldn't look at you anymore. None of the manor families. Too bad. But you have to realize that marriage is—"

"What is marriage? What do you know of it?"

"Emily, you need to be able to—"

"Face the facts? That's what mother says. Now. Will you promise to listen and not tell anyone if I let you know our idea?"

"Of course."

"The ice wall on the east can be climbed. We could go the way you came. With plenty of supplies. We could make a new start. Not with the Soarers you talk about. We could go beyond them. Perhaps go south. You've said there's a lot of open country. Plenty of game. Now don't look like that. You're thinking I don't know the difficulties. Perhaps I don't. I do know what it's like to be here. I'll never be anything. Live all my life in this stone house, drinking spruce tea. Growing old. Hearing the wind blow the snow all winter. No. That's a slow death and dying all the way. Besides—"

"There's more?"

"We'd all go."

"All who?"

"The carleyboshers—except that insect, Pennybacker. Jean is married. His wife agrees. They all agree. We were thrown together by adversity. And Jean says his two brothers will go. It'll be a party. The Monets have been up on the ice face already this summer practicing. We won't hurry. We'll all practice. It all depends on Roland's being able to walk."

"Do you really love him?"

"Of course. It's not only . . . our misfortune."

"You're sure, Emily?"

"Yes. I thought you had such an intuition you would know."

"I thought so when he was hurt. But that was a time of great tension. Well, I'll do my best by him."

"Good. He's waiting. In the small receiving room."

"What if—"

"No 'what if.' We knew you'd help." Emily threw her arms around Tor and rested her cheek against his chest. "You should be shorter for a kiss," she said.

"When you've been on the ice for about forty days, you may not want to kiss me," Tor mused.

The Shumai had all been runners in the old times, and they had come to know much about therapy for runners. Tor visited the Fenbakers for several days, getting Roland Thebeau started. It was not easy. In spite of his claim to patience, Thebeau wanted immediate results. Tor tried to calm him by explaining the other skills he would need, listing them and setting up a program for learning them.

In his spare time, he tried to visit the young Raider and get him to talk. The few words the man did use were not comprehensible. Then the sectorjudges moved the man to the southsector prison to get him away from the farmers. Tor occasionally met some of them in Boiling Springs. He silently took their verbal abuse and stood aside for them, yet he always managed to remind them that the season was not over, and they would need to defend themselves. He himself began to feel increasingly tense and restless. Finally, with little explanation to the Fenbakers, he left for the west ice wall.

He stayed in the forest, occasionally noting signs of a patrol of the sheriff's men, including Bob's unmistakably giant tracks. One night he started for Boiling Springs to study again his records of the previous raids, but as he left he saw the sky was suffused with pearly moonlight. He stopped. The Ice Valley divided the year into fourteen months of twenty-six days, the last one always having twenty-seven. He made some rapid calculations. Translating the records into the thirteen Shumai lunar months, he saw that the majority of the raids had come on the night before the full moon. That was, he saw, the next night. He turned and began to run west again.

As he passed farm after farm, he found they were sleeping, as though the ice wall were an ayas high and unbroken. Finally, past high night, near the westward rise, where the forest began, he saw a large fire and headed for it. A knot of men was standing around it. He stopped back from the firelight and called, "Johnny."

"Who's there?"

"Tor."

"Scum," said a man. "Troublecauser. Come into the light so we can stick you with one of these."

"Mosquito bait," another muttered.

Further shouts and curses were interrupted by the sheriff's man, who yelled. "Silence, you gang of sheep skinners! Tor, what is it?"

"Come out here."

Johnny left the others and came out into the darkness. "What?"

"I finally fit in the last piece. Your calendar doesn't fit the moon. Most of the raids came the night before full moon."

Johnny paused. "That would be tomorrow night. Tor, I'm worried. Bob and the men didn't come back."

"Bob? Either they're holed up somewhere or the Raider scouts got 'em."

"What, then? What should we do? We can't go after 'em."

"I'll go. You prepare the farms all along the west border. Those men. Will they listen?"

"Likely not. But I'll go see."

Tor waited as the men conferred. He could see them arguing. Finally he came forward. He recognized Jase Smythe from his encounter at Johnstons'. "All right," he said. "You can't afford to argue. I'll need one man with me to try and find the sheriff's men—unless you're too sheepish. Johnny, divide the others to warn the farms. No lights tomorrow night. Nothing obvious. The women, children, and the old have to be drawn back from the ice wall. We have nearly eighty kilometers to cover. We have to get started."

"Listen, savage, we don't even know there's a reason to do anything."

"Then what're you doing out here? Waiting for Bob's men? To play games?"

"Why lose a whole day's work? Snow's comin' soon. We'd be fools. Scare everybody."

"Smythe. Come with me. Help me find Bob's men. How many are there?"

"Eight," said Johnny. "I'll come."

"Then who would direct things if we don't get back? No. Somebody else. Smythe likes to fight."

"I'll go," said Garey Blake, a small man Tor had met in prison.

Tor looked at him. "Good," he said. "We'd better move. Johnny, leave somebody here. We'll come back here."

"All right. The Lord keep you."

About that time, just passed high night, Elayna softly opened the back door of the manor house and let herself in. She turned, her light dress rustling, and saw a lamp flare. Her mother had just uncovered it. "What?—"

"Get Tristal, please, Elayna."

"At this time of night?"

"You just left him, didn't you? Get him."

"How could you dare to—"

"Get him. This is important. Or I'll ask Randall to—"

"No. No. I'll get him."

Dame Arbyr sat rather grimly in the light of the small lamp waiting. Her dark hair, streaked with gray, was parted in the middle and combed down the sides of her head, each gathering bound lightly with yellow linen. She wore a dark night robe and sheepskin house boots. Her hands lay entwined in her lap.

Rubbing his eyes, Tristal entered behind Elayna. He stopped when he saw Dame Arbyr's expression.

"Now," she began. "Your dogs left the sheep this morning."

"Which?"

"Two. Raran and Lady. They've never done that. Billy said Raran really didn't want to go. She apologized for it. But she couldn't contain herself. Lady followed."

"I'll find them in the morning."

"What does that mean?"

Tristal seemed to ponder.

"You know. It means your uncle is in trouble."

"He generally is."

"Sit down. Look at the record. Ah, well. What could I expect of you? You keep no promises. I had trusted you about Elayna. At least the dogs have a sense of loyalty and honor."

"Mother. I don't have to hear this!"

"Then go. I'm not concerned with you."

"What concerns Tristal concerns me."

"How cute. I know it's over seventy kilometers, but something is going on in the west. The dogs are gone. Tristal, I know you're tired of going to Boiling Springs to do my bidding. I won't ask you after this. I promise. But you can run like none of my men can. And you can use that weapon. You must go. You must start now, even though you're tired from all that exercise you've just had."

"Mother!"

"Why lie? You know what I think? I think the Raiders have come and your uncle is in the middle of it."

"What can I do about that?"

"Not much here."

Tristal pondered. "All right. I will go." He looked at Elayna.

"Then go," said Dame Arbyr. "And you. You'd better do some good washing before you go to bed."

"Mother!"

"When you finish, come back. Well, Tristal, are you going?"

Tor was grateful Blake had come. The small farmer walked more softly than any other Ice Valley man he'd met. They moved through the forest toward the ice face for a quarter of the descending night when Tor stopped and reached back and stopped him with a gentle touch to his chest. He knelt down and Blake did the same. At first they saw and heard nothing, but then, very slowly, a multiple presence seemed to suffuse the forest ahead like faint woodsmoke. Tor wondered if Blake could sense it. He put his mouth to the farmer's ear and said, "They're here. We'll have to stay put all day tomorrow or back up very, very quietly."

"You sure?" Blake replied.

Tor stayed silent. The man had sensed nothing. It would be better to wait. They remained still while late mosquitoes whined around them and drank blood unrestrained. The pearly sheen of the sky faded. Finally a branch snapped up the hill, then another. Blake squeezed Tor's arm. They turned and moved down the slope.

It was a long way to travel in the dark in silence. As they went, they heard sounds behind them, and once a voice. Ahead they could see Johnny's fire far out on the fields. Spaced out to the north two more distant fires flared up. As they reached the alders, the sky in the east began to lighten with early dawn.

"How are you at running?" Tor whispered.

"Right now, very good," Blake returned.

"They're coming down behind us. When we pass that clump of trees, we'd better move."

They did, Blake sprinting on ahead. From behind them they heard shouts. Tor glanced behind him as they ran and saw several men coming through the trees. Blake was tiring, slowing, as they neared the first meadows. Tor stayed behind him. He saw an arrow coming and dodged aside, then drew out his axe as they ran. Another arrow passed over his head and narrowly missed Blake, then a third, right behind it, took the farmer through the leg. Tor heaved him up and ran on, out into the meadow, then turned and set him down.

"Can you walk at all?" he asked.

"I—no." Blake crawled and hobbled. Tor picked him up again and began walking backward as rapidly as he could. Suddenly eight men ran to the edge of the woods. The mournful note of a ram's horn sounded behind him. It was picked up to the north and south, traveling along the line of west farms. It looked as though the Raiders wouldn't wait for darkness now they knew they had been discovered. Tor put a boulder between them and the Raiders, moving back carefully. A flight of arrows came over it, but high.

Tor cried out, then ran as fast as he could with Blake on his shoulders. Ahead he made out Johnny coming with several of the farmers. Tor turned in time to see one of the Raiders round the boulder. The man aimed an arrow at him, but had to dodge several arrows from the farmers, so his own went wide. He started to nock again, but a crossbow bolt took him through the chest. The farmers cheered as he went down, but then Raiders in large numbers began to come out of the woods. Tor continued to run with Blake, passing the thin line of men who came out to them.

The farmers began to back up in front of the oncoming Raiders, who yelled in a high falsetto as they came. One man, panicked, ran by Tor, who shouted to him to take Blake. The man didn't stop, but the next man did, trading Tor the wounded man for a crossbow and quiver. Tor turned and tried to hold the farmers from fleeing. Raider arrows began to drop some of the men as they ran. Others, more stubborn, only walked backward, awkwardly shooting arrows at the advancing men.

Soon more farmers began to arrive, thickening the ranks. Their longbows had a longer range than the bows of the Raiders, but their aim was wildly inaccurate. The farmers continued to fall back until they reached the first line of snake fence, climbed it, and stood behind it. The Raiders lined up out of range, yelling derisively.

Something was wrong with this. Tor looked around. Far to the north he saw a column of smoke from a burning building or haystack. "Johnny," he shouted. "They mean to hold us here. There are others somewhere else. Can they get behind us? What about the woods to the south?"

The men looked apprehensive. Tor took five men and ran south toward a tongue of evergreens that followed a rocky ridge into the meadowland. As they neared it, they saw a body of men in the woods. One of the farmers blew his ram's horn. He was answered by a horn from the farmhouse to the east. Tor spurted ahead, soon coming into arrow range. He slung the crossbow and knocked aside several arrows with his axe. Ahead a line of six men stood calmly with bows drawn, aiming at him.

He felt a moment of panic, then, as he looked for a place

to dive, saw Raran and Lady, loping from the east, speed up and race for the men. The Raiders released, Tor dove to the side, one arrow passing through his blouse. He rolled over, hearing the dogs, and ran for the men. Two were down and the others were hacking and stabbing at the snarling animals. Two turned toward Tor, one nocking an arrow, the other rushing him with a strange sword. Tor swung his axe into the man's arm, rushed by, knocked the other man's bow aside as he drew, shoved him back, and finished him. Raran was down, with two arrows in her, as Tor, in a cold fury, finished the other men. More arrows came from the woods. Watching, Tor knelt by the dog. Lady, with several wounds, dragged herself to him. Raran's sides heaved as Tor touched her while watching for arrows. Then he felt her side shudder under his hand and grow still.

For an instant he couldn't believe it, then a wild grief went through him—after all they'd been through together. A line of men came out of the trees at him, yelling. He stood over Lady and Raran, suddenly drained. Longbow arrows arched over him. The Raider line wavered but advanced. Tor stooped to pick up Lady, but she, too, lay limp and still. He unslung the crossbow, loosed the bolt, laid the bow down, and with a wild yell, ran at the men. He heard shouting behind him as the line of men parted in front of him. He stretched out to his left with the axe as he passed through it, felling one man. A glance behind him showed more farmers running from the tenancy to the east. In a numb fury, Tor worked down the line of Raiders, felling them as he went with sweeping arcs of his axe.

The rest wavered, then broke in front of the advancing farmers and ran for the woods. Tor never hesitated, but followed, hacking at stragglers. Somehow, no arrow struck him. He could see men in the woods ahead and swerved aside as he neared, then backed up slowly as they pecked away at him with occasional arrows. He saw the Raiders were massing again and trotted back toward the line of farmers, who were bringing up long shields from the farm and handcarts with shield fronts. Tor was astonished that they had remembered so much and improved on what they had discussed in earlier training.

In a loose line, the Raiders again advanced from the woods, then, with their wailing yell, broke into a running charge. The farmers fell back to their shield line and tried to hold. Few panicked. Arrows began whacking into the shields, and some into the men behind them. But Raiders were dropping, too. Nevertheless they did not waver. They swept up to the farmers, leaving their wounded behind, and tore away the shields in a fury. The men behind them held their ground, fighting with bows, knives, and farm tools.

Tor saw clearly that the farmers' desperation was their support; their families were not far behind them. Finally the Raiders wavered, then turned and ran. But Tor saw a farmhouse behind him go up in flames, then a barn. He yelled and pointed. The retreating Raiders jeered as they ran. Tor yelled out, "Every other man go for the farm." The farmers hesitated, then some left. At that point the sheriff from Boiling Springs arrived and took over that sortie.

They found twenty Raiders, who ran eastward out of the burning buildings only to find themselves facing a band of sheepherders running from Rockridge Manor. The men hesitated then fled northward, trying to skirt the farmers, but they found that impossible and gathered into a small circle on a knob of rocks and trees.

Meanwhile, Tor led a group of men with shields toward the point of woods. The remaining Raiders retreated into the thick spruce trees. Tor drew back and held them there. Johnny's men still held the fence. The Raiders there were standing at ease back out of range.

The sheriff's men surrounded the Raiders who had fired the farm. He said, "All right. These we'll eliminate. Now, get some shields. We'll walk a body of men to the east side and fire the brush. Won't take long to move them out. Not one gets away. Understood?"

They followed his lead. When the fire took hold, the wind, blowing westward, took the smoke and flame through the small hill of rock and trees. The Raiders had to make a run. They tried to go north, breaking through the line of defenders, but the others were on them. The fight was short but sharp. Not one Raider surrendered. When all was finished, sixteen defenders lay killed or wounded.

The sheriff shook his head grimly and said, "All right, men. Now we get those men off the field." Again they advanced, behind their shields, climbing the snake fence. The Raiders walked back through the meadow in front of them, jeering as they went. As the sheriff's men neared the alders, suddenly a large band of Raiders advanced at a run from the trees, shrilling their wailing cry.

The sheriff's men ran back, some dropping their shields, but when the Raiders closed on the snake fence, they found themselves facing a deepening line of men and outnumbered at least four to one. They also found themselves with few arrows. When the Ice Valley men began to advance across the field behind their shields, the Raiders could do nothing but jeer and retreat, and as they did, the sheriff split a body of men from the main group to join Tor's men to push the Raiders up through the point of woods. Halfway across the field he dispatched another body to cut off the neck of the woods and block the Raiders in.

Seeing this, the main body of retreating Raiders sent up their shrill yell and ran to intercept the second group and save their fellows. The sheriff's men pursued. A sharp fight followed. Blood ran freely on both sides, but Ice Valley men continued to arrive, now from the manors farther eastward, and the Raiders finally had to break off and run. The men in the point of woods were surrounded and cut off.

"It's a shame to waste those trees," the sheriff said, "but we're going to have to root 'em out." They fired the woods at a number of points, and the Raiders ran out in a body, southward, breaking through the line of defenders and racing for the ice wall, leaving scattered dead behind.

After all the Raiders had been pushed into the woods to the west and the men had cut a fire break, the sheriff said, "Now, Tor, what do you think?"

"If you cut off their retreat up the ice wall, you'll kill nearly all of them. But you'll lose a lot of people. If you hold this ground, I suspect they'll leave."

"What would you do?"

Tor looked at the ground. "It's hard to know. I hate to see anyone killed. I'd say let 'em go. But if they come back as a result, more may die."

"Have we punished 'em enough?"

"I think so. These people aren't fighters. The Shumai would follow them all the way, but a lot would die. The Pelbar would let them go and then build walls. It's up to you to say what Ice Valley will do."

The sheriff surveyed the wreckage around him. "We'll let 'em go, set up a guard tonight, then search the forest tomorrow. Where's Bob?"

Tor winced. "He's up there...somewhere. I fear..."

"Well, he'd be only one of a lot of good people, then. It all hurts, doesn't it? But you're used to this."

"You never get used to it."

As the day advanced and the defenders put out the fires, gathered their wounded, and began burying the dead Raiders, Tor found himself looking at the strangers closely. A great many seemed unhealthy. Some had a strange line in their teeth. He had noticed they weren't remarkably strong or fast. Many seemed oddly white.

He wondered what that meant, but when he mentioned it to one of the Boiling Springs physicians, the man frowned and shook his head. He examined several of the bodies, then said it was obvious something was wrong, but he couldn't tell what.

It was late afternoon before Tristal arrived, exhausted from his long run and loss of sleep. He found Tor asleep by the snake fence. As he knelt down, Tor opened his eyes. "Raran? Did she come here?"

Tor looked away. "Yes," he replied. "And Lady."

"Where are they?"

Tor rolled over, his back to his nephew. Tristal waited, kneeling, looking around. He put his hand down on the ground and drew it back dark with thickened blood. "They're over there," Tor finally said. "Near the point of trees. Away from the Raiders. Both in one grave."

 XIX

Tristal helped with the wounded as the day waned. Once, while he carried water, a man called him over and murmured, "I...need Tor. Get him for me. Tell him it's Garey Blake."

Tristal was puzzled, but went for Tor, who still lay resting by the fence. When told, he immediately rose and trotted toward the hay barn in which the rows of wounded men lay in the dusty driness. He knelt by Blake, who smiled wanly and said, "You have to help me. They took my daughter. Renee. Only fourteen. They must have her up on the ice by now. What am I going to do?"

Tor sighed and looked up. Several men were watching, tense. "All right," he said. "I'll need about eight men. We'll have to go up into the woods. There may be some danger."

"Eight?" one man snorted. "We'll all go."

"The wind is still right," said Tor.

"Not another flight!" Tristal moaned.

Tor laughed. "In a way." Then he frowned down at Garey Blake and said, "I'll come back with her or not at all."

Blake started to open his mouth, then stopped.

Tor and twenty-eight men toiled up through the woods to the logger's shack, which the Raiders had fired in their retreat. Tor trotted up the hill behind the shack toward a boulder pile and, leaning hard, shoved one large stone aside. He knelt and began pulling on a massive package inside. "Help," he said.

Soon the odd parcel—a great deal of linen and several lengths of wooden piping—was on its way down the hill. "Take it to the steam spring south of that point of woods," Tor said.

Once there, as the sun bathed the clouds in the east with pink, he had two men climb nearby trees and string across a line threaded through a ring fastened to the long, sewn mass of linen, which had been stiffened with thin spruce gum. When the line pulled taut, the folds of linen hung stiffly. Tor then connected the pieces of pipe, long logs burnt hollow through the middle with an iron rod, and fitted it to the connections from the spring. Steam flowed into an opening at the bottom of the linen, which slowly filled and rose against the upper line.

Tor got people from the growing crowd to hold lines looped around the structure, relieving the pressure against the upper line. He grinned. "I think it's going to work," he said to Tristal. "Remember? Eolyn called it a balloon. I worked on it up in the woods."

"I don't understand," said Tristal.

Tor turned and fastened a blazing torch below the hoop in the bottom of the tall linen bag, then sat in a double loop of rope below it with three jugs of sheep fat in his arm. With the heat from the torch, the balloon began to strain at the guys. "Cut that rope," he called to one of the men in the tree. "Down below! Be ready to let go. Don't hang on. Tristal, wait by the ice face. It may be awhile. Just hang around. I may need some help. Now, let go!"

The linen bag hovered for a few moments, then started a slow rise. The crowd cheered as Tor rose up beyond the long shadow of the ice face, catching the final sun rays and drifting toward the southwest.

"I'd never believe that if I didn't see it," the sheriff muttered. "What's next with that man?"

"Well," said Smythe, whose arm was in a sling. "What's next is he'll have to snatch Renee Blake out of the hands of that whole mob of murdering hugger-muggers."

Tor continued to rise, drifting much south of where he wanted to be. He was alarmed at the rate at which the torch used his fuel, which he poured into a wooden bowl below the thick rag wick. He hoped he would make it to the ice wall. But closer to the wall he caught the updraft, and somehow, in the coolness, he rose faster, passing the near edge of the ice, still rising, noting the mass of perhaps one hundred fifty Raiders in the distance to the northwest as dark flecks, and then seeing, to his surprise, far to the west, a dark band he recognized as forest. He was much relieved at that, but he was also growing cold. He stopped adding fuel to the torch, then tried to snuff it out so he could descend. Above, he saw a rip begin in the linen, then lengthen. His descent quickly became more rapid than he wanted. Fortunately, fresh snow had fallen on the ice—and it seemed much less fissured than the eastern ice wall.

As he neared the surface, he wriggled out of the harness and hung, dragging his feet, then let go. The balloon collapsed like dissolving smoke. Tor found his legs asleep and tingling as he started to walk, then trot, toward the Raiders. He saw now why they picked their raids so they could retreat during the full moon—the rising moon bathed the ice in weird light, accentuating the depressions. Tor fought down his fear of fissures and trotted through the ankle-deep snow.

It was high night before he saw, to his north, some

stragglers of the Raiders, all wounded men and those help-ing them, moving slowly across the ice, well spread out.

He picked the last group, of four men, only one of them whole, and, rising from behind a jutting ice fold, struck them down with quick whirls of his axe. Then he took one of their long, furred coats, uncovering the black leather they all wore during the battle. A shaggy hat helped hide his braid of light hair. He trotted forward, dragging the sledge with one body on it. Soon, striding with his head down, hand behind him as he pulled the sledge, he caught up with another group of three.

One of the men spoke to him. He seemed not to hear, then dropped the rope and swung his axe, quickly killing all three. This is no way, though, he thought. Sooner or later they would get him. After all, he estimated from the balloon that the group contained at least a hundred fifty men.

Soon he drew abreast of a lone man, and killed him, but the man cried out. Far ahead, a group of three turned around. Tor pretended to be helping the man up, throwing the corpse's arm over his shoulder and moving him to the sledge. One of the men ahead called back to him. He waved. They turned and plodded on.

Tor slid the sledge around behind another fold in the glacier surface and abandoned it. He trotted ahead, heading southerly, hoping that any prisoners would be with the stragglers. Eventually he cut back, seeing he had passed most of the long tail of Raiders. Selecting a shadowy cup of snow-covered ice, he crouched down and watched. Seven groups passed before he saw them—a girl holding what appeared to be a baby, and a young boy, herded along by five men. All the men appeared strong and unwounded.

Tor found his heart pounding as he slowly fell in with the men, stooping to hide his height. As the spaces between men constantly shifted, he tried to find that perfect moment when he knew he could get them all. From far back came a faint shout—Tor knew that meant some of the bodies he had left had been discovered. Two of the men turned, then the others. Tor plodded on for three steps, then swung his axe, in spinning arcs, downing all the men.

The girl cried out. Tor grabbed her and said, "Renee? Your father sent me. Come." He scooped up the boy and baby together and led her, running southward, dodging behind the ice ridges. Even with his burden he outdistanced her and had to wait.

Finally, she came up, crying, and panted out, "I can't. My feet. My feet are freezing."

He saw she had thin summer shoes on. "Ahead," he said. "Can you count to four hundred?"

"Yes."

"Walk for four hundred steps. Then I'll fix your feet. Some."

Tor kept behind her, looking back. No one followed immediately, but soon after he had begun to rip the Raider coat into strips to wrap her feet, he heard the shout of discovery. Trying to stay calm, he wrapped her feet, then those of the boy. Then he handed her the baby and said, "See that point of ice? Down there? Go there. Get behind it. I'll follow. Now. Run. I know it's hard, but it's for your life." He watched them go then followed, dragging the remains of the coat, obscuring the tracks somewhat in the moonlight. Then he smoothed out a section of them completely and made a side track, still dragging the coat. He led this around a depression in the ice, jumped back in the old tracks from above, and ran backward about twenty arms. Then he jumped down into another ice gully and smoothed out the snow behind him until he curved around a promontory of ice. He turned and looked, then raced away, hearing the shouts of pursuers growing louder behind him.

He found the children crouched behind the high jut of ice, shivering. "I've led them astray for a short time," he said. "Come. We have a long way southward to go."

"Home is east," the boy said.

"The way down the ice is southeast," said Tor. As they went, he sliced up the Raider coat further and put a wide strip of it around the shoulders of each child. Then he took the baby and wrapped the rest around it. Despite all the activity around it, the infant only whimpered occasionally while it slept. But by the time the east again grew light, the children were completely fagged out and the baby cried lustily. Tor checked behind him continually, but heard only distant shouts. He hoped he could find the balloon again.

Fortunately, their recent reverses had instilled caution in the Raiders. Never before had they been followed up onto the ice so they may have anticipated an ambush ahead.

They also must have been extremely tired. Not only had they fought much of the day, and been severely defeated, but they climbed the high ice face again and retreated without rest. Tor at least had rested during the previous afternoon and rode up onto the glacier.

As the sun rose, Tor kept the children in ice gullies as much as possible, but he also kept them moving. He tied a small gag over the infant's mouth. Outraged, it tried to cry until it nearly choked with the mucous in its nose. It was not a gentle day at the nursery.

Finally they found the balloon. Tor sent the children on ahead as he dragged it across the ice, trying to slice it into sections as he went. Behind, he heard a distant shout and turned. In the distance he saw small dark flecks. The Raiders had seen him. He sent the children into a stumbling trot and followed, dragging the fabric.

It seemed easier for the children as they began a steeper descent near the edge of the ice wall. Tor had to shout ahead to warn them not to run too fast and slip. He also made better time on the downslope. When the edge came, he was surprised to find how abrupt it was. He got the children to crouch down in the snow, and, giving the infant to the boy, got Renee to help him rip the fabric into large strips. She was crying.

He heard a closer shout. Quickly, he cut loose the binding ropes, began tying strips of balloon together, and made two loops in the end.

"Renee," he called. "You take the baby." He slipped the loop around her, tied the boy in the other loop, and payed it out over the edge, saying, "When you reach the end, you have to find someplace to stick fast. There's no choice. Then bring the rope down, loop it, and go down half a length. Can you do that?"

"I—I think so," Renee called.

They went out of sight over the edge. Tor shouted after them, "Renee, I'm going to let go after I've let it all out and I've waited. You'll have to figure it out from there."

"What about you?" she called back. Indeed. What about him? Tor didn't know. He said nothing.

He ran out of fabric strip and held on for a time. Then he threw the end outward, closing his eyes a moment with a sickening feeling of fear for the children. Then he turned. Six Raiders were above him, closing in.

Scrambling up, he ran north along the edge of the ice, jumping over wide fissures. The first Raider arrow zipped by him. He knew there would soon be another. He then ran up a fissure, out of sight, scrambled up it, and jumped over, right in front of one of the Raiders.

The man cried out as Tor hit him with his shoulder, jerked his axe free, and finished him. Then he ran up the fissure, away from the ice wall, vaulted over the edge as it grew shallow, only then feeling the sting of an arrow that had sliced along his side, waist high. He scrambled over two more of the fissures when he saw, above, three Raiders with a rope. They hadn't yet seen him.

He shut his eyes a moment wondering if he could take them, bit his lip, and ran up the fissure, then, gauging where they might be, climbed the side and jumped. The men cried out, but before they could react, Tor was on them, with one stroke for the first, an arc for the second and third. Downslope, others had seen him. He scooped up the rope and ran, choosing a fissure and running down it toward the ice face, expecting a Raider to come over the edge as he did.

He reached the edge, knelt, made a loop, spread it over a wide knob of ice, and lowered himself over the edge. He had the rope wrapped around his right arm and held on with his left hand, sliding down as rapidly as he could. Seeing a rough ledge, he stopped, bracing himself, keeping tension. As he suspected, the tension released, the rope snaked down by him, ending with the cut loop. He let out a wild yell, ended it abruptly. Looking around, he saw nowhere to fasten the rope end. He took his axe and cut a ledge back into the ice face. This high it didn't crumble off as it did below, but he knew he was in a tight spot. What of the children? Now he had a clearer idea of what he had abandoned them to.

From above a large ice chunk rumbled down and bounded off the surface of the ice, passing close by him. The Raiders were making sure. Tor settled down to wait and rest, so fatigued that he couldn't imagine much further effort. Below he could see he had about two hundred arms of ice wall to descend. He couldn't see much close to the ice face, but after a time, as he sat in a quandary, he smelled smoke. Tristal, he thought. He's letting me know they know we're here.

Tor eased around in his precarious position, took out his axe, and began to cut back into the loose ice, enlarging the cut into a small cave. Above he heard another rumble. A huge chunk fell by him, and with it a Raider, screaming as he went. Tor hoped that the people below were well back from the ice wall. As Tor rested in his ice cave, he began to realize it was too cold to stay in. He took his axe again and cut a large knob in the firm ice back in, then passed the center of the rope over the knob and ventured out again, keeping the entire rope in a loop with the knot at the bottom.

He lowered himself to the end of the rope and sat in the loop cutting another small cave back into the ice. Again he made a firm knob, untied the rope, and tugged it loose from its hold above. Nine times he did this, growing more tired and cold each time, and each time wondering how he ever could have abandoned the children to the ice face. It was like killing them.

The tenth time Tor cut back into the ice, it seemed rotten no matter how far he went, and he feared the roof of his little cave would fall in on him. Below he heard shouts, and looking out, he saw a growing crowd, but up close he could see nothing.

He turned, spanning the fissure he was in, to test the wall, but as he did, the ice beneath his feet gave way, and he fell, wedging a moment in the ice, splitting more loose, sliding and bouncing down the ice face, finally stopping with a sickening jolt. He was aware of hands on him, of being lifted, of stabbing pain in the side. "The children," he murmured. "The children."

"They're getting them. Look."

Tor tried to shake the blackness out of his eyes and finally said, "Put me down, then."

They did. Gradually his eyes cleared, and he saw a train of ladders up the side of the ice, with a crowd of men tying more on and lifting them, with side poles and guy ropes. It looked very rickety. At the top he could make out two children clinging to a fissure. As he watched a man started up the ladder. Then everything grew dim.

Tristal came and spread a wool blanket over him. "Here's your axe," he said. "It got down before you did."

"That's a brave girl," Tor murmured. "Let her grow a little, and you could go anywhere with her."

"You're too old for her."

"Too bad. Too bad."

 XX

It took Tor a long time to recover, at first at the Blakes' cottage, then for a time at Judge Fenbaker's. Finally, when he could walk, he set out for Dame Arbyr's to spend the winter, hoping to earn enough for linen for his next balloon. Tristal had returned there two weeks earlier, just before the first snowfall. .

As Tor walked slowly down the wagon-rutted road, he felt immense relief that now, after five winters, he knew the way out of the Ice Valley. But if Tristal left with him in the spring, he would have only two years to keep his promise to Fahna. He passed into the southsector near the manor of Clear Hill and turned south with the road toward Blue Lake. Finally he came to the upper end of Blue Lake, where the road turned eastward, and soon after he saw three men coming from the town after him, running. Seeing the uniform of the sheriff's men, he waited.

They came up to him, panting. "Tor," one of them said, catching his breath. "Come with us."

"What's this about?"

"Sheriff . . . wants to talk to you. Don't know about what."

Later, in the sheriff's office, Tor watched the man nervously looking on his table for something, his hands trembling. "Oh, yes," he finally said. "Here. An order from Southsectorjudge Morton. You are to be held until a full investigation is made of possible complicity in the recent horrors in the west."

Tor stood silently a few moments. "What's the real reason, the real beef, as you people, without knowing the delights of that meat, put it?"

The sheriff looked at him, openmouthed, then said to his men, "Put him away. Not here. In the prison."

Tor did not resist. There seemed little point. It would all come clear soon enough. But when the thick, nail-studded door closed on him, he felt a sinking of the heart. He turned in his cell and saw, by the dim window light, the young Raider he had captured over a month ago. The boy stared at him, then turned on his bench bed and covered up his head.

Far away, at Northwall, it was midautumn. Fahna was walking down the path from her house to the river. Horns had sounded indicating the arrival of strangers from upriver. Suddenly Bravet emerged, as though from nowhere, and stood next to her. She started. He took her arm.

"I . . . want to tell you something."

"Yes?"

"It's been years now. You won't ever talk. Even last spring—it was . . . such a short conversation."

"It was too long. I know what you want. I've been promised. You know that."

"Any man in his right senses would be back—would be here for you by now. He's not coming."

"He . . . is. What did you want to tell me? Please. I want to see what's coming down the river."

"I've got a small band now. We're tired of logging for the Pelbar. The whole of the plains is deserted. We're going out again to follow the herds. I'll be the axeman. They've agreed."

"Ah. That . . . will be nice. When do you leave?"

"Spring. Third month. I'll be here two springs after that, too."

"Why?"

"To see you pass the seven-year promise limit. Alone."

"I can wait all my life if I choose."

"A waste. No such beauty as yours is anywhere in the whole river valley."

"You've looked?"

"Please. Don't be nasty. I can be rough."

"No doubt. Now, I must go. Please let go."

"I'll come."

"If you want. Just take your hand off me."

The two walked in silence down the bank to the river,

where a strange flotilla of five boats neared the landing area. A line of guardsmen waited for them. It was a mixture of rough hunters, old men and women, one young woman, and her two small children. A guardsman set a plank for the lead boat, and a large man jumped ashore with a leather line and pulled the boat up.

"This is Northwall," said the guardcaptain. "You are strangers? How can we help you?"

"Place for winter. We'd like work. Any place to stay. Is this Pelbar?"

"Yes. The north Pelbar city, though now a home of all people."

"Good. My name is Dardan. This is my wife, Orsel, and other from far north, near ice."

Fahna uttered a short, sharp cry. Several guardsmen turned to see her covering her mouth with both hands. "The short-sword. It's Tristal's short-sword," she shrilled.

"Tristal. He gave it to me," Dardan said. "Late summer. Now...four year ago. His uncle—Tor—wanted to cross ice. Haven't seen them since. We were leaving and had only stone tool. He gave this."

Fahna ran down the bank and took it, drawing out the blade. It was well worn and the blade end of the handle was slightly charred.

"That," Dardan said, pointing, "was done before. By mad Shumai. They heated it and burned him across chest."

Fahna gasped. "His chest?"

"He is all right. It healed. Just a scar."

"Dardan," Orsel said, "there'll be time. Let us get ashore. Baby need cleaning."

"He usually do." Dardan laughed lightly.

"I will get you a new short-sword if I may keep this one," Fahna said.

"Take it. It was gift. Glad for new one, though."

Two days later, Fahna left for Pelbarigan to study again with the Dome woman, Eolyn. She sat on the deck of an old Tantal sailing ship holding the damaged short-sword in her hand, occasionally looking down at it, touching the blackened guard and the charred wood of the handle next to it.

Tor had been in his cell for six days before the Raider said anything to him, and then it was contemptuous. He said it coming back from work cutting stone, which Tor was not required to do.

It sounded like "bik."

"Bik?" Tor questioned.

"Bik!" the Raider asserted.

Tor mused awhile, then said, "Vizkud. Is that right?"

The Raider stared at him. "Visgud," he replied, and spat.

"Well, we've established that you speak a variety of common Urstadge," Tor said. "Look. Let me see your hands."

The Raider drew back. Tor held out his fist, closed, then opened his fingers, one at a time. "One, two, three, four, five," he said.

The Raider stared at him a long time, then looked at the floor and said, *"Aan, duwo, dray, vur, vif."*

They continued to exchange words for some time. Slowly the young man took up Tor's words, frowning. But at last he seemed again to turn himself inside out with rejection.

By the time an Ice Valley month was up, though, he was quite friendly. Tor questioned him as intently as he could about Raider society. The young man clearly was proud to be a Raider—a Sgenamon, as he called them.

The first day of the second month, the guard summoned Tor to the foreroom, where he found Southsectorjudge Morton awaiting him, flanked by two armed sheriff's men. Tor said nothing.

"We are gathering evidence to support the charges," Morton began. "It will take some time. But it is winter, and perhaps you would be idle anyhow."

"You nether aperture, only the unjust arrest people and then hunt for evidence to keep them. It's nonsense. You know I wouldn't be idle. How am I ever going to earn my way out of this giant sheepsty if I can't work this winter?"

The judge stared at him, flushed. "I needn't talk to you, then," he said, rising.

"No, fish guts. Pinkeye. Pile of sheep manure. Flea scruff. You were mothered by an eel and raised by maggots. You..." The judge had left by that time.

"You had no call for that," said one man. "It'll go harder."

"What will? I've done nothing. You know that. What's it about, anyway?"

"Not for me to say. But Dame Arbyr's mourning is over."

"Oh. That's it. Protecting the rich. She needed to fear nothing."

"She? She doesn't fear anything. But there's your nephew, you know. Negotiations are underway for Elayna."

"Negotiations? Is she a nation?"

"Now. Back to your cell."

The young Raider was there when Tor arrived. He looked up quizzically, and said, *"Fut det ul poot?"*

"Nood mudge. Lut ef pider."

"Pider? Ni. Biter."

"Oh. Biter."

The young man smiled slightly as Tor turned and winked to the astonished guard.

That evening, Tor tried to explain as openly as he could about the battle. He encouraged the young man—who told him his name was Peelay—explained what had happened and described the wrongness of the raids. But the boy clearly exulted in them, explaining that they were necessary to replenish the population since the Raiders had few children.

Tor discussed what they knew about the Time of Fire and the fact that other groups of survivors had had problems with residual pollution then asked if the Raiders passed over the highly radioactive empty places. Peelay frowned. It was clear he had never seen one. Tor encouraged him to continue talking, and during the next several evenings he did.

Late one night, as Tor asked him to describe their food, the boy mentioned soft, gray pots.

"Gray pots?" Tor asked.

Peelay, who translated the altered sounds quite readily now, stumbled through an explanation of how they were found as long pipes in a tangle of ruin. They were easily cut into sections, then pieces were fused across the bottom with heat. Cooking was done in them by dropping in heated stones, since they would melt if put over a hot fire. But they were valuable because, though heavy, they didn't smash like pottery.

Tor had a strange feeling about this. Sterility, he knew, developed from poisons. He fell into musing.

Peelay asked him, *"Vatz run?"*

"What's wrong? I think—I don't know. We'll see to-morrow."

The next day he got a friendly guard to bring in a piece of lead. It was rare in the Ice Valley, but some pieces were used as weights in stretching cloth. Tor didn't know their source. The guard handed it to Tor, saying, "I hope you'll tell no one about this. I don't understand."

"If the Raiders are cooking in this, and got it from some ancient construction, it may be what keeps them from re-producing. So it would be the reason they need to raid."

"Oh," the man said, musing. "You think so?"

"Stay here. He'll be in soon. See."

Peelay came in, tired from his rock shaping, curious about seeing the guard. *"Vo hay voor?"* he asked.

"Peelay, he brought...you understand?..."

"Prood?"

"Yes. He brought this. Is this what the gray pots were made of?"

Peelay took the lump of lead and frowned at it, creasing it with his nail. He smiled up and said, *"Eis. Datz zeem tun."* Then he shaped his words carefully. "That's the same thing."

"We call it lead," Tor said. "The Sgenamon can't cook some things in it and stay healthy."

Peelay frowned again, slowly making out what Tor said, as Tor returned the lead to the guard with thanks. The man seemed amazed at the progress Tor had made with the Raider.

After the man had gone, Tor said, "Now, Peelay. Why did they send you down the hill? You were so much younger than they."

Three nights later, Tor lowered tied strips of wool blanket out the barred window of their cell, which they had after long effort succeeded in weakening, and let Peelay out. He followed. They dropped into the howling cold of a full winter storm. Tor hurried the young man to the rear of the sheriff's quarters, pried open the door, and found winter clothing and skis. Silently they set off northward through the drifts.

It was morning before their escape was discovered, but word spread rapidly, and a watch was set on all the roads. Sheriff's men headed out toward Boiling Springs and Dame

Arbyr's, and the first group found in a sheltered cove the tracks of two pairs of skis. By nightfall, the secondsector sheriff had been alerted and sent his men out to warn the farms.

Shortly after, Tor and Peelay arrived at the Johnston farm near where the young Raider had been captured. Tor rapped on the door, the sound muffled by his thick mittens. Stanley Johnston opened it, his mouth dropping. "You!" he said.

"What is it, Stan?"

"The savage and the Raider." He moved to block them, but Tor pushed into the warm central room. An old woman and three children sat there.

Mother Johnston stormed into the room with a pan of hot fat. Tor snatched up a child and held her in front of him. "Listen a moment!" he shouted. Then in a soft voice, he said, "May we sit down?"

"You won't get away with this. The sheriff..."

"Just listen." Tor's voice had such definiteness that they stopped. "This young man I think is your son, Billy," he said abruptly.

They stared at him. "No," said Johnston.

"They sent him down the hill because he'd been here before. I've been talking to him in prison. There's no 'th' sound in Sgenamon dialect, but he picked it up easily. He must've known it. It's a hard sound to pick up. They only changed his name slightly—Billy to Peelay."

The young man had been looking at them all with great suspicion; he couldn't follow all of what was said.

"Mother, put down the fat," Stanley Johnston said.

She looked down absently, then took it back to the rear fire and reemerged without it, smoothing her hands on her wool pants. She looked again at the young man and said, "No."

"I'm a Sgenamon," Billy said slowly. "Not one of you."

"That's common," said Tor. "Young children taken early enough become full members of their new culture. They are proud of it. They despise the old one, even that of their parents."

Mother Johnston said again, "No." Then she said, "Show me your side. Right here." She pointed at her left side at waist level. Tor helped Billy off with the coat and pulled up the prison jumper, revealing an old burn scar. Mother

Johnston gasped, putting her hands to her face, then reaching out to his, saying, "Oh, Billy, what've they done to you?"

"I'm a Sgenamon," Billy said, now nearly smothered.

Stanley Johnston looked at Tor. "What can I say?" he asked. "I'd of killed him. Mother demanded it. What can I say?"

"Don't say anything. Why not give your son a hug? I hope you realize how hard getting him used to Ice Valley ways again will be."

"You know how hard it's *been*? Endless crying and middle-maddle? Endless."

The next day the news of Tor's escape reached Dame Arbyr's, brought by a sheriff's man as they sat at supper. They added a place for him at the long trestle table, and after an embarrassed silence, Randall Stonewright said, "So you think he'll be coming here?"

"No need to be afraid of that, Randall," said Dame Arbyr, sighing. "He knows enough to get out of the south-sector. He knows my brother runs the area not for justice but for his own designs."

"A representative of the law cannot be expected to listen to such talk," the sheriff's man said as he rose.

"Young man, sit down and eat," Dame Arbyr called. "After all, I am his sister. It would be easier not to be. It is known to all that Tor wants to leave Ice Valley. It is also known well enough that I would have him master of this manor. Strangely enough, the judge is using my fondness for Tor as a lever to pry me away from marrying Randall—are you surprised at my openness?" She laughed lightly. "Perhaps it's the barley wine. Maybe I'm too old to play these silly games. I don't know why Tor escaped, but I do know that if he makes it to the secondsector, Fenbaker will never turn him back to Morton. And if Morton came for him, the whole population would rise up against his men. Tor is hero enough to them."

"What about the Raider?" the man asked grimly.

"I don't know. We'll learn in time. He has some idea. But he's given me my freedom. Morton wanted to arrange a match with the Thirdsector Fitzroys. I think he has Hercule in mind. Pfaahh! Randall, now that Tor is gone, I think we need to..." She paused, looking playfully at the sheriff's man.

"And what of me?" Elayna asked. "You're not thinking at all—" She paused and looked at Tristal, who sat astonished, his thoughts racing.

"You are provided for, my dear," Dame Arbyr said. "Don't ask me to be consistent, after all. I did give in to Morton in that game, knowing your wishes."

"Smithson?" she whispered.

"The very one. Now, I am almost drunk," Dame Arbyr said. "Tristal, you seem disturbed. Well, you ought to know the basic human rule—property first, then emotion."

Tristal stood and glared at Elayna, who looked down, red-faced, then glanced up, turned, rose, and left the room.

"You savage," said the sheriff's man. "I need to take you with me. For safekeeping. Only at Flatrock. It'll be all right."

"You just try it, cowboy." Tristal sneered at him.

"You all have witnessed it. Resisting arrest," said the sheriff's man.

"I don't think we've seen anything of the kind. Do you, my dear?" said Randall Stonewright.

"No. Not at all."

"I certainly haven't," said Unsit. "Tristal, may I get your coat?"

"Now see here!" the sheriff's man said.

"Drunk and abusive. And while on duty!" said Dame Arbyr.

"How can you be such liars?" the man yelled.

"The sectorjudge's man asks an odd question. Sit down. Have some more wine."

The man tried to stand but two of the manor workers leaned on his shoulders.

"I'm sure we can be amicable," said Dame Arbyr.

Outside, Tristal strapped on skis. Allen, a kitchen boy, brought him a food parcel and silently put it in his pack. "Randall says to head for Alder Glen," he said. "You'll be in secondsector by morning then. He says he'll send you the value of your work to Fenbakers'."

"Thank him for me."

"Here. A note from Elayna."

"Keep it, Allen. I—"

Allen put it back in his pocket. "Even a boy knows,

Tris. You don't cross class lines. It was impossible. Remember it as fun."

"Well, good-bye, Allen." Tristal took up the poles. "Good-bye. Don't stand downwind of the slaughterhouse."

"Right. Don't wet your flax in the sheep trough." Allen watched Tristal ski off into the dark.

Three days later Secondsectorjudge Fenbaker sat on his dais in the sector courtroom. Seats had been brought in, and the room was crowded with people. Sitting with Tor, still grim and silent, was Tristal. West manor farmers, workers from Boiling Springs, and manor folk all crowded in together. Billy Johnston, now dressed in Ice Valley wool, but with his ritual facial scars, sat in the front row.

"Young man, if we release you to the Johnstons, will you agree not to give away anything about us to the Raiders?"

"Eis, I akree," he said. "Put I em Sgenamon sdill."

"I have a thought, Judge Fenbaker," Tor said. "How would it be if Billy comes with me when I leave in the spring? He can return to the Raiders and explain to them what I think of how they are poisoning themselves."

"No! Never!" Mother Johnston cried.

"Just a thought," said Tor. "If they knew, they might avoid it and so have their own children and little need to raid. Even more, they might trade with you over the ice. Billy is a natural link—the first one. It might stop the raiding. It might bring you products that aren't here in the valley. It would give you a market outside yourselves. Who knows? Maybe some of you will leave the valley for a time. I saw the forest beyond. Billy says it isn't far. Maybe thirty kilometers."

"Never. Don't even talk about it," said Mother Johnston.

"Just a thought."

"Tor, your thoughts have an odd way of changing things," Fenbaker commented. "We'll have to think about that one. Now, Billy, did you understand what was just said?"

"*Zum*. Eis."

"What do you think?"

"I . . . ton'd knuw. I . . . would dry."

"Er . . . ah, yes, try, eh?"

"Eis."

"Well, now that you've lost a lot of the winter, the west manor people tell me they'll help with the . . . balloon, Tor. I take it that it'll have to be bigger."

Tor looked at Tristal, who dropped his eyes. "Yes. Quite a bit."

 XXI

TRISTAL thrust the bowl of burning fat up under the opening of the tall, bulging balloon. It expanded further, straining at the ropes. "Now, I think, Tor," he called.

Tor reached over with his axe and rasped the master restrainer in two. All the guy ropes fell free of their loops and the balloon rose rapidly, carried on the east wind, higher and higher, toward the ice wall.

From below a general cheer rose, and much hand waving. Tor looked over at Billy, who clung to his harness in fear, looking down at his parents and most of the population of the west manors, waving and shouting. As they rose higher and passed away from the large steam vents, they came to the spruce forest, a sudden band of dark green, with its scattered pockets of late snow. Then it thinned out closer to the ice wall, where travertine buildup and smaller steam vents and hot springs, in an occasional, irregular line, faced the tall, already crumbly, contorted mass of ice. They rose rapidly, cresting the high ice.

"Ah!" Tristal called, seeing out beyond the ice wall the far dark of forest to the west. Then he added, "Billy, is that more ice?"

"Eis. Nod so wide. The rifer goes through id. Zomedimes dangerouz. I—"

"It's not so bad if you don't look down," Tor called.

"Worz iv you loog up," Billy replied.

"We may make it all the way across," Tor said.

"Not much choice. Either climb down the ice or hang up in a tree," Tristal replied.

As they ran out of fuel and the balloon slowly settled, they could see the face of the ice was rough and steep. Their feet touched, in harness, then they lifted off, dragged a short distance down the slope, and settled, cutting loose quickly.

Getting down the ice was not very difficult there. They dragged the balloon down and stored it in a shelter of boughs, in case it might be of use to the Raiders in recrossing to talk to the Ice Valley people. Otherwise, they could use the cloth.

The three hiked down through the trees to a stream running with melt water, southward. Here the two Shumai parted with Billy, who hugged them both formally and then left, following the stream, a valiant adolescent attempting a fearsome undertaking. He said the Raiders would be a long way off, preparing springtime incursions against the widely scattered settlements amid the vast forests and rivers of the west.

Tor and Tristal crossed several ridges and valleys, sometimes in snow. On their second day they came to the Sgenom River, which had given the Raiders their name. They caught some cottonwood logs and tied them together into a massive raft, which they shoved into the rapid stream. The second afternoon a giant ice wall loomed ahead of them where the river passed through a narrow gap between two mountains. They were moving fast at the time, and as they rounded the last bend, they saw they would pass into a tunnel through the ice.

Tor cried out, took his axe, and began to hack loose the side log, freeing it as they rumbled in under the ice, the roof rapidly squeezing down. "Jump on, Tris," he shouted.

"What?" Tris yelled, reluctantly abandoning the splint basket he was making.

Ahead, in the weird darkness of the ice tunnel, they heard a roar. Tor shoved the rest of the raft off and ahead. It scraped the roof at one point, while the single log barely cleared, then they were ahead of it. Tor began shoving wildly at the roof, steering them across the current. "Duck!" he yelled. The river rolled into the ice and dove under, except for a narrow chute into which Tor steered the log. They shot through and suddenly emerged into the light, soaked and shivering.

They paddled to shore, using numbed hands, and waded

in, shaking. Once they had built a fire and dried, Tristal took his bow and walked back to the riverside. Soon he had returned with a large fish. "Look, zamu—that's what Billy called it. Big, eh?"

Tor seemed gloomy. "What is it?" Tristal asked.

"I could have killed us both back there. And I think there's one more ice wall ahead."

There was, but it was warmer ahead and the two Shumai rafted through a narrow chute where the water tossed and thundered but was not very dangerous.

Soon they found themselves beyond the ice, on a flatter river. Seabirds were flying above, and tall, ancient, unfamiliar trees grew by the river and on the sides of high, rounded mountains. The mountains were crested with snow and running with narrow ribbons of water, which fell hundreds of arms downward to small runs that fed the Sgenom. Mist rose and curled its coils around the mountains, obscuring then revealing them. Rain fell in drifting fogs and steady downpours.

The two improved the raft while drifting, and on it Tor began building another boat, shaping its members with his axe. He took special pains to explain to Tristal every step and get his help. Before they finished it, the river had slowed further, and, looking up, Tristal saw a small settlement by the shore, plank houses with sheets of smoke hovering over it.

"That would be the Carfers Billy described," said Tor.

"Hostile?"

"No. Only to the Sgenamon looking for their children."

XXII

As their boat grated on the shore pebbles, and Tor stepped out into the shallow water, he paused and ran his eyes across the scene ahead. No one. It seemed still, ominous, but as he searched his instincts, his finest senses could taste no real danger.

He turned to Tristal and motioned for him to come forward unarmed. They pulled the boat and raft up farther and walked toward the low-roofed houses. Massive carvings, blooming with eyes, enlivened the surfaces of the buildings. Posts and fire-cranes showed similar carvings of animals, birds, fish, strange machines, dwellings, and human body parts, all highly stylized, ritualized, remarkably vital and vibrant.

Frowning over the settlement, on either side, two dark mountains loomed, running with water and shaggy with tall, thick trees. The two Shumai took it all in, walking slowly up onto the crown of the settlement, glancing at each other, finally sitting by a smoldering fire, which Tor idly fed with chips and splinters. After a time, during which he and Tristal remained silent, Tor not so much heard or saw as felt someone approach.

An old man with long gray hair combed down the sides of his round, dark face came and squatted down with them.

"This is my nephew, Tristal. I am Tor. We are Shumai, from far to the southeast, beyond the ice. We are going westward."

"Not much farther lies the sea."

"So we understand."

"From whom."

"From Billy, an Ice Valley boy taken and adopted by the Sgenamon."

"You have been with the Sgenamon?"

"No. Only Billy. They raided the Ice Valley last season

and Billy was retaken. We got over the ice and let Billy go to see if he could arrange for some kind of peace."

"You don't make peace with some things—great toothed fish, winter storms, falling trees."

"But they are men, and you and I are men."

The old man spat in the fire of chips. A small hiss sizzled and died away. Tor turned to look at him and smile.

"What do you want with us then?"

"Company. A place to build our boat." Tor made as if to stand up, but the old man laid a hand on his arm.

"Do not stand now. You are watched, might be shot. I will stand first. Come then. Let us look at this boat of yours. My name is Nuchatt. This is Shoulder Mountain Camp. That axe. That is truly an axe."

"Ah. Yes. It's come a long, long way."

"Give it?"

Tor slowly unsheathed his axe and passed its handle over to the old man, who, humming softly, held it at arm's length squinting at it and passing his hands over its surface. Then he held it gently, staring out across the broad river and handed it back.

"For fighting," Nuchatt mused.

"Yes. And other things."

"Leading men."

"Yes. Maybe it will help with boat building."

Nuchatt chuckled. "Maybe. But we have other tools. You hungry? We might put the fish back on the fires." He gestured over his head, then walked over to the makeshift log-craft Tor and Tristal had made. He whistled softly, laughed, and shook his head.

Tristal ventured the first look behind them. The village was alive with people, and a line of six young men, armed with bows, stood in a line in front of the others.

Nuchatt waved a dismissal to them, and all but one turned and walked quietly back among the others. "We live this way because of the Sgenamon, you see."

Tor replied with a light laugh then said, "They don't make things easy for anyone. But they may change. I think they will. I think—"

"What?"

"They have been poisoning themselves."

"How do you poison poison itself?"

"No. They are men. Maybe the poison can be removed. At any chance, I see they give you no trouble."

"They do. The trouble of watching. Constant watching. But they and the slavers are no problem anymore except when they come in force enough to burn what they can see."

Tor let his eyes sweep the village.

"Yes," said Nuchatt. "You are seeing little. I suppose you knew that." He gestured and called in another language to a young man nearby, then turned his back and grasped Tor's boat. The young man came, and with him Nuchatt rocked and lifted the boat off the raft and shoved it out into the river. Then Nuchatt spanked his hands together.

"Come," he said. "We will eat. Then we will build you a proper boat." The young man laughed.

That night the Shumai slept on the beach by their raft. No one had invited them into any of the buildings, and they had not asked to go. Four unarmed young men slept with them, partly, it seemed, to guard them, partly out of hospitality. In the distance, they heard singing, in unison, of endless, chanted songs.

In the morning Nuchatt reappeared and led them around the camp in close to the plunging rock of the mountain. Under a rough shake-roofed shed a number of logs lay on trestles. The old man mused at them with pursed lips, then turned and smiled. Striking one with his hand, he said, "Good. Just the right one for a two-man boat."

With the help of a number of young men, they dragged and rolled the log down to the beach, and immediately several men set to working on it with mauls and chisels, splitting off the top and shaping the ends. They worked steadily, often singing together, never measuring except with the tools. Nuchatt stood by, hands in the pockets of his leather apron, occasionally making suggestions in a gentle voice. The young men always did what he proposed.

By noon they worked amid a semicircle of people, older women weaving fibers, or methodically beating them across logs to separate the strands, men carving, chatting, or playing a curious game with pebbles in bowls, children running among the group.

Tristal observed that Nuchatt made certain he saw exactly what was going on. He didn't understand why the old man paid so little attention to Tor's contribution, as the older Shumai worked steadily at rough shaping with accurate strokes of his long-handled axe.

As the afternoon progressed, a large iron kettle was hung on a heavy tripod over a fire. Out of the corner of his eye Tristal saw fish, meat, and herbs tossed in it as a succession of children stirred. An ambiguous scent began to drift toward the beach, but by this time the young Shumai was hungry enough to find it pleasant.

"No need to worry, Tristal," Nuchatt remarked. "It will be good. We have eaten it for many years and still live."

Tristal smiled weakly at him. It was as though the old Carver knew his thoughts. He began to worry about a repetition of their experience at Sedge and started to hold his thoughts on facts and absolutes as Tor had counseled during their previous flight. But somehow Nuchatt seemed genuinely kind, though wary.

As it turned out, the strange stew was good. The Shumai dipped their noggins in it, standing in a circle with the villagers, who dipped in their wooden bowls.

The next few days repeated their experience of the first, but eventually they saw a large boat, with a sail and a number of paddlers, plowing upriver. It sounded a mournful horn, and the Carvers answered with a similar call on a curled sheep's horn.

As the boat slipped into a landing ditch dug from the shore sand and lined with rock, the young people greeted the visitors, obviously more Carvers, with waving fronds of fern and cedar as they chanted in a language strange to the Shumai. Each person was handed a square of fried seal blubber on a peeled wood shaft as he stepped ashore.

Most prominent among the visitors were four women dressed in hooded capes sewn with pieces of shells outlining the same kinds of shapes as those in the carved houses. One, a large woman whose cheeks ballooned outward and forward as far as her nose, and who leaned on a carved staff, was led up the rocks to a large chair which had been set up for her.

Tor and Tristal stayed by the boat, though they did little work because it would obviously have been impolite. For a time the woman and the older people of the village held a conversation, with gestures and some gutteral exclamations. Then she pointed at the Shumai, and all heads turned toward them. Tor laid down his axe, smoothed his hands on his pants, and walked up toward her, Tristal following.

"You," the woman said, in a surprisingly deep voice, "You call yourselves...what?"

"We are Shumai," Tor replied. "From the plains far to the south and east, across the ice."

The woman snorted and spat. "Tell me about it then," she murmured, with a slightly sardonic grin which showed many teeth missing.

Tor sighed and sat down on the rock near her. "It will take a long while to tell only a part of it."

"I have no baskets to weave. You, young one, you may go work on the boat. I will ask you later."

"To test my truth? You will find it will let in no water."

"Tell. I will judge."

Tristal returned to the boat, which was now completely roughed out and mostly trimmed. He watched over his shoulder now and again as Tor talked, gesturing with his one arm. The talk went on until Tristal was bored with being alone smoothing and shaving the swelling middle section of the boat.

Finally, Tor came down, with all the people watching, and said, "Your turn."

Tristal handed his uncle the Carvers' draw knife and went to sit where Tor had been. He looked up at the old woman's watery eyes.

"Your uncle has told us of wonders not to be believed by anyone," she remarked. "Of great crowds of animals, weapons that can burn an arm away or explode a tree, men whose faces are eaten off, and the like. Now you tell. Just of your trip. Your coming. Tell."

Tristal felt a moment of fear as he looked around at the dark-eyed faces around him. The men were well armed. Why did Tor seem so nonchalant about it all? Suddenly it came clear to him—all he had to do was tell the truth as well as he could. Then it would mesh with what Tor said. Clearly the Carvers had reason to fear strangers. They were only taking reasonable precautions.

Tristal talked as the shadows lengthened. Occasionally the woman questioned him, and he tried to explain more fully what he had said. Finally she slapped her hands on her thighs and rose heavily, reaching out for someone to lean on.

"Evidently Nuchatt was right," she said. "You are what you say you are. It seems impossible, but it is clearly so. Now I need something to fill my belly. I assume there might be some old stew."

A young woman from Shoulder Mountain Camp laughed and led her toward the largest of the plank houses. The whole party followed, leaving Tristal behind, with Nuchatt standing near. The old man smiled at him, then laughed and followed the others.

That evening the two Shumai sat alone by the river, with a noisy celebration going on behind them in the plank house.

"I don't understand—their not inviting us," Tristal said.

"They don't want us to see the inside of the house," Tor replied. "We will see then that no one lives there."

"No one lives there?"

"No. They live under the mountain. The one to the south. They use the houses but do not live there. The old woman is a leader of six settlements. She . . ."

"How do you know that?"

"Her cape. It has six segments, and the lower right one has the strange bird symbol we see all over here. They signaled for her the first day we got here. It took a while . . ."

"They signalled? How?"

"The large metal disk. Up there on the pole. They reflected the sun on it, sending a message over to the point downriver."

"I didn't see that."

"On the second day, I saw a return flashing. She lives much farther off, though. The paddlers were tired. It was clear they started out in the early morning. They had coats which they had taken off. I imagine she lives in the center of this group of settlements, and not under rock. Shoulder Mountain has to be especially careful, being more isolated and without watchers farther inland. They send workers here to help with the work in the rock."

"In the rock?"

"Yes. Did you see the broken rock lining the boat ditch? And did you notice several of the paddlers greet in-laws?"

"In-laws?"

"Yes. There was friendship but not the closeness of blood."

Tristal stared out across the water. "I've been just sitting here not seeing any of that," he muttered.

"You will. If you looked you would. You will learn to look. We are fortunate in Nuchatt. He is curious about us. His mind ranges freely. We mean something special to him. He has even kept Akeena away from you."

"Akeena? Who is Akeena?" Tristal asked.

In the morning the sailing canoe left with its entourage. They paid little further attention to the Shumai, other than to stare again. After they left only Nuchatt helped on the boat with one other man. Clearly the old woman thought it was well enough to be distantly friendly to the strangers, but not to welcome them into the society. That was all right with Tristal. He wanted to finish the boat and be off. Several times he caught himself looking upriver with a certain longing, but he shook it off. The Ice Valley was far in his past already.

Two weeks later, Tor and Tristal paddled into the morning sheen of the wide river, the new boat finished and much improved by the help of the Carvers.

A young woman cleaning fish paused a long time in her work, watching them. Then she laid down her knife, rinsed her hands, and walked up the rock to where her grandfather sat, also watching.

"Do you think they will return, Grandfather?"

"I think not. Perhaps the younger one, but likely not, Akeena."

"That is too bad."

"Did you sleep with him, then?"

"No. He was grieving over something and the thought never occurred to him."

"You would have, though?"

"Yes. He is so tall. His hair... it's not copper. Too light and..." Her voice died.

"Like dried grass wet with mist?"

"Yes. Like that. I cannot understand them, especially One Hand."

"I never thought I would see this day, Akeena, and them."

Akeena's eyes widened. "What, then?"

"No. They are not gods. But they are the first, the re-opening of the world. We were here before the ancients. I know that, but not how I know it. We have been here through that time that left the ruins on Oval Island. It is their language we speak, as well as the private language of the gods. Now it is starting over, reopening, after the long sleep. It is One Hand's spirit that is doing it. He is drawing the other one, Tristal, the way you would pull a captured seal behind a small boat."

"Why? Why could he not leave him with me?"

"The boy would not stay. He would go, too, but he does not know how yet. That is why One Hand will betray him."

"Betray him? His own flesh?"

"Of course. Soon, too. Why did you think he made Tristal pay such close attention to the building of that boat? One Hand will soon enough paddle off in it. I feel it."

"An awful thing."

"Not awful. He does not even know he will do it yet. I can feel it. It is the betrayal of the world. Mona betrayed me, you know, by dying."

"How? Dying? She would have stayed if she could."

"Yet I am left to be alone, to grieve for her all this time. It was her betrayal because she was part of the rhythm of the world, and betrayal is the way the world moves. If One Hand never betrayed Tristal, the young one would never grow. He grouches at it, but he looks to One Hand for judgment, for guidance."

"But to take the boat—"

"Tristal has the means to build his own boat now. It is inside him. One Hand saw to that. And so did I. I saw it and I helped him. As he pushes it into the water, he will be saying to himself, 'This is my boat, my life, my own future. I am the only paddler now.'"

"It is good, then, you were here to help them. It wasn't going to be a very good boat, was it."

"They have not lived in boats, though they know the feel of rivers."

"The eyes you carved. They will help them see. How will Tristal know to carve the eyes?"

"The carved eyes are only the mark that they themselves see. A part of Tristal's seeing is asleep, and One Hand has striven vainly to awaken it. Soon enough it will be startled open by the cold water of One Hand's betrayal. We will not see it. But I know it in the same way One Hand knows it."

"He is a prophet, then?"

"Yes. And his reward will be cold wind and driving

water. He has an iron heart, child. It has been beaten upon but has not broken. In its strength, and in his seeing, we shall all be changed."

"Changed, then? Not blessed."

"Blessed if you can bear change. Look at me, Akeena. My gray hair runs down my head like streams of water from the mountains. I am part of what has always been here. I am the same, and will endure through all change. But change is not a part of me, so the blessing is not. But it is there, after all."

"All the same, I wish he had left Tristal. I would like to reach across in the morning and touch his yellow hair."

"You will have to touch the sunlit planks of the wall. You are the mountain, too. Think of him as a stretch of moving sunlight that has crossed the mountain. Then the clouds return, and the deeper moods of your eyes. They are deep, you know. As deep as the sadness of rain. Now. It's time to finish with the fish, Akeena."

"Will you make the splints?"

"Yes. Not now. My soul is too full. I have to absorb the meaning of their coming."

"It is their going that troubles me. Look. The mist has swallowed them. There is only river now."

"There is always the river. The fish, Akeena. The fish."

 XXIII

As Tor and Tristal paddled steadily among the misty, evergreen-covered islands, flocks of gulls slowly appeared and faded away into the mists. Seals, which the Carvers had described, rose and sank in the wind-roiled water. Tristal paused and dipped his fingers in the water, then tasted them. "It's salt, Tor!" he exclaimed, grimacing.

"So we've made it all the way to the western sea—the one Stel set out for so many years ago."

"What has it done for us? Look at all the scars you've

picked up. There's nothing particular here. It's new, I admit, but . . ."

As though in answer to his remark, the water to the west of the boat stirred and poured away, as an astonishing black bulk rose from the sea, then rolled forward. A humped, sliding shape vanished, only to rise beyond, spewing spray from behind its head, rolling under once more, then appearing, rising far out of the water, flipping out an astounding broad tail, and sliding under again.

The two Shumai held their paddles poised in awe and disbelief. Farther off the shape appeared again, spewed mist again, and once more rolled under, the sea folding together as the height of the creature's back sank away.

Tor began paddling rapidly in the direction the beast sank, but it didn't reappear.

"What if it's hostile?" Tristal called.

"I think it's what Nuchatt called a whale—of some kind," Tor said. "The biggest animals anywhere."

"Look. Another."

Another shape rose from the water and rolled back, then rose again, shooting its whole front half free of the water, shaking and twisting long flukes, and flopping back onto the water with a heavy splash. Then two more rose beyond it and again disappeared.

Tor was silent a long time, looking.

"That island good enough?" Tristal asked, stirring him from his reverie. "For supper. For camp."

"Oh. Any. We have water."

"We need to turn south, to go far beyond the ice."

"Yes."

It was a fairly large island, and while Tristal cooked fish, Tor walked around it, returning and saying it had its own small spring.

Tristal looked up, his eyes shrunk with smoke. "It's a barren place, all rock and trees and this endless mist. I'll be glad to be back on the plains in Shumai country."

"A long way."

"If we run into the problems we did coming out, I'll be an old man before I get back. Fahna will have grandbabies."

"Fahna? I thought maybe you forgot her."

"Forgot her? Why? Because of Elayna?" He paused a long time while he moved the splinted fish to cook the other side. "How do you think it was for me? Everybody isn't a sterile old man. If I am to be any good for Fahna, I can't be—"

"Pure? Chaste?"

"Dry. Shriveled. Or starry-eyed, designing wings that don't fly."

"Or balloons that do."

"Suffering black flies, Tor, I'm just not cut out for this heroism, this emptiness. You can drive a person just so far. Across all that ice, fleeing from those mind-takers. Hanging over your death held only by a rope in the hands of a one-armed man. Cramped in a valley full of complacent farmers and sheepherders, run by rich families and unjust judges. Some wood just doesn't make axe handles. It might be a good cabinet or a beam in a house. But all this shock, shock, shock will splinter it."

"You're referring to yourself? You underestimate yourself."

"I know myself. You keep saying that, dragging me across ice and beyond to prove yourself right."

"No. It's right that you go home. What are you going to say to Fahna?"

Tristal paused. "Nothing. I suppose you will."

"No. Not my affair."

"Very funny. You're not a leader, Tor. You're a madman."

"She'll know."

"Fahna? What? She'll know what?"

"You'll hold her in the manner of someone who's held a woman before."

"She won't know that unless she's been held by someone who never held one. And then it won't matter."

"All this time and trouble, and you still see so little about knowing. Well, it's just as well. Hopes sometimes are not realized. That doesn't always imply failure. Only a different direction."

"More riddles. More arid philosophy. I'm tired of it, Tor. I'd as soon not hear another word of it. Ever. You aren't my idea of success. Any idea you'd have for me would be running with blood, most of it mine."

"Perhaps you're right. You ought to acknowledge what we did, though. We broke up a tyranny victimizing the man-lovers. We freed some people from the domination of mind-takers. We crossed ice that no one ever has before. We were the first visitors to the Ice Valley other than the Raiders—and we changed the valley people. They'll defend themselves better now. Perhaps they'll get out. We were the first outsiders the Carvers have seen since ancient times. Nuchatt told me. All that isn't a waste of time."

"Unless you'd rather be doing something else. All those years have crumbled in my hands like dead leaves. I feel half used up for nothing."

Tor said nothing, scanning the sea for more whales. The two ate in silence, prepared for sleep in silence. Finally, Tor said, "Pray with me, Tris. Just this time."

"What should I pray? Ice Valley prayers?"

"No. They aren't prayers. Only memorizations, recitations. Let the songs of things tell you your oneness with them, and feel the complex harmonies—like Pelbar choir song. Feel the rhythm and pulse that underlie everything. It is perfect, Tris. Even if the surface of things go wrong, there is underlying perfection imperfectly perceived. It declares itself, uttering its own goodness in spite of hunger, theft, imprisonment. They are only violations of the song, failures to hear it. The bad silence of emptiness, deafness."

"None of that means anything to me, Tor."

"Think about it. Promise me you'll think about it."

"Why? Why should I promise that?"

"Why? I have no good reason. I'm your uncle. I've loved you and tried for you, even if I'm so strange. But I see it all much more clearly now. Even that was worth all our trouble."

"See what? What could be worth the trouble we've had?"

"What I was just saying. The rhythm and pulse that underlies everything. It is perfect. It really is perfect. All the Heart River religions see it. Well, they glimpse it. Then they say to themselves that it's very nice, but won't weave cloth or hunt down wild cattle. So they begin to hedge with it, shove the core of their perception of Aven into the small inner pocket in their winter coat, and begin relating, relating it to their own lives."

"What's wrong with that?"

"Nothing... as long as they don't forget that it is the core—the absolute perfection which they see must be the fact about all things, even though we may not see it. The ministers of Aven see it. Surely the intuitive ideas about

Sertine are based on it. Even the Sentani Atou implies that at its core, though they are not a very religious people. I imagine that is one of the most ancient facts about people— that they do not really accept experience as we see it as being ultimate. But almost no one takes it literally. Nuchatt did, I saw it. He did."

"How do you know that?"

"Because of our rapport. We may have been killed but for Nuchatt. He came to us at the fire. He is able literally to accept the idea of the inner perfection of things. I begin to think that all explorers, all inventors, all planners even, have a glimpse of that. And that must mean that all things are interconnected as one, because that is the only way they could be perfect, the way every individual number in a complex calculation fits into the perfect solution of the problem. It doesn't disappear, but belongs to the whole. The way in Pelbar harmonies every note belongs. You can still hear the note, but it is also part of the chord."

"You are talking about a chord far too complex to hear or sing."

"For us, perhaps. For us. But there is always Aven. We look across this misty sea to where the sun strikes those fir trees, and we call it beautiful. Some say that which we see is only there, and we ourselves supply the notion of beauty. I think that the same thing that prepared the eye and mind to see beauty there provided the beauty to see. What we see is a community of trees in the repose of action, growing, holding the mist droplets blowing through their needles, swaying in the wind, all immensely complex, but all simple when seen as a oneness. Ah, there's one."

"One what? Oh. Another whale."

"Three. No. Four."

Tristal fell silent again, wondering if it were the silence of emptiness Tor spoke about. Well, who cared? Not him. He was so far from home his whole heart cried out when he thought of it.

"Tor, I can't understand you. Maybe all this is so. Maybe you are superior. But I . . . can't simply forgo things like family, the love of a woman. I'm not sterile."

"I can't understand why people keep calling me sterile. Well, maybe I can. It isn't so. But everything finds its own shape, even love. Especially love. After what my mother did, I can't . . . get myself to depend on any woman. It is a partial dependence, an individual dependence. It lacks the inner perfection by ignoring it."

"Your mother? I thought she died."

"No. It doesn't matter. She did what she felt . . . right. But it resulted in my spending much of my boyhood slaving for the Alats. It was severe enough. Then . . ."

"Then what?"

"Look. Look at my right arm. Ruthan did that. Gentle Ruthan."

"It could have happened any time, the way you've lived."

"But it didn't. And Eolyn. The lovely Eolyn. She would have killed me."

"Aven, Tor. You aren't saying you fell in love with Eolyn."

"Fell in love? Is that what it's called? I don't know. She is a kind of thinking so opposite to mine that . . . it's hard for me to conceive of it. But the poor thing. Raised underground in a dome. My heart leapt out to her. Don't wince. It's true. She was warped by it, even though so beautiful. I could have . . ."

"Could what? She thinks you're a savage."

"I know. I know. Poor Dailith. She'll chew him up— without knowing what she's doing. I could have supplied what she lacked so easily, it . . . simply confirmed me in perceiving my destiny. I'm content with it, you know."

"Your destiny! But not mine."

"No. My destiny. Your education. After all, something ought to happen to you before you become your staid, middleaged self."

"But this! All this! We're at the far edge of all Urstadge. You're insufferable. I can't believe this."

"That's what is so curious. We are at the far end of Urstadge, only to discover it isn't an end at all. It's the beginning of something else—or more of the same thing. The name is arbitrary."

Tristal looked at him in anguish and disbelief, and refused to say any more.

At dawn he woke to hear Tor say, "There's one. Another. Look. Right close in." He ran off. Tristal heard the boat grate on the rocks as he pushed it off, throwing his pack into it. He watched Tor paddle rapidly right toward the nearest whale, a large one with visible barnacles as it rolled up out of the water. Tor for a moment seemed to be right on it, crying a wild Shumai yell as its tail rose, seemed to hang right over him, and slid downward as he reached out his hand to touch it. Then the whole scene faded into a drifting mist.

Tristal called out for Tor, waiting for a reply that did not come. He called again, standing on the shore a long time. Finally he turned and mounted the rock again, seeing only then his own pack, and jutting from it, the handle of Tor's axe.

For a moment he was bewildered. He took the axe up in his hand. The sheath was with it, polished and tooled. Why had Tor left it? In his pack? Then Tristal realized— Tor had left without him, leaving him. On an island. To get home alone. Tor wanted to go on. Tristal beat his fist on the rock in rage, then took the axe and sent it spinning far out in the air, realizing, before it came down, that he would need it to build a boat, running to see where it would fall. He watched it plunge into the dark water.

He spent much of the day diving for it, finally hooking the sheath. Shivering, he brought it up to the large fire he had built. He dried himself, and the axe, in the heat, then settled down in fatigue and despair. So this was it. His education. 'Get home, Tristal. I've brought you out. Get home by yourself. Then you'll be worthy of something I think you ought to know, however much you don't feel it.'

Well, there was no way out of it. He would have to do it. He set about looking for a cedar to begin splitting for his boat.

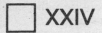 XXIV

TRISTAL'S boat was small and hurriedly built since he wanted to be on his way. It leaked. The fourth day, between islands, with a sea running, it sprang a seam, and the water began running in rapidly. Tristal stuffed a fold of leather into the opening, baled, and paddled rapidly, making it to an island exhausted and wet.

In the driving mist and rain, he made a fire only with difficulty, then warmed himself with long shivering. He stared at the boat for a long time, then took Tor's axe and chopped it up. Piece by piece he added it to the fire.

His next boat took him three more weeks of hard work. It was a single cedar log, hollowed out and shaped. He marveled at how the axe would hold an edge and could be used as a draw knife. He decided to make templates, to measure and to refine the symmetry of this boat. In the end he even added Carverlike eyes to the prow with his clasp knife.

It sat well in the water and rode high and straight. He added a short mast and a sail sewn from three sealskins. The seal meat he dried carefully and stored in a tight-topped wooden box.

Working his way south through the misty islands, he felt unutterably lonely. He saw how his uncle had not only been company, but a sort of window through which to see the shape of the place and day. Not that he himself was dull minded. He was keen-eyed and capable, but he found only a small measure of his uncle's abounding delight in his surroundings. Several times he saw whales, feeling only outrage at Tor's fascination with them. Once he found his boat surrounded with elephant seals, even, at times, pushing them away from the boat with his paddle—but without any enjoyment of their swelling presences churning the water.

At times he seemed lost in a maze of islands, but knew that if he kept his course southward, he would eventually go beyond the region where the great walls of ice were possible. Once he passed a tiny settlement of Carvers, but he kept away, and when a boat put out from the shore, he only waved his paddle aloft and kept going.

Summer was waning when he finally began to respond to the dark, wet beauty of the scenery, with misty mountains falling into the water, heavy with tall trees, with inlets and looming islands, and the great mammals of the ocean, rising and blowing, then submerging again. Sea lions rode the rocks in groups as thick, from a distance, as handfuls of bean pods, and above them clusters of gulls filled the air and limed the tops of the great boulders. Often the high-finned orcas waited for seals and sea lions offshore.

Somehow, Tristal didn't fear them. Nuchatt had said he carved their eyes on Tor's boat so the orcas would recognize him as their brother, but he knew that was only a pleasant tradition. Finally, though, he began to feel it.

Eventually he realized that the passages he was in were narrowing and had no real access to open sea. By the time he finally beached the boat as far south as he could go, the cottonwood leaves were yellowing and the evening air cooling. When the air was clear, he could see, far off to the east, a gigantic snow-covered cone, but even so he felt he was south of the great masses of ice. He decided to turn east.

The next morning, though, he was awakened by the distant barking of dogs. He rose and began a run away from them, but they drew closer. He counted nine, heading straight for him. He shot the first three with quick arrows, then unsheathed Tor's axe and killed four more as they leaped at him in a rush. The other two kept their distance, barking and howling. Tristal could hear more coming, then saw them, and men behind them armed with bows and spears. Tristal began to run south again, but the swarm of dogs finally forced him to climb a tree.

At last the men ran up, panting, and surrounded the tree. "Well, you up there. You sure killed enough dogs. Not very friendly, that. You've got a choice. Throw down those weapons and come down, or we'll shoot you out of there and let them eat you."

Tristal threw down his bow and two remaining arrows.

"The axe, too."

Tristal threw it down, feeling somehow empty.

"Now you. Climb down. You're going to go to work."

Tristal climbed down, suddenly feeling weary and futile. Had he come all this way to be killed or enslaved?

He stood in a circle of men and dogs, while one man tied his hands behind his back, beating off the dogs. Another went over his things, frowning at the clasp knife, not knowing what it was.

"Who are you?" an old man asked.

"My name is Tristal. I am a Shumai from far to the east."

"Where are the others?"

"I am alone. All alone."

"What are you doing here?"

"Trying to go home. Only trying to go home."

The man laughed. Then one of them said, "Well, you might as well forget that."

Their dialect showed some curious likenesses to that of the Soarers, though it was a bit closer to Tristal's own. As he stood there regarding them, Tristal seemed to hear Tor's voice saying, "Be patient. Be patient. Never despair. There will be a way."

They began to walk him westward, across a peninsula and toward the coast. Soon they met another party that had killed two deer, animals Tristal had never seen before. They untied his hands and made him carry one end of a pole with a deer on it.

In the evening they made him clean and butcher the deer for drying, then tied him again. Most of his captors seemed wholly indifferent to him, but Anse, the old man who questioned him first saw that he was fed then questioned him further. By nature he was kindly and curious, as well as amazed at Tristal's height and strength. On the second night, Tristal told him the Shumai names for all the stars and the Shumai speculations as to their nature and distance. Anse stared and thought, finally saying, "No. That is impious. You are in darkness. They are the souls of great ones. The rest of us are the darkness between them. So say the priests."

"The priests? I met priests of the ice far in the north. Do you know about them?"

Anse looked shocked. "No," he said, and rose to leave.

Tristal found that the old man avoided him from then on—
except to see he was fed.

In the morning, Tristal caught sight of a smoking mountain far to the south, but soon they passed into a forest and
it was lost to view. That evening they pressed on until past
dark, using a trail obviously more worn than the scant track
they had been following. Finally they emerged on an inlet
near the sea where houses and torches showed a large
settlement. One man led Tristal to a stockade near a high
cliff.

"We found this stray," he called to a guard in a bastion.
The man pushed Tristal through the log gate, then two
others led him to a rope that dangled from the top of the
cliff.

"Put your foot in that loop," one said. He loosed Tristal's
hands. "Hang on. You're going up."

They hauled on the rope, lifting Tristal to a cave pierced
in the cliff. "Get off there, sea slug," one called up to him.
Tristal stepped onto the cliff edge at the mouth of the cave
and crawled forward into utter darkness. Dimly he saw the
rope move away. It was cold and damp inside. He had not
been fed and was thirsty. Groping around, he found an old
fur robe. He curled up in it and stared at the darkness. He
was miserable.

But he roused his mind, knowing it was a time for resolve. Gritting his teeth in the blackness, he decided he
would endure whatever had to be endured. He would hold
his mind poised to be aware of any advantage, any possibility of escape, he could. He would preserve his strength
as well as he was able. He would be honorable to his fellow
captives, knowing there would be plenty of them. He would
prevail. And he would recover his axe.

For a moment all these resolves seemed absurd, but then
Tristal put that aside in his mind and took them into his
spirit. In a flash, he saw that had been Tor's attitude of
mind in the Ice Valley. There had to be a way out. But he
was approaching the sixth winter. He had a year and a half
to get home.

The next evening, standing on the rock patio outside the
cottage of Stel and Ahroe far off at Pelbarigan, Bravet
reminded Fahna of the same thing. She and Eolyn were
having tea, talking with Ahroe, the Pelbar guardchief, about

the first summer of negotiations toward forming a federation of Heart River peoples. Bravet had mounted the pathway to the cottage uninvited. He had cocked out his right hip, with its axe, and made his announcement to Fahna. She had stared at him, then dropped her eyes.

"Would you like some tea?" Stel asked.

"Tea? No. Water's good enough."

"Some water," said Ahroe. "I never liked water from prairie streams myself. Never knew what was in it, especially with all the wild cattle around."

"You've been in Shumai country?"

"Yes. With Hagen and by myself. And I've been beyond. Garet here was born in a Shumai camp. Then we came home, Stel and Garet and I, all the way from far into the western mountains. It seems an age ago. Did you like the mountains?"

"The mountains? We . . . didn't go there. Plenty of game on the prairie."

"Yes. Of course. No tea, then?"

"No." Bravet glanced at Fahna, who regarded her feet intently. Then he sauntered down the path toward Pelbarigan.

"Fahna," said Stel. "You sprout admirers the way a garden does weeds."

"Weeds," she said. "Weeds it is."

 XXV

UNTIL he thought about it, Tristal was amazed at how wholly incurious about him his captors were. He was, to them, a commodity, a means of accomplishing work.

The attitude seemed not calculated, but it was contagious. Tristal found himself alone in any obvious desire to escape. The other slaves, ninety-two living in the high caves, and a few others coming from and going to far off work, seemed largely impassive. Almost all of them were shorter, darker-skinned people, not unlike the Carvers, though those people, as Nuchatt had explained, had long ago developed means of defense that rendered them immune from capture from raiders. A few slaves were black-skinned, and some had light skin and various shades of brown and red hair.

The enslavers called themselves the Iyunwah and their habitation Shagrock. It was a place of geological tumult near the sea, occupying the flat land adjoining a small inlet and the surrounding hills and cliffs. The slave cliffs were separated from the shore by a rocky hill, so Tristal learned little about the Iyunwah community itself, which lay on the western slope leading to the stony beach. Earth tremors were common, and one of Tristal's early terrors was that the rock face of the cliff on which he lived would shift some night and the roof would subside, crushing him.

At first, Tristal was put to copper mining with most of the other slaves, but as autumn advanced, they dug potatoes in the wide fields near the stream that entered the inlet. These were sorted and stored underground, the poor ones being saved for the slaves. Turnips were also grown and stored, as were beans and corn. The slaves helped with fishing and drying the catch. They had plenty to eat, mostly fish and potatoes, because the Iyunwah, who thought of themselves as an intelligent people of enterprise and leisure, regarded this not only as humane but also sensible, since it maintained the strength of their workers.

Tristal had not been there long, though, when he saw a slave severely lashed for obeying a command slowly and, it was said, insolently. For the Iyunwah, the beating was simply discipline necessary for keeping order. They didn't think of it as cruelty.

After that, Tristal resolved to be of as little notice as possible. This was difficult because of his size and yellow-blond hair and beard, but he compensated for it by attempting diffident obedience. He found it hard, though, not to adopt this attitude within himself and become simply a slave, especially as winter set in, with its infinite boredom, its fog and rain, slack tide and full, the endless slop and wash of gray water, the undulating of the limp kelp—vegetation trying to become water, the rocks and forest soggy, his Ice Valley wool shirt always wet, always smelly, the fires all smoky, even the waves themselves beaten by rain.

At night especially, he felt despair. Unlike the other

slaves, he occupied a small cave alone at the end of the line. He came in tired from the day's work, only to have the Iyunwah guard lower the ropes from their pulleys at the top of the cliff, which was sheer and about forty-five arms high. Being so large, Tristal generally had to haul many of the slaves up to their caves, trudging away with the rope as they stood in the loop at the end. He himself usually went up last, pulled up by five guards.

Once, toward the end of his lifting slaves, he slipped and almost dropped a man. He was beaten for that, but he was also given some help.

The other slaves were hesitant to trust Tristal; he was an anomaly, perhaps even an informer, and they tended to isolate him. Perhaps that helped him not to give in to his situation, though, since he had no company to make his enslavement convivial. It was oppression from beginning to end. But he saw no chance to escape.

In spite of his continuing anger at what he saw as Tor's unconscionable abandonment, he found himself asking, on winter nights in the entire blackness of his cave, what Tor would have done. He knew his uncle would think, would create mathematical games, would observe stars, and all these he did as well. He also saw that Tor would pray, and this Tristal avoided, not through a purposeful distaste, but because it seemed to him irrelevant. But as winter grew old, and seemed to continue forever, Tristal began going over the set prayers of the Pelbar and Shumai as well as he could. He found them of little use, even when he tried to think them out.

He finally gave it up in favor of disciplines of the mind and body he could practice at work and in private. The other slaves began to resent the force and accuracy of his arching blows with the rock hammer when they wedged chunks of ore off the walls of the pits.

"Easy," one would say. "No hurry. We have all our lives."

Tristal would smile slightly and slow down for a while, but then the idea of the perfection of the act of hammering began to fascinate him again, more than going easy on himself or covertly resisting the Iyunwah.

Finally an older man, wrinkled and leathery, sat by him at their noon break. "You want to work less, yellow-hair."

"Work less?"

"Don't know why you do it. But they notice. Never good to be noticed by the Iyunwah. Always trouble."

"Why are you telling me?"

"Trouble for one is trouble for all. I see you're not making problems on purpose. No need. Besides..."

Tristal looked at him.

"You're Shumai. I've seen Shumai. I'm not one of these north coast fishermen. I'm Forman—from east of here. Got in trouble and had to run. I ran too far. But that was long, long ago. I'd like to go home before I die. Never thought of it until I saw you."

"How do you know I'm going?"

The man chuckled. "You're Shumai. You have the wild spirit. I see it when you hit the rock rod. Every strike is the swing of an axe to you. But you can't do it. You are letting them know, too. Swing like a slave, but don't think like a slave."

"That what you do?"

"No. I tried. It went to sleep through the years. You've aroused it. You'll find a way out. I want to go. Take your time. You get only one chance, then they hang you on the pole inside the stockade to die slowly and rot in front of all the night caves. The smell of death sometimes fills the caves at night. Hard to breathe. Impossible to forget. Very effective. In all the years I've been here, I've seen only four people hung up like that. The others remember. They tell the new ones. Know why you're alone?"

"No. The others don't like me. They don't want trouble."

"Not it. The Iyunwah fear your effect on the others. Even when you try to be like a slave, you aren't. They're watching. Even when they seem not to notice."

"What's your name?"

"Rizon."

"Tristal."

"I know." The man rose, dusted his leggings, and sauntered away to work.

Spring seemed to delay endlessly, as further fogs and cold rains swept in from the sea, but finally the weather moderated and the trees and grasses began to respond. For Tristal it was a time of even greater stress, as he watched the stars shift and finally knew he had exactly one year to get home. It seemed wholly impossible. He was no nearer escape than he had been. He knew there were mountains to the east and didn't want to cross them in winter. Much further delay would mean hard winter travel. He tried again to pray.

Far to the east at Pelbarigan, Fahna also watched the stars approach and pass the spring equinox. She stayed close to Eolyn, the dome woman, avoiding company. When Bravet came with his growing band, largely composed now of restless young men, she managed to avoid him. He hung around for two days, restless and angry, but finally had to leave for the summer hunt so his followers wouldn't think him weak. But on the morning of their departure, the Pelbar found the number one scratched in stone walls, drawn in giant figures in the river mud, put on scraps of paper on trees, and even hung in a great banner from the top of a tree on one of the river islands.

A few guardsmen knew what it meant, so soon the whole city knew. Fahna remained more secluded than ever. Eolyn kept her continually busy.

☐ XXVI

TRISTAL was swinging his heavy mattox in a potato field as the commotion filtered faintly up from the inlet. The Iyunwah were cheering the departure of six slavers, large, low sailing vessels on their way to scour the far north for fishermen to capture. Tristal stretched his back, looking, then went back to his rhythmic chopping before the overseer could chastise him. Inside he felt a deeper bitterness toward these strange people, with their entire blindness toward their captives.

For a moment he felt inclined to send the slavers off with a curse of the priests of the ice. Tristal was overwhelmed by vitriolic rancor when he thought of his situation and how Tor had in a sense abandoned him to it. But then he seemed to see Tor's face and hear him ask, "Where is your honor, your sense of truth, your justice, your love?"

"What chance have I at them?" he said aloud, then looked sideways as several nearby slaves paused to look at him.

"Keep at it. Silence," said a nearby guard patrolling with two of the enormous Iyunwah dogs.

Tristal wondered if he was going mad. He would have to assert a greater self-control. Just then his mattox struck a round, alluvial stone, splitting it cleanly, like one of the stones Tegrit worked. In an instant Tristal wondered where his mind had been—he was surrounded by the material of tools and weapons! He wished now he'd paid more attention to Tor and Tegrit, though he had worked at tool making some in the Ice Valley prison. Here was a real start at resistance. First he would have to enlarge the hidden storage chamber in his cave to keep materials in. With stone tools, he could make other weapons. He would be infinitely careful. But he had less than a year to get home. It couldn't take too long.

That afternoon, two guards came and pulled him aside. He was needed for gravedigging duty. That he had done before, high on the rocky headland over the inlet where the Iyunwah buried the common people. Digging was difficult, and it promised to take him well into the evening. There was also danger; he had heard of cases where the Iyunwah, drunk from the mourning party, would kill the slave who dug the grave and throw him in the pit with the coffin.

It was past slavesupper when Tristal, nearly finished, learned that the grave was for Anse, the old man who had been with the hunters who captured him and the only Iyuwah who had ever shown interest in him as a human. Somehow this brought a further sinking of his spirit.

Soon the burial party was toiling up the hill, led by a young priest whose dress, Tristal noticed, was astonishingly like that of the priests of the ice. He suddenly realized why Anse was shocked when Tristal had mentioned them—the northern group might somehow be an offshoot of Iyunwah.

He knew nothing of Iyunwah religion other than that they had one but seemed very lax in its observance. The priest was scarcely more than a boy, slim and brown-haired. He carried the long chain of his office, swinging it like a pendulum before him and singing in a toneless chant. The mourners straggled along behind him. Tristal noticed with alarm that they lurched and stumbled as they made their way. He thought he saw some apprehension in the priest's face as well.

They reached the graveside and dumped the coffin on the unmounded side. The young priest held up his hands for silence, but the mourners kept muttering. Finally he began a set speech, which he recited very rapidly, too rapidly for Tristal to pick up clearly. It was something about joining the forces of the world until somehow "it is determined that Anse is to be another star or one of the dark spaces between—"

"Yeah, yeah, Ambel. We know all that. Sure Anse is going to be"—the drunken young man paused and spat— "one of the stars. A big one. One of the very biggest." The crowd laughed.

"You must show respect for your own dead," the priest said, somewhat plaintively.

"Respect for the dead. Respect for the dead," an old woman shrilled. "You call that empty basket of words respect for the dead? That slave could make a better speech. You..." Her voice died off as she clung to a young woman in slightly tipsy grief.

"Yeah. Get the slave. Let him talk. Get away, priest. Ambel down the hill." The crowd laughed again.

A fat man from the back said, "Yeah. Let the slave talk. If we don't like it, we can dump him in with Anse. Then the priest on top of them."

"The slave. The slave," another voice yelled from the back. He was joined by a general clamor. A dirt clod arced over the pile Tristal had made and splatted into the young priest's face, cutting his lip. He began to back up, wiping his eyes, as several men chanted, "In the hole with the priest. In the hole with the priest." He finally cleared his eyes, turned, and fled down the hill, pursued by several mourners. All but one fell down in their drunkenness. That one caught up with the young man, and for a time the whole group stood watching the two wrestle on the ground, the priest's robes now torn and begrimed, as two guards ran up the hill toward the pair. They all stared as the guards separated the two. One led the mourner back up the hill, to general laughter.

"Hey, Alby, that was pretty good," one man called. "You can almost crunch a priest. Some fighting that."

"All right," the guard said. "Do what you want with slaves, but any more of this brawling and you'll all be pulling plows. You'll be paying a triple priest fee. One more word about it and it'll double again."

Another clod of mud soared over the pile. The guard ducked, drew a curved sword, and rushed forward. The mourners scattered. The man then stood on the pile and addressed them. "I've warned you." He put his sword away. "If I draw this again, there'll be blood on it before it's sheathed." He looked around. The crowd stood silently, as though strangely balanced, afraid to move lest they fall. The guard then turned and strode down the hill, saying over his shoulder, "Just bury your man and get it over with."

As the guard grew more distant, one man began to laugh. "The slave. Let the slave give the oration," he shouted.

Tristal gripped the shovel, but he knew he would have no chance against the crowd if they really wanted to kill him. As the murmuring group turned toward him, he heard a bird below piping in the bushes and found himself astonished at listening to it. In a flash he remembered what Tor had said about everything singing itself.

He laid down the shovel and raised his hands. "All right. I will give you the oration," he said quietly. He stepped up on the dirt pile. "This man, Anse, is the only one of you who ever showed the slightest kindness toward me. He saw I was fed when I was captured, and he tested my wrist cords to see I didn't lose my hands. He was a good man, as far as any of you know how to be good."

"Keep that up and you'll be in the hole," one man growled.

"Quiet!" the old woman yelled. "Let him talk. At least something will be said at Anse's burial."

"I gather that you think death is the end of things, except for the talk about becoming stars or darkness. You know well that is just talk. The Shumai, my people, know the stars enough to tell when a new one appears. That almost never happens, and when it does, they last only a short time. But death is not the end.

"I know you might like some evidence of that assertion, and who can give that clearly? We have only hints and surmises. But some of them are good ones. I would like to tell you about several of the best.

"First, an example. I came here from far to the north, where my uncle and I had traveled from a great distance to the east, passing over ice barriers and living between two of them for some time. My uncle is the best man I ever knew, though I've been angry with him often enough. He cared for me after my parents were lost to a prairie fire."

"A what? What's that?"

"Quiet, sea slug," the old woman said.

"When we reached the sea and made a small boat, my uncle Tor became fascinated with whales. The Carvers had told us of them, but only when he saw them did he realize how immense they were. One morning he paddled off into the mist following one and never returned.

"I have no doubt that he is still alive. But he is dead to me. I do not grieve for him, though, as one does for the dead. He simply had an interest, and pursuing it took him beyond my interests, beyond my horizon.

"It is the same with Anse. Think of it this way. He has had an interest that has taken him away, never to return. We also have hints as to what that interest is. We watch people age. Perhaps we might think of aging as resulting from the body's inability to sustain itself. No. This is not so. It is the growing dissatisfaction of every person with the limitations of the world. He doesn't even realize he is dissatisfied. But he is. His body shows it. His mind is turning elsewhere, and the body reacts by diminishing."

"What a pile of crap!" the man called Alby shouted.

"Quiet, you stinking brawler!" the old woman yelled back.

"His body diminishes because it sees itself as less necessary. The spirit instinctively understands its dissatisfaction with the body, and since that is what animates it in the first place, the body begins to sink away like an empty waterskin.

"You may think that is fanciful, and perhaps it is, but it agrees with another hint. We see our fellows as qualities. In the short time I was near the deceased, I saw the qualities of curiosity, kindness, awareness, concern, sturdiness, and selflessness—all rare enough ones among you."

"Cut that, you yellow-haired pile of fish entrails."

"These qualities never leave us. They arise, re-form themselves, appear over and over. They are closer to our identity than the shape of our nose, the color of our hair, our station in society. They are us. Wherever I see kindness, I know the presence of Anse, because that which he embodied is there. Wherever I see concern, he is there, too. Not because he owned those qualities, but because they owned him. They are a larger thing than humans.

"These things are not only limited to humans, but are found throughout the world around us. The mother bird feeding her young is simply another voice of the quality of love. The wild rose radiates the qualities of gentleness and beauty. We know this because all our poetry associates things which may appear to be different but which share these qualities. Even the most degraded people exhibit them. They are the stuff and fiber of being. They show at base the . . . singleness of all good things."

Tristal fell silent without thinking about it. He had been desperately making up talk to calm the Iyunwah and forestall any attempt to kill and bury him. In the process he had wandered onto the thing Tor had tried to tell him over and over. In this context he found himself believing it. He desperately tried to think of something else to say. He bowed his head and said, "As you lower your friend into the grave, you are only taking the final step which he began, as you all have as well, long ago, of moving beyond the body.

"Anse has done that. He is through with his body. He does not need it anymore. But you are not through with him. You will see him when you are kind, when you are curious. You will deny him, kill him, when you are cruel and dull. No one wants to feel himself cruel. Or dull. Or nasty. That is a good thing and shows our love for the identity which speaks through us. That is the way Anse is still alive and the way you can keep him alive in your thought. Because it is not him you keep alive only. It is yourselves and all things. You are illustrating your oneness with them. Now, perhaps he has been kept waiting long enough and would like his body to be put out of sight so his loved ones can become more aware of the true part of him."

Tristal clasped his hands in front of him and looked down, wondering what would happen next.

"You're just saving your own life, entrails," a fat man muttered.

"Shut your fat mouth and put Anse in the grave," the old woman shrilled. "You've just heard the best oration ever and you want to smear it up!"

Several people laughed and moved toward Anse's coffin, lowering it into the grave and throwing handfuls of dirt on it. They seemed more sober. As evening deepened, they shuffled down the hill and left Tristal to fill the hole alone. He began. His hands trembled at first. Then fear subsided in him. What had he said? Where had it come from? What did it mean? He wasn't sure that he believed it, either, but he knew it had saved his life.

Before he finished, a guard with a dog trudged up the hill for him. The man had food. Tristal had thought he would miss his supper, as was usually the case, but he was being given seal meat, well cooked and seasoned, and potatoes in a delicious sauce.

The guard stood in silence as he ate it, then said, "You. Clean yourself up now. You're to see Governor Watomie."

Tristal had not so much as heard of a governor. Whatever it meant, he was sure it wasn't good. The cardinal rule of being a slave is going unnoticed, and seeing a governor was a poor way to do that.

He was more sure of it when he walked up the wide stone steps of the governor's house, between guards, and passed by the great carved doors. He was then led down a corridor, with people watching him, and halted in front of another set of doors. Here a red-haired guard clamped copper handcuffs on him and the doors were opened on a large, stone-floored room with high windows on three sides. The right wall was divided by a gallery held up by enormous, intricately carved wooden columns. Ahead of him stood a dais on which a long-faced man sat behind an ornate table with a carved front embossed with hammered copper. The man wore a finely woven robe, dark blue with white piping. Around his neck a heavy copper chain hung, with a medallion that rested on the desk in front of him. The man motioned to the guards to bring Tristal forward. When Tristal came close, the man rested his chin on his hand looking at him.

"You," he began, in a deep, gravelly voice. "I hear that you gave a fine funeral oration. I wish to hear about it."

"I . . . only said what came to mind to keep them from killing me. It was nothing, I'm sure."

"I've been told the ideas in it already. Even though the Campban family was drunk, we are a people of ideas, and we don't forget them. Very interesting. Where did you learn those things?"

"Sir, I've traveled a long way and lived among a variety of people. I just said what came to mind. The Pelbar know far more about such things than I ever will. The Ice Valley people—"

"The Pelbar? Who are they?"

"They live far to the east, across the mountains and plains on the Heart River."

"You came from there?"

"Not directly, sir. I went with my uncle to see the ice country. Eventually we went all the way to the seacoast, and then I came down here and have become your slave."

"How far is it?"

"I think about two thousand ayas, which is about thirty-two hundred kilometers."

"What is it in tidespans?"

"I don't know, sir. I've never measured in them."

The governor tapped his fingers. "Well, I've been asked by the Campbans to reward you. What reward would you wish?"

"Reward? To be given my axe and be let go, certainly."

The governor regarded his fingernails. "You have asked for two rewards. Which would you prefer?"

Tristal hesitated. Of course he wanted to go, but it seemed impossible for him to leave without Tor's axe, irrational as he knew that to be.

"Perhaps then I could ask to be left as I was before your people found me."

"That's very clever indeed. Tell me, why is the axe so important? It makes a fine wall decoration but seems not worth freedom."

Tristal followed the governor's gaze and saw the axe hanging on the south wall, on the face of the gallery. His heart surged and he felt his own muscles knot up.

"It isn't important. I will go without the axe if that is all that's possible. It's a symbol, the Shumai spirit of liberty."

"The spirit of liberty? That's not a real answer to my question, slave."

"The axe was my uncle's. It's all I have from him. It's . . . a badge of office—or used to be. I am a Shumai, and my uncle carried it as the leader of a band of hunters."

At that point another earth tremor shook the hall, at first slightly, then with increasing force. The governor gripped the table in alarm. Tristal stood as he was impassively. Finally the tremor subsided and the governor regained his composure.

He stared briefly at Tristal, then said, "If we were to give you the axe without freedom, then of course it would immediately revert to us, since slaves hold no property— especially such dangerous property. If we were to free you, you would of course have to leave all your clothing, since that is ours, and when you stepped from this room and building, you would be rearrested for indecency and would give up your freedom. You must learn to choose modestly."

"Choose modestly? Is that the purpose of this charade? What would you suggest, sir?"

The governor rose, angry. "Charade?"

"Does that offend you? I'm not sure what it means, really. It's what the Pelbar call a pointless game. But if I must choose modestly, perhaps then I would like another seal meat dinner sometime. If that's acceptable."

The governor stared at him until Tristal dropped his eyes. At last he said, "It is acceptable. Guards—remove him. Squadleader, stay." He clapped his hands, and the two guards yanked Tristal around and led him out. After he had gone, the governor regarded the squadleader silently, finally saying, "That man is dangerous. He must be watched."

"He's never given the slightest trouble, governor."

"All the more. He has a mind. He's been places, seen things. He wants to be free. If you must, find an excuse or two to beat him. If things seem even slightly wrong, hang him up to rot."

The squadleader shuddered. "You have no idea how bad that smells, governor."

"Do it."

"Yes. Of course. If anything seems even slightly wrong."

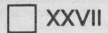 **XXVII**

It was midsummer. Tristal's arms were stretched wide, over limbs, with ropes held by guards. An overseer counted as a third guard whistled the whip across his back. It was the third time he had been beaten, always on minor pretexts. Tristal had given them no cause they knew of to punish him.

"Twelve. Enough," the overseer cried. The guards let go of the ropes and Tristal slumped to the ground, rolling over onto his wounds, wincing, rolling back away, the bloody welts now covered with dust.

"Up now. Back to work. No more shirking," the overseer barked. Tristal struggled to his feet. The guards removed the loops from his wrists. One man handed him a copper-headed hoe. The whole scene seemed to whirl around with frantic pain for Tristal. He took the hoe and walked to his row, the guards watching. Tristal began chopping weeds in the potatoes, faltered, straightened, began again.

"How can he do it? He's one tough man," a guard muttered.

"Nothing wrong with him. A pity. A fine man. Too fine to be a slave. I feel rotten about this."

"Governor's orders. He's only a slave."

"I know. But it stinks."

Somehow Tristal made it through the day, and when the slaves were herded to the shallow draft boat he took his place at the oar bank, keeping himself from wincing only by gritting his teeth. The center of the boat was occupied by a party of nine Iyunwah, a family and friends who had been on a day outing. They laughed and chatted until one of the women glanced at Tristal's back and gasped. The others turned and looked. Then they turned away. The overseer sensed their silence and felt a tide of anger rise.

214

He had only done his job. The damned yellow-hair always made trouble, just by being around.

One of the passengers, a girl about nine, began to cry, then stumbled across the boat toward her mother, tripped on a thwart, and fell over the side with a hollow splash.

"Hold, hold!" the overseer shouted. The oarsmen paused. The girl's mother shrieked. The girl must have gone under the boat. Several moments passed as all stood, nonplussed. Then Tristal stood up and dove over the side. The guards sprang up and drew their curved swords.

One shouted, "No one else move or you die right now."

The boat drifted, turning slowly, as the girl's mother wept and everyone watched the surface. Nothing came up as enough time passed for a small flock of gulls to fly slowly overhead, crying harshly, swerving away from the boat, and heading north.

Tristal swam down into the murky water where he thought the girl had fallen, reaching and groping. But he found nothing. His back stung and his lungs began to strain. Still his reaching arms found nothing. He grew desperate, saying silently, "Aven, Sertine, Lord, whatever you are, ordering and governing, you have to help this girl. You have to. There is no other possibility. It is all that order can bring into experience." Still his waving arms found nothing. He turned to swim out a little before his lungs, crying for air, would force him to the surface. Suddenly he found the girl's heel in his hand. He gathered her in and scissored rapidly toward the surface.

Behind the boat the water suddenly surged as Tristal appeared clutching the girl.

"Backwater! Easy now!" the overseer shouted. The boat was brought alongside. Tristal grasped the gunwale as guards leaned over and lifted the girl into the boat.

"You. Climb in or be left," the overseer shouted.

Tristal looked up, his mouth wide open as he gasped for breath. He tried four times to lift himself over the side but couldn't. The girl's mother shrieked. "She's not breathing. She's dead."

A guard leaned down toward Tristal, who gasped. "The girl. Lie her down. Help me in. She'll breathe." The guard looked at the overseer, who nodded. Tristal was hauled into the boat. He slid over the near oarsmen and crawled toward the girl.

"No. Here. Like this." He rearranged her, knelt by her side, faltered, still panting hard. Then he felt her neck for a pulse and said, "Good. There's heartbeat." Then he leaned over her, cleaned out her mouth, tilted back her head, and breathed into her, pinching her nose shut. He set up his rhythm, his chest heaving, gesturing one of the men of the party to sit across from him, and working him into the rhythm. He rechecked the girl's pulse. The process continued, the Iyunwah taking over. Every time Tristal leaned forward his ruined back exposed its watery red to the circle of viewers. It intensified the mother's distress, and she sobbed continually. At one point Tristal, looking up, caught the eye of two of the slaves at an oar. They were angry with him. He couldn't help that. He never could be sure of any of them anyhow.

"Let her alone. It's unseemly. She's gone," the overseer said.

"Sometimes it takes many sunwidths," said Tristal. "You can't give up until you know she's gone. She has a pulse. Put your hand there. You can feel it."

The overseer glared at him. "I'm sorry," Tristal said. "She's only a girl. She deserves a life. I hope you'll forgive me my disobedience. When God, whom the Pelbar call Aven, led me down through the water and put her heel into my hand, I knew then she would be saved. But we have to carry it through."

"Let him alone!" the mother shrilled at the overseer. "Can't you see he's trying to help?" The man turned angrily away.

Soon the boat came alongside the dock and the slaves were led off. "Don't break the rhythm," Tristal said to the man. "I have to go."

"You can't go," the mother shrieked.

"Whatever you say," Tristal replied.

"You, Noute—stay and guard him. Bring him back when this is settled." With that the overseer turned his back on them and left.

Tristal shivered in the cold wind, but no one seemed to notice. The process continued as the sun waned. Finally the girl coughed, and Tristal held out his hand, stopping the man who was trying to resuscitate her. The girl coughed again, retching and gasping, then opened her eyes, as her mother caught her up. Tristal looked up at the guard, who jerked his head at him. Tristal climbed the ladder to the dock and walked ahead of the guard down the dock. The world began to swim again, but he forced it back to steadiness.

"I don't understand you," the guard said.

"I needed to wash my back."

Once again Tristal stood in the governor's chamber flanked by guards. "I don't ever recall a slave brought before me twice," the long faced man began. "It seldom happens once. But again I have been asked to reward you. I trust you understand what modesty is in such things."

Tristal smiled slightly. "Yes. I do. Might I rest in the cave until my back heals, please? I hope that is modest."

"It is. You may do that." He began to wave his hand to dismiss Tristal and his guards, then paused. "If—"

"Yes?"

"If you answer a few things. This axe. You said it represented the..."

Tristal filled the governor's pause. "The Shumai spirit of liberty? Only to me, sir. It's only an axe, a tool."

"Poorly designed, too."

Tristal smiled. "Yes," he said. "But if you hold the wings of the blade, you can use it as a draw knife. If you strike with the center, you won't destroy the wings."

The governor regarded him drily. "Don't be ingenuous. I know what it did to the dogs."

"Yes. They were careless dogs. They mistook me for a gopher."

"Of course. Now, the other thing. On the boat, you said that God led you down to the girl, Dacey. What did you mean?"

"I—I don't know. An extraordinary thing. Everybody was just standing there like posts. I suddenly realized you were all cold-water people and probably didn't swim. I swam down without knowing where she was. I felt *guided* to her. It was dark, my eyes were weeping with salt and cold, my back felt like fire, and I asked in my anxiety to be guided to the girl."

"That's nonsense, you know."

"No doubt. It seems so, doesn't it? I don't understand it. She must be beloved of something powerful, though, when so poor an instrument as I was allowed to lift her up out of the water."

The governor regarded him coolly. There seemed nothing else to say. Inside, he felt a kernel of fear seem to burst, slight but unmistakable. It was like an earth tremor, but within. "You've done this before, then?"

"I've tried. It never happened. It was a matter of wanting, though."

"Ah. You mean if you wanted to be free hard enough, it would happen."

"I don't think so."

"You don't?"

"No. It is a righting of balances, of order. It isn't a matter of personal benefits. I think. I don't know. Certainly you know more about these things than I."

The governor regarded him in silence. "You may rest until your back heals. That is a modest request."

"Thank you, sir." Tristal bowed slightly, and as the guards marched him out the door, the governor saw the red bands of his wounds spotting through his fresh shirt.

The governor sat in the flaring lamps, staring at Tor's axe high on the wall. An orderly asked if he wanted anything, but he waved her away. Another slight earth tremor shook the building. The governor saw the axe tremble slightly on the wall. It was too late now. With a single act, Tristal had made it nearly impossible to hang him up to rot. The Campbans and now the Lotts would rebel at that. Well, he was just a slave. He seemed willing enough to work. Perhaps it was a needless worry. And yet . . .

High in his cave the next day, in sunlight, Tristal shaved the stock of his crossbow with a fresh stone knife. He would give himself two days, then return to work. If he were to make it back, he'd have to start soon. Still he had no plans. And he felt feverish. They had pushed his body very far and it seemed to be reacting.

Once again he paused. He had told the governor the truth. His *wanting* had led him down to young Dacey Lott. He had not simply asked his prayer. It had been a yearning. Is that what Tor had meant all along? It was hard to say. Perhaps it was just coincidence, too. After all, he had marked where the girl went down, and anyone who had dived in the muddy Heart River had practice in finding things purely by instinct and feel.

Tristal wiped his brow. It seemed oddly sweaty. He felt dizzy. He pulled aside the rock door and deposited his tools and materials inside the storage chamber. Then he looked at it. No, it could not be detected. He lay down, as the cave seemed to eddy and churn. It was not an earth tremor. Something was wrong.

Four weeks later Tristal still lay in his cave, cadaverously thin, but recovering. The young priest, Ambel, sat by him, having brought him food.

"Who is Fahna?" he asked.

"Fahna? A young woman."

"You love her?"

"I . . . suppose so. I'm promised to her. Was. It looks like that is over."

"Yes. Are you well enough to tell me more about what you said at the burial?"

"I've told you everything. You're the priest. You're supposed to know about such things."

"I don't. I don't think any one of us does. Religion and philosophy mean little to us—just forms politely adhered to, a fuss made so we will think certain events have formal significance. Nothing more. For you it is a living fire."

"Hardly. I haven't taken to it as some know it. I'm only a baby. When you go, please tell the guards I think I can work tomorrow. I thank them and you for keeping me alive while I was ill."

"You won't tell me then. You mean to use it as a weapon against us. I guess we deserve it."

"One thing I'm sure of is that no good thing can be used that way. It only works in favor of people. They fall afoul of it when they go against the welfare of everyone. You Iyunwah are faltering as a society. You are in decline. You cannot last. No one needs to act against you. You've acted against yourselves by your oppressions."

"You don't understand."

"Probably not."

Outside Ambel heard a distant shouting. He stooped to the mouth of the cave and looked out, shading his eyes. "The slavers are returning." He paused. "Only two. They are late and there are only two."

He called the guard and they lowered him on the rope. Tristal rose and walked unsteadily to the cave mouth. Far off, coming around the rise to the west and into the inlet were the two slave ships he had seen leave earlier. They must have traveled more or less the same route he used coming south the previous year, then gone beyond. Only two of six? Suddenly Tristal chuckled to himself. He knew as well as if he had been there that somehow Tor had a hand in that.

Then his bleakness returned. He knew that with his condition and situation, he would never make it back to Northwall by the spring equinox. As he leaned on the rock wall, it trembled under his shoulder.

He sat a long time in the entrance, leaning back, as guards, with dogs, were bringing the new slaves to the compound by the cliff face. Twenty-two new people had been torn from their lives for the benefit of the Iyunwah. Shading his eyes, Tristal could see three women among them. All were dark-skinned, with long black hair, like most of the present slave population. Tristal knew the Iyunwah had been hoping for at least four or five times that many to replace the dwindling slave supply, for in spite of all the efforts of the Iyunwah, the slaves refused to breed.

Some time later, in the dusk, Tristal's loop was lowered and a new slave forced to stand in it. The guards hauled the rope. Tristal stood to help the new person, and as he reached out he was surprised to find a woman, younger than he. That complicated everything. Perhaps it was hopeless to think of escape. They would have something in mind, putting her with him—perhaps she was an informer.

Her name, she said, was Tingli. She and her brother, Unger, had been captured in the early summer when the Iyunwah made a quick raid on their island village. They had never before had to defend themselves and so had offered little resistance.

But as the slavers moved west among the islands, they had found only abandoned villages, eventually realizing that the villagers were fleeing their homes ahead of the invaders. The slavers captured only one more fisherman, and he said that a one-armed man had convinced them to set up sea-watches and establish food caches and escape routes.

Eventually the slavers had found a village that seemed

peaceful and unaware, but when four of the Iyunwah boats beached on the rocky shore and stormed the still houses, they were met with a flight of arrows and fish spears. They tried to shrug off the initial shock, but they had lost a full third of their men and half the dogs. They fell back toward their ships, but by then a cloud of small skin-covered boats had paddled around a point and headed for them. Tingli watched the sharp flight from offshore until the Iyunwah made the captives kneel with their faces to the planking. But she could hear the shouting and screaming, and smell the burning Iyunwah ships.

Then the fishermen turned toward the remaining two slaver craft and the slaves were made to sit up and row. Tingli said her heart leaped with pride at the villagers' defenses even though she was lost herself. She thought they would be the end of the periodic slave raids.

Tingli had been hurt when captured, and she had not mended fully. "We will be infirm together," Tristal told her. "I will be your brother."

"That is not what they hope. You see, we will not..."

"I know. Neither will I. Your people don't trust me anyway. I don't need any more hatred."

That night, with Tingli's head pillowed on his bony shoulder, Tristal stared into the dark. How could he finish his crossbow bolts with a stranger present? He was losing his chance to keep his promise. He sensed this more strongly every day. Tingli squirmed a little, pressing her round cheek against him. He felt her weight sharply in his back, but he held himself against moving and disturbing her.

Bravet's band was growing. They returned early from the summer hunt, heavy with hides and dried meat. Several fights at Northwall resulted from the scorn of the old hunters for the swaggering young men, cocksure and muscular. They would have none of Pelbar softness. The old Shumai way was superior. They enjoyed impressing young women, but seemed unable to convince any to join them; hide scraping and childbearing out on the vast plains had little appeal.

Bravet himself left for Pelbarigan, seeking Fahna, only to learn that she was living in the Protector's apartment and working with Eolyn. In some way she eluded him while getting from one place to the other. The young hunter grew more frustrated and angry as he realized the guardsmen were watching him with slight amusement.

His third evening in the Pelbar capital, he wandered down to the riverbank where a small cluster of men were working on an experimental boat of some kind. It looked very strange. As he walked around it, frowning, his eyes met those of Stel Westrun, and the Pelbar builder invited him to sit on the framework and share some tea.

"No, water's good enough," Bravet said.

"Come. This is just flavored water. Got honey in it and some herbs. Are you in a hurry? Here. Got some cakes, too."

On an impulse, Bravet put his hands up on the boat ribbing and vaulted lightly up by Stel.

"How was the hunting this summer?" Stel asked.

"All right. Plenty of wild cattle. Very easy now. Some wild horses now, too."

"Be here long?"

Bravet looked at him narrowly. "You know why I'm here. You all know. It's fishgutted poor to make fun."

Stel put his hand on Bravet's arm. "No. No fun. You need to understand, though. She will do her own choosing. She has chosen. No one knows why people choose the way they do. But her choice is made. You can't change it. You have to make another choice."

"Have you seen her? There is no other."

"She is lovely, isn't she? But you don't marry loveliness. You marry a person, a background, a family, tastes, fears, awarenesses, weaknesses. I know you won't believe that—until you are older. Her choice was made before you came. And when you came, you used an approach . . . well, you must see she has always been stared at, slathered after. Only Tristal didn't. He was shy and friendly. His mind was elsewhere. She chose for him. You have to understand that. Let it go. Here. Have another cake?"

"What kind of a fungussniffing choice is that? I understand she simply told him he was hers as he was leaving. And he hasn't been around for almost the full time. He won't come. He may be dead somewhere. He may have forgotten. Who knows? All this time she stays so muddigging remote from everybody. Wants to die virgin. A waste."

"Would you take her out on the prairies to run in the heat and rain? Ahroe might do that awhile, but not Fahna."

"The guardchief? You know her?"

"Yes. Don't you see?"

"I would give it all up tomorrow for her."

"It's what you are now. You are too deep into it. You can't become something else. I'm afraid, Bravet."

"Afraid?"

"Of what might happen. You won't harm her...will you? You have to know that she is loved. She is Jestak's child. The whole wide plains won't hide you if anything happens to her."

Bravet looked at Stel and then spat off the side of the boat into the mud. "So that's the way it is, is it?"

"Yes. That's the way it is."

"I suppose you would come after me."

"If it came to that."

"What good would that do, old man?" Bravet jumped lightly down from the boat.

"Maybe none," said Stel. "But I would come."

☐ XXVIII

IT was late winter and the rain drove down steadily. The smell of death filled the slave caves. Rizon, who had been roused to the thought of freedom by Tristal, despaired of following him when he grew ill. So he had tried it on his own, but the dogs had caught him on the third day. It hadn't taken him long to die on the pole, ripped as he had been. Now he hung there, black and bloated, disgusting even the guards with the intolerable rankness of decay.

Tingli was still with Tristal. They had developed a relationship of fraternal trust and respect. On Tingli's part this was mingled with awe when she realized that the Tor Tristal spoke of was the man who had saved her people. Tristal made her promise to tell no one because if she did somebody was sure to inform on him, bringing down more beatings and perhaps death.

She assured him that no one would do that.

"But look at Rizon rotting out there. Someone told on him. He would have had another quarter morning."

"But they would have known that Agli was aware of it. If Rizon escaped, Agli would have been hanging there."

"Even so."

She turned her back on him. He paid little attention. "I have to work on my bow bolts. You going to tell?"

"I hate you."

"All right. I'm used to that."

"No, I won't. No. But you have to take me when you go."

"Take you?"

"If you don't, they will know I kept secret your weapon. I will hang there."

"Not if you tell them it was hidden and must have been made before you came."

"But the bowstring is made of my braided hair?"

"It could be anyone's. Most people have black. Besides, if I'm successful, the bow will be with me."

"Why do you fight it, Tristal? You are the leader. You've said yourself you can't get back in time. Do what . . . what's the matter? Oh. Well, you'll have to stand that."

"I suppose so. I've found no plan, though. No chance to make a set of wings here and glide out. No balloon. It may have something to do with the earth tremors, though."

"I don't understand."

"If a really bad tremor comes but doesn't crush us, it may really disrupt the Iyunwah. One of Tor's old principles is that if you give people enough to worry about besides you, they tend to ignore you."

"Unger will help. He has got Olert and Ingcon to agree."

"Much more of that and we might as well tell the governor."

"Tris, you have to trust us. We know what we are doing."

"Trust you? You, all right, Tingli. But all of you?"

"Anyone we trust."

Tristal stared out at the rain, the odor of what had been Rizon rank in his nostrils.

At the same time, three young men sat by a fire about forty ayas northwest of Northwall. It was snowing on their fur hats, their heavy coats, the heavy leather of their pants as they sat cross-legged. They seemed not to notice.

They sang a Pelbar hymn in harmony, then took it apart and put new words to it, ribald and only roughly cobbled to the music, laughing all the while.

Finally one of them said, "I'm getting wet. I think I'll crawl in that fishsucking tent before I'm made of freaking mud."

"Stoke the fire first."

"My turn? It was my turn last."

"No. Mine. I'll help. Not too big, though. Tristal might see it. Bravet would froth."

"Tristal's not in this end of Urstadge. If he has any sense."

"What's the matter? Don't you like sitting out in the brush all winter? Beats working. Or choking in mudsucking Pelbar city smoke."

"All the same, a house and a girl would be nice."

"You have a Pelbar soul. Don't tell Bravet."

"No fear. Seriously, what would you do if we did meet Tristal?"

"String up his thumbs. Skewer his gullet. Sprain his ear."

"That's not seriously."

"No need to be serious. We won't. We never will."

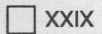 XXIX

EVEN though the twilight sky was dark with rain, Tristal knew the spring equinox had come. His promise was broken. Anger and depression almost overwhelmed him. His profound discouragement seemed to wash away, though, strangely leaving him alert with the fine attentiveness of desperation.

He had helped haul most of the slaves up to their caves, and finally it was his turn. He put his foot in the loop and four slaves strained to raise him, slipping in the mud and almost dropping him. He gained the ledge with some relief, seeing Tingli dimly back in the cave. He turned, still holding the loop a moment, and saw, below him, one guard holding the rope, its loose end twined around his leg. The man was directing the last three slaves. No dogs remained inside the palisade, and only two guards stood well down the line of caves. The man above remained back in his shelter and hadn't come for the rope yet. It was an unmistakable moment of pure opportunity.

Tristal turned to Tingli and said, "This is it."

"What?" she said, gasping as he disappeared.

He had thrust his foot back into the loop and leaped out. The guard below shot upward with a yell as Tristal plummeted down. He let go as he hit, and the man whizzed down, thudding nearby in a sodden heap. Tristal had the man's sword out in an instant as the other two guards, drawing theirs, ran at him, shouting.

He ran toward them, and as he neared, they split up. Tristal took the one on the right, parried then arced the sword deep into his neck. Turning, he dodged the other man's blow and drove the sword through his midsection.

He swept up another sword and ran for the palisade as the guards on the bastions began to shout the alarm. Tristal scrambled up the wall and vaulted over, almost into three dogs. With a fierce pleasure he killed one, the second, and chopped away the front legs of the third. Then he headed for the rocky hill toward the sea. He would get Tor's axe and leave or die in the attempt. What did it matter now they had held him from his promise?

As he ran up through the rocks, hearing dogs baying behind him, he suddenly realized how unplanned and foolish his escape had been. He was committed to it now. He would carry it through as long as he could lift an arm. With an unexpected rush a dog hit him in the chest, knocking him down. He struck out with one of the swords, then right back with the other. The dog had dodged the first, but the second caught it in the chest. It shrieked and dropped. Tristal finished it, listened a moment, and continued running.

Far behind, one of the guards, panting, asked another, "Where's he going? Right into town? Madness."

"It's yellow-hair. Knew he'd be trouble."

"We'd better head for the governor's."

"We are."

Eight dogs later, Tristal reached the unmistakable, imposing building, in which lights glowed. Hearing dogs and shouting behind him, he ran around the side, caught the edge of the roof of a garden walkway, and scrambled up on it. He had recognized the high windows of the receiving chamber. They were covered with scraped hide, and one of them quietly split as Tristal cut a cross in it with his curved sword. He stepped through onto the gallery. Below some kind of evening gathering was taking place. He slipped down the slanted gallery, crawled to the middle, looped his belt over and around the handle of Tor's axe, pulled it gently tight, and jerked it over the rail, triggering two swords, which flailed out at nothing above the startled crowd.

A woman screamed and as Tristal ran for the window, an arrow passed him and thudded into the wall. He turned, saw an archer, and flung one of the swords spinning toward the man.

When he emerged from the window, the garden was full of dogs and men. He turned, mounted the high roof, ran over the ridge, and leaped across to a lower nearby dwelling. Then he ran down the far end, wormed down to the heavy wooden guttering, hung off, and dropped.

For a moment the dogs were baffled, then they heard him and set off, baying. As he ran, Tristal's legs trembled and almost buckled from another earth tremor. He ran south through the rainy streets, hearing several dogs catching up fast. He turned just before the lead dog jumped, swept it aside with the sword, taking the second and third with quick sweeps of the axe. Two more hung back. Tristal turned and ran again. After six steps, he turned and clove the skull of one dog. The last one shied away, yelping. Tristal spun the sword at it, catching it in the legs. Then he finished the animal with the axe and took up the sword again.

Behind him the guards were at a fault. "If he goes south, he's in for a surprise," one said. "He'll be forced onto the beach."

"Or the sea. He swims, you know."

"The dogs can swim."

"If any are left."

No one watched the hill; the guards never imagined that Tristal would head back to the slave compound. He was breathing hard as he came over the crest. Again several dogs were on his trail. Hearing their approach, he jogged down the hill as silently as he could on the wet ground. Ahead he saw an arc of torches as the guards lit the area of the caves.

The lead dog rushed Tristal with a snarl, but an axe stroke chopped it off in a short squeak. Two more hung back, harrying him. He tried to run and watch them at the same time, now hearing Iyunwah shouting far back on the hill. Tristal ran ahead, trying to listen, catching one dog in its final rush with a quick backstroke of the sword. The third would not approach within reach, but followed baying.

Ahead all was not calm. Guards were spaced out inside the palisade, back from the caves. Four were lying on the ground closer in. No one paid attention to the dog behind Tristal except the three remaining dogs at the slave compound. When all four rushed him, outside the palisade, Tristal caught the first two before one fastened on his arm. He hacked the dog away as the last one hit him high on the back, but he spun and sliced the beast across the stomach. As it shrieked, the guards in the bastions turning, Tristal hurtled beneath the wall, dodged through the gateway and up the bastion stairs, pitching one man over the wall and killing two others.

He ducked an arrow from the sentry across the gate, grabbed a torch and lobbed it at him, then swept up a bow, nocked, aimed, and loosed an arrow at one of the guards on the interior perimeter. It took the man in the leg. Another dog was scrambling up the awkward stairs as Tristal nocked again. He quick drew and pierced the animal as he saw someone coming down a rope from the caves. Two of the guards started for him, but a bolt from above took one man and the other retreated. Tingli had the crossbow!

Tristal heard guards and dogs running down the hill and knew he was in a tight spot, caught between the two forces. Well, he didn't care to live that much now anyhow. On impulse he rushed down the bastion stairs, swept away another dog, sent an arrow up into the bastion on the other side of the gate, and followed it up with a curdling Shumai yell. Two men jumped off the wall and ran. The other one was dead.

Tristal ran down the stairs and began shutting the heavy

gates. A dog ran in, and the guards inside began running toward him, but they were pursued by several slaves, and more were slithering down the ropes. The dog slashed Tristal's thigh as he severed its spine with the axe. It slumped away and he shut the gate and threw the small inside latch across it.

Then he turned to face the guards, eleven of them, two armed with bows. One bowman buckled and went down. the other took careful aim at Tristal, as he started running along the wall north. The man shot and missed as three men with swords tried to head Tristal off. Yelling insanely, Tristal rushed at them. They scattered, only one venturing a thrust, which Tristal parried. Then he leaped at the man, slicing him across the chest with the axe. He had made it through to the gathering slaves. In the gloom Tristal made out two slaves who had reached the top of the cliff and were letting down all the ropes.

Somehow they must have killed the three guards always stationed there. Nevertheless, despite the good beginning, some of the slaves refused to descend from the caves. But enough did so they began to force the remaining guards back, some throwing heavy rocks and others wielding swords from the downed men. Tingli was using the crossbow, methodically loading, aiming, and shooting guards as though she were cleaning fish. She had taken out the sentries' only remaining bowman first; the others were comparatively helpless. They clustered, rushed the gate, and ran outside, the last of them falling in the doorway, a short bolt in his back. The guards dragged him out, closing the gates and throwing down the heavy outside bar.

"On the bastions," Tristal yelled. Once there, outside, in the deep gloom and rain, they saw Iyunwah gathering.

"Must be over a hundred at least. Not many dogs."

"They all took pieces out of me," Tristal said. "I scattered dogs from here to the governor's. See? Got my axe."

"Now what do we do?"

Tristal sighed. "I don't know. I just began this on an impulse. Didn't know you'd follow. What about the clifftop?"

"It leads nowhere. There's a big gap in the back all the way across."

"Can we climb down it?"

"Then we'd be stuck in a narrow canyon. They could stop both ends. Probably already have."

"How about climbing the other side of the canyon?"

"It's sheer. I was back there moving logs for them. Near the inlet. With bows they'd have us before we got up. They could shoot across from our cliff."

"If they could get up."

"True. But it can be climbed on the north end if not on this face."

"Yellow-hair, what'd you get us into this for?" a small man shrilled.

"You didn't have to come. Could stay in your cave," another answered.

"Wouldn't miss it," someone called. "Like a good whale hunt."

Back in the dark, Tristal could hear the sounds of chopping as a man hacked down the pole holding the remains of Rizon. As they dug down in the stony soil to bury him and his pole, because no one could bear to touch him, the Iyunwah began lighting torches in a semicircle around the compound.

"We need about eight people to go up on the clifftop so they don't climb it and shoot down on us," Tristal called. Instantly he had twice that number.

Ahead he saw that the Iyunwah were building light log frames to use as shields when they advanced against the palisade. The situation didn't look good. Tingli stood next to Tristal, still holding the crossbow. "You want this?" she asked.

"No. I have my axe. I may make a longbow later. Much more used to it. I had to make that out of firewood. All short pieces."

"Works well. Will we get out of this?"

"What do you think?"

"I'm frightened. I don't think we will. I don't want to rot on the pole."

"No. I didn't expect to get this far. We'll get out. We have to."

"Is that any kind of plan?"

"No. Do you think I could get everybody to climb to the clifftop?"

"We'd be trapped."

"Yes, but we can't hold this wall once morning comes.

There are too many of them. I'd rather climb it in the dark than when they can shoot us as we do it."

By morning they were on the clifftop, slipping away in the dark and rain as the Iyunwah assembled and prepared outside. They watched as the guards and volunteers from Shagrock eased the barriers forward in the dawn. Several of the fishermen chuckled, but Tristal told them to be silent. They watched as the Iyunwah entered the compound and fanned out facing the cliff. Tristal sat still making a longbow and instructing a circle of others how to do the same.

The Iyunwah shouted up toward them, but they couldn't be heard. Then they scratched a giant message in the dirt of the compound: "Give us the yellow-hair and you can go." The fishermen couldn't read it, so Tristal read it to them.

"You can give me to them if you want to. It makes little difference," Tristal said.

"No use. A lie. They'd never let us go anyhow," said one old man.

Two weeks later they were still on the clifftop, surrounded now by a thin ring of Iyunwah. They had enough water, but had soon killed and eaten the clifftop animals they could catch. They had plenty of time to practice their archery, but they were starving, rebellious, disheartened.

"Still feel we are going to get out, yellow-hair?" one man croaked, derisively.

Tristal looked at him. He didn't know. "I'm sure you are," he said. "As to me, I care little." At that point an earth tremor made the whole ground jump, then leap in waves, harder than any they had felt so far. The face of the cliff sheared away as they scrambled back. Below Iyunwah were sprinting away. Some of them had been caught in the rockfall, others sent sprawling by it. The trembling slowed, then another tremor hit, and below the whole landscape seemed to undulate. Then the motion died away.

"Unger," Tristal called. "Have some people check the perimeter. This may give the Iyunwah an easy way up."

"Or us a way down."

"Or that. Now that we are fully armed and they've been stood on their ear, maybe we could make it to the inlet and across."

Unger and several men left to check the tablelike cliff-top. It was a full quarter ayas in diameter, and Tristal didn't expect them back soon. As he waited, he became aware of smoke rising over the hill toward Shagrock.

"Look, Tingli. They're having some trouble over there."

"None of them are leaving."

"Not yet. Wait."

Soon some Iyunwah sentries did leave in response to messengers from over the hill. And Unger returned to say there was a fairly easy way down the cliff on the north side toward the inlet.

"Let's make a run, then," Tristal said.

"Yellow-hair, none of us have the stinking strength to run."

"A crawl, then. Let's make a crawl."

Someone laughed. They all walked to the north perimeter, now a slanted jumble of rocks. "I don't want to be on that if there's another tremor," Tristal said. "Let's try it, though. Look. Some of them are waiting for us. We'll have a fight. Got your bows?"

Some of the fishermen shrank from the idea of another fight, but no one refused to go. As they climbed down the loose rock, they could see more Iyunwah gathering. Escape was not going to get any easier. But Tingli suddenly pointed out that the water was draining out of the inlet. At first slowly, then more rapidly, it quickly passed the low-tide level, then beyond, sucking down the central channel, leaving wide mud flats with distant fish flopping.

"What?"

"Up the rock. Quick. Back up the rock!" Unger yelled, waving his arms. "Wave. Big wave. Quick."

Below, the gathering Iyunwah jeered and began to rush them. Tristal formed a line of bowmen and sent the others back up the rock. One ragged volley of arrows held the attackers back. Suddenly one of the Iyunwah happened to turn around. He began to shout frantically. They looked and began to run east. Simultaneously Tristal heard a rumble and saw an incredible wall of seawater rushing up the inlet, curling into the slave compound, gathering, pouring up the north side of the cliff, as the fishermen frantically clambered upward. The water caught, lifted, and obliterated the running Iyunwah. Then it began to flatten, turn, and drain back, taking with it trees, portions of palisade, two wrecked boats, and, somewhere under the surface, the entire Iyunwah siege force.

Tristal and the fisherman stayed on the cliffside silently, in awe for a time. Then one old man said, "Well, I see a couple of beached fish, and I'm hungry." He began climbing down. Others followed.

"What was that?" Tristal asked.

"An earthquake wave," the old man said. "Sometimes come when the earth trembles. Sometimes just appear out of nowhere. When the sea drains back, you run. Out fishing, you never really know they are passing. Don't come often. I've seen two before."

The next day, Tristal and the fishermen, well armed, walked down the street of what had been Shagrock. Many of the buildings had been thrown down by the tremor, and then the tidal wave had washed up over most of the entire settlement. A dog barked at them until a man sent an arrow into it.

They found thirty-two survivors in the governor's hall, which had cracked and buckled but still stood.

As the fishermen walked in, they backed down the hall, swords ready. Tristal stood in front of them.

Watomie, the long-faced governor, sat at his table, surrounded by a ragtag collection of survivors. "So this is what I get for sparing your life," he said.

"What? I didn't send the tremor or the wave. If we'd been in the caves, we'd all be dead because the rock face broke off and fell."

"What do you want? Our lives?"

"Do we look like blackhearted Iyunwah? No. Do you need help? We're leaving soon."

"Help? Help from you?"

"Have you looked in all the buildings? Is anybody trapped?"

"I...don't know. But go. We can take care of our own. Just go."

"All right. Just remember. If you're ever tempted to attack your neighbors again, they know to appeal to the Shumai. We'll come, no matter how far. We are allies now if they need help. I imagine they know enough to manage."

"Attack? With what? You crazy?"

"Probably. Slavery will do that." Tristal turned and they left without another word.

Tristal turned to the others. "Come," he said. "You take the one boat. I'll leave you at the inlet."

"No. I'm going with you," Tingli said as they passed beyond the door.

"You? I'm going to travel about two thousand ayas. Much of it running."

"I, too," said Unger. "No reason to stay. The village all gone, killed or scattered."

"If you can't keep up, I'll have to leave you. I've broken my promise, but I must go back."

"Just in case you leave them behind, I'll come, too, and be with them," another young fisherman said, grinning.

They heard a noise behind them and turned to see Ambel, the young priest, running toward them. "I want to go with you," he said, panting.

"Go with us?"

"I have no reason to stay. Never did anything anyhow. I want to meet Pelbar. I want to go where the earth doesn't shake."

"It's a long way."

"All right. I have all the time of my life."

At that moment, Fahna knelt with her head in Eolyn's lap, sobbing convulsively. "It's all right. He may come still," Eolyn said.

"He broke . . . his promise."

"He couldn't help it. I'm sure. Besides, you told me how that promise was gained."

"He should have kept . . . his word. What will I do now? Everybody will be laughing—the proud beauty brought down by her sky nose. And what about that awful Bravet and his bullies?"

"Don't worry. We have guardsmen to keep them off."

"I'm afraid. Stel is gone, and Ahroe. I can't stay with the Protector forever. If I go home . . ."

"Yes?"

"There are others. And my father will be ashamed."

"Jestak? Never."

"Oh, Eolyn, why does everything have to be so . . . wretched?"

XXX

It was past midsummer as Tristal and his twelve fellow travelers sat in a grassy circle with the Forman ironworkers, high in the mountains near where the hot springs and geysers made clusters of rising cloud. Tristal had told them about Rizon and how he had died.

"He left a long time ago," one man said in the same sharp, crisp tones Rizon had used. "He murdered a man, a cousin."

"Why?"

"Something about a woman. It seems he paid for it. Now, do you need anything? Supplies? Dried meat? We have ample. Need knives? I see stone tools. A lovely axe, that. May I see it?"

Tristal gave it over, handle first, and the old Forman studied it closely, running his fingers over it, holding it away at arm's length. Then he gave it back with a smile. "I'd like to meet the man who did that work."

"It's a long way. We're going there now. I assume he's there. He was seven years ago."

"I'm too old for such a journey. But some may go with you. Ib? Jost? What about it?"

The two demurred, but six men and the young wife of one decided to go. All were young and strong, with the typical stocky build and black hair of the Forman primitives. Their skin was very white where the sun hadn't burned it. Some had blue eyes, but most had dark brown.

Two hundred ayas west of Pelbarigan, Bravet stood with his men on a height of ground and said, "This will be fine. We'll build a log stage there. Seats around. A log house over there—small—and a big one down there."

"What's this for?"

"My wedding. To Fahna."

"She's agreed then?" One freckled man whooped and tossed his pack in the air.

"She hasn't agreed. We're going to take her."

The group fell silent. Tension and wariness hung in the air like clouds of gnats.

"Anyone who won't doesn't have to. I claim the loyalty of your silence, though."

"Shumai don't do that, axeman."

Bravet turned, enraged, and rushed the man who had spoken, an older man who had come for the experience of hunting again. He threw the man down and stood over him, axe at the man's throat. "I say what Shumai do. I'm Shumai, and I do it."

The man said nothing. Bravet stood back from him and looked around. "Now. Any other objections?"

The freckled man let out a long yell and tossed his pack in the air again, shouting, "Now finally we're going to get some excitement around here." A number of the younger men laughed and cheered.

"Now," Bravet said, "Let's get to work. We'll need a carcass, the whole thing. Who wants to hunt? And we'll start with clearing the brush. Got those axes?"

As summer died and turned, and the prairie insects churred among the brown grass and goldenrod, Tristal moved eastward, restively, with his small group. In the eighth month, they met a group of nine horse Shumai hunting for the Emeri, and soon after struck the Isso River. They started down it on crude rafts, constructing boats as they went. The river was lethargic and criss-crossed by bars, so they made poor time at it. Tristal longed to leave them all behind and strike eastward running. But his dread of returning and meeting Fahna grew with the late summer days.

Fall brought tumult and rejoicing at Pelbarigan for Stel arrived from the Bitter Sea with the second Pelbar steamboat, bringing a large numer of Peshtak he had freed from Tantal slavery. The Tantal had been defeated at Ginesh, then again in a lake skirmish at Iver, and finally at the Portage. South at Threerivers sound progress was being made on the Heart River Federation of peoples.

After the general celebration, no one noticed anything

unusual as Bravet's running band returned. The normally loud young man seemed quiet and well ordered for a change. Even the Pelbar guardsmen saw nothing in their behavior to criticize.

When they vanished, no one marked the event. Two days later, Eolyn remarked to Ahroe, "I don't understand it. I thought Fahna was recovering from Tristal's not returning. But she's gone home, or something, without a word. Right in the middle of an experiment."

Ahroe was preoccupied and had said, "What?"

Eolyn repeated her remark, adding, "And that dreadful Bravet didn't even bother..." The two women looked at each other a few moments. "No," Eolyn whispered.

Ahroe bolted out the door of her cottage and raced down the pathway yelling for the guardcaptain.

Four days later Tristal called for the boats to beach on the east bank. When they were together, he said, "I don't understand it. I'm uneasy. Something's wrong. It has the feel of...I don't know what. I have to get on. I'll leave a trail. If you want to come this way, then follow it. Otherwise, follow the river until it flows into the Heart, then paddle north."

"How will we know the Heart?" one young fisherman asked.

"If you walked into a wall, you'd know it. The Heart is the mother of rivers."

"What's the matter? Danger?"

"No. Yes. I don't know. There's something in the air— like before we met the mad running band in the north. Or so Tor said. I didn't understand it then. Besides, I have this feeling about Fahna. What if I ran all the way from here. I'm thin enough now. She might...she might accept me anyhow if I come worn down and thinner yet. It's worth a try. I have to try. You understand—we've tried enough together."

"We'll keep up," said Tingli.

"No. If you can, all right. Now, I know this seems irresponsible, but you can get along. You've come this far. You'll like the Pelbar. I'll meet you there if I can." He turned and began a slow run through the high grass. Looking back, he saw the group was following him, but as he ran on, most of them quickly strung out far behind.

He headed east, feeling the joy of being Shumai on the vast prairie, but still a strange anxiety. Two days later he picked up a trail near a creek. A running band? He followed it. Here they had camped. He studied the muddy rim of the stream. Here was old Sark's running boot track, with his lazy S stitched across the seam. It walked along the muddy shore, upstream, with occasional barefoot tracks alongside—a woman.

Here the woman had bathed, as Sark kept his back turned. How careless he'd become—in the old days no one would have left all these... Tristal felt his mind pause and a strange creeping sensation along the back of his neck. He looked at the woman's tracks. Here they stood in an H shape, a lovely arc of spread toes, delicate arch, fine, narrow heel. It...was Fahna's. There the left little toe curled slightly under. Yes. H. A message. Sark knew it. What was it? He touched Fahna's track with his hand. What if it was a call for help? H? Was it an accident? No. The tracks stood apart. They were clearly printed.

Tristal made a marker for his group, wherever they might be, and set off after the running band at a hunter's pace. They seemed to be heading for the old gathering place east of where the Longwhip River flowed south to the Isso. They would reach there by evening—with Fahna. Tristal quickened his pace, running at the top of his breathing, following the long trace of bent prairie grass.

As Tristal had surmised, Bravet's band arrived at the height of land shortly after dark. He had sent two hunters on ahead to build a fire and put meat over it. As they strode into the cleared area, Bravet called out, "Look, love. Your wedding site."

"I'll never marry you while I have breath or sense," Fahna said, gritting it out through tight lips.

"No? Ah. We'll see. There are alternatives. If you won't, these men may each test you out and see if they would like you. Nice? Nothing but the nicest cuts of meat for my men."

The freckled man yelled and threw his pack in the air. "Don't take him, woman. You won't like him at all."

Bravet gave him a hard look, just as Sark, the old hunter, stepped in front of him, his worn spearshaft ahead of him. "Shumai don't do these things. I come along with you for the hunting—like the old days. But this is no running band.

It's a mob of rapists. Come to your senses, man, you—"

Without a word, Bravet had knocked the spear aside and struck Sark's neck with the flat of his axe. The old man crumpled. Fahna shrieked and ran to him, kneeling by him.

"It's all . . ." the old man murmured, as Bravet dragged her away.

"Leave him. A reminder to anybody with ideas." His eyes swept the band, now silent, staring. "Anybody? Want to join him?"

"Nobody?" Fahna screamed. "Not a man in this gang of cowards."

Bravet slapped her across the mouth and pushed her up on the log platform. She wrestled away from him, crying out, but he caught her and shoved her ahead of him, calling back, "Ony, bring that rope."

Laughing, the freckled man brought a leather rope, which Bravet looped around Fahna's neck, shoving her back to a skinned pole emplanted on the platform and binding her neck to it.

"All right, beauty, which will it be? Me or them? You choose."

"I chose," she gasped.

"You chose! The whimperer! Tristal the orphan! His crippled uncle always backed him. I'll give you the options. Which?"

"Tristal," she gasped.

Bravet slapped her across the face. "Tristal," she said again.

Bravet slapped her again.

"Hey, axeman. Easy. Leave us some," an older man said. A number of them laughed.

Bravet leaned in close to her and whispered, "This is your last chance, sky nose. It's life or death. It's gone too far. Take me. I'm not so bad. I won't be scorned all my life. I'll give you to them. I really will."

Fahna reached out and bit his ear as he drew it away. It streamed blood. He touched it and looked at the blood on his hand, then at her. Then he grabbed her arms and whipped them behind her, tying them with the rope. Facing her again, he took his belt knife and slowly slit away her light coat and then her shirt, tearing them and tossing scraps of them behind him. When he stood aside, she was naked to the waist.

"How's that?" he yelled, a strange tension in his voice.

Ony shouted again, and some of the younger ones took up the yell.

Bravet faced her again and said, "Your last chance. Choose or it's too late."

"I'm . . . so ashamed. Let me go," she murmured.

"To them?"

"Home, you maggoty-meated mud turtle," she shrieked.

Bravet took out his belt knife again and slit her cotton pants away, running the blade down her thighs, one at a time. Some of the men shouted and crowded forward. He turned and raised a hand, grinning. "Easy. One at a time, later. Easy." He ripped the cloth off her completely and flung it away. Then he stood aside again, spreading his arms. Fahna lowered her head as much as she could, standing in blue cotton shorts and her boots alone.

Ony yelled again, leaping up and down, shouting, "The rest, the rest." Several others took up the chant, but as the shouting died down, it seemed strangely prolonged by a Shumai greeting yell from off to the east.

Instant silence fell over the group. "Who's posted out there?" Bravet shouted.

"Nobody. All here," someone said.

Bravet strode down from platform and advanced across the circle as Tristal entered the east side. "You gave no answer. Anything wrong?" Tristal asked calmly, his chest rising from his running.

"You're not welcome," Bravet said, his hand on his axehead. "Get out."

"You're not Shumai then?" Tristal looked across Bravet's shoulder at Fahna tied up. "No. I see you're not. Shumai don't treat women like that. Who are you then?"

"Listen, fishguts, I asked you plainly to leave," said Bravet, slightly rattled by Tristal's size and calm voice. Everything about him radiated the traditional Shumai axeman, the figure of legend, burned hard in stark sunlight and adversity, straight as a spearshaft, lithe in every motion, quiet and watchful, his eyes glittering like blue jewels.

"And what have you done to Sark?" he asked, stepping around Bravet and stooping toward the old man, who feebly lifted an arm.

"Tristal," he murmured. "Good you're here."

"Get out, you promise breaker. Get away." Fahna's voice was shrill.

Tristal glanced at Bravet, then said, "Fahna? Is that you?"

"Get out of here, you stinking no good. Can't a person even get married without your breaking into it?"

"Married? Tied to a post?" He laughed. "While I'm here I might as well apologize," he said, stepping up on the platform.

"Get off there, pigweed," Bravet shouted after him.

Tristal turned and raised his hand deferentially. "Soon," he said. There was something almost hypnotic in his actions, his stance. A slight wave of embarrassment went over most of the men, knowing they were seeing the real thing, realizing the falsity in their position, play-acting in the grossest way. Even Bravet was momentarily nonplussed. He had imagined Tristal as frail and dependent. There was something dangerous about this man. For the first time in his life, Bravet tasted real fear. He'd have to back his moves now, and he already sensed the outcome.

Tristal walked up to Fahna, who hissed at him, "Get out of here. They'll kill you. Why didn't you come? Look what you caused."

Tristal flicked out his axe and drew the edge of it across the ropes as they crossed between Fahna's breasts. The ropes fell cleanly away. Then he ran the blade down the cord binding her neck. "Wrists, too?" he asked mildly.

"Get away from here," she screamed. "Can't you see this is where I want to be?"

"Fine. Be here. But decently." Tristal cut the wrist ropes and slipped off his shirt, putting it around her.

"Oh," she murmured. "They did burn you." She shuddered. "And those four lines. What happened to you?"

Behind them, Bravet, seeing his whole little world melting away, shouted and drew his axe, but as he ran toward Tristal, Sark lifted the tip of his spear, and the young man ran it through his belly, crying out, gulping, and falling across the old man, shrieking in his pain.

"You, pull him off," Tristal said to Ony. The man looked at Bravet, then at Tristal, took up his spear and threw it, but Tristal knocked it aside, then stepped down and advanced on him. Ony turned, looked at Bravet's axe, then at Tristal, then ran across the circle and out into the darkness.

"Are there any Shumai here?" Tristal asked.

Five of the oldest men came forward and stood by him, facing the others. Then two more came. They confronted nineteen young men, all armed with traditional Shumai spears.

"Well, what'll it be?" Tristal asked. "A fight? More death? Or an end to this stupidity? We can all walk away from here together if you want."

"What's wrong with a good fight?" one man asked.

Tristal looked at him a long time, then said, "Whichever of you may survive will spend the rest of your lives running from the Pelbar guardsmen. It's all the same to me. Please yourself." Behind him he heard Fahna gasp slightly.

"Where's your running band, big axeman?" another asked.

Tristal laughed. "They aren't much at running. They're coming along sometime. They are sea fishermen, a Shagrock priest, and some curious Forman primitives."

"What sea?"

"The shining sea of the west. If you have so many questions, why don't we sit down and talk—after we see to these men."

"No hurry. Both dead," said one man.

"That Tor's axe?" another asked.

"It was. He put it in my pack and paddled off in the fog chasing a whale. I never saw him again, but later he banded the north fishermen together against the Iyunwah slavers."

"How do you know?"

"I was one of the slaves. Tingli and Unger, whom you may meet, saw it all happen."

"What's a whale?"

"A sea creature about seventeen arms long—at least the ones I saw."

A couple of the men laughed at that. "Did you kill them with your axe?" one asked.

"No. They spear them with barbed spears attached by rope to barrels or air-filled skins. Then they follow as the whale wears itself out towing them and finally spear it through its blowhole. Whales breathe from a hole on top of their heads."

Again one of the men laughed.

"No. It's true," one said. "Samme told me. In the South-ocean the porpoises breathe that way. But they aren't so big."

"You've been to the Southocean then?" Tristal asked.

"Not me. The Atherers have come north."

"I've been gone a long time," Tristal said.

"Just finding that out?" Fahna remarked drily.

"Sure you didn't enlarge the sea beasts, axeman?"

"If you wait around, you can ask Tingli."

"Did you find the ice? You went looking for ice."

"Never want to see so much ice again. Tor and I walked across ice for over fifty days, then spent five years trapped in a valley between ice walls. There was a whole society there."

"How'd you get out?"

"Finally Tor built a balloon. Something Eolyn had told him about. We floated out over it."

There was no laughter this time. "All right? Is it friends?"

"Might as well," one said. "Don't want to fight a man who climbs ice mountains and eats giant fish."

Tristal smiled slightly. "Good. Now. We ought to bury this man here by his skinned pole. If we can wrap Sark up, I want to take him to a valley east of the Heart and put him with Dard. His son."

Late the next day they met Tristal's companions. Fahna had remained noncommital toward Tristal, and he hadn't seen her in private or poured out the apology he felt, but when she saw Tingli, Fahna moved slightly closer to him.

As the two groups ate together, Tingli and her brother stood as far apart as the length of a whale and explained its habits and uses. The groups intermingled, fascinated with each other, talking late, and when the fishermen explained Tristal's escape from the Iyunwah and the subsequent mass revolt, Bravet's young Shumai hunters listened eagerly, taking pleasure from such tumult.

"It sounds better in the telling," Tristal said. "A lot of it was nasty work."

"What was the best part?" someone asked.

"The friends. The country, of course, in its incredible vastness and change, but the friends. You find them everywhere; people have goodwill." He smiled at Tingli and Unger, glanced at Fahna. "The guardsmen will be here in a while. How about it? You men with Bravet—you done anything they'll want you for?"

"They did nothing," Fahna said. "Only him. They only followed him. I'll say so."

Several of the men looked relieved, but none spoke up. It was midmorning of the next day before Blu and a line of guardsmen were in sight. The two groups kept away from each other while Tristal and Blu strode forward, Blu recognizing him, letting out an endless Shumai yell, high and trilled, and running to hug him. The two stood a short while and talked, then beckoned the groups together. The guardsmen were tired from their long run, so the whole party sat down together for talk and rest.

Finally Tristal was able to draw Fahna aside, though standing away from her and not touching. "I'm sorry," he said. "Once we got into the journey, there was no way of coming back in time. I tried. Tor even told me I could have the boat when we were only a week into the trip. It . . . isn't exactly a tender courtship, is it?"

Fahna looked up at him, and her eyes went fiery, then grew mild again. "No. You aren't much of a lover, are you? You'd have gone off and never come back if I hadn't made you promise. It seems a long time ago. We were children then." She paused and looked at him hard. "Well, are you just going to stand there? I can't . . . I can't do all the . . ."

"Marry me then, please?"

"What of Tingli?"

"She's a sister."

"It doesn't seem that way to her."

"Yes, it does. I talked to her about you often enough when we were captives."

"Together? In your own . . ."

Tristal stopped her with a long kiss. When they drew apart, she said, "I thought you never would."

Two weeks later, Tristal and Fahna were married in the Northwall chapel, with a crowd in attendance that flowed out the doors. This was followed by a public feast that Jestak said would set him back a year's work. Almost a month later Tristal and Fahna accompanied Sark's coffin down the Heart and then inland to the small valley where his son, Dard, was buried. Up on the hillside, Dard's grave was brown with fallen leaves, but the sun shone down through the thinned foliage with the fierce joy of autumn.

Digging was hard in the rocky soil, but at last Sark was lowered in and a Pelbar hymn was sung by the assembled guardsmen. Tristal's eyes filled as he thought of the last time hymns had been sung there, for Dard and the others. Fahna clung to his arm.

Before they began filling the grave, Tristal slid Tor's axe from its sheath, knelt, and laid it on the coffin. As he stood up, many looks questioned him. "It's all right," he said. "Tor left it behind. Perhaps I can, too. It is Sark's by right. It is a true blade, and so was he. He never counted the cost of his sense of honor, but stood to it, and in doing that he touched immortality, because wherever courage is, he will be there, since he made it his own."

They mounded the dirt and rock on Sark's grave and turned away toward the river and the waiting boat. Fahna murmured, "He did that for me."

"Not only. For himself. For Bravet, even. Bravet is only pitiful now. Otherwise he might have been a monster. Sark drew them all back from it. I doubt if any of those men had killed anyone before. Sark spoke the thought of half of them if they had the courage. The way was prepared for me. The weight was even on the scale, and I just stepped on."

"Don't be so modest."

"It's impersonal, I think. A person is no tougher than an apple. I would have died there, very easily. It was the ideas that changed everything. That's what has happened all along to Tor and me. You can't just live along like Bravet's followers. I've certainly seen that somebody is always trying to use you to carry out his designs. You have to illustrate the values larger than you are, and then..."

"And then you may die like Sark."

"Sometimes. But all the best lives do that. They lean on the strength of the true nature of things and so seem much stronger than they are alone."

"The axe. Why did you give it up? I should think... I'm glad you did. Even as famous as it has become."

"It's a sound axe. But my hip feels much lighter without it. Even Tor knew it was the idea of the thing that was important. I still have that."

Fahna ran her arm around his waist and put her fingers

down into the empty axe sheath. Somehow this struck her funny, and she gave out the first laugh after the burial. Several heads turned, but not in reproof, and an exchange of smiles lightened the mood as they walked through the fallen leaves.

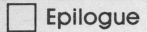 Epilogue

AHEAD, Tor could see no more islands—only the ubiquitous fog, washing and blending across the slightly swelling sea. From behind him came the distant cries of gulls. He turned and saw the dim shape of the last island massing vaguely up.

Far back, the fishermen had told him there were no more islands, but he had found a few, beyond where they had ever gone, struggling above the sea surface.

He had lived there with the short, dark people for some time. Early in his stay he had taught them how to gather a large force from their scattered groups, to retreat, scout, and mount an attack in concert, defeating the Iyunwah slavers in their many-oared sailing vessels. Then he had lingered with the fishermen. They had fished together, hauled drift logs back to the tundra covered islands, built peat-roofed houses, hunted seals, and sung their epic songs, some of a time of giant metal boats and rainbow patterns on the water. He had learned enough of the different language of the remote western settlements to converse quite easily. More than one fisherman had tried to marry Tor to a daughter.

But, as usual, Tor had grown restless, though in an expansive and leisurely way, and his interior voice spoke softly to him again of something he needed to do beyond where the sun sank into the water. Now he would go see what that was.

He shaded his eyes with his hand, lifting aside the thick fur cap. Nothing lay ahead but mist and water, and for a few moments, the mist seemed to form a tunnel into which he was sailing, a dim, strange place fringed with light.

He eased back, contented, adjusting the sail. Ahead of him lay seven pouches of dried seal meat and three large woven water bottles, pitched and greased, as well as two oil bottles. His crossbow lay neatly in its case, and next to it a thick sheaf of bolts in a waterproof quiver. Jutting up from the bow a heavy-shafted harpoon with a polished bone head pointed its finger at the sea, then the sky, as the boat pitched.

Close to the boat, a dusky sea lion rose up through the water, spewing spray. It regarded Tor briefly with one large, liquid eye, then rolled forward and sank again back into the darkness of the cold ocean.

About the Author

A native of New Jersey, Paul O. Williams holds a Ph.D. in English from the University of Pennsylvania. Following three years of teaching at Duke University, he settled in the tiny Mississippi River town of Elsah, Illinois, where he is currently a Professor of English at Principia College, teaching American literature and creative writing. He has two children.

His response to his small community has been varied, including helping to found the Historic Elsah Foundation and direct its small museum, and serving as the president of the local volunteer firefighters. His poems, essays, reviews, and articles on literary subjects and midwestern history have been widely published. While he has written largely on nineteenth-century America and served as a president of the Thoreau Society, he has also developed a deep interest in science fiction and fantasy.

The Breaking of Northwall, *The Ends of the Circle*, *The Dome in the Forest*, *The Fall of the Shell*, and *An Ambush of Shadows*, his first five novels, are set against the same background as *The Song of the Axe*.